# Back To You

## C.J. MIRANDA

*Back to You* © 2017 by CJ Miranda

All rights reserved. No part of this book may be used or reproduced in any written, electronic, recorded, or photocopied format without the express permission from the author or publisher as allowed under the terms and conditions with which it was purchased or as strictly permitted by applicable copyright law. Any unauthorized distribution, circulation or use of this text may be a direct infringement of the author's rights, and those responsible may be liable in law accordingly. Thank you for respecting the work of this author.

*Back to You* is a work of fiction. All names, characters, events and places found therein are either from the author's imagination or used fictitiously. Any similarity to persons alive or dead, actual events, locations, or organizations is entirely coincidental and not intended by the author.

For information, contact the publisher, Hot Tree Publishing.

www.hottreepublishing.com

Editing: Hot Tree Editing

Cover Designer: Claire Smith

Formatter: RMGraphX

ISBN-10: 1-925448-74-6

ISBN-13: 978-1-925448-74-0

10 9 8 7 6 5 4 3 2 1

# Dedication

I'm dedicating this to other young writers, those who spend their time in worlds other than the real one. You have a gift. You should embrace it. It took me far too long to realize this.

# BEFORE

I just can't handle it anymore.

All the smiles, all the hugs, all the congratulations, they're all just so damn fake.

None of them will touch on the elephant in the room, comment on the woman who isn't there.

They won't act like my mom's just bailed on me and my dad; no, they're all so damn proud of me for graduating high school that it doesn't matter.

It's suffocating.

So I slip out the front door and plop down on our porch steps, hugging my knees to my chest and then crying for what feels like the millionth time this summer.

It's too much. All of it is just too much.

That's why I'm getting the hell out of this place at the crack of dawn tomorrow. Instead of going to the state school just a short ride across the interstate, I decided at the last minute to accept the offer from the school in Shreveport, the city farthest from home where I'll still get an in-state tuition rate.

It killed my dad, of course, to hear that I'm leaving. He'll never say it aloud, but it's like I'm doing the same thing my mom did to him. I know that. Of course I know that, and it kills me to know I'm hurting him.

But I feel like an animal with its hind legs caught in a trap.

I'm just so desperate to get away from this place, to get away from the memories of this household, of happy parents in my happier childhood. I can't stand to keep walking the streets of the town I love, the town my mom claimed she loved until she said in her goodbye note that "it was just too small." I can't see the sympathetic faces of our neighbors, hear their pitying sighs as I walk by.

It's overwhelming.

I need to get the hell away from it, to breathe.

And breathing in a town so close to the gulf that there's a constant cloud of humidity lingering in the air isn't exactly the easiest thing to do.

Especially now, now that it's the middle of summer, now that it's nighttime and there's that lingering scent of oncoming rain. The moisture in the air is practically suffocating, but I'll take it any day over being in that kitchen and having to act like going off tomorrow is more exciting than it is necessary for survival.

My cries are softening up when I hear footsteps, and I reluctantly look up. My heart gives a dull thud against my chest when I see the tall, wide frame of Weston Alcorn, the boy who's lived across the street from us for as long as I can remember, the boy who's really a man and who's now become an intimidating six foot and some inches tall.

His eyes have that same pitying gleam in them, the one I've seen a million times in the past three months, but for some reason, I can't find the urge to want to smack him. Maybe it's because they're so damn green I can't think of anything but that, or maybe it's the soft little smile stretched across his full mouth.

I don't know what it is, but when he asks me softly, "You mind if I sit?" I find myself shaking my head and scooting over so there's room for the guy twice my size.

My fingers reach up to wipe away the tears lingering on my cheeks, and I curse when I look down and see the black streaked across them. Today was the first time in weeks that I put makeup on, and now here I am, crying it all off and completely regretting that decision.

He's quiet for a long while, which doesn't really surprise me.

Weston has always been a quiet guy, always polite and willing to make conversation when necessary, but never really jumping at the chance to do so.

It always kind of stressed me out, honestly, his reluctance to converse. I'm the kind of person who can only handle silence around people I'm truly comfortable with, and when I'm not, I feel panicked and anxiety-ridden every time things go quiet.

Not right now, though.

No, right now it's kind of nice.

I feel him look down at me after a few minutes, and I can't find the willpower to look back up at him, not when I know how pathetic I look. I'm sure he heard me crying and that's why he walked over here, but that doesn't necessarily mean I have to acknowledge the fact that I was crying. Right?

"That bad, huh?" he finally asks, his voice low and gruff and yet still sounding so very loud.

I snort a laugh, tears burning my throat for another split second. Reaching up to once again wipe at my eyes, I say, "They're being too nice, actually."

"Ahh," he muses, and once again I feel his eyes on the side of my face. "The avoidance. Used to be my favorite part."

The sarcasm gets through to me, and I finally turn my head and meet his gaze, my breath catching in my throat when I see just how close he is to me. Our porch stairs aren't incredibly wide, of course, seeing as how our house barely hits a thousand square feet, so his broad and warm body, I now notice, is flush against my own.

"Your brother?"

He nods. "When he died, not one person came up to me and said what I wanted to hear. They just.... They said something ridiculously sympathetic, and then, after a few months, it's like they forgot it even happened."

"What'd you want to hear?" I ask softly, running my eyes over the chiseled planes of his face and thinking how utterly crazy it is that I feel comfortable sitting here with him like this.

He meets my gaze again, the green in his eyes scorching as he says, "That it fucking sucks."

"It really does," I agree, my voice cracking as I feel the tears start to work their way back up my throat. He gets it. Finally someone fucking gets what I feel, or at least will tell me about it instead of acting like being angry at fate is ridiculous.

"Hey," he says, picking up on the incoming emotion and then reaching to grab at my hand. Our fingers instinctively interlock, and my eyes divert from his heated gaze to look down at our hands. His are so large, his fingers warm and rough, while mine are dainty and smooth. But yet they fit together so perfectly, so soothingly, and it's like warmth has been directly injected into my bloodstream.

Before I can take another breath, his other hand reaches out, his fingers lightly grasping my chin to pull my gaze up to meet his again. He says, "I'm not going to spew some shit about it getting better, because honestly it doesn't, but it does get easier to forget about it. It's like each day is practice and, after a while, you become skilled at not thinking about it."

"Thanks," I murmur, feeling better even if it's only just for now. "I... I don't know why you decided to come up here and talk to me, but I'm glad you did."

He smirks and then drops his hold from my chin, only to let his fingers briefly graze against the sensitive skin of my jaw. My breathing picks up as something strong ignites in my belly, and before I'm even aware of what I'm doing, my eyes drop from his to his lips, and I find myself wondering what it'd be like to feel them against my own.

My heart is racing, my adrenaline thumping, and when he says my name to get me to look away from his mouth, it takes every ounce of willpower I have not to lean forward and take what I now think I want.

But when our eyes meet again, I can see the fire behind his gaze. I can practically feel him wanting to lean in too, and I just can't stop myself.

I surge upward and kiss him, my body roaring to life as I *finally* let myself give in to an emotion other than anger or grief. My free hand slides up the wide, hard expanse of his chest only to bury itself into the thick hair at the base of his neck, and it's then that Weston finally begins to respond. With a groan, he winds his free arm around my waist and jerks my body against his, my legs instinctively lifting and draping themselves over his.

With his mouth slanting over my own, he unleashes everything I've been feeling back into me, giving me an onslaught of emotion that I can so easily give back. And boy, do I ever. I kiss him with a relentlessness I've never felt before, a wildness I've never once thought I possess. Everything I have I pour into him, into this kiss.

I grab on to him—to his hair, his shoulders, his shirt, anything I can get my hands on—in a fierce desperation that's almost painful. He doesn't seem to mind, though, as he seems to be reciprocating equally, his fingers digging into my thigh, his mouth unrelenting against my own, his hand grasping the back of my neck so I can't move away from him.

Not that I'd ever want to.

Until, of course, I can no longer breathe.

I wrench away from him with a gasp, the intensity of our kiss having made me completely forget how to inhale.

My chest is heaving, my lips plump in a way I know will lead to bruising, and my body aching to be one with his again.

"Iris," he rasps, seemingly trying to cover up the fact that he's out of breath but completely failing. "I—"

"There you are, Iris!" a voice calls, making me jump about an inch off the steps. Quickly disentangling my legs from where they're still draped over Weston's thighs, I look behind me and try to quell the blood rushing to my cheeks.

Standing there with her head stuck out the door is Mrs. Fredrickson, owner of the best bakery in town and also resident busybody. I curse internally when I see her big eyes take in the scene, our heavy breathing, my red cheeks, and his mussed hair.

It would take an idiot to not figure out what was going on out here.

"Oh!" She giggles, her dainty hand reaching up to cover her mouth. "Oops. I am so sorry, you two, it's just... Iris, your dad was looking for you."

"Um," I start, desperately looking over at Weston and seeing him eying his home across the street like it's a cool glass of water and he's been stuck in the desert for two months. I turn away from him, the blush on my cheeks still raging, and say, "Okay, tell him I'll be right in."

"Will do, honey," she says with a sly wink before disappearing back into the house and shutting the door.

Yeah, by early tomorrow everyone in town is going to know what Weston and I were getting up to out here.

My heart's still pounding against my chest, and I have no idea what needs to be said, but something definitely does. What happened out here... it was so sudden, so rushed, so... *frenzied*. It was everything I needed at the moment, a momentary distraction.

Do I regret it? Not even a little bit. Do I want to talk about it? No.

I want to go inside feeling better, feeling better from our little tumble out here, and just end the evening, go to sleep, and then get the hell out of this place tomorrow.

It's all I want.

"Weston, I...," I begin, only for him to lean in again. His face is so serious, his lips red and delightfully plump, and just looking at him, him being this close, it all makes me want to kiss him again. I didn't think I'd want to, but then... but then he just came near.

He reaches out so his rough fingers can skate over my jawline, making that warmth in my belly reignite. God, I've been looking for chemistry like this all of high school, and now that I find it, now that I find someone I could actually be close with... I'm leaving.

Fate is such a fickle little bitch.

He says, "We'll talk about it later, okay?"

I nod, his intense gaze and nearness making speaking nearly impossible. He gives me a little smirk, obviously noticing how dazed he's made me, and then says, "Bye, Iris."

"Bye...," I breathe, my words stopping when he leans in to press a kiss against my forehead.

The next minute, he's gone.

And then, the next morning, I'm gone.

# DURING
## Chapter One

To say I feel strange the minute my car forges back into my hometown would be a vast understatement.

It's been four years.

I haven't stepped foot in this place for four years, and now... now I'm back for good.

It's slightly terrifying and incredibly weird.

As I force myself to drive slowly down the main road of town, I look around and take in all the changes that have occurred—not that I'm expecting there to be any. Our small town has never been one for big changes, always wanting to stay the same despite the urbanization of every single city around us.

Back in high school, I loved it.

Now, though, since I've lived in a semi-big city for the past four years, it all seems just so... underwhelming, I guess.

But my dad refuses to move elsewhere, and until I can find a job and income to pay for my own place, I'm living with him in the same little house I grew up in.

*Back to You*

It only takes me five minutes from the main road to pull into my dad's gravel driveway, his house looking about as unchanged as the town does. Still small, still homey, the weeds in the flowerbed still just a little bit overgrown.

Once I park the car, I sit there for a moment, letting what's happening fully sink in.

I'm back home, and I really don't know how I feel about it.

I've missed my dad more than words can explain, only ever having seen him during short breaks where he'd drive in, lodge up in a hotel in town, and we'd go out for a few meals and maybe see a movie. I could never come back here, not when I'd just gotten out, and luckily he'd understood that. Honestly, I think he was just glad to escape for a little while too.

Last time I saw him, though, just a couple of weeks ago for my graduation, he said that pretty much everyone back here had found something else to talk about. He said that my mom bailing had been pushed onto the back burner, and that people only ever commented about it on their anniversary or something.

Of course, I don't think my mom leaving will ever be pushed to the back of my dad's and my minds, but at least we're not constantly being reminded of it by the townspeople's "neighborly concern."

When he told me that, some of my worry had disappeared and I'd gotten kind of excited over the prospect of returning home. Despite the pleasantly freeing anonymity I'd felt in Shreveport, nothing can ever beat walking into Meg's diner and getting a huge hug from Meg herself while being asked how that test you'd been worrying about went.

The people in our town may have slight boundary issues, but love has never been a problem. There's always been an abundance of that.

I'm just about to hop out of the car when I see the blue front door open and my dad pop his head out. When his eyes land on my car, an excited smile graces his handsome face right before he bounds out of the house and over to me.

I just saw him two weeks ago, nothing like the months I went without seeing him while in school, but still, seeing him and *being home* makes it feel like I haven't seen him in years.

"Dad!" I squeal happily, throwing my door open and then leaping into his arms when he extends them.

God, he smells just like he always has; the spice of his cologne, the mint of the mouthwash he uses after every meal, and just the slightest touch of dish soap. The familiarity of it has tears burning my eyes, causing me to bury my face against his shoulder. I knew I'd missed him, missed home, but it never really occurred to me just how much.

"Hey, honey," he greets warmly, placing his large hand against the back of my head.

After a few moments the heavy emotions lift, so I sniffle them away and then pull back from my dad's hug. We both chuckle when he notices the tears still lingering in my eyes, and he asks, "What're you so sad for?"

"I'm not sad," I insist, shaking my head. "I just…. I guess I just didn't realize how much I'd missed it here."

"Well it missed you too," he says with a small smile. "I've had death threats hurled my way if I don't get you into town later on today. You coming back has been all anyone can talk about."

"Oh *yay*." I groan, rolling my eyes. While the love I've gotten from all our neighbors and friends has always made me happy, I've never been too comfortable with the attention that seems to coincide with it. It's too much sometimes, and today it's going to be attention four years in the making.

It's going to suck.

"You'll be fine." He winks, chuckling, before stepping to the side and looking in the back seat of my car. "Now let's get your car all unpacked before the rain comes."

*Back to You*

I hadn't even noticed that overwhelming scent of a brewing storm in the air, one of the things I missed most while being away at school. A good rainstorm has always been my favorite thing in the world, and waiting for them has always given me the same kind of thrill as a kid waking up on Christmas morning. In Shreveport, though, you could never really smell the rain approaching, what with all the buildings around.

But here, it's just as good as I remember.

I smile. "Let's do it."

By the time we're lugging my last box through the front door, it's started sprinkling, and before I let my dad get too comfortable inside, I ask him, "Coffee on the porch?"

His tall, wide frame turns from where he'd been approaching the couch, and I see some kind of nostalgic emotion take over his large blue eyes. His voice is thicker than normal when he says, "Sounds perfect."

He quickly whips us up a batch of coffee and then after I fix mine how I like it—more creamer and sugar than actual coffee—we quickly head out onto the porch so we don't miss any of the rain. I'm pleased when I see that the rain's picked up, the branches on the trees across the street whipping through the wind, the sound of it heavy on the pavement.

I follow my dad to the far side of the porch and then take a seat in the rocker beside his, sipping at my coffee and then humming to myself in absolute contentment.

This, right now, is absolutely perfect.

"How'd your finals go?" my dad asks curiously. "We didn't really get to talk at your graduation with all the people around."

By people he means my mom's parents who, despite her disappearance and the fact we've never been close, were still adamant about coming to the ceremony and taking up all of my time.

I smile as I remember just how disgruntled he'd been at the

time, and then quickly launch into the stories accompanying my last semester of college. It'd definitely been one of the easier semesters, as pouring myself into my course work to avoid thinking about my mom had left me with a pristine GPA that even failing a few finals couldn't have hurt.

It'd been the hardest one emotionally, though, saying goodbye to the few close friends I'd made. They were all moving off back home or to graduate schools in different states, and despite how intense we'd all been about staying in touch, we knew it wouldn't truly happen.

I'm busy telling him about the time my roommate and I had just gotten back from some banquet, all dolled up in dresses and heels, and with the help of a few beers we'd decided to tag all of our friends' cars with window paint. It'd been absolutely hysterical running around the parking lot in our fancy clothes, ducking behind cars every time we heard voices. He's laughing as I relay it to him, looking thrilled that I was able to make such good friends.

The sound of a vehicle coming down the road cuts into my story, and when I look up and see a black truck pulling into the lot across the street, the Alcorns' lot, my heart stops.

In all the preparation for coming home, I never let myself think about the last night I'd been here.

The night with Weston Alcorn right here on this porch.

The night I'd thought was just a rush of vulnerability, only to discover much later when I was trying to let myself feel for guys at school, that it'd been so much more.

I can feel my dad's concerned gaze on me, but I can't seem to tear my eyes away from the scene across the street as the truck gets shut off and the door opens. My breath catches in my chest when I see the painfully familiar body jump out of the front seat and then rush up the stepping-stones to the home's front porch. I'm starting to feel better when I know the next step is to disappear into the house so I won't have to look at him anymore, but unfortunately he doesn't do that as soon as I'd like.

Instead, he turns around and looks over here, and even through the rain I can *feel* it when his eyes land on me. My nerves begin burning through my skin, my heart thudding hollowly, and even as I see that unhappy frown mar his lips, I can't take my eyes away.

I can't do it until he's turned back around and stalked into the house, slamming the door so hard that I can hear it all the way over here.

It's then I can finally breathe, but even so my body still feels like I've shoved a finger into an electrical socket.

"You okay?"

Forcing myself to snap out of it, horrified at the thought of my dad seeing how much Weston affects me, I wrench my eyes away from the Alcorns' front door and look over at him.

His eyes are wide with concern, but I see just a little sparkle of knowledge in them as well. He's noticed, I realize. How could he not have? The effect Weston has on me is absolutely unreal.

"Yeah, Dad," I answer, and then swallow. "I'm fine."

"Okay...." He trails off, his brows a bit furrowed as if he doesn't quite believe me. I don't quite believe me either, if I'm being honest.

Figuring the best thing to do is make a question out of it instead of avoiding it like a guilty person would, I ask, "Weston still lives there?"

"That he does," my dad answers, taking a long sip of his black coffee. "He moved out for a little while, but his parents retired and decided to move to Florida. They wanted to keep the house in the family, so they told him he could have it if he helped with the monthly mortgage."

I'm really not that surprised to hear that. There are two kinds of people who grow up here: the leavers and the lifers. Weston is without a doubt a lifer. It's just in his attitude, the way he looks, and the way he talks. He was born to stay here.

"I bet he loves that," I comment as nonchalantly as I can, reeling a bit over the fact that this now means he's going to be just across the street from me again.

I was able to ignore it in high school, what with him being two grades ahead of me and the two of us only ever interacting on the school bus or when their family came over for dinner.

Now though, now I'm not so sure I'll be able to ignore him. Not after that night four years ago. Not when I learned how incredible he felt that close to me, how much pain he could make me forget.

"I think he does," my dad says, breaking me out of my thoughts and also making me realize I've been staring across the street for the past few minutes. "I talk to him pretty often, you know. Sometimes we'll meet up for a drink, or if I have leftover food I'll offer it to him."

This catches my attention. I look over at him with hitched brows. "Seriously?"

"Yeah. It's really just the two of us down here, you know? The Danielsons at the end of the road keep to themselves and the Sills moved a couple months ago."

"Huh," I say, finding it incredibly strange that my dad is friends with the guy I made out with the night of my going away party. Part of me wonders if there's any way my dad could possibly know about that, but another part of me knows that there's not a chance in hell Weston would have ever told him.

Unless my dad heard about it from Mrs. Frederickson after she interrupted us.

No. There's no way, right? He surely would've said something by now.

I decide to not let myself worry about it any longer; instead just finishing my coffee, watching the storm, and listening to my dad catch me up on all the town's drama I missed while away.

---

"Oh darling, look how much you've grown!"

My cheeks are on absolute fire as all the patrons in the diner turn around to see what Meg's talking about, and I have to seriously fight the urge to sink into my seat when they realize it's me.

Meg has owned the ever-popular diner for as long as I can remember, and she's about as subtle as a bulldozer. She's forever been like a second mom to me though, consistently keeping up with what I have going on and always making sure that I'm okay. So I guess I can't be too mad at her for drawing so much attention to our booth.

"She doesn't look that much different, Meg," my dad says while shooting me a comforting wink across the checkered tabletop.

"She looks like a woman," Meg insists, making the urge to dig myself a hole even stronger, "but you just don't wanna see it."

"That's disgusting." My dad cringes, drawing a loud laugh out of both Meg and me. "Don't talk about my girl that way."

"She's twenty...." She trails off, her eyes wide, before she looks at me and asks, "How old are you again, honey? My memory is not what it used to be."

My dad hitches up an untamed brow. "And yet you're here taking our orders?"

"Hush now," she scolds lightheartedly, leaning over to swat him on the shoulder. "It's not like I don't know your order anyway. You get the same thing every time."

"Well that's 'cause I'm scared you'll mess anything else up!"

"Dad!" I gasp, laughing at the exchange between the two of them. "Stop being so horrible to her!"

"Yeah, Steve!" Meg taunts, coming over to wrap one of her arms around my shoulder in thanks. "Listen to this smart, college grad daughter of yours."

"Where you think she got her smarts from?" he teases, looking over at me with a bright, unabashed smile.

Shaking my head at my dad's apparent new, incessant need to be Mr. Funny Man, I look up at Meg and declare, "I'm twenty-three, Meg."

Her eyes practically bulge out of her skull. "Are ya serious?"

I chuckle. "Yes ma'am."

"Damn." She whistles, shaking her head. "We must be getting pretty old, huh, Steve?"

"I'm like wine." My dad laughs. "I get better with age."

At this, Meg and I simultaneously groan, not at all ready for another round of him attempting to be funny. "Dad, come on."

"Sorry, sorry," he says, raising his hands in defense.

"So anyway," Meg starts, giving my dad an accusatory side-eye before looking my way, "what're you going to be doing now that you're done with school? You found a job yet?"

"Not yet," I say, "but I'm definitely looking. I don't want to freeload off my dad forever."

"Amen," my dad pipes up.

I roll my eyes at him, and then Meg says, "Well, honey, I actually may know of something. It's not exactly a career, but it'll tide you over until you find something else."

"Yeah?" I ask, perking up and wiggling in my seat as I sit up straighter.

I shouldn't be too surprised that she knows of something; working here she overhears pretty much everything that's going on in town.

"Yeah!" she says happily. "You know the lawyers in town, Poole and McNabb?" When I nod, she continues, "Well, their receptionist is knocked up and pretty far along too, and I know they're looking for someone to take over while she has the baby and then for the first year or so, I think. That gives you quite the cushion to keep looking."

"That'd be perfect," I tell her, already beginning to get my hopes up. I thought the only openings in town would be here at the diner or maybe at a fast-food joint, which I was definitely not excited about. I'm socially awkward enough; having to serve people and be around them every second would not work out so well. Sitting in a desk and answering phones, though? That sounds right up my alley.

"Have they put an ad in the paper, or...?"

"I'm not sure," she says. "I think they're asking around for now. The girl there now has a month or so until she's desperate to take her maternity leave, so they're not really rushed yet."

"Well, I'll call 'em first thing tomorrow," I say, knowing that a job like that will be snatched up in seconds around here. "Thanks, Meg."

She grins widely, pleased she was able to help. "Of course, honey. Now, what do the two of you want? It's on the house."

"Meg...." My dad trails off, as if it's an argument they've had before.

"It's her first night back in town, Steve! Give me this one, at least."

"Fine," my dad huffs. "But you're getting an over-the-top tip."

"Oh, I'll be so wounded," she says sarcastically, placing her hand over her heart.

Almost two hours later, my dad and I are finally walking out of the diner; Meg having stopped by to check on us so much it took forever to get to eating our food. My stomach is completely bloated now and I'm drooping with exhaustion. That four-hour drive this morning is finally starting to catch up to me.

All I want to do is crawl into bed and sleep the night away.

The sky is black when my dad pulls his Suburban into our gravel driveway, and as I climb out of the passenger seat, I can't help but notice that the light across the street is still on. It is only eight thirty or so, so of course he's not in bed yet, but I am just a bit surprised by how wholly aware I am of him this quickly.

All throughout high school, I never really paid that much attention to Weston. He was older than me, so we never really saw each other at school, except on the bus. We might've exchanged a few words while waiting on it in the mornings, but once on, he always sat in the back with his cool friends and I sat up front so I could listen to music without being interrupted.

I'd known he was there, of course; I'd always been slightly attracted to him. Pretty much every girl at the school was, if I'm remembering correctly. He never really dated though, except for this one brief fling with a cheerleader in sophomore year.

Despite having the looks to be this massive popular jerk and date every pretty girl, Weston was just too quiet to do it. He talked to his friends, sure, and I don't think he was necessarily shy, but he just wasn't really a talker. He always seemed content to keep to himself, and that was amplified even more when his brother died. After that, people kind of steered clear of him. He made it completely obvious he didn't want people's sympathy, nor did he constantly want to be reminded of it.

So Weston and I never really interacted with each other until that night on the porch, and the way that night ended has stumped me ever since. I know why I kissed him: vulnerability and the fact that he was even hotter up close. Why he kissed me back, though, I still have no clue, and he *really* kissed me back too.

Maybe it was because he felt bad for me, with everything going on with my mom?

"You coming?" Dad asks, and I jump, realizing that I've been staring across the street for far too long.

"Yeah, sorry," I murmur, turning away and ignoring my dad's curious eyes as I head up the porch stairs. "I'm so tired from the drive, I must just be out of it."

"Yeah," he agrees, sliding the key into the doorknob and then pushing it open. "I'm sure you're exhausted. That drive is a long one."

I follow him into the house and then watch as he pushes the door closed behind us and flicks the locks. "I'm going to bed," I tell him once he's done, taking a few steps forward so I can give him a hug. "Night, Dad."

"Night, sweetie," he returns, giving me a kiss on top of my head before letting me go. "I'm really glad you're back home."

"Me too." I smile at him, and no matter how much I may want to admit otherwise, I realize I'm not lying.

I *am* glad I'm home.

# Chapter Two

The next morning, I sleep in much later than I usually do, not rising from my bed and heading to the kitchen for my morning coffee until around ten thirty or so. I guess yesterday really did wear me out, as I'm usually a pretty early riser.

My dad's already gone to work, of course, leaving me to an empty and completely silent house.

I can't just jump into being lazy, though, as my first and only goal of the day is to call that law firm Meg was talking about last night and ask about the receptionist job. This may be the only job I can find for a while, and I definitely need to take advantage of it. While lazing around sounds incredibly appealing, it doesn't exactly bring in an income, and that's something I'm in dire need of.

Even though I love my dad and everything, being in this house with him is soon going to get old. I can feel it. I love being home, the comfort and familiarity of it, but it also houses some pretty unpleasant memories that I absolutely hate reliving. I've managed to make myself busy enough to not really think about my mom leaving for four years; I'm not going to start slacking now.

So after I slurp down a whole cup of coffee and then start the machine on another one, I pick up my cell phone, swallow my nerves, and quickly dial the number Meg scribbled down for me on a napkin. The phone only rings twice before I hear the click of it being picked up and someone saying, "Good morning, Poole and McNabb, this is Miranda."

"Hi," I say nervously, my voice squeaking just a little bit. "My name's Iris Tilley, I was calling about the receptionist job opening."

"Oh?" the lady asks slowly. "You're trying to take my job, then?"

My cheeks catch on fire and panic surges deep in my gut. "No! No... I mean, well yes, I guess, but only while you're on leave. You are going on maternity leave, right? That's what I—"

My horrified babbling is cut off by her loud laughter, making my cheeks burn even hotter. "I'm just kidding! I know they've been looking for someone to take over for me, don't even worry about it. Let me transfer you to their assistant."

"Okay," I manage to croak out, still a bit terrified of her from the earlier joke.

"This is Jenny, how can I help you?" a new voice asks a minute or so later, this one having a much more evident southern twang than the first.

"Hi," I say, before repeating the exact thing I first said to the receptionist.

"Oh, that's great!" she coos. "We haven't even put an ad out yet. I've been on their cases to get to work, but they kept saying we had time, and I was like, no you don't! Miranda's leaving in four weeks!"

I laugh, my nerves still there and churning, but put at ease just a little bit by how friendly she sounds.

She says, "They're free tomorrow afternoon if you want to come in for an interview. Would that work for you?"

"Oh my gosh," I breathe, excitement and nerves battling it out in my stomach. I have an interview... tomorrow? That gives me little to no time to have the freak-out session I know is on its way. "Yes, that'd be perfect."

"Great, I'll schedule you in for two thirty. How does that sound?"

"Sounds good," I answer.

"I will see you at two thirty then, Ms. Tilley!" she exclaims happily, and then quickly follows up with, "Also, if you really want to impress them... wear something purple and gold. Okay? They're kind of crazy about LSU."

I chuckle, not at all surprised. Everyone around here thinks the Tigers are more of a religion than a college. "Will do. Thanks for the heads-up."

"No problem," she says, and I can practically hear a smile in her voice. "You have a good day, Ms. Tilley."

"You too." I grin, hanging up the phone and then all but falling onto the sofa beneath me. My breathing's slightly quicker than normal, but I'm still thrilled. If I get this, if I can manage to beat the recent college graduate's shitty job outlook, then everything will fall into place.

And that's all I want.

After reveling in my good luck for about twenty minutes and also simultaneously freaking out because I've never had a legitimate job interview before, I remember about that coffee I set to brew. After running over to fix it how I like it, I look around the empty, cluttered kitchen, and decide that I'll tell my dad the good news over a nice dinner.

I've never really been much of a cook, always too lazy to make anything other than an easy pasta dish or a piece of chicken on the George Foreman grill, but I guess today I'm just in that kind of mood.

The only grocery store in town other than Walmart is one of those rich people organic stores, and my dad and I have never quite been interested in a diet that doesn't include greasy hamburgers and french fries. My not-quite-so-flat stomach has never really thanked me for that, but my soul always has.

So even though I hate Walmart, I turn my car in that direction and then pull into the dismally populated parking lot five minutes later.

After parking and hurrying into the store to escape the sun, I grab a cart and get to pushing my way over to the food aisles.

Over the next fifteen minutes, I grab all the food items I think I'll need, and then head to the back of the store to grab some nice wine for the two of us. It's as I'm passing the nonalcoholic beverage aisle, though, that a terrifyingly familiar figure catches my eye. My feet stop moving forward for some unknown reason, my heart catching in my chest, and my grip on the shopping cart tightens.

It's Weston.

He's here, and he's just a mere three yards away from me.

While his eyes are trained in front of him and haven't yet spotted me, I quickly look him up and down, taking him in since I wasn't really able to yesterday through all the rain. He's in dirty, brown-specked jeans and a blue striped button-down with the sleeves pushed to the elbows, and through them I can tell just how much he's bulked up since I saw him four years ago.

Weston's always been a large guy, incredibly tall with deliciously broad shoulders. He's always had a body that other guys would kill themselves in the gym for, and here, now, I can tell he's only improved on it. I can see the cords in his forearms working as he leans forward to grab a case of bottled water and settle it in his buggy, and as he grabs another one to match it, the muscles in his chest flex through his shirt.

A particular warmth settles in my belly and my mouth goes completely dry.

I know that I either need to say something or get moving, my gawking at him having gone on for far too long, and it's when I'm finally about to decide to just move on that he takes the decision right out of my hands and glances my way.

My breath halts in my chest when his eyes meet mine, then his bright green gaze fleetingly looks me up and down before settling back on my face. I definitely don't miss the appreciation cross his face as he takes in the bareness of my legs, but I'd feel much better about it if he hadn't tensed up painfully right after.

His sharp jaw clenches, and it's then I grasp just how utterly not pleased he is to see me here, standing right in front of him.

My throat works as if it knows it needs to say something, but my mind doesn't seem able to fathom up anything. It's like everything inside of me has come to a screeching stop.

"Iris Tilley," he says after a few moments, his Adam's apple bobbing up and down.

I try to fight how good my name sounds on his tongue despite how unhappy he seems to be saying it, and say weakly, "Hi, Weston."

He doesn't say anything back immediately, instead letting us both just awkwardly stand there looking at each other, silently fighting over who needs to talk next. I know I definitely need to say something, since I'm the one who disappeared the day after we kissed, the day after he said we needed to talk about it.

But I can't.

It's like he's robbed me of every solid thought I have.

"You're back," he says, grabbing his buggy to turn it in my direction so he can take a few steps the same way.

I swallow. "Um, yeah, I am. Finally finished college and all that."

He nods. Being just that much closer allows me to get a good look at his face. It hasn't changed as much as his body has, only losing that slight boyish roundness. With his wide yet sharp jaw, a strong, slightly bent nose, and bold brows, he'd be the epitome of strong masculinity if not for his pink, plush lips and his overtly beautiful green eyes rimmed in enviable lashes.

It's hard for me to imagine this man, this absolutely gorgeous man, kissing me with those lips of his, those strong hands clenching his shopping cart shoved in my hair or gripping my thigh.

How on earth did that night, that kiss, even happen?

Bringing me back to the present, he asks, "You staying with your dad?"

"Yeah." I nod, nervously tucking a piece of escaped hair behind my ear. "Until I save up for my own place, of course."

"Of course." He grins wryly, his voice turning just a smidgen darker.

My brows furrow in confusion. Is he... is he mad about that?

"Um." I swallow. "Yeah. So, uh, I heard your parents moved? That you're keeping their house?"

His eyes darken just a smidgen. "Yep. Didn't want to just leave it to another family."

"I guess that's true," I say, attempting a small smile but absolutely failing. "So, um, what do you do now? My dad never—"

He cuts me off, nodding toward the cases of water in his cart. "I'm in construction. On site today, actually, so I came out to get these. Really need to get them there, so...."

I don't miss the obvious hint he's just hurled my way. He wants me to leave him the hell alone is what he's really saying, and it makes my stomach feel distastefully hollow. "Oh," I say, blushing as I move my cart so he can get his through. "I'm sorry. I—"

He cuts me off again. "See you, Iris."

And then he's gone.

My feet are rooted to the spot, my mind whirling with his nearly palpable dislike of me. Was he.... Was he really that affected by my leaving after that night? That kiss couldn't have affected him nearly as much as it did me, right? I mean, obviously it got to him a little bit, judging by the intense reaction I got out of him, but never in a million years would I think it was enough to make him this cold toward me.

He had to have understood why I left town, right?

I look over my shoulder and see him hurriedly pushing his cart down the large walkway toward the registers at the front, his

25

shoulders tight.

Well... maybe he didn't.

---

"I think I speak for both Chet and me when I say we'd be happy to have you aboard," David Poole, one of the lawyers at the firm, says with a handsome, perfectly straight-toothed smile.

I can't even help myself. "For real?"

I realize what's come out of my mouth and how informal it was, and my cheeks burn in humiliation. I mean, yeah, it definitely did seem like the interview was going well and I was somewhat expecting to land the job, since their assistant, Jenny, had told me that no one else has been interviewed and they'd waited until the very last minute. But never would I have imagined they'd give it to me right here and now.

Luckily they seem to be more amused by my immature outburst than angered, the two middle-aged and handsome men throwing their heads back and laughing together in a way that's almost harmonized, telling me they probably spend far too much time together.

Chet McNabb, the other partner, says once he's done laughing, "For real, Ms. Tilley. You seem like a perfect fit here, whether or not it's just temporary. And I'm sure Jenny will be thrilled to have someone her age around here."

"Thank you so much," I say with the biggest, cheesiest smile. "This is incredible. I never thought I'd get it today."

Chet shrugs his broad shoulders encased in a nice suit and says, "It's a small town, Ms. Tilley. We've been putting this off for so long because we knew the kind of characters we'd get in here. You don't seem to be one of those."

"I'm not," I say earnestly, shaking my head. "I promise you."

"Good," David says, running his hand through his curly blond hair before shutting the interview book with a thud. "Now, we need to talk to Miranda and see when she's willing to have her last day. She's been doing us kind of a favor staying on for these past few weeks. We'll have Jenny call you."

"Sounds perfect," I say, rising when they do. "I could start tomorrow if you needed."

"We're thinking more along the lines of next Monday," Chet says, adjusting his thin black tie.

"Whatever you need," I say, praying I sound less desperate than I think I do. My dad said to be as accommodating as possible, that I need them more than they need me, and that's what I'm trying my best to do.

The two tall men come around to my side of the table and take turns shaking my hand and saying that it was nice to meet me and that they'll see me when they see me. Despite the expensive-smelling cologne coming off them, they both seem like such down-to-earth and nice guys. I was so intimidated when I first walked in since I know the two of them have money, what with being the only law firm in town. But I quickly relaxed when David smirked and said, "Go Tigers," when he saw my purple pencil skirt and gold jewelry, and when Chet accidentally let out a burp in the middle of the interview.

So hopefully I'll feel at home here, despite the enviously gorgeous Jenny who greeted me when I first walked in.

She's definitely going to take some warming up to.

She's incredibly friendly, as nice in person as she was on the phone yesterday, but she's got the whole blonde-haired, blue-eyed, perfect-chest thing going on and it's a bit of a hit to my self-esteem. I don't want to be petty, but it's hard not to be jealous of someone who looks like that.

Thankfully, I don't see her again as I walk out, instead only seeing the pregnancy-rounded face of the redheaded receptionist I'll be stepping in for.

"How'd it go?" she asks, her eyebrows raised.

"I got it." I smile proudly.

"I'm happy for you," she says, tipping her head toward me. "Just don't get too comfortable, all right? I love my job."

Her bluntness renders me speechless for a quick second, but I do have to admire her for it. Telling people how I feel has always been difficult for me, and I respect people who are so easily able to do it.

So I just say, "It was nice meeting you, Miranda. Congratulations on your baby," and then head on out of the office and into yet another blisteringly hot day outside.

I'm dying to get out of these damn heels, never having been one to normally wear them. They're the one pair I own, wide-heeled black pumps, and the only reason I got them was because my best friend back at school thought it was ridiculous I didn't have any. I love how they look on me, having spent just a second longer than normal looking at my reflection in the mirror this morning, but the pain they are causing is just not at all worth it.

As soon as I climb into my car, I rip them off my feet, tossing them into the passenger seat before I start the engine.

And then it hits me.

I just got a job. A real, adult job. Of course it's only temporary, but still... I have a job, a paycheck.

Smiling to myself, I pull my phone out of my purse and dial my dad's number, praying that he's not too busy at work to answer my call. He's an accountant and an absolute nerd when it comes to numbers, so sometimes it's hard to pull him away.

Luckily, he answers after the fourth ring.

"How'd it go?" he immediately asks, letting me know he's been eagerly waiting for my call.

"I got it!" I squeal, trying my hardest not to do a happy dance since I'm still in the parking lot and anyone inside could walk out and see me. "They offered it to me right on the spot."

"Iris, that's incredible!" He cheers for me, making me smile even harder. "We have to go out and celebrate tonight."

"Okay." I grin. "Whatever you want, Dad."

"You're the one who got the job, sweetie, so it's whatever you want. Just think about it until I get home and let me know when I walk through the door, okay?"

"Will do." I laugh, once again reminded of how great my dad is.

We hang up after our goodbyes, and I hurry home so I can beat the usual after-school traffic. I pull into the driveway and hop out of the car, carefully walking across the gravel since my feet are bare.

It's while I'm having issues putting the key into the doorknob that I hear movement behind me. My heart leaping painfully in my chest and the hair on my neck rising, I slowly turn and look over my shoulder.

All breath leaves my body when I see a large golden dog trotting from Weston's front yard over to mine. "Hi boy," I coo in a high-pitched voice, dropping to my knees as he darts up the stairs to my lap.

His tongue is hanging out of his mouth and he pants excitedly as he leaps onto my outstretched thighs, his face lifting as if to lick mine. "Aww, no." I giggle, pushing his head away so he doesn't lick me, but scratching the top of his head.

"Who do you belong to, honey?" I ask, even though I know he won't answer me, my fingers coming in contact with his collar.

I have to dodge his head coming at me to pull his collar around to look at the tag, relief hitting me when I see a name and number etched into the silver circle. "So your name is Thumper, huh?" I ask, running my hands over his ears and laughing when I hear his breathing increase happily.

"Come on, let's get you out of this heat," I tell him, standing upright and finally getting the key into the lock and pushing it open. He cheerfully follows me into the house, his large tail wagging energetically.

I fix him a bowl of water, as I'm not sure how long he's been outside, and as he quickly starts lapping it up, I finger his collar again and type the number etched into it on my phone. I pet his head quickly as the phone begins to ring, and then walk over to sit on the couch.

Whoever it is doesn't answer, so I'm preparing myself to leave a voice mail when I hear the voice on the voice mail recording. "Hey, this is Weston Alcorn. I can't come to the phone right now, so just leave a message and I'll call back."

His voice is strong, deep, and leaves that same ring of fire circling around in my belly that seeing him in person does. This is absolutely ridiculous. I should not be having these feelings for someone's voice mail, especially since it belongs to someone who's made it pretty obvious he hates me.

It does make me feel a little less intimidated by him, though, knowing that this adorable and friendly dog belongs to him. Maybe he's not as intense and broody as he likes to make out to be? No one with a dog that acts like this could be as cold as he tries to come off.

"Hey, Weston, it's, um, it's Iris," I say after the beep, feeling ridiculous for how nervous I am just leaving a voice mail. "Your dog... he was outside and saw me on my porch and came running over. I have him at my dad's since it's so hot, and I'm guessing you're at work, so uh, I guess you can just come get him when you get home? I'll be here, so... so yeah. Bye."

I hang up the phone with burning cheeks, my heart racing as if I've just run a marathon.

After four years, after just one kiss, after being with other guys, how do I still feel this way? How am I still so affected? How the hell am I getting so flustered over his voice mail?

It's horrifyingly pathetic.

I fall back onto the sofa, prop my feet onto the armrest, and take a deep breath, attempting to quell all this adrenaline.

Before I know it though, golden paws are leaping onto the sofa, propping up Thumper's large body so his chocolate brown eyes can meet mine.

My heart warms.

Maybe I need a dog.

---

It's around five fifteen when I hear a knock at my bedroom door, and my dad calls out, "Weston's here!"

My stomach lurches. I'm both nervous to see him and disappointed that he's here. I've been having such a nice time with his dog, all cuddled up in my bed with me and watching a Kardashian rerun, and I'm really not that ready to give him up.

Sighing in defeat, I attempt to sit up, but it's quite hard with a dog half my weight on me. Smiling at how cuddled up he is, I run my fingers through his fur and say, "Come on, man... time to get up."

His eyes slowly open. He seems quite lethargic after his nap, but then Weston laughs loudly at something from the den, causing Thumper's eyes to widen. Letting out a happy bark, he quickly hops off my bed and pushes through the cracked open door.

"Hey, big man." Weston chuckles, and I can hear the dog leap on him and start begging for his attention.

Well, now I guess I don't feel quite as loved.

I'm dreading going out there to face Weston after his brush-off at Walmart yesterday, but if I don't go out, then I'll be the one in the wrong and that's not really something I want. Sucking it up, I head out of my room. Weston is sitting on the edge of the couch with Thumper's front legs propped on his thighs. The dog is eagerly wagging his big tail as Weston scratches behind his ears.

He and my dad are talking about something fishing related, but when I come in Weston finishes up his sentence and looks over at me. I changed out of my job interview outfit earlier and am now clad only in a thin tank top and cotton shorts. If I had any sense at all I would've changed into something a little less revealing, but I've been hot from having such a large, furry dog lying on me.

And besides, if I had changed, then I wouldn't be feeling the slight feminine gratification that accompanies his lingering glance over my body.

After a moment or two, long enough that my dad notices Weston's focus and clears his throat, Weston shakes away his stare and says, "Thanks, Iris, for letting him come in. I must not have shut the door all the way this morning."

"It's no problem," I say in complete honesty, satisfaction tingling in my chest.

My dad looks between the two of us before settling on Weston and saying a bit uncomfortably, "He and Iris are buds now. He hasn't left her side since I got home. Never seen that before."

"Really, now?" Weston asks, his eyes still intent on me as he hitches an eyebrow and makes everything south of my ribcage clench.

God, the man really is too damn good-looking.

I swallow. "Um, yeah. He was superfriendly. Kept me company the whole time he was here."

"Huh." Weston exhales, finally dropping our stare and letting my breath come back to me. He scratches Thumper's back as he says, "Yeah, that's pretty odd for this guy. Usually he's not too taken with strangers."

My dad looks at me and smiles. "Maybe he's just a good judge of character."

Despite him being nice to me when I walked in, I definitely don't miss the sarcastic grin that stretches Weston's lips when he says, "Must be."

I flush in disappointment, not at all happy that he's once again decided to not like me, and just as my dad opens his mouth to say something, Weston rises to his feet and says, "Well, I'll get out of y'all's hair then. I'm sure Thumper here overstayed his welcome."

"Not at all," I say civilly, my blush burning even brighter when his eyes meet mine once more.

My dad quickly breaks the silence, saying, "We were actually about to head out to BR for dinner. Iris here landed a job today."

"Really?" Weston says, sounding surprised. "That quick, huh?"

"Yeah, I guess," I say, nervously tucking a piece of hair behind my ear. "But it's just temporary. The woman I'm stepping in for is about to have a baby."

"Well that's too bad," Weston says. "But still, congrats."

It doesn't sound even slightly genuine, but the awkwardness of the room is starting to get to me, so I push the maybe-insult to the back of my mind and just respond cheerily, "Thanks."

He gives me a small, fleeting smile, and then turns to my dad and tells him he'll see him later, sounding much friendlier with him than he did with me. Feeling pretty damn insulted, I purse my lips, looking to the ground, and don't look up until I hear the front door shut.

When I do, my dad's looking at me, and before I can even say anything to brush away what just happened, he comments, "Well, that was weird."

"Um, yeah," I reply with a harsh swallow, my chest suddenly feeling tight. "That it was."

# Chapter Three

My mom and I used to be close.

I try not to think about how good she was to me during my childhood; it makes the reality of her leaving even harder. But she was... she was good to me. She'd take me shopping for new school shoes every year, she'd always do my hair, and she would never hesitate to take me somewhere when I asked.

She always did it with a smile too—that beaming megawatt smile my dad was always obsessed with.

Not once did I see that smile waver, that cheerful spirit diminish, and so when she left... when I came home from school to find a note taped to the fridge explaining why she could no longer stay here, I was stunned.

There'd been not one warning sign.

In fact, I'm pretty sure the night before she left she and I were up late into the night giggling about how I was almost done with high school and how I'd soon get to meet a bunch of cute college guys.

She was a perfect mom until the second she left.

You'd think that would make me hate her less, make me not

resent her as much for leaving. But it's the complete opposite, in fact. What she did, how she handled the whole thing, made me hate her even more.

If she'd given me just a few signs, then maybe I would've been more prepared. I wouldn't have been so shell-shocked, so unable to wrap my head around it. For the first couple of days, it was like I hadn't even gotten the note. I wasn't able to admit it to myself.

But then after a week or so went by with no word from her, it slowly started sinking in that she was truly gone.

I still don't think it's fully hit me yet. Sometimes I'll catch myself reaching for my phone to text her if something's happened. It's gotten rare nowadays—it *has* been four years—but it still happens.

It kind of happened this morning.

It was my first morning of my first real job, and she wasn't here to tell me what to wear, how to act, or how I should do my hair. She wasn't here to give me a little pep talk over our morning coffee. She wasn't here to witness this milestone in my life, and it left me pretty damn depressed on my drive to work.

Once I got here, though, at nine o'clock on the dot, I pushed it to the back of my mind and didn't let it get to me again.

Despite this being only a temporary job, I still want to do my best so that once it's all over they'll give me a glowing recommendation.

I'm really starting to get the hang of it as well, and I'm not lying when I say that I find answering the phones strangely enjoyable. The first few times I answered, I nervously stammered through the greeting Jenny taught me, but now, just three and a half hours later, I'm breezing through it.

"I'll transfer you," I say, the words already an instinct. "Just one moment."

As I push the few buttons to transfer the call to Chet's office, Jenny strolls into the lobby.

Dressed in all black but with the contrast of her platinum blonde hair, Jenny is the spitting image of everything my self-confidence hates. She's freakishly beautiful but also incredibly kind, making it impossible to dislike her.

"Hey, Iris," she says with a smile once I hang the phone up, strolling over to my desk and resting her forearms against its black surface. "What are your plans for lunch?"

"Um, I don't know," I say truthfully, having been so nervous and caught up in my mom-lacking emotions this morning that I didn't even think about it. "I hadn't really gotten that far."

She giggles. "That's perfect. There's this amazing café up the road and they have the best salads. I was going to go there today. You want to come with?"

"Sure!" I agree happily, feeling lucky that I've already made a friend at my new job. With my friends from high school having gotten out of this town and my friends from college hundreds of miles away, I'm in desperate need of someone to hang out with other than my dad. "That sounds perfect."

"Great," she says. "We close the office from twelve to one for lunch, so let me just go get my purse and we can head out."

"Okay," I agree as she makes her way out of the lobby, the four-inch heels on her shoes making a professional clacking sound against the shiny black floors.

Five minutes later, we're pulling into the parking lot of a little shop strip, and I see the café she mentioned wedged between a nail salon and an antique shop that belongs to the mother of some girl I graduated high school with.

I quickly hop out of the car, not having realized with all my nerves today how hungry I was, and gladly follow her into the cozy-looking café. With one glance I see just how popular this place is since there's only one empty table, and I can't help but ask, "Is this place new? I don't remember it ever being here."

"Yeah, I think so." She nods as the two of us fall into the line of people. "I just moved down here a year ago and it was here, but I have no idea about before."

"Oh?" I ask curiously, wondering what on earth made her move down here. The only people who live here now have had relatives living here forever, and so it's pretty uncommon to hear of a newbie. "Why'd you move here?"

"It's a long story," she says, tucking a piece of blonde hair behind her pierced ear. "Basically, I followed an old boyfriend down to Baton Rouge for school, and then we graduated and I couldn't find a job there, so here at the firm was the closest. He dumped me, moved to Tennessee, I think, and so I just decided to stay and get an apartment here."

"Where are you from?" I ask her. "'Cause most people would never want to stay in a place like this."

"Houston," she says. "And I hated it. It was too big, too urban. I didn't know 99 percent of the people I graduated with. Then, you know, I start working down here, meeting people in town, and I loved it. I love how everyone knows each other, you know? And everyone's just so friendly. So when Dalton left I decided to stay."

I nod, trying to wrap my head around someone actually wanting to leave a place like Houston for a place like here.

She smirks. "Why? Do you hate it here?"

"No!" I exclaim, shaking my head. "Of course not. I mean, sometimes I hate how small it is and how everyone knows your business, but... but most of the time it's pretty awesome how nice everyone is."

She smiles and the two of us move up in line as a middle-aged redhead grabs her drink and walks off. "Exactly. So what about you? Why do you live here?"

After I tell her my little backstory, the person in front of us grabs their drink and leaves, allowing us to step up to the counter and place our orders. We both order salads and iced coffees, and then as the barista gets to work on our drinks, she looks over at me and asks,

"Tired of it here, then?"

"Yes and no," I answer her, loving how she actually seems interested. "I don't know. I guess I'll see how I feel when Miranda comes back."

The barista comes up and hands us our coffees, telling us that our salads will be out soon, and Jenny and I head on over to a booth in the corner that a group of teenagers just deserted.

Starting up where we left off, she says, "God, I hope she never comes back. She was such a bitch."

I laugh, taking a sip of my drink and savoring the caffeine, and then listen as she dives headfirst into telling me all the gossip accompanying the law firm.

---

The rest of the day passes by pretty quickly, and at five o'clock on the dot, I'm waving bye to Jenny as we part ways to our cars.

Outright pleased with myself for how well today went, as well as completely exhausted, I quickly back out of the parking lot and start on the short drive back home.

As I drive, I decide that I'm too tired to cook, and swing by the one Chinese place in town, texting my dad that I've got dinner covered before driving the rest of the way home.

As I turn onto our street, I notice the black truck behind me in the rearview mirror, and one heart-pounding moment later, I divert my eyes from the truck's hood to the driver. Swallowing hard when I see Weston's face, I quickly focus on the road ahead of me before taking the right turn onto our gravel driveway.

Fighting the urge to be pathetic and wait in my car until he's inside his house, I throw my door open after cutting the engine and reach over to the passenger seat to grab my purse and the large brown takeout bag. I know better than to call over to him like most friendly neighbors do, so I ignore the sounds of him exiting his truck and instead just head up the driveway and the porch stairs.

And then I'm falling.

I vaguely hear the sound of takeout containers splattering on the porch's wooden beams, but it's drowned out when I feel the scorching pain slide up my thigh. A scream escapes my throat as the burning hurt intensifies, my eyes swimming with tears and my heart pounding with raw adrenaline.

It takes a few seconds for my mind to register what's happened, that I must've fallen through a faulty plank, and it's right as I'm looking around and gauging how painful it'll be to pull myself out of here that I hear the sound of pounding footsteps. It's hard to see through the tears, but it's not that difficult to figure out that Weston must've seen what happened and decided to run over.

"Iris!" he calls when he hits the stairs leading up to the porch. I watch through blurred vision as he carefully walks around the hole I'm in and then squats so we're at eye level. "What the hell...? Are you okay?"

I squeeze my eyes to slightly quell the agony radiating from my thigh, and then manage to say, "I think... I think so? But my leg is.... I don't know, but it hurts really bad and—"

"Hey," Weston interrupts my rambling, his voice uncharacteristically soft. "It's going to be fine, but I got to pull you out of there and it may hurt, okay?"

"Okay." I swallow hoarsely, the compassion in his green eyes sending comforting waves down my spine.

He rises up just a little bit and then extends his arms to me. My heart catches in my chest when I have to wrap my arms around his neck. It's as he starts to stand up fully, bringing me with him, that I feel the rawness on my thigh scrape against the jagged edge of the porch.

A high-pitched scream escapes my throat, and I clench my eyes closed as fresh tears begin to build.

39

"Shit," I hear him murmur, before I feel him take a step closer to the hole so that my body can move back and not be so close to the splintering edges.

I instinctively burrow my face into his chest as he finishes pulling me out, and I can't find the will to be embarrassed about my tears leaking into his shirt. Once I'm out, he attempts to set me on the porch, but the pain in my left thigh has that leg crumpling against the pressure my weight puts on it.

His arms squeeze me against him when he realizes I can't stand on that leg, and then he lifts me up again and carries me over to the wall beside the front door. Looking up at him, I see his wide gaze trained intently on my thigh, his teeth gnawing on his bottom lip.

I try to look down at my thigh to see why it has him so worried, but he grabs my chin and makes me face him instead.

"Where's your key?" he asks.

"Um...." I take a deep breath, his closeness diverting the pain. "It was in my hand.... But they fell. They're probably—"

"I'm going to go inside and get a wet towel for your leg, but it's a pretty deep cut. When is your dad getting home?"

I shrug helplessly, my mind whirling. "I don't know. He's... he was saying last night that he's been kind of swamped at work, and when I texted him 'bout dinner, he didn't respond, and he still never replied saying he'd left, so I'm guessing he's still there?"

"Fuck," he curses, shaking his head. "Well then, I'm going to have to take you to the hospital. That thing," he says, motioning to my thigh, "is going to need stitches."

"What?" I ask, panic surging in my throat. "No... it can't—"

"It is," he cuts me off dryly, looking quickly down at it once more. "Just don't look at it, okay? I know you're not good with blood."

"Wait," I start, trying to remember exactly how he knows that. I would've remembered us talking about it, because I'm not exactly proud of the fact that, despite my high pain tolerance, the sight of blood always renders me dizzy. "How do you...?"

I trail off, noticing that he's moved away from me and is now leaning over to grab my keys from the porch. "Which one?" he asks when he stands back up, referring to the ring of keys all painted different colors of nail polish.

"Purple," I answer.

He disappears into the house, and while I hear him banging around in the kitchen, I have to try my utmost hardest not to look down at my thigh.

Weston comes out of the house just a minute or so later, locking the door behind him and then falling to his knees in front of me. "I'm going to wrap this pretty tightly," he says, "so it's going to hurt. But I have to put pressure on it or the bleeding won't stop."

"Okay." I swallow, my nerves not nearly what they would be if he weren't here. Despite him having been nothing but rude to me since I've been home, the sight of him, him being here, still comforts me.

I feel the lightest brush of his fingertips against my exposed thigh, my work skirt having been hiked up during my fall, and then right as I feel my hormones surge and my breathing stop, the coolness of the wet rag presses against my cut.

It doesn't really hurt until, after he's placed the wet rag against the cut, he takes a piece of gauze I didn't see before and ties it tightly around my leg. "Oww," I whimper, my eyes once again scrunching shut.

The pain is a horrible throbbing when I hear him stand up, and it takes everything in me to open my eyes. He's right there in front of me again, and his eyes are so intensely focused on my face that it's hard to remember just how much he dislikes me.

"You think you can walk to my truck?"

I look over his shoulder to the black truck parked across the street, and as much as I don't want to, I have to shake my head. With my thigh hurting as much as it is, it'd be impossible for me to walk all the way over there.

"Come on then," he murmurs, leaning down and swiping one arm under my knees and the other against my back.

The moment I'm in his arms, his scent wraps around me like the comfiest and warmest of blankets. The pain fades into the background, and my nerve endings crackle to life like a candle being lit. But still, I'm comforted. No matter how awkward we've been around each other, him holding me like this, *cradling* me, makes it seem like we have never been closer.

After tenderly depositing me in the passenger seat, he quickly backs out of the driveway and starts us in the direction of the hospital, my dangerous feelings evaporating as quickly as they arrived.

An hour later, after checking in and trying not to stare at the other patients in the emergency room, I'm being settled in a wheelchair and Weston is following the nurse as she pushes me back into an open room. She takes all of my vitals and then peels open the gauze Weston wrapped around me, her eyes sympathetic as she looks at me and says that the doctor will be in soon.

She's gone after that, leaving Weston and me alone in the small, white, bleach-scented room.

I know I need to say something since this whole situation is so awkward and random, and I'm pretty confident that Weston won't say anything first. Instead, he's sitting over on the chair in the corner, looking tense and uncomfortable and like he'd rather be anywhere but here; completely opposite of how comforting he was being earlier.

I swallow, nerves inching in, and say quietly, "Thanks for this, Weston. I know you probably have better things to be doing."

"It's all right," he says, looking down at his hands and starting to pick at his nails.

Completely underwhelmed at his response, I let out a quiet sigh and then lean back against the stiff pillow behind me. I'm trying my hardest not to think about the pain in my leg or the fact that I can *feel* the cut bleeding, and the only other thing my mind can find to concentrate on is the man sitting just a few feet away from me.

Which is equally as painful.

Sudden vibrations in my pocket distract me from my thoughts, and when I pull my phone out, I sigh in relief. It's my dad. I called him on the way here and he never answered, probably busy at work or the ringer was too low for him to hear, so I sent him a text relaying what was going on.

The poor man's probably freaking out.

I hold it up to my ear. "Hey, Dad."

"You're in the hospital?" he demands hurriedly, his voice overcome with concern. "What...? Who's with you? Are you okay?"

"Dad, I'm fine," I assure him, feeling horrible that he's so worried. "One of the boards on the porch must've been old or rotten or something, and when I was walking up from work I fell in and cut my leg up pretty badly. But Weston saw and wrapped it for me and brought me here."

"Thank God," he breathes. "I'm on my way there now, okay? Have you seen the doctor? What'd they say?"

"Saw the nurse," I explain. Weston looks over at me as I continue, "She said it's definitely going to need stitches. We're waiting on the doctor to come back now."

He says, "I knew I needed to get that porch fixed. I've just been putting it off and... and I don't know. Honey, I'm so sorry."

"Dad, it's not your fault." I chuckle. "Just rotten luck. It could've been a lot worse." And then before I can think twice about it, I add, "Thank God Weston was across the street. I don't think I would've been able to pull myself out."

I can practically feel Weston's stare burning the side of my head, making my cheeks flush, but he needed to hear it. Despite how big of an ass he's been since I've been back, he really did save me today. If I'd had to pull myself out, the cut would've been much worse, and I don't know if I would've been able to drive out here."

"Well, tell him I'll buy him a beer sometime or something as a thanks, okay? I'll be there in twenty minutes if traffic lets up."

"I'll tell him," I say. "Bye, Dad."

We hang up and I slide my phone back into my pocket, hesitant about looking over at Weston, although I still feel him staring at me. I do, though, because if I don't it'll just make this whole situation weirder.

I tell him, "My dad's on his way, says he'll buy you a beer for helping me."

He just nods, his hand reaching up to run through his dark blond hair. Once again feeling like a burden, I say shyly, "You don't have to.... You don't have to stay here, you know? Since he's coming. You can leave if you want."

His eyes flash darkly. "Do you want me to leave?"

"No," I say with a shake of my head, tucking a loose piece of hair back. "That's not what.... I don't know, you just... you just seem like you don't want to be here."

I'm sure my cheeks are practically fire truck red at this point, but I had to say something. He's made it so obvious that he doesn't like me, that he doesn't want to be near me, and even though I have absolutely no idea *why*, I don't want to make him feel obligated to stay with me if he despises it so much.

He doesn't say anything; instead just deciding to continue sitting there in silence, and it starts to piss me off.

I open my mouth to say something to him, but before I can there's a soft knock and the door is pushed open. A tall, handsome man in a white coat steps in, softly closing the door behind him and then putting his focus on me with a comforting smile.

"I hear someone took quite the nasty fall?"

"Guilty," I reply, blushing, sticking my hand in the air like I'm in school and saying I'm present.

He introduces himself and then pulls his rolling chair over so he can sit, gesturing for me to move my leg toward him. I avert my eyes to the ceiling as I do so, and then cringe when I feel him start to undo the bandage.

Luckily, he asks me questions as he looks over the wound, effectively keeping me distracted.

"You fell through a porch, right?"

"Yes, sir," I answer apprehensively, biting hard on my bottom lip when he moves the bandage a bit to the side, causing it to tug against one of the raw edges.

A second later he's closing it, though, and gently placing my leg back against the bench I'm on. Taking that as a sign it's safe to look down from the ceiling, I meet the doctor's gaze as he begins to talk. "Well, I'm definitely going to have to X-ray that first, just to make sure nothing else snuck its way in. After that we'll stitch it right up and you'll be good to go."

"Sounds great."

He looks over at Weston with eyebrows raised. "Boyfriend?"

"No," Weston says gruffly, giving me a quick glance with furrowed brows. "Helpful neighbor."

"Well," the doctor says to him, motioning to the bandage on my leg, "I'm assuming you did this, then?"

"Yes, sir."

"Beautifully done," he says with a nod. "May be a little messy now, but it kept her from needing a transfusion."

"A transfusion?" I gulp.

"Oh yeah," the doctor says, chuckling at my unease. "This is a damn deep cut, honey. I saw a little muscle tissue down there."

Nausea starts to swirl in my belly. "You're serious?"

He nonchalantly waves his hand. "It's really no big deal. I can get you a mirror if you want to see—"

My heart is throbbing as Weston cuts him off, his voice a bit edgy as he says, "Probably not the greatest idea, Doc."

"Oh?" the doctor prompts, his blond eyebrows rising as he checks back with me to see if it's true.

I grimace. "Yeah. I just.... It freaks me out, I guess. Don't know why."

"Most people don't like it," the doctor says kindly. "I'm just around it so much I'm a bit immune, and I forget not everyone's that way."

"Thanks," I murmur, my cheeks still burning. The color begins to fade, though, when Weston adjusts himself in his plastic chair, and I'm once again baffled as to how he knows I'm so badly affected by blood.

And then it hits me that Weston interrupted the doctor right when I was starting to panic, as if he knew it was going to happen.

As if he were being nice.

I'm lost in confusion when I vaguely hear the doctor clear his throat. Knowing that I've been caught dazing, I flush even deeper as I mumble to the doctor, "Sorry."

He continues, "All I was saying was that I'm going to get a nurse to come grab you and bring you over to X-ray, and then once that's done and I've looked it over to make sure there's no splinters, we'll get to stitching."

"Okay," I answer, wondering just how long I'm going to be stuck here.

He leaves, saying a nurse will be in "any moment," and when the door is shut, I once again peer over at the large blond occupying the corner. His green eyes are trained intently on his hands as if he's about to start picking at his nails again, and I begin to think maybe it's something he does when he's nervous.

Feeling a bit more warmed up to him after realizing this, I don't have to force out the words when I say, "Thank you, Weston. You know, for stopping him when he was talking about the... the... *you know* in my leg. I was starting to freak."

He snorts, a light and heart-stopping beginning of a smile touching his lips as he chuckles. "I could tell."

"How do you...?" I start nervously, knowing that it's an awkward question but just *having* to know. "How do you know I'm not good with blood and stuff? It's not something I really tell people."

He finally looks up from his hands, my chest clenching when his gaze touches mine, and the feeling of it is so distracting that I almost don't see the pink shade his cheeks. But I do notice, thank God, and once again it has me wondering if maybe he's not the untouchable enigma I think he is.

He looks back down, his hands running harshly from his thigh to his knees, and asks me, "You remember our PE classes were at the same time, right?"

I have to think back on it for a second, but of course it doesn't take me long to remember. Although I may have never caught myself doing so back then, I was always subconsciously aware when Weston was around.

Which makes it easier for me to remember and respond, "Yeah, you were a senior I think, because I was a sophomore."

"Yeah," he says, looking back over at me. "Well, there was that free day near the end of the year. A lot of guys were playing basketball, and that guy got conked in the face with the ball."

"Oh yeahhh," I drag out, remembering that day pretty vividly.

He's right; it was a free day, something they gave out with more and more frequency as the end of school year got closer, because I remember sitting on the bleachers and making note cards for my finals.

I recall hearing a bunch of shouts, so loud that I could hear them over my headphones, and then looking up and seeing blood gushing out of this poor guy's nose. "I do remember that."

He nods before continuing. "And then when you saw, you leaped off the bleachers and ran into the locker room. When you came out, it was obvious you'd been throwing up."

"Oh my gosh," I mumble, feeling a ridiculous second wave of embarrassment from an event so damn long ago. Running my cold hands over my warm face, I say, "I can't believe you remember that. I always told myself that no one noticed just to make me feel better."

I hear him chuckle again, and the humiliation starts to fade when it hits me that this is the second time in five minutes I've had the pleasure of hearing the sound.

Dropping my hands from my face, I watch him curiously as he says, "I just remember thinking that it was weird, you know? You'd always been so intense with your grades and stuff, and seeing you act so... I don't know, human... was weird."

"I was human!" I exclaim with a laugh, my chest flushing with warm, happy jitters as it sinks in that he actually paid some attention to me back then.

My reputation in high school was pretty lackluster, boring, since I'd just been the smart girl who was going places, a rarity at the school.

I was never picked on for it. I just think that the majority of students thought it was strange. At such a small school in such a small town, a high school diploma was only a pit stop in a life consisting of young marriages, lots of kids, and jobs you got because you knew someone.

I never wanted that for my life, not that I thought anything bad about it.

No, I was perfectly fine to blend into the background, hang out with the few friends I had when I wasn't working hard enough to get a scholarship, and then go to college where I'd never be the odd one out again.

Which is exactly what I did.

And it was the best thing I could've done too, because now I'm much more comfortable with myself because I was in an environment for four years that didn't give weird side-eyes to people doing homework during their free time.

The door opens before either of us can say anything else, and a tan-skinned woman who looks to be in her late thirties pushes a wheelchair inside the room. "You ready to go?" she asks me.

"Yes, ma'am," I answer, glancing over at Weston and feeling my happiness from mere moments ago wavering when I see that he's once again picking at his nails.

Is our brief moment over already?

After she situates me in the chair, her glance latches on to Weston and she asks, "Staying or coming?"

He looks up from the torn skin around his thumbnail and his eyes slide over me before he replies, "Staying."

My gut telling me that the nice Weston from a few minutes ago is probably gone for good, I tell him, "My dad will probably be here by the time this is done, so you can leave if you want."

He looks back to me and I barely see the emotion, if that's what it actually is, flash in his eyes before he places his hands on the armrest of his chair and pushes himself to his feet. "I'll go, then," he says, his jaw tight.

The nurse says, "Follow us and I'll show you the way out."

He does just that, and when he turns in the direction she's pointed him, I can't help but watch him walk away and feel immensely more confused than I was before.

# Chapter Four

After the next day at work, which was full of answering questions about why my leg was propped up underneath my desk, I'm exhausted and more than ready to be in my bed when I pull into the driveway.

I'm careful to step around the hole in our porch, my dad having marked it early this morning with a This Area is Wet sign he stole from work, and then let myself into the house.

Knowing that my dad will kick my ass if I cook for him tonight, I quickly change into some sweatpants and a thin camisole and take up residence on our couch, burrowing into a comfy blanket and switching on Netflix.

Before I know it, though, I'm asleep and then being forced awake by the sound of heavy footsteps on the porch and then the door being pushed open. Groaning, I tighten my grip on my blanket and snuggle deeper inside it, my quick nap only having made me feel more tired.

I close my eyes again, knowing that my dad will evacuate the room the minute he realizes I'm asleep, but when I hear a masculine voice distinctly not belonging to my dad, I know that's not going to happen.

By the time I'm sitting up and looking down at my top to make sure my breasts haven't come out during my nap, my dad is already through the door and Weston is following him in with a delicious-smelling pizza in his hands.

"Oh no, Iris," my dad says, looking down at the disheveled sofa and then over at me. "We didn't wake you up, did we?"

"It's fine," I say with a wave of my hand, rising to my feet and then pulling my sweatpants up a little bit since they'd ridden down enough to show the skin of my hips.

Weston's gaze snaps away from me the minute I catch him looking, and I try to forget about the warmth curling in my stomach by telling my dad, "I wouldn't have been able to sleep tonight if y'all hadn't."

"It's probably the pain medicine," he responds, grabbing the pizza from Weston's hands and placing it on the table. "Those things tend to wear you out."

"Yeah, I guess," I say, folding my arms across my stomach.

"You did okay at work, though?" my dad asks me. Weston coldly brushes by me as he heads toward the food.

"Yeah." I swallow, feeling incredibly self-conscious now that I see Weston's back to his old cold self.

I thought that yesterday at the hospital the two of us had made just the smallest bit of progress, that even though we'd probably never be friends, he wouldn't be this standoffish toward me, but I guess I was wrong.

"Other than to use the bathroom, I never left my desk. That girl I was telling you about, Jenny, she went and got me lunch."

My dad smiles over at me from where he's now sitting at the table and says, "Well, that sure was nice of her."

"She's pretty awesome," I respond, letting Weston grab his slices and a beer from the fridge before I even dare move into the kitchen.

Once I've grabbed my plate and drink—no beer for me since I'm taking strong medication—I sit down next to my dad and keep quiet as the two of them lose themselves in a conversation over how they think the LSU baseball team will do in Omaha.

Weston's as friendly as ever to my dad, of course, his face open as they chuckle over jokes and disagreements. It's pretty infuriating, the fact that he can be so nice to my dad and yet so callous toward me. I feel like I don't belong sitting at my own dad's kitchen table.

My gnawing thoughts are cast aside when my dad cuts through by asking, "You okay? You haven't eaten much."

"Oh, I'm fine," I assure him, ignoring a set of bright green eyes boring into my forehead. "The medicine might've messed with my appetite a little."

"But you've eaten today, right?" he checks. "You ate what that girl brought you?"

"Yes," I insist, and then figuring that he won't calm down until after I've eaten a little bit more, I make a show of picking up my one half-eaten slice and taking another bite. "I'm fine, Dad. Don't worry."

"I always worry," he says. "Especially right after you've fallen through a rotted old porch. The doctor did give you a tetanus shot, right?"

"He did," I promise. "Right before you got there."

"Good," he says, looking considerably more settled. "I'll feel better once the porch is fixed, though."

"When's it getting fixed?" I ask curiously, and take another bite of pizza.

My dad narrows his eyes at me, and when I glance over the table I see that Weston's looking at me strangely as well.

Well, more strangely than normal.

I'm about to ask what's wrong, when my dad says slowly, "That's what we were just talking about, Iris, before I asked you why you hadn't eaten."

"Oh," I whisper, looking down as I feel the blood rush into my cheeks. "Sorry, I probably... spaced out, I guess, when y'all were talking about baseball."

"You sure you're okay?" my dad asks fixedly, like he's terrified I have some deadly disease and haven't told him.

"I'm fine," I insist once more. "I just got up from a nap and I'm on pain meds. I'm just out of it."

When it looks like he's accepted my excuse, I ask again, "Now... when's the porch getting fixed?"

My dad looks across the table at Weston, who says, "We'll start this weekend. Whoever wants overtime can come help, and then we don't have another major project until next month, so we can work during our spare time. Shouldn't take too long if we come as often as we can."

"Wait," I cut in, not realizing what I'm saying until after the words are out of my mouth. "*You're* the one working on it?"

If he is, that means he's going to be over here a lot more, on our porch, in the hot sun, sweating, most likely taking his shirt off and throwing hammers and shit around and.... Dammit.

"Is that a problem?" he asks matter-of-factly, raising one of his thick dark blond brows.

My dad's looking at me and, realizing what I've done, that I've made it sound like I don't want him here, I start to panic as I say as convincingly as possible, "No... no, I just.... I'm surprised that it's so quick. I figured y'all would be busy and it's on such short notice...."

Weston explains a bit coldly, "We're in between big jobs at the moment."

Okay, well that makes sense, but still. This means Weston's going to be at the house more often, and him being here is going to have me constantly on edge. I can barely breathe normally around the guy, so why does he have to be here when I'm trying to adjust to my first job and heal from an injury?

"But your boss," I start, grasping for straws as I try to say something he hasn't thought of yet, "he's cool with that? I mean, I'd be pretty pissed if all my workers spent their hours doing that big a favor for a friend."

My dad chuckles underneath his breath as Weston gives me a dry, tight grin. "I am the boss, so no... don't have a problem with it."

"You're the boss?" I ask, completely bewildered and caught up in the panic of this whole situation. "But at Walmart, you were.... You had dirt on you and...."

"Sitting at a desk all day drives me crazy." Weston shrugs, somehow managing to look nonchalant and proud of himself all at once. "If I'm needed at the office, they'll call me, but most of the time I'd rather help with the hard work outside."

"Oh," I say, feeling foolish for how I've reacted. I've made an ass out of myself, and I'm sure that once Weston leaves, my dad will waste no time in asking what's gotten into me. I can always use the pain meds as an excuse, I guess, but my dad would never believe that.

He's definitely going to know that something's wrong.

In a desperate attempt to salvage what's left of my dignity, I say, "That's incredible, Weston, that you're in charge. I couldn't ever imagine being the boss of something so young."

He doesn't look at all grateful for my sentiment, but he still says, "It is pretty great."

Feeling even more self-conscious and desperately in need of an escape, I shrink into my seat and pray that the next few minutes pass by quickly so that I can excuse myself without making it look like it's because of what just happened.

Still feeling my dad looking at me, I meet his gaze and silently beg for him to take over so that I no longer have to talk.

Thankfully, he understands.

Turning his attention to the only sane young person in the room, he tells Weston, "I'll go and have you a key made, West, so that if neither of us are here y'all will still be able to use the bathroom and get water and stuff. I'm about to be traveling for work a bit more often, and I know Iris would hate to have to ask to leave her new job to come let you guys in."

"That sounds good," Weston says, the tension in his voice now evaporated since it's no longer me on the receiving end of his words. "And there shouldn't be too many of us here at a time, since it's a small area. I know you want the whole thing redone, but having all of us out here would get in the way more than it'd help."

"You're redoing the whole thing?" I sheepishly ask, hating that I have to bring attention back to myself but really wanting to know.

Having the whole thing redone is going to be a hell of a lot more expensive than just the hole, and my dad doesn't have the biggest wallet in the world.

My dad nods. "I am. Yesterday reminded me how old the thing is, so I might as well. Don't want anything else like that ever happening again."

I know I shouldn't say it, but I can't help myself. "Won't that be really expensive, though?"

Weston says, "We have a lot of leftover wood from previous jobs, and really it won't take that long or too many of us."

My dad grins over at Weston before looking back down at me and saying, "He cut me quite the deal, honey."

"That's really great of you," I tell Weston, truly meaning it.

Despite how horrible he can be to me, Weston *is* great to my dad, and my dad's someone who really needs it. After what my mom did to him, how badly she broke him by leaving like she did, Dad's pretty hesitant toward people. He'll never in his life admit it or act like it, but I know it's true. It's why he jokes so much; if he plays off everything like it's funny, no one will know what's important to him and use it against him.

No matter how much I hate how Weston is around me, I need to suck it up and not care. I can deal with the cold shoulder and the random backhanded jabs all day if it means my dad has someone he can trust.

Weston just gives me a weak attempt at a true smile, but this time I'm determined not to let it get to me.

I'm not giving Weston that hold over me any longer.

---

Sooner rather than later, I realize that my little self-declaration to not let Weston's rudeness bother me hasn't worked.

At all.

In the past two weeks, he and three other construction workers have been to our house to work on the porch five times, and each time just drives me even crazier. It's not the weekdays that are so bad, mainly because I'm so exhausted from work by the time I get home that I can't deem it necessary to care when Weston brushes off my greeting to them all.

The weekends, though, are the worst. I've always been an incredibly early riser since getting things done when I know most of the city is still asleep gives me a weird sort of peace. But they've gotten here so damn early that I haven't had any time to curb my grogginess with coffee or change clothes.

The first Saturday morning they were here, Weston and some stranger I was later introduced to as Bobby came into the house for orange juice when I was still sans bra. They walked in the kitchen right as I pressed the brew button on our coffeemaker, and when I heard them, I immediately had to dash around the corner into my bedroom.

By the time they went back outside and I felt it was safe to come out, my coffee was already lukewarm.

I understand why they get here so early; the Louisiana afternoon heat is positively fatal most days, and on others there are highly powerful storms that pop up just to combat the severity of it.

But the earliness isn't the only issue.

Having Weston here, just like I knew would happen when they told me about all of this, puts me constantly on edge. Since I never know when he's going to come inside for the bathroom or a drink, I usually just hide out in my bedroom until they're gone for the day.

And if I do see him, he's usually without a shirt. The sight of his chest, all tan and broad and rippling with muscles, is nearly painful.

I try not to let it distract me, but that's something I've recently learned I have no control over.

I do have control over the cleanliness of this house, though, and for that very reason it has never been cleaner.

I've always been a stress cleaner, swapping sadness or anxiety for a broom and some Lysol, so that's why Wednesday night, when I get home to see Weston busy hammering away, I immediately find myself thinking that the countertops in the kitchen must need a good cleaning even though I scrubbed them just this past Saturday.

His head comes up when he hears my car hit the gravel driveway, but by the time I've climbed out of the driver seat, he's put it back down and perfected the art of pretending he doesn't see me.

"Fuck it," I murmur to myself, ignoring him completely even when I have to walk just a few feet from where he is.

After letting myself into the house, the door already unlocked since Weston's here, I change clothes, feeling much better in cotton shorts and a T-shirt than in the white dress and purple cardigan I've been in all day.

I tie my hair into a ponytail and head on into the kitchen, figuring that Weston is almost done and probably won't come back inside, since it's getting late and he's the only one here. I put two chicken breasts into the sink to thaw like my dad texted me to do, and then grab the Lysol and new package of sponges I got Monday evening.

I'm busy scrubbing down the half of the sink that the chicken's not in when I hear the door open, and my dad calls out, "Iris, I'm home!"

57

"Hey, Dad," I respond, laughing at his shouted greeting, since he didn't realize I was mere feet away in the kitchen.

"Oh...." He trails off, chuckling to himself. But then his eyes meet mine and he takes in what I'm doing, and his grin falls as he asks, "You're cleaning again?"

I toss the dirty sponge into the sink and start the water on it as I answer with a lie. "Yeah, I've just been on this big cleaning kick lately. Don't know why."

"I noticed," he says, sitting as he loosens his blue-and-black plaid tie. After I turn the water off, I look at him and see that his eyes are concerned, his lips flat, and before I can ask why, he says, "Are you upset about something, honey? I haven't seen the house this clean since... since your mom... you know."

I feel a crack in my chest at how worried he looks, and the horrifying thought of him thinking I'm getting sick of this place like my mom did enters my mind.

"Dad, no!" I say urgently, crossing my arms over my chest. "That... that was different. I cleaned so hard back then that my hands would crack from all the soap and bleed everywhere. That's not.... Look, I don't know why I'm doing it, but I'm not upset about anything. I promise. I'm really happy, actually."

The lines in his face ease just a tad, but I can tell that I still haven't quite convinced him. He asks, "You're sure? If it's something I'm doing, just let me know. I know living with me again is an adjustment, but—"

"*Dad*," I cut him off desperately, hating that he's been thinking this. "Of course it's nothing to do with you. I love living here, seeing you all the time. I hated never seeing you while I was gone. I think getting away from here, from all the... you know, mom stuff, was good for me, but I hated that I had to be away from you to get away from that too."

"Well, is that it?" he asks, looking a bit pained at my words no matter how reassuring they were meant to be. "Is it being here with all the memories and stuff? I got rid of her things while you were gone. I don't.... I thought that—"

I cut him off again, my heart tearing at what this ridiculous attraction-based cleaning spree of mine has done to him. My dad absolutely hates showing emotion like this, this kind of vulnerability, and I know showing it to me is killing him. His goal in life is to be my strong, funny, teddy bear of a dad, and I know that, to him, this is equivalent to failing at that.

"I barely even think of her anymore," I tell him honestly. "Sometimes, yeah, I do. I did the first day of work, when I wasn't sure what to wear or how to do my hair because that's... that's mom stuff, you know? But most of the time I'm perfectly happy with how things are. Aren't you?"

I don't think I realize how much this whole scene has gotten to me until my voice cracks as I ask him that. Seeing my dad upset over me is one thing, because I can fix that, change whatever I need to change, but seeing him upset over my mom is a whole other story.

How can I try to fix that for him when I haven't really fixed it for myself?

I don't think of my mom most days simply because I have other things to do, because other things have happened and I've gotten so used to not thinking of her. But other days it's still like the day after she left, when I holed up in my room and cried into my pillow for a solid twenty-four hours.

It's like what Weston told me that night on my front porch, about how the hurt never gets better, but that we just get better at not thinking about it.

"Of course I am," my dad says, rising to his feet and walking over to me. "Having you here is the best time I've had since you left, Iris. Watching SVU, going outside to watch the rain, just drinking coffee with you in the morning.... I love all that."

"Me too," I say, my voice cracking again.

Feeling like this whole emotional and pretty painful conversation is almost over, I try to speed it along by saying, "Look, Dad, why I'm cleaning is silly, okay? It's not.... I just do it to keep my mind off other things. It's not solely a thing I do when I'm depressed."

"What are you—" he starts, his brows furrowed, but before he can finish his question the loud banging sound of Weston nailing a board into the porch echoes throughout the house.

And then my dad's eyes widen, his mouth drops open, and dread quickly replaces the negativity our conversation brought on. "Iris," he says, and looks over his shoulder out the window for a moment before looking back at me. "Does this.... Does this have anything to do with a certain neighbor being around all the time?"

"Wha...?" I gape, my heart pounding. Even knowing that I've already given myself away, I have to fight it. "No! Dad, of course not! No!"

A mischievous grin touches my dad's mouth as his mind begins to work, his lips stretching further and further with every passing second.

"*Dad, stop*," I beg, hating that he's putting together every embarrassing thing that's happened these past few weeks.

He exclaims happily, "You know, I knew something was going on! You two are on such thin ice around each other all the time, and I thought maybe it was just me seeing things or looking too deeply into it, but...."

When he trails off, I have to ask him, "Why are you so happy about this? Do you know how horrible this whole situation is?"

His smile begins to fade as he asks slowly, "Why's it horrible? He's not...?"

"Dad, in case you haven't noticed, Weston hates me."

"No he doesn't," he says, aghast, as if I'm stupid for even thinking that. "Why would you think that?"

"Are you blind?" I cry. "He hasn't made it very subtle. Like the other night for dinner, he was so rude to me and so nice to you."

"That's because you sounded horrified he was coming to work here," he points out. "Of course he was going to be offended."

"I was only horrified because he's been rude to me ever since I've gotten back. That was the first time I was the first one to dish it out, and I didn't even mean to do that! I told him how awesome it was that he was so high up in his job!"

"Iris." He chuckles, looking at me like I'm demented. "I think you may be misinterpreting things. Weston's a quiet guy. He's not going to just come up to you and be nice."

"Quiet is fine!" I hate that he's not understanding me. "But that's not what he's been toward me!"

"Hey, hey," he says, placing a hand on my shoulder, his voice much less teasing than before. "Calm down, okay? I don't think you're seeing things right, but even if Weston has been rude to you, it's probably just because he's scared of you."

"Scared of me?" I ask disbelievingly, rolling my eyes. "Why on earth would he be scared of me?"

Taking his hand off my shoulder, he smirks and heads to the sink, placing his hand in the water to check the chicken before saying in a playfully bored tone, "Don't think I don't know what happened between you two during your party."

My eyes practically bulge out of my skull. "Wha...?"

After pulling the chicken out and wiping his wet hand on the folded towel on the counter, he says, "If you think for a second that Mrs. Frederickson wasn't inside cooing to everyone who'd listen about you two, you're crazy. You know her mouth is constantly running."

My cheeks burn as horror creeps into my gut. "What do you mean... everyone?"

He continues, "I doubt anyone even remembers, Iris, what with all the drama your mom leaving caused. But yes, she came in and immediately told me that she'd found you but that you were a little occupied with the boy across the street."

"You didn't.... Why didn't you...? What? Why didn't you say anything?" I stammer out, this new information making me feel just the slightest bit nauseous. I always knew that the odds of Mrs. Frederickson blabbing about what she saw were much higher than her not, but I guess hearing that she actually told everyone makes it feel real.

He shrugs. "You were eighteen years old, honey, almost nineteen. I knew something like that was bound to eventually happen, and I've always liked Weston. And besides, it was a rough time for us. You needed something to get your mind off it."

I open my mouth, but he just keeps talking. "So when I say he's scared of you, I really think it may be true. Despite what most people think, boys feel just as hard as girls do, and knowing Weston and how quiet he is, him doing something like that must've been a damn big deal. And then you left the next day."

"But you know why I left," I say, trying my hardest to defend myself. I've never been proud of how I handled what happened that night, but I've never made it sound as bad as my dad just did.

"Of course I do," he says, grabbing a knife from the drawer and starting to cut up the chicken. "I think you did what you had to do for you, and that always needs to be your first priority. But just because you did what was right for you doesn't mean what you did to other people for that to happen is immediately excused, you know? You always got to look out for yourself, yes, but never forget to factor in other people as well."

Feeling completely overwhelmed by what this conversation has turned into, I bury my face in my hands, trying to calm my mind down. My dad is totally and completely right, I know that, and in knowing that, I come to realize that what I did four years ago was even more wrong than I'd thought.

I should've told Weston that I was leaving the next day; I

shouldn't have just let him walk off thinking that we'd talk soon.

It was selfish of me.

I can make excuses all night long about why I did it, but I still did it.

I guess I just never realized how much one kiss between us would mean. I always knew it'd mean a good deal to me, of course, being that it was my first and that it made me feel so good during such a bad time. I just never allowed myself to think that maybe it'd affected him too.

But what am I supposed to do about it now? Go out there and apologize for something that happened so long ago? It'd be the most uncomfortable conversation of my life, and not only that, but what if my dad's wrong? What if that's not the reason Weston's mad at me, and when I go out there and apologize, he just shrugs it off as no big deal?

If he reduces the quality of something as meaningful as that kiss was to me, I don't think I'll be able to handle it.

Taking my hands from my face, I lean against the counter and side-eye my dad, asking, "Can we just.... Can we just not talk about this anymore?"

"Fine by me," he says, leaning up to grab some flour and spices out of the cabinet. "Just give me a little heads-up next time you have a crush on someone, okay? That way I won't have to worry about picking up after myself for a while."

# Chapter Five

By the time Friday rolls around, I'm desperate to do something that gets my eyes and mind *off* Weston Alcorn. Ever since the conversation with Dad Wednesday night, I haven't been able to get that kiss out of my head, and when my dad told me that they'd be working on the porch all weekend, I knew I had to be proactive.

Except for a few stress-driven nights in college where I was craving to let loose, I've never really been the type of person to initiate a night out. I've always found it more fun to stay home and be in comfortable clothes and to only have to regret the amount of junk food I've consumed the next morning.

But even with my dad being back to normal after our talk and me wanting to assure him I am as well, I know I won't be able to get everything Weston-related out of my head if I'm at home.

Which is why at work, even though I was pathetically nervous of her rejection, when I saw Jenny coming back from lunch I asked her to do something with me tonight. She agreed, thank God, and since neither of us wanted to spend our time in one of the several redneck-filled bars around, we decided on the one club in town, the Boot.

*Back to You*

The Boot's been around forever. My mom and dad used to talk about their wild escapades there, and it's one of those places that's kind of a landmark in town even though there's absolutely no reason as to why. It's located in an old warehouse, the large space having been renovated fifty years ago into an oversized dance floor, bathrooms that have needed cleaning since the nineties, and two always crowded bars. It's a place that you'd see from the side of the road and be a bit nervous to walk into, what with its industrial-grade tin roof and roughed-up red brick walls, but on the weekends it's always wall-to-wall with people.

It's eleven thirty now. We've been here for well over an hour, and I'd be lying if I said I wasn't having an absolute blast. Despite finding Jenny completely intimidating, she's once again proven to me that she's probably the nicest person I've ever met.

Not only that, but she seems to be as thrilled about our new friendship as I am, if the three shots she toasted to us being "badass motherfuckers" tells me anything.

Currently, the two of us are on the jam-packed dance floor dancing together to some country song that sounds more pop than anything else. We're drawing a good bit of attention too, attention that, if I were sober, would make me uncomfortable.

But thanks to the shots we've had and the two mojitos I've downed, I'm actually enjoying the attention, especially coming from this one cute dark-haired guy sitting at a table with a few of his friends and smirking over at me every few minutes.

Unfortunately, though, there's this empty space in my cup that desperately needs filling.

Once the song ends, I quit dancing and grab Jenny's arm so I can lean in and tell her, "I'm going to the bar!"

"Okay!" She nods energetically, squealing happily when she hears the next song come booming over the speakers. "Oh my gosh, I love this song!"

I laugh at her, absolutely loving how she's one of the few people I know who'll go out simply to have fun. Since the minute I arrived on her doorstep, her only goal has been having the time of our lives, and it's really worked.

"I'll be right back," I tell her, looking around quickly to make sure I don't see any lurkers waiting for their chance to get Jenny alone, and then making as quick of a getaway as I can with the crowd pulsating around me.

I dodge the heavy traffic to the bar, and then I'm quickly slinking up to the wooden countertop in a small free space between two groups of people.

The DJ switches songs, this time swapping out the slower, sexier song for something with an effervescent beat. Cheers erupt on the dance floor as Nicki Minaj's voice rings out, and I'm smiling at the sound when I feel something in the atmosphere switch.

The song quickly fades away in my mind and the hairs on the back of my neck stand tall. I brace my hands against the bar's edge when I feel someone come up behind me. I want to look over my shoulder and see who it is, but the slight retreat of my tipsiness has swept away any ounce of flirtatious bravery I possess.

I'm telling myself to relax, to not let the warm body behind me distract me, but the effort is pretty much in vain. Whoever it is has a scent so intoxicatingly rich and male that doing anything other than being hyperaware of him—like catching the eye of a bartender—is a lost cause.

My heart starts pounding when the people to my left leave, and I feel him move so he can fill that space. Out of the corner of my eye I see strong forearms, beautifully emphasized by the rolled back sleeves of his linen shirt.

After a few moments of shameless and hopefully sneaky ogling, I allow my gaze to roam up the line of his arm, tracing over his strong biceps, wide shoulders, and....

Shit.

My breath catching in my throat and my brain roaring how stupid I am, I snap my gaze back to where it belongs, watching as the redheaded bartender makes his way over.

I can't believe Weston is here.

Why is he here?

He doesn't seem like someone who'd enjoy coming out to places like this. He struck me as the type who'd rather sit at home with his admittedly adorable dog and think about how much he hates me. It's immature of me to think that, I know, but how can I not?

Luckily he hasn't recognized me—at least I don't think he has—and now all I have to do is remain meek enough so that he doesn't look down at me.

I can do that, right?

In the midst of my internal freak-out, I almost don't realize that the bartender has stopped in front of me and asked what I wanted.

"One mojito, please," I say, and then I remember Jenny complaining not too long ago about how she was almost out of beer, so I quickly add, "And an Ultra."

He nods at me, and then I watch, panicked, as he turns his attention to Weston and prompts, "For you?"

My heart plummets when I see Weston take a quick side glance at me, and as I listen to him rattle off his boring order of a Bud Light, I curse inwardly. Of all nights I have to see this guy, of all places he could've gone instead, it has to be tonight and it has to be here. This night was specifically to get my mind off him, and now that he's here and has already rattled my hormones, it now qualifies as a bust.

And I'd been having such a good time, too.

As the bartender walks away, I feel Weston look down at me, and knowing that I can't just ignore the guy, I return his look. He looks damn good tonight too. My earlier ogle of who I thought was a stranger didn't do him justice. The usual scruff on his jaw is a bit scruffier than usual, probably due to him being so busy helping with the porch, and his wavy blond hair looks perfectly disheveled.

"Iris Tilley," he greets, his voice neither cold nor warm. "What're you doing here?"

"It's a bar," I reply dryly, the shameless sarcasm in my voice telling me that there's definitely still some liquid courage lingering. "What do you think?"

He smirks in response before shifting his weight, leaning just a bit closer to me. "What I meant was," he says slowly, his voice deep, "that you've been in town for over a month and this is the first time I've seen you do something outside your dad's house."

*Jackass*, I think to myself, hating the way he says it. It sounds like he's saying I don't belong here, in this town, like I'd rather hide out at home than try and set up social ties. Maybe I don't fit into this town as well as he does, maybe I'm not as stereotypically Southern as he is, but that doesn't mean I'm inherently snobby.

"I've been busy," I say defensively, watching the bartender out of the corner of my eye as he starts in our direction.

I lean in to tell the bartender to put it on my tab, but before I can open my mouth Weston has placed two ten-dollar bills on the countertop and said, "For both of us."

The bartender gives me a fleeting look before grabbing the cash and walking off, and once he's gone I mutter a begrudging "thank you" to Weston and take a long, much needed gulp of my drink.

Pleased at the warmth immediately spreading through my stomach, I turn back to Weston and say, "As I was saying, I've been busy. With the job, my dad, the whole leg thing. I haven't exactly had a chance to come check out the *incredible* bar that is the Boot."

I say the last bit sarcastically, causing his eyes to flash in annoyance. "Oh, I'm sure the places wherever the hell you left to go were *so* much nicer than this."

"They were," I insist. This place is great, and I know bashing on it makes me look like a snob, but I'm so far done with Weston and his superiority complex that just seeing him annoyed makes me feel better. "I'm sure there's a reason this place is named after a dirty-ass shoe."

I watch as he takes a long, drawn-out sip of his beer, his eyes never leaving mine the entire time. It's completely obvious that I'm pissing him off, but instead of being upset about it like I normally am, I'm going to throw it all right back at him.

"Then why're you here, huh?" he asks, the strobe lights over the dance floor flickering over his hardened face. "If this place is so beneath you."

I have a feeling he's referring to the town in general and not just here, but I let it slide. He's obviously made up his mind about me and thinks I'm some snooty bitch, but at this moment I'm done with caring about him and about what he thinks of me.

I'm done remembering our kiss as if it were some important, life-changing thing.

I'm just done.

I'm not letting him have the power to make me feel small and in the wrong anymore.

"I'm here," I say, taking another huge gulp of my drink to help get the rest of the words out, "for a fucking drink. To have a good time. You know, what people usually do at bars? I'm not here to be a complete dick to someone who's never been anything but nice to me!"

My heart is pounding yet again and my breathing is coming in short, shallow pants. I've finally called him on his shit, and while a huge part of me feels so good about it, another part, the small, sober one, can't help but think I've just made this whole thing between us even worse.

His jaw is twitching in anger as he stares harshly down at me, clearly trying to think of a response.

Before he can say anything, though, a familiar and completely inebriated voice calls out, "Iris!"

Wrenching my stare from his, I look to my left and see a grinning Jenny hurrying over to me, her hand reaching out to grab my arm once she gets close enough. Her blonde hair, perfectly curly before we came out, is now falling in beautifully effortless waves down the slim curve of her back, her slightly rounded cheeks flushed with a mix of exertion and alcohol. "I was making sure you were okay. You were taking a while!"

"The line was long," I tell her, grabbing her beer from the bar and handing it to her. "But here, I got this for you too."

"Oh okay." She grins happily. "Thanks!"

And then after she takes a long swig from her brown bottle, her eyes fall on Weston. Her eyes widen just a little bit more, and before I know it, she's taking a poised step forward, so graceful it's like she hasn't been drinking, and extending her hand toward him. "I'm Jenny. Who're you?"

"Weston," he responds gruffly, reluctantly turning his attention to her. He takes her hand and shakes it.

"And how do you know Iris?" she asks sweetly, giving me a genuine smile before turning back to look up at him.

"She lives across the street from me. Always has."

"Oh, that's so cool!" Jenny exclaims, before giggling. "So small-town, too. I grew up in Houston, so people knowing their neighbors, let alone being friends with them, was so rare."

"Oh?" he asks, and I watch in absolute disgust as his face softens and an easygoing smile takes its place. "Houston, huh?"

Nausea starts churning in my stomach when I see him lean back against the bar, his arms crossing over his chest like he's setting himself up to be there for a while. I shamelessly reach for my half-empty mojito and down the rest of it.

I have no right to be upset about their flirting, and knowing that only makes me more upset.

Weston and I had our moment four years ago and, along with every ounce of damage that happened to me that summer, I abandoned what could have been the result of that. I was so damn fearful of that kiss being anything other than the lifeline it was to me, that I gave up any right to think I have some sort of hold over Weston.

I don't. He's free to do what he pleases and, unfortunately, *whom* he pleases.

And it's that very thought that has me waving the bartender over and ordering another mojito and a shot of tequila. I know it's not good to mix alcohols, but at this point I can't bother to give a shit.

All I want now is to pretend like this isn't happening.

---

"Oh my God!" Jenny exclaims through her laughter, sitting down across from me at the same café booth we sat at my first day of work. "But Friday night, though!"

Despite it being Monday and my hangover from Friday night being long gone, I still haven't quite mentally recovered from our night at the Boot.

Saturday morning I woke up on Jenny's couch feeling like I'd been hit by a truck, and when I looked at my phone I saw flirty text messages from an unknown number indicating that we'd done something naughty. I've felt this overwhelming cloud of shame and guilt since.

Not only that, but even though I blacked out during the end of the night, I explicitly remember the flirting that went on between Weston and Jenny, since it's the whole damn reason I got as drunk as I did, and I'm still bitter about it. I know I shouldn't be mad, as he and I were never together, but I can't help but be irritated over how easy it was for her to bring out his nice side when he's done nothing but be harsh to me.

She's my only friend in town, though, and really she did nothing wrong, so I know that I'll just have to deal with it.

As I sip on my coffee while waiting for our food to be delivered, she asks me with a silly grin, "So how much do you actually remember from Friday?"

"I remember introducing you to Weston," I say, hating that I have to bring it up. "And then nothing."

"Oh God!" She laughs loudly, tilting her head back. "That's so funny! Things got so crazy after that!"

"Did they?" I ask nervously, that same sick feeling of shame washing over me yet again. "What all happened?"

"Well Weston and I were talking, which is a whole other story I have to tell you later, and then we look over and you're making out with some guy!"

Completely horrified, my eyes bulge and I ask quietly, "Seriously?"

"Yeah!" She giggles. "He was really cute, though, and following you around like a lost puppy after that, so I definitely don't blame you."

"I think he texted me," I muse.

"No," she gasps. "Really? After everything that happened?"

"Wait...," I start, her words not making any sense. "What else happened?"

"Weston punched the guy," she says, wrapping her tiny fingers around her coffee mug. "The place was about to close and you weren't feeling so good, so we were helping you to my car. That guy hadn't been around in a while, mind you. After y'all making out at the bar, I dragged you to the dance floor and we didn't see him again."

"Until the parking lot?" I clarify, my mind whirling.

"Yeah." She nods, taking a sip of her latte and then continuing. "We were trying to help you into the car, and I guess he saw you and came running over and was trying to take you from Weston, and so they started arguing and the guy said something about you wanting it, and Weston just snapped. Punched the shit out of him."

"Oh my God." I exhale, dropping my face into my hands.

Obviously I made a fool out of myself that night, and I doubt I'll ever forgive myself for making out with a stranger in front of Weston, but for him to do that for me when I was that drunk and had just yelled at him is incredible.

"I can't believe he did that," I can't help but murmur out loud.

"Why?" she asks, and when I drop my hands from my face I see that she's looking at me curiously, her eyebrows raised. "He said y'all were friends."

"He said that?" I ask dubiously.

"Yeah." She nods, tucking a piece of her hair behind her ear. "We were really hitting it off, you know, and he wasn't trying to make any attempts to get in my pants or anything, but it really seemed like he was interested. When I saw him freak out on that guy so bad, it had me kind of worried, you know? I thought maybe you two had a thing and I hadn't bothered to ask first or.... I don't know. So I asked him straight up what the deal was, and he said that y'all have lived by each other forever, and that he was just really protective."

Although it's kind of painful to hear that the two of them hit it off so well, to know that he thought enough of me to lie to her and tell her we're closer than we are means a lot. A part of me thought he would just tell her how the two of us don't get along, but him telling her that we were close means he doesn't want her to think badly of me.

Which means he cares, no matter how little.

The rest of the lunch she spends gushing to me over Weston and how different he seems from her ex, Dalton, and how she can see something happening between them even though they only had the one conversation. It's a painful lunch from my side of things, but she seems so happy that I can't cut in and switch topics like I want to.

By the time work is over and I'm on my drive home, I can't

seem to fight the overwhelming urge to tell Weston thanks for what he did. He didn't have to stick up for me like he did, and him punching someone like that could've ended much worse. He could've been arrested for assault or something, and even though everyone in town knows the cops wouldn't actually put him in a cell, the fact of the matter is that he still took up for me.

When I pull into the driveway and don't see Weston working on the porch or his truck across the street, I know that now's the only time I have. I can't do it in person because I'd just choke, but I have to do something. He has to know how grateful I am.

So I take the coward's way out and text him.

**Me: Thank you.**

Feeling much better after that, I make my way inside the empty house and immediately head toward my closet. After changing into my pajamas for the night, despite it only being half past five, I head back into the living room and plop on the couch in front of the TV.

Five minutes later, my phone buzzes with his response.

**Weston: No problem.**

# Chapter Six

For the next two weeks, things are relatively calm.

I slowly get into the swing of my new job and having a new friend, the wound on my thigh no longer hurts, my dad starts spending more time at work due to an upcoming client meeting, and Weston and his guys finally finish up the porch.

I'm starting to feel more at home here than I did at school, and while it's sort of bittersweet, I'm also so happy with the way most things are going here.

My dad and I have never been closer, for one. When my mom was around, he was always kind of the third wheel, and then when she left, things were so awkwardly tense that we never solidified our relationship before I moved away. Now, though, I can definitely say our relationship is as healthy as possible, and I absolutely love it.

Except for when, of course, my dad was able to convince me to tell him what happened that night at the Boot and he reacted even worse than I thought he would. When he finally stopped teasing me about this crush he thinks I have on Weston, he waved it off as nonchalantly as only he could and said that Weston's smart enough to have known it was just the alcohol making me yell the way I did.

Even though I did mean the majority of the things I said.

I regret how I went about it, of course, but it doesn't mean I regret finally telling him how I was interpreting his behavior.

It's still as awkward as ever around the frustratingly handsome neighbor, though, and my dad's insistence on the three of us hanging out so that I'll have another friend in town besides Jenny is downright insufferable.

Luckily, Jenny and I have completely forgone the normal hesitancy that most new friendships have, which keeps me out of the house and with things to do more often than not.

Unfortunately, though, this closeness has made me quickly learn that Jenny's the type of person who includes her friends in every aspect of her life.

Including her love life, which, I just found out two nights ago, has taken quite the leap now that Weston finally asked her on a real and true date. So, because of us being such fast friends and her being as charmingly convincing as she is, I'm currently driving my car from work to Jenny's apartment so I can help her pick out something to wear for their dinner tonight.

I'm once again having to reinforce the notion that I need to accept the two of them dating, because a person like Weston, when I really think about it, is perfectly suited for someone like Jenny. Her outspokenness will compensate for any lack of conversation he offers up, but she's not so bold as to go where he'd get annoyed.

So, in all truths of the matter, I should be thrilled for them.

But for some reason, whether it be because I'm still hung up on Weston's and my kiss or if it's simply because I'm just a horrible person, I'm not. I have to pretend to be, though, because Jenny's so damn over the moon about this whole thing that I'd be an even worse person if I brought her down.

Later, when it's closing in on six o'clock, a whole hour before

*Back to You*

Weston's supposed to be here, I'm pouring both Jenny and me hearty glasses of white wine so that her nerves will be soothed and mine won't be so on edge while dealing with hers.

She's trying on her third and hopefully final outfit of the night, a cute and casual navy blue dress that plays up her enviable figure without looking too formal. He told her that he'd made a reservation at a nicer place in Baton Rouge, which is only a quick drive across the interstate, but both of us know that even the nicest place there doesn't constitute anything too dressy.

When I make it back to her room, I see her standing in front of her bronze floor-length mirror at the opposite side of the room, and in the reflection I can see her large, expressive eyes nitpicking every little thing about the dress.

"Stop it," I scold, taking the few steps to reach her and handing her one of the glasses. "You look incredible."

"Really?" she asks nervously after taking a sip, her teeth jutting out to nibble on her bottom lip as she looks back at herself. Her free hand flits over invisible wrinkles and imperfections, and for a few brief moments I'm horrified to admit that seeing her so insecure feels kind of good.

After my short stint at being a jealous adolescent, though, I give her my honest opinion and gush, "Yes! That dress is perfect, actually, and those wedges you wore the other day would go super well with it."

She agrees and quickly gets to work on her makeup, and after I take a sip of my drink, I ask curiously, "So what're you doing for the Fourth? It's Wednesday, isn't it?"

"Yep," she says, sweeping her brush a couple more times before tossing it into the small cosmetic pile beside her thigh. "I'm going out of town actually. A long-overdue family get-together."

"Oh that's cool," I say, slightly disappointed that she won't be in town and available to drag to the barbecue at Meg's. "Where are y'all going?"

"Destin," she answers, sounding a bit more enthusiastic. "My uncle has a condo there, and he and his family usually have it for the Fourth, but he's got some work stuff keeping him home, so he's letting us use it."

"I'm so jealous." I sigh, taking another, this time longer, sip of my wine. "I haven't been to the beach in ages."

"You didn't go for spring break or anything when you were at school?" she asks curiously, meeting my gaze through the mirror.

"Nope," I say with a shake of my head. "That wasn't really my or my friends' scene, you know? We partied and everything, but spring break on the beach has always scared me. Too intense."

She shakes her head at me. "You're nuts, Iris. Me and Dalt went the summer after junior year when we were finally legal, and it was *the* best week of my life." She pauses for a moment and then laughs. "It was crazy, though, I'll give you that. I don't think either of us were sober for four days."

"Exactly!" I exclaim, my point proved. "And that's just not my thing, I guess. I'll go for a few drinks as much as the next person, but going that hard for a long time would be so hard for me, with how sick my stomach is the next day."

"True," she relents, right before teasing, "You did go pretty fucking hard that night at the Boot, though."

My cheeks flare with heat just at the memory of it. I still have yet to forgive myself for getting so hammered and acting the way I did in front of Weston, Jenny, and whoever the hell that guy I made out with was. "Let's not talk about that night. Please."

She giggles at my disgust. "I don't see why you're still so hard on yourself about that. Everyone has those nights where it just hits 'em harder than normal."

We're quiet for another few minutes. She starts in on her eye shadow while I finish up the rest of my drink and try to forget my indiscretions. As I place the empty glass on the end table beside the bed, I ask her, "So it's just you and family going?"

"Yeah." She nods. "Which I'm dreading, but kind of glad too. The four of us haven't seen each other like this for a while."

"Four?" I say softly, trying to remember the people she's told me about. "You, your dad, your brother, and... what's your stepmom's name?"

"Clarissa," she answers, right before cursing when she accidentally pokes herself in the eye.

I remember the conversation we had about her family just a few days ago. Her mom and dad split when she was young, apparently, but she and her younger brother always remained close to both, doing that whole every-other-week thing so many kids of divorce have to do.

"How long have they been married again?"

"Mmm...," she says, pausing her mascara application so she can think it over. "Nine years, maybe? I think I was sixteen when they got married, 'cause I remember driving my new car there."

After doing some quick addition in my head, I ask in a high, surprised voice, "You're twenty-five?"

The scathing glare she sends me in the mirror's reflection definitely does not go unnoticed, but I can't help but be surprised. In all of the conversations we've had about each other, her being two years older than me never came up.

"Yes," she answers simply, her voice having lost all color. "Let's not talk about it."

"Aw, come on!" I giggle, finding it funny how sensitive she seems to be about the subject. "It's not that bad!"

"It is that bad," she urges, dipping her mascara wand into its tube for the third time. "I'm five years from thirty and still have no actual future with someone to make a family with. Hell, by the time I find someone who wants to marry me, all of my eggs will be dried up."

"Oh shut the hell up," I exclaim, thinking that I'd throw one of her many throw pillows at her if she didn't have a glass of wine sitting right beside her. "It's not like there's any sort of time frame for that kind of stuff anymore. It's pretty rare to be married and have kids now at twenty-five."

"Not down here," she points out, which does have a bit of truth to it.

More than half the people I graduated high school with are already expecting their second kids, and they're all about two years younger than Jenny is. I will admit that on some occasions I've had a sudden, random want for domesticity, but just as soon as it comes on it passes, and I'm left absolutely thrilled that I only have myself to take care of.

"Jenny, most people that get married and have kids that young don't go to college, and the wives rarely, if ever, have jobs of their own. You did all that stuff. You had more aspirations, and there's nothing wrong with that. Hell, to me, I think that's better than settling down so early."

"I know," she says begrudgingly. "And I do love that I'm so independent. But, I don't know, some days I'd love for my husband and me to be woken up by our curly-headed babies jumping on our bed, you know?"

"You still have plenty of time for that," I point out. "And the ones who've already settled down, they don't have plenty of time to do what we're doing, you know? They don't get to go out without worrying about their kids, and they—"

She cuts me off by looking at me over her shoulder with a wicked grin and saying, "Don't get to make out with strangers against a bar."

"Do you want me to throw something at you?" I ask her with narrowed eyes, the urge getting stronger the more she giggles. "'Cause I will."

After she stops laughing, she turns back to start digging in her makeup bag again and says, "You're right, though. Most of the time I love that I can do whatever I want."

"Exactly!" I agree wholeheartedly, and then before I can think twice about it, my wine has me saying, "And who knows? Maybe this Weston thing will pan out and you can have his curly-headed babies."

"Maybe," she says, grinning sheepishly at me in the mirror before turning her attention to framing her lips in a rusty pink lip liner.

As she's in the middle of doing so, we both snap to attention at the sound of a knock echoing through the apartment. I feel a deep thud in my chest knowing that Weston's here, and when I glance over at Jenny, I see panic coating her face as she hurriedly attempts to finish.

Knowing what I have to do even though I hate it, I murmur unhappily, "I'll go let 'im in," and then clamber off her bed and head toward the front door.

Haphazardly pulling at the risen hem of the pencil skirt I wore for work, I take a deep breath while telling myself I can do this without making it awkward, and then pull open the front door.

The first thing I see is his large tanned hand extended in front of him and upward, his fingers curled into a fist as if he were just about to knock again. Trembling nerves start to race across my skin as I watch him realize it's me at the door and not Jenny, his bright green eyes turning to hardened glass as he slowly lowers his fist.

"Hi," I say meekly. "Jenny's almost done."

With that, I shakily step to the side and motion with my head for him to follow me in. I shut the door behind us and then inhale deeply through my nose, trying my hardest to ward off all the anxiety-ridden hormones that Weston seems to carry over him like a storm cloud.

Once I feel as calm as I think is possible, I step away from the door and follow him to where he's sat down on the beige sofa I drunkenly crashed on just two weeks ago.

He looks up at me and I see his throat work before he asks, "Why're you here?"

Folding my arms over my chest and trying not to be annoyed at the surliness of the question, I answer, "I was helping her get ready. I followed her here after work."

This doesn't seem to surprise him, as he answers with a brief nod, and so before I can let my anxiety make me believe that staying here with him to make conversation is a good thing, I hurriedly scamper away from him and back into Jenny's bedroom.

She looks much more at ease than she did when we heard the knock, and when my eyes fall upon the newly empty wine glass on her dresser, I know exactly why. She's picking up a pale pink glass bottle of perfume when I come in, and when she looks over at me I tell her, "I'm going to head out, okay?"

"Okay," she says softly, glancing briefly over my shoulder. "Thank you... for helping me."

"Of course," I say genuinely, giving her a smile that's only a little bit shaky. "Have fun, okay? Weston's a great guy."

This seems to ease whatever leftover nerves she has, her chest deflating with an exhale, and she says, "I think you're right. I'll text you the details once it's over."

Even though a huge part of me would love to never hear of the two of them together again, a small masochistic part of me has to know how it goes. So after I tell her that she better and wish her good luck one more time, I delicately close her bedroom door and head back into the living room.

Weston looks up at the sound of my footsteps, probably hoping for Jenny to make her appearance, so before I can let myself read into the disappointment most likely on his face, I tell him, "She'll be done in a sec."

"Okay," he says gruffly.

I head over to the kitchen table to grab my purse and then move toward the front door, but before I can let myself out, I feel words working in my throat and I know I'll be miserable if I don't say them now.

"Weston?" I call, yards of distance now between us. He looks over at me, his eyes hesitant. "Please don't hurt her, okay? She needs this."

Jenny's one of the most independent girls I know, what with having stayed here by herself three years ago and having a steady, well-paid job and a nice apartment. Being independent doesn't necessarily mean not being lonely, though, and in that brief period of time where she took her guard down and mentioned her fears, I realized just how lonely she really is.

Jenny needs this, even if it doesn't move on from this first date.

The chiseled planes of Weston's tense face begin to soften. My stomach warms at the realization I've made him feel even just a little bit better, and my eyes can't move from his face as he says, "I won't, Iris."

Those three words making me feel infinitely better, I smile softly and let myself out of the apartment.

---

It's Tuesday right after lunch, and the excitement of tomorrow being a holiday and a paid day off from work is practically tangible throughout the law firm, especially because everyone except for me is taking off Thursday and Friday as well.

As for me, though, with my dire need of a deposit for an apartment as well as a lack of plans to actually take time off for, I'm staying here until five today and all day both Thursday and Friday.

The phones have been practically dead today, too, and since everyone here is so eager to get out for the afternoon, they're putting off giving me things to do which leaves me incredibly bored.

In fact, at this moment, I'm currently busy beating my high score on some incredibly addictive puzzle game on my phone and not caring that either of my bosses could walk through at any given time.

"Shit," I curse, that round only having been one hundred points away from beating my high score. With my elbow propped up on the desk and my fist digging into my cheek, I tap the replay button for the millionth time today.

Suddenly the front door opens, the painfully intense July sun breezing in through the space and immediately warming my exposed arms. Cursing to myself again because I've now been caught not working, I hastily turn my phone's screen off and then take my elbow off the desk.

My heart racing at the prospect of getting into trouble, I reluctantly look up to see who's come in, praying it's not Chet or David, and then feeling so much better when I realize it's not.

An unfamiliar guy, appearing to be around my age with the sharp angles of his face and obvious lack of lines and wrinkles, is walking in my direction and staring straight at me.

"Hello," I greet politely, stretching a professional grin across my lips despite having just spent the last hour playing a childish phone game. "How can I help you?"

Once he reaches my desk and casually places his hand on it, I let myself quickly get a look at him. He looks somewhat familiar, his light blond hair wavy and tucked behind his ears, his bright blue eyes large and expressive. I can't pinpoint it, though, and I have a gut feeling I'm going to spend the rest of my afternoon combing through Facebook to determine how I know him.

"Yeah," he says lightly, glancing behind me at the tinted glass wall ornamented with Poole and McNabb's last names. Then, giving me an easygoing smile, he says, "I'm um, I'm looking for Jenny. Jenny Turner."

"Oh?" I ask curiously, thinking she shouldn't have an appointment for this afternoon since she's leaving for the beach in close to an hour. "Do you have an appointment?"

He chuckles. "I'm her brother."

"Oh!" I exclaim, suddenly feeling silly. No wonder he looks familiar. "I'm so sorry, I should've realized."

"No big deal," he says, still tittering underneath his breath. "I'm kind of glad you didn't catch on. Everyone always thinks we're twins and it gets really old."

Gratefully smiling, since he's trying to make me feel better, I attempt to quell the heat in my cheeks when I respond, "Well, you're welcome then, I guess? Are you here to pick her up for Destin?"

"That I am," he says, looking pleased that I know that. "You and Jenny are friends, then?"

"Yeah." I nod happily, tucking a piece of hair behind my ear. "I just moved back from school, and the receptionist needed to take her maternity leave, so I was given the temporary reins of the phones. Jenny showed me the ropes and we just got along really well."

"That's great," he says. "She needs friends here, you know? My dad and I worry about her all the way out here by herself."

"Yeah, Houston's pretty far," I point out. "You still live out there?"

"I do." He nods, before explaining further, "But I'm actually starting to look for new jobs out this way, to get out of Texas."

"So you're just gonna slide on over here?" I ask dubiously.

He chuckles. "Maybe? I just graduated in engineering and I know BR has a bunch of plants, so...."

"They do have that," I agree. "Not much else, though. But yeah, I just graduated too, actually."

"Yeah?" he asks, his grin stretching to reveal a perfectly white smile. "With what—"

"Here you are!" Jenny's voice exclaims, ringing through the lobby.

Turning my attention away from the cute boy who surprisingly wanted to talk to me, I watch as Jenny hurries over to her brother, leaping into his arms for a big hug.

"I missed you so much," she says, the excitement in her voice getting lost since her mouth is against his shoulder, his hand coming around the back of her head to keep her steady as he places her back on the floor.

As he pulls away from her embrace and brushes the hair out of her face, he says genuinely, "I missed you too, airhead."

"When you texted and said you were here, I thought you'd just come back, but then you were taking forever and now I find you out here flirting with my friend!" She punches him on the shoulder, her huge smile stretching when she sees the light blush illuminate his high cheekbones.

Which makes me blush too.

"We were just talking about how awful you are," he teases, lightly returning her punch with one of his own.

"Bullshit!" She laughs, looking the happiest I've ever seen her. Even after Weston asked her out, even after their first date went incredibly well, even when we were drunk off shots and dancing our hearts out on the dance floor... I've never seen her as happy as she is right now. "You both love me."

Her brother rolls his eyes before saying, "*Anyway*... Dad's in the car singing show tunes, and I think Clarissa's going to kill him if we don't get going soon."

She laughs as if that's a common thing. "Sounds perfect. My stuff's in my trunk."

He looks back to me. "It was nice meeting you...?"

"Iris," I answer.

"Iris." He smiles before extending a strong arm toward me.

"I'm Campbell."

# Chapter Seven

"Oh there ya are, honey!" Meg greets me happily late the next afternoon, her bright red lips stretching into a smile. "I was just asking your dad when you were gonna show up."

"Sorry I'm late," I say sheepishly, returning the hug she gives me. "People are already out with the fireworks, so it took forever to get through the streets."

"Rednecks and their explosives." She clicks her tongue disapprovingly, shaking her head. "Anyway! Food's already out. Beer's in the fridge and in the red cooler out back."

"Sounds great." I smile, looking around at the already crowded diner.

It's the Fourth of July and everyone in town knows that means a barbeque and party at Meg's, complete with an awesome firework show once the sun's gone completely down. It's been a tradition for years, and I'd be lying if I said there was something else I'd rather be doing, even if people I haven't seen in years are here and just waiting to bombard me with questions about college.

I grab a beer from the kitchen first, of course, and then after taking a nice swig of it, I set off in search of my dad. We came in separate cars because he offered to help Meg get everything ready, and I was in no hurry to leave my bed on my first weekday off in a month.

After getting stopped by two of my dad's old friends and catching up with them, I spot my dad's tall frame in a corner booth, Meg sitting at his side. They and two other people clink their beers and laugh about whatever toast one of them made, and as I get closer I see my dad look down at Meg. The sparkle in his eye when she gives him a coy little smile is impossible to miss.

My feet stop moving and my mind starts racing, my stomach churning with something indiscernible as it occurs to me that my dad and Meg may have something going on between them other than just a lifelong friendship.

I must've missed it my first night here when Dad and I came to eat, but there's no way I could miss it now. I've seen my dad look at only two girls that way: me and my mom back when she was still around. Even from yards away I can see the softening of the lines beside his eyes, the glittering of his eyes.

He's totally hot for Meg.

And I'm totally not sure how I feel about that.

Still, though, I know I need to go and say hey to him. He's been so busy at work lately that I haven't gotten to see him as much as I did when I first came back. But now... now that I think about it, what if he's not been busy with work and that's just been what he's telling me? What if he's been going to see her instead?

The churning in my stomach intensifies.

"Iris!" I hear him call, shocking me out of my thoughts.

I wrench my eyes away from where I'd been staring into the distance and instead focus them on my dad, seeing how utterly happy he looks and feeling the unpleasantness in my gut start to dissipate.

"Hey, Dad," I say, hurrying over so I can reach down and give him a hug. "I've been looking for you, but I got stopped by Paul and Frankie."

"Yeah, those two have been drunk since around noon, I think." He chuckles. "You just get here then?"

I nod, glancing over his shoulder at Meg, who's talking to the couple across from them like nothing's different, like I haven't just figured out that something is going on between her and my dad.

"Yeah, so I'm going to um... I'm going to go get some food," I say, thinking that'd be a good escape.

"Okay, honey." He smiles. "You can come sit with us unless you find some younger, cooler people to hang out with."

Meg and the other two people at the table laugh at his joke, which makes my face start to burn for some reason. I nod awkwardly and turn away, my mind racing again now that I can finally breathe normally.

The table set up in the middle of the room is filled with typical barbecue food, and I waste no time in getting myself a heaping plate of it all. I haven't eaten since around seven this morning, when I left my bed to grab a Pop-Tart.

Instead of retreating back to my dad's table to eat, though, I decide to head outside and see if there's anyone else I know here.

The back of the diner has always been a bit of a hangout zone. Wooden picnic tables are spread out on a large, raised deck, the upright beams on the edges decorated with white twinkling lights.

I've always loved it out here, and even right now, when it's crawling with people I haven't seen in ages, it's still so beautifully peaceful.

Letting my eyes rake over everyone's faces, I recognize about 90 percent of them. My third grade teacher is sat at a table in the corner, along with four other people I recognize from the local elementary school; the grocery store manager with the funny goatee is sipping a beer and flirting with a woman I recognize from the bank; and at the table closest to the grill, laughing along with the high school football coach, is Weston.

Realizing that my only options are either by myself, with all of the school staff, or with Weston and Coach Hopkins, I'm overly thankful when a shrill voice calls out, "Iris Tilley!" making the decision for me.

Mrs. Harris, my third grade teacher, is waving me over, so after letting out a huge sigh of relief, I hurry to her table.

"How've you been, sweetie?" she asks once I've sat down.

I talk with her and the others for a good half hour, long enough to finish my plate, my first beer, and the second one the librarian from my junior high brought me. It's been a strange conversation, that's for sure, but hearing the ladies who taught me when I was prepubescent talk is incredibly amusing.

Once I finish my second beer and promise to not be a stranger, I grab my trash and head back on inside.

It's empty in the diner, thanks to everyone being outside and readying for the fireworks, so I throw my things away and head toward the kitchen fridge, remembering the librarian told me it was where all the good beer was being kept.

After I grab one, I start back outside to see how large the stash of explosives is this year. If the firework shows from past years are any indication, no one spared a penny.

As I'm walking across the sticky tiled floor to the front door, I hear the one in the back open, and when I look over my shoulder, my breath gets caught in my throat. Weston seems to have stopped in his tracks as well, his bright green gaze meeting mine across the room.

"Hi." I speak first, my heart pounding.

"Hey, Iris." He nods, pulling the back door completely shut and then tossing a silver beer can into the trash bag. "Happy Fourth."

"You too," I say with a small smile, glad and just a little bit surprised he didn't completely ignore my hello. "You been here long?"

"Maybe an hour or two," he answers easily. "I offered to help with the grilling, but Meg said she had it covered."

"Of course she did." I giggle. "That woman will never let a man do anything for her that she can do herself."

He grins at that, making my heart pound just that much harder.

"She's a ball of fire, that one."

"She is," I agree with a smile, but it disappears as I remember how I saw her and my dad looking at each other earlier.

The beer in my system must make me think it's okay to tell him, "I think she and my dad are seeing each other."

His eyes widen in shock, his thick eyebrows rising. "What, really?"

"Yeah," I say with a nod, tucking a piece of hair behind my ear. "I mean, they've always been friends and all, but... I don't know. The way they were looking at each other today... it's how he used to look at my mom."

"Jesus," he says with a shake of his head, taking a step toward me before stopping himself and crossing his arms over his chest. "How're you.... I mean, are you okay with that? Meg's got to be the first since...."

"Since my mom," I finish for him, biting down on my lip. Not knowing why I'm talking to him about this, but feeling like I have to keep doing so, I shrug. "I don't know, actually. Technically he's still married to my mom, so yeah. It's weird."

"I'm sure it is," he says openly. "I'm surprised he didn't tell you, with how close y'all are and everything."

"That's just my dad," I say with a wave. "He'll do anything so that I'm happy, including leave out things. He just hates negative confrontation."

He nods, his eyes meeting mine again. The attention and understanding in them makes my breath catch in my throat, and I can no longer fathom up words.

Luckily he can.

"They'd be good together," he says, sounding uncomfortable, as if he's afraid of stepping over some imaginary line. "Your dad and Meg, they... they make sense, you know?"

"They do," I hesitantly agree, thinking back to how well they'd gotten along at dinner my first night back. I see the worry in his eyes blur away as I add, "Meg's incredible, and my dad definitely needs someone like that after... well, you know."

"Yeah," he says with a brief chuckle.

A slight awkwardness falls over us, as I'm not sure what to say and I'm sure he feels the same way. Something has to be said, though, what with how everything's been going between us since I've been back. Although the odds of Weston and I ever being friends are incredibly slight, I'd still like to be comfortable around him.

It's such a small town, it's not like I can avoid the guy.

"So... um," I start clumsily, my chest all jittery with nerves from the silence. "You and Jenny, huh? I heard y'all's date went really well."

Immediately after the words are out of my mouth I want to smack myself. Talking about the girl he's dating, my newly appointed best friend in fact, with our sorely brief romantic past is probably not the smartest thing to do.

It was just the first thing that came to mind, unfortunately.

"Um, yeah." He nods, sounding about as uncomfortable as I did asking the question. "She's great. She's... really nice, you know?"

"Yeah," I agree. "Y'all work well, I think."

"Yeah?" he asks, raising a brow.

"Yeah," I say once again, hating that it's the truth. "Both blond, both... I don't know." I giggle. "Y'all both love it here."

Something dark flashes in his eyes at that, right before he says tightly, "I guess you're right."

Crossing my arms over my chest and feeling suddenly very small in his presence, I anxiously realize that I need to wrap this conversation up quickly. It's turning painful, and I hate it.

I need this to end on a good note.

"Thanks for listening to me, you know... about Meg and my dad. I know it was probably so random for me to—"

"It's no problem," he cuts me off, before adding, "and I won't say anything... since you aren't entirely sure."

"Thanks," I say with a small smile, still feeling highly self-conscious but glad he thought to say that. "Are you... are you going out for the fireworks?"

"Yeah," he says, motioning with his head toward the front door and causing us to both head in that direction. "I hate missing them, and Lord knows those old guys need some good eyes lighting everything."

I chuckle along with him and then follow him toward the front door, my breath catching in my throat when he holds it open for me and I have to brush by him to get through, my front briefly skimming his. I feel my nerve endings crackle to life, and when I chance a glance up at him I see that he's not entirely unaffected by the contact either, his jaw clenched and his eyes flashing.

I feel an incredible satisfaction at that, but then right after, Jenny's face flashes in my mind and the feeling crashes down into guilt.

Damn it.

Pushing everything to the back of my mind, I skim my gaze over the front yard and my dad immediately gets my attention by waving in my direction. Before I go to join him, I turn to tell Weston bye and to thank him again for talking to me, but he's not there, his large and easily identifiable body already having disappeared.

My chest tightening, I whip back around and then quickly spot him walking through the crowd, his shoulders tight and his pace hasty.

It's like Walmart all over again; he just can't get away from me fast enough.

Feeling the hopes that had risen after our talk inside, no matter how awkward it may have been, come crashing down and settle into something comparable to indigestion, I hurry over to my dad and hope he can cheer me up.

As soon as I see the intoxicated and giggly Meg at his side, I realize that's not going to be the case. Even though my talk with Weston

93

slightly warmed me up to the idea of my dad and Meg together, it's still weird and my feelings are still bruised from the fact that he didn't tell me, whether or not he did it thinking it was better for me.

Yes, my dad deserves happiness, and yes, I am so very happy for him because it seems like he's found someone. It's just... it's my dad, and it's proving impossible for me to picture him with someone other than my mom.

Anyone at all, in fact.

Is everything going to be different now?

Are our rainy afternoon porch coffees going to be extended to her as well? We only have two porch chairs. Am I going to get kicked off mine so she has one?

Is she going to start coming around for dinner? Am I going to have to set three places instead of two? Am I going to have to text her too, to make sure she's okay with what I'm craving?

I don't know how okay I am with any of that.

"Hey, pumpkin." My dad smiles at me, wrapping an arm around my shoulder and pulling me into a side hug, completely oblivious to my inner chaos.

"Hey, Dad," I say, pulling away from him so that I can cross my arms across my chest. I can smell the beer on his breath, and it annoys me more than it should.

I'm twenty-three years old. My dad having a girlfriend should not bother me this much.

But it does.

I just can't help it.

"You okay?" he asks, his perceptiveness working when I *really* wish it wasn't. "I haven't seen you since you got here."

"I'm fine," I assure him, giving him my best attempt at a smile. "I was sitting out back with Mrs. Harris and the other teachers. And I was just inside talking to Weston."

His expression perks up at that. "Oh really? So you and Weston are okay now?"

"Dad," I groan. "We know each other, of course we can talk."

"I was just asking," he says defensively, giving me a guilty grin so I know he's still teasing.

"Shut up." I laugh and push his arm, my mood lifting just a bit at how happy he seems to be.

"Iris, honey!" Meg coos, coming around my dad to give me a slightly uncoordinated hug. "How are you? I haven't seen you since you got here!"

"I'm good," I assure her, feeling suddenly tense. Usually Meg's hugs are about as familiar as my dad's, but now... now not so much. "And I've been here, you saw me say hey to my dad earlier."

"Oh I did, huh!" She laughs loudly, looking at my dad and smacking him on the bicep like I did less than two minutes ago. "Your dad here was probably just talking my ear off about something stupid and I forgot!"

The laugh that comes out of me is completely disingenuous, but I attempt it nevertheless.

"Meg," my dad says, apparently finding it necessary to intervene. She's a bit drunker than I initially thought, and she's not bothering to try and hide how much she and my dad are hanging out. He grabs her arm and pulls her away, saying, "Let's get you a coffee, okay?"

"Steve." She giggles, shaking her head and causing her crazy blonde ringlets to bounce around her flustered face. "I think I'm a wee bit drunk."

"I think you're right." He chuckles, smoothing back some of her hair before looking at me and telling me he'll be right back.

As I nod, my eyes fall to where Meg's threading her arm through my dad's and stepping close to him, closer than two friends should be standing. Feeling my chest squeeze painfully at the movement, my eyes lift and then immediately come into contact with my dad's.

He looks guilty, and I purse my lips.

How long has he been lying to me about this?

Has it been the whole time I've been back?

The two of them turn away and he leads her back into the diner, and even when they're yards away I can hear her drunkenly laughing and cooing at whatever he's saying.

My throat is burning with tears as the two of them disappear inside, and I'm swiping underneath my eyes for any possible wetness when I catch Weston looking at me. He's a good distance away from me, with a small group of guys behind one of their truck beds as they go through all the fireworks, but I still don't miss the concern flitting across his gaze.

And for just one short moment, I feel better.

# Chapter Eight

"So how was the Fourth?" Jenny asks me early Monday morning at my desk, all bronzed and relaxed from her time on the beach.

I try my hardest not to wince, remembering how after my dad brought a very drunken Meg inside, neither of them came back out until the fireworks were over and I was telling everyone I knew goodbye. Seeing as how I was asleep by the time he got home and he's been gone on some business trip since then, we still have yet to talk about him and Meg, and I'm still very much unsettled by it.

But that's a conversation for another day.

So I just say, "It was fun, but I'm sure yours was a lot better. How was the trip?"

"Incredible," she coos, flicking her blonde hair over a tan shoulder bared by the thin straps of her sundress. "Hot as hell, of course, but so worth it. I was not ready to come back home yesterday."

"I bet," I muse.

"Speaking of my trip," she starts, a huge, white grin stretching her glossed lips. "I have some major things to tell you at lunch today."

"Really?" I ask her, my eyebrows raised. "About what?"

"You made quite the impression on my brother the other day," she says, her smile only broadening. "But I'll tell you later, okay? Chet will have my ass if I'm not back there on time."

Blushing, I just nod and say, "Okay."

The rest of the morning goes by in a quick haze, the phone ringing every two minutes with new clients wanting to sue someone for something that happened over the holiday.

By the time lunch rolls around, I realize that I've been too busy to notice how deprived my stomach is of food, and when Jenny comes out I can't leave with her fast enough.

Instead of our normal place, we decide to splurge on some Taco Bell, as Jenny's apparently hormonal and craving the cheap Mexican food. I'm happy enough to comply, and right after we slide into a sticky booth, I'm tearing into one of my tacos.

We make small talk about things that are going on at work, as she has some new gossip about David and his wife, but it only lasts a couple of minutes. She seems to be itching to tell me what her brother said about me.

"So," she says seriously. "What'd you think of Campbell? And tell me the truth. Don't leave anything out even though he's my brother."

I swallow the last bite of nachos in my mouth, and then say to her honestly, "He's cute. We didn't really talk for long, so I can't really say much else."

"Well, he's super interested." She smiles widely at me.

Warmth floods my chest at that, but I still can't help but say, "He lives so far away though, Jen. I don't—"

"That's the best part!" she squeals. "He's been wanting to move around here 'cause he's starting to hate the city, and I think if he had more of a reason to—"

I cut her off, starting to feel overwhelmed. "He'd move here for me? When we talked for literally three minutes?"

I feel a little bad when I see her smile falter, but it's something I have to ask. Campbell was attractive and easy to talk to, yes, and I'd be glad to go out with him, but him moving states to do so is too much.

"Well, not just for you," she points out, her voice now less excited. "I just think he was nervous to come here 'cause he has friends and stuff in Houston, but if he had me and a girl he was interested in, then... you know. He'd feel better about the move."

"I don't know," I say with a sigh. "I just... I'd feel major pressure if he moved here and we went out. Like what if he took me out and it didn't go well? Then half the reason for his move would've been for nothing."

She shakes her head. "No, it's nothing like that! Come on, Iris. I mean, if you don't like him that's fine and I get it, he *is* my loser brother. But if you are interested, then you should totally let me know. He really wants to come here for work. He just needs one extra little push. It's not like he'd blame you if he came and y'all didn't work out. He's not like that, I swear. Campbell's way more chill than that."

I open my mouth to say something, but she quickly adds in a soft voice, "And I'd get my brother back, Iris."

My mouth snaps shut at how desperate she sounds about this. I can't help but mull it over. She's telling me directly that even if we didn't work out it'd be fine, so what's the harm, really? If he came, she'd get her brother and I'd get someone else to hang out with.

Not only that, but if there were a new guy in my life, then maybe I'd stop thinking about Weston so damn much.

I'd stop replaying that dark, intense look he gave me when I brushed by him at the diner Wednesday night.

And I'd stop feeling so guilty every time I remember that he and Jenny are an item.

Giving her a smile that's not entirely sincere, I say, "Okay then, fine."

"Dad?" I say Wednesday evening when I walk into our house. It's the first night since the night before the Fourth of July that my dad's Suburban has been in the driveway before my car.

A part of me is thrilled that he's back, as this past week has been quite lonely without him here. Our house is pretty small, but it felt pretty damn spacious when I was here by myself, and not in a good way.

Another part of me is dreading seeing him, though, since the topic of him and Meg direly needs to be discussed. Being alone with my thoughts did help, and I think I'm more open to the idea now than I was when it was first shoved at me. Of course it's still going to take some getting used to, but at least now when I think about it I'm not overcome with dueling needs to cry and punch something.

"On the couch!" he calls in response, and when I take a couple steps further inside, I see the back of his head as he points the remote toward the TV and mutes the nightly news crew.

I walk over to him and return the big hug he gives me, plopping down beside him on the couch and getting to work on removing the wedges I wore to work today, a purchase from two weekends ago that was heavily influenced by Jenny and her insistence that I had incredible legs and needed to showcase them more.

"How was your trip?" I ask, my feet screaming in relief as I toss the black shoes to the side and prop them on the coffee table in front of us.

"It was really good," he says, turning to face me. He looks quite tired, I notice, the skin underneath his large blue eyes a bit darker than normal. "It was a trucking company so everything was really casual, and there weren't a lot of people in the office which was good. Their finances were in such shit shape, though."

"That's good, though, right? You love stuff like that."

He chuckles, his eyes sparkling with a bit of life. "I do. The first night I don't think I slept at all. The hotel they put me up in had an all-night coffee bar in the lobby, so that definitely helped."

"You're such a nerd." I laugh, shaking my head. "You should've just stayed longer and gotten paid more. It's by the hour when you're away like that, right?"

"Yeah." He nods. "But it was driving me crazy, so I had to work on it. There's no way I would've been able to sleep. And I hate staying away from home that long, especially knowing you're here alone."

"It did get pretty lonely around here," I say truthfully, sinking into the sofa and casting a quick glance at the TV.

"Unfortunately I have a few more trips coming up, but none of them should take that long. They're mostly small companies."

"Anywhere interesting?" I ask.

For a little bit longer we talk about his upcoming trips, the coolest place he's going being Nashville, and before I know it, he's ordered a pizza and we're pigging out and he's telling me the news said it was most likely going to be an active hurricane season this year.

It's as he's cleaning up our napkins and empty beer bottles that he finally decides to bring up the Meg situation.

"So, Iris," he says, intentionally avoiding eye contact with me and wiping down imaginary dirt on the kitchen counter like I do when I'm stressed.

"So, Dad," I say tauntingly, attempting to deflect the awkwardness with humor like *he* usually does when *he's* stressed.

Maybe my dad and I are more alike than I originally thought.

"About the party at the diner, about the whole... about the Meg thing...." He trails off, finally stopping with the cleaning and leaning against the counter, crossing his arms over his chest.

Knowing he feels as weird about this as I do, I say, "Yeah. I kind of noticed that."

He nods, and after a tense moment says, "It's very new, Iris, and

I don't want you thinking I've been hiding this from you, okay?"

Breathing out a huge sigh of relief, I ask, "So y'all... y'all *are* a thing, then? Like is it official, or...?"

He chuckles, his head lifting and his eyes briefly meeting mine. "I don't even know how this whole dating thing works, Iris. You'd probably know better than me."

"Okay," I drawl, my chest oddly tight. "But... I mean, is it...?"

For once deciding to not beat around the bush, he says firmly, "We've been on a few dates, that's all. Our first was right before you came back to town, and I would've told you, but I didn't know how you'd feel since this is the first since, you know... your mom, and I didn't want to tell you anything, get you all worked up, unless I thought it was something that could last."

"And you think that now?"

"I do." He nods, looking back down at the tile floor.

"Well that's...," I start, even though I have no idea where the words are going, my voice trailing off as I start trying to decipher how I feel.

I've had a week without him here to think about it, but that was before he actually made it real. Now that it's real, now that I know for damn certain that my dad is dating the woman who was a second mother to me growing up, I'm once again unsure.

But I am happy that he's happy.

That's something I know will never change, despite how challenging it may be for me to accept that a new woman is the source of that happiness.

So I swallow back any hostile emotion that may be lingering in my voice and tell him in all honesty, "I'm happy you're happy, Dad. That's all that matters."

A bittersweet smile stretches his face when I say that, and it hits me that maybe dating someone other than my mom is as hard for him as it is for me. He and my mom were middle school sweethearts, as they started dating in eighth grade, and in the twenty-four years that they were together before she left, I know he never looked at anyone else.

"Thank you," he says after a pensive silence, and when I hear the catch in his voice I feel tears start to climb their way upward.

This is all so much to take in, despite my dad dating someone new having been an option for over four years now. I just.... I think it took so long for us to grasp the fact that the rock of our family, the one who was always there, had left us.

It took four years for us to get used to our family being just the two of us, and now that I think we've done that, we can finally start letting other people in.

It'll be hard of course, if this whole Meg thing is any indication, but being truly happy has never been easy, and for the longest time my dad and I were too busy recovering to even try.

Now we can, though, and I think we're both ready.

---

"So where are you and my brother going tonight?" Jenny asks me slyly two weeks later, having approached my desk just an hour before closing time.

Two days after I gave her the okay to tell Campbell I was interested, she blissfully told me that he was starting to look for jobs in town and that he'd stay with her when he had interviews. Turns out that a guy who graduates with honors in engineering can get interviews pretty quickly, which means he's been in town since late last night for two interviews he had this morning and is going to drive the four hours back home tonight after our date.

I'm certainly feeling pressure because of that, and because Jenny's been talking about this date tonight like it's the start of our path to being sisters. Already a part of me regrets agreeing to it, but then I remember how well Campbell and I got along and how cute he was, and I try my hardest not to let Jenny's overenthusiasm ruin it.

"That new steak house, I think," I answer, remembering how Campbell and I laughed together over the phone when he told me about this place before checking to make sure I wasn't a vegetarian.

"Ooh," she coos, "I've been dying to go there! Maybe I'll get Weston to take me this weekend."

It barely affects me when she says it, as she's been telling me for days now that their relationship is definitely going somewhere serious. They've been on two more dates since their first, and even though she's bummed he hasn't tried sleeping with her yet, she hasn't lost hope that it's going to happen soon. I know this because she's made damn sure to chronicle every moment between the two of them to me. It's incredibly annoying, and it gets to me way more than it should.

"I'll let you know how it is," I tell her.

"Good!" she exclaims. "He's coming here at five, right?"

"Yeah, right around closing time. My dad brought me here so that Campbell can just drop me at home."

"Well, I'll make sure to come out and say something embarrassing," she jokes threateningly, right before the office phone goes off.

"Yeah?" I answer, knowing by the ring that it's someone in the office.

Chet's recognizable southern accent comes gruffly over the line. "Our assistant in there?"

"Yes, sir," I say while trying to hold back laughter, looking up at Jenny and signaling her to go back to her desk. Her eyes widen in panic before she hurries out of the lobby as quickly as she can in her heels, and I tell him, "She's coming back right now."

The next hour goes by pretty quickly, and before I know it, Campbell is picking me up in his sleek black Acura and he's driving us to the city while I'm asking him about how his job interviews went.

"Really well actually, thanks," he says, tossing a perfect white grin over at me. "The first place was an engineering firm just like the one I'm at now, but they were a lot more casual than I'm used to, and the second one was at Exxon, which is my first choice, but usually you have to know people to get in there."

"Exxon, really?" I ask, raising my eyebrows. "It's impressive you even got an interview there."

He chuckles. "I guess. I don't know how the interview went though. The guy was kind of a hardass."

"Well, I mean, you are dealing with chemicals and gas and all that stuff, right? You've got to take it a little bit seriously."

"Very true," he agrees, giving me another smile as he pulls the car off the interstate and comes to a stop at an intersection. "And that's how where I am now is, all very intense. That's the only way I work well."

"Really?" I ask before saying, "I'm the opposite. When I'm stressed or overwhelmed, I kind of just shut down. Or babble, which is even worse."

"Babbling's cute, though," he says, his blue eyes glittering as they meet mine.

"Oh my gosh, no it's not!" I exclaim, laughing. "I always say things that make the situation even worse. It's so awful."

"Well, if it's a job you love, then stress isn't really so bad, at least that's what I've come to notice. It's more of a fun challenge, kind of like a puzzle."

"That's what my dad says," I say. "He's an accountant and an absolute math nerd, so he loves his job."

"What about you?" he asks, and through the windshield I see the steak house's sign come into view. "What do you think a job you'd love would be?"

My cheeks start to burn slightly. "I'm still not really sure, which is horrible since I'm twenty-three and already graduated. Nothing calls to me, you know?"

"Yeah." He nods, pulling into the packed parking lot and quickly taking a spot that some BMW is pulling out of. "I was really lucky when it came to that. My dad's an engineer, and so I always got to see what he was doing, and it interested me more than anything else. So that's what I did."

After undoing our seat belts, he cuts the engine and then tells me to stay put so he can get the door.

He puts his hand on the small of my back as we walk across the sidewalk to the front door, and the warmth of it seeps through the fabric of the purple dress I'm wearing. Once we're inside, he leads me up to the host stand and tells the girl there of our reservation. Ten minutes later, we're seated across from each other in a dimly lit booth and a soft-spoken waitress is pouring white wine into our glasses.

We're both quiet as we skim through our food options, the waitress having told us she'd be back in a few minutes for our orders, and when I finally decide what I want and close my menu, Campbell is looking straight at me with this contented gleam in his eyes.

"What?" I ask, suddenly feeling shy under his gaze.

A little smile touches his pink lips before he shakes his head. "Nothing. I'm just really glad you decided to come out with me."

My heart warming at how sincere he sounds, I can't help but say back wholeheartedly, "Me too."

"So," he says in a playfully serious voice, "tell me about yourself, Iris Tilley. How's work going? You like what you're doing?"

Briefly feeling my stomach clench at the use of my whole name, something Weston tends to do a lot, I shake it off before I nod and say, "I really do like it there. The guys are awesome and I love Jenny to death. But it *is* only temporary, so I'm trying not to get too comfortable."

"Yeah, you mentioned before something about maternity leave." He nods, making me happily realize that he remembers our first conversation almost a month ago. "What do you think you'll do after?"

"I have no clue," I sigh, reaching forward and taking a sip of my wine. "I have a guaranteed year though, so I'm not in too much of a hurry to be looking. Right now I'm just focusing on saving money for an apartment."

"Where are you staying now?"

"With my dad," I answer. "Which isn't bad or anything, but he's got his own life, you know? And I'm working on getting mine. Plus, that house is really small and it's the one I grew up in, so I'm kind of sick of it."

"Makes sense." He smiles, taking a sip from his wine glass as well. "What about your mom? What's she do?"

My heart stops beating for a quick, painful second. I manage to say somewhat smoothly, "I'm not sure what she's up to, actually. She left me and my dad, right before I graduated high school."

"No way," he breathes, and I see the horror in his eyes. "Iris, I'm so—"

Not wanting him to think he's upset me, I cut him off with a shrug and say, "It's totally fine, you didn't know. My dad and I are in a really good place right now, so it's not bad."

"Still though," he says, his voice distant like he's trying to wrap his mind around things. "Right before your graduation? That's terrible."

"It was," I say, desperately wanting to change subjects. "But I'm fine now."

He's still stunned into silence for a couple moments, but thankfully he decides to drop it. "So what college did you go to? LSU like I'm sure everyone around here does?"

Even though the change of topic is brisk and a tad awkward, I'm so incredibly thankful for it. I quickly dive into telling him all about my time at college while he adds his own little undergrad stories here and there.

Our dinner comes and we continue talking about anything imaginable as we eat and finish our glasses of wine, my mind still in complete shock that I'm able to talk so comfortably to someone I haven't known for years. Maybe it's because he's Jenny's brother and I'm so comfortable with her, or maybe it's just because our personalities mesh incredibly well.

I realize with a start that since he called me by my whole name, I haven't thought of Weston once. That's quite the accomplishment for me.

In fact, by the time he's paid for our bill and he's leading me out of the restaurant, his hand once again fit intimately against my lower back, I start wondering if maybe Jenny had a valid reason for being so excited about this date.

Maybe something really great *will* come out of this.

We talk about his impending drive back to Houston on the way back to my house and, the wine from dinner making me a little sleepy and lowering my jitters, I lean contentedly back in my seat and look at him as he talks. His sharp jawbone is incredibly attractive, and when I'm not watching that move, I'm looking at how soft his blond hair looks as it curls above his ear.

He really is very cute.

I stop gawking at him as I direct him toward my dad's house, and after he puts the car into Park and I open my mouth to say thanks and goodbye, he says, "I'll walk you up."

Knowing that a kiss is very much a possibility, nerves start fluttering around in my stomach but, I realize contently, not in a bad way.

"Thanks for coming out with me tonight," he says as we walk, his hand seeking my arm out to help me up the porch stairs.

My skin buzzes at the warmth from the skin on skin contact. When I stop in front of the door, my eyes meeting his, I notice that he's moved close to me and that his face has gone softly tender and determined. My heart is pounding, and for some awful reason I suddenly remember that I haven't been kissed in months.

And then I pray I haven't forgotten how to do it.

He doesn't immediately lean in to kiss me, though, so I find the nerve to say faintly, "Thanks for inviting me."

My breath stops when he takes another step toward me, our noses a hair apart, and he asks, "Is it okay if I kiss you? I don't want to be too—"

My heart fluttering in my chest, I slowly nod and breathe, "It's okay."

And then his lips are on mine and my instincts have taken over, my mouth meeting his kiss for kiss and my hand sneaking out so I can rest it against his clean-shaven cheek.

The moment doesn't last long and it never goes past a few slightly heated pecks, but that doesn't mean I'm not feeling warm and sated when it's all over.

"I'll call you next time I'm in town?" he asks, his fingers brushing a brown wave of hair off my forehead.

I nod and watch as he heads down the stairs back to his car.

"Drive safe!" I call out, suddenly remembering that, while I get to go lie in bed and replay every pleasant moment of our date, he's got to drive the four hours back to Houston.

He gives me a smile in return, waving goodbye before hopping in his car, and as he pulls away I notice movement out of the corner of my eye and then hear the slam of a door. When I look over at Weston's house, I see the old screen door still slowly closing in, and my heart suddenly goes cold.

Was Weston outside during all of that?

Did he see me kiss Campbell?

Feeling unnecessarily perturbed at the thought, I let myself into the house, tell my dad everything was fine and that I'm going to sleep, and then fall face-first onto my bed.

And then the nasty thought flashes across my mind.

Why is it that one thought of Weston can interfere with what was an amazing, picture-perfect first date?

# Chapter Nine

The next couple of days go by quickly, and by the time Friday night rolls around, I'm completely desperate for a quiet night home in front of the TV. Work's been incredibly busy for some reason, and Jenny has been handing me some of her duties so I can help out.

Thankfully though, Jenny has plans with one of her friends from college tonight and my dad has a date with Meg, so I'm not obligated to do anything.

Which is why, at six o' clock on a Friday evening, I'm eating a bowl of mac and cheese while curled up in a large knit blanket on the sofa, *Scandal* playing on the TV in front of me.

Suddenly barreling out of his bedroom, my dad asks hurriedly, "Does this look okay?"

After swallowing a bite of my dinner, I look over at where he's standing and see that he's dressed himself handsomely in black slacks and a blue button-up shirt that I know, up close, makes his eyes pop. His thinning hair has been styled neatly and his face is cleanly shaven, and I feel a goofy smile touch my lips at how adorably nervous he is.

"You look great, Dad!" I tell him. "Very handsome."

"Really?" he asks, reaching up to fidget with his hair. "I mean, this is something I'd wear to work and—"

"Well, you are working," I tease. "*Working for her love.*"

He narrows his eyes at me, and as he starts to fidgets again, this time with the sleeve of his shirt, I ask him curiously, "Why are you so nervous, anyway? Y'all have been out before."

"Yeah," he says, "but now that you know and now that we feel comfortable telling people in town about it, it's just more serious. More's on the line."

"You'll be fine." I grin enthusiastically at him. "It was obvious at the party that she's really into you. Where are y'all going anyway?"

"That steak house that guy took you to Tuesday night. We've been everywhere around here, and you said that place is really nice...."

"It is really nice," I assure him. "And Meg's going to love that."

I watch in amusement as he grabs his things off the kitchen table and shoves them in the pocket of his slacks before making his way to the small mirror hanging on the wall by the front door.

He starts fidgeting with his hair once again, so I yell at him, "Dad, go! Jesus!"

"Fine," he grumbles, taking his eyes off his reflection and looking at me angrily. "And you better start being nice to me. I'll kick you out on your ass."

I laugh loudly at that, knowing he would never even dream of doing such a thing. "Yeah, okay," I say sarcastically. "Now leave. And good luck."

I hear his Suburban pulling out of the driveway a minute later, and so I once again get comfortable on the couch and settle in for the next couple of hours.

Around nine o'clock my phone goes off, and when I grab it off the coffee table I see that it's just a text from my dad.

**Dad: Staying at Meg's tonight. Can you please bring the garbage can out before morning?**

Grimacing at the thought of my dad and Meg sleeping together and feeling much worse about their date than I initially did, I reluctantly send back that I will and then try my hardest not to think about it.

Him going on dates with Meg is one thing; staying at her house is a complete other.

I try to get back into the hang of watching the TV, but after his text I can't seem to concentrate on anything other than that, so I decide to call it quits for the night.

After rounding up the trash from inside the house and bringing it outside to the big can, I start rolling it across the grass in our front yard to set by the road for collection tomorrow.

As I'm cursing the humidity for the millionth time since living here, already feeling my hair start to frizz after less than a minute, I hear the rumble of a car's engine coming down the road. Glancing curiously in that direction, I see a cab round the corner and slow down.

When it stops in front of Weston's house, I can't help but feel my curiosity stretch further.

Why is Weston getting a cab at nine o'clock on a Friday night?

Figuring I should probably go inside so as not to gawk, I start to head in that direction, but I'm stopped in my tracks by the sound of Weston yelling. Turning to see what's going on, I see that the cab's back door has been opened but no one has gotten out.

And then a familiar voice starts yelling, "I'm not going to fucking give you more money for a tip than I am for what the fucking ride cost! Are you serious? It smells like Pringles and ball sac in here!"

What the *hell*?

Even though it's probably stepping over so many lines, I find myself hurrying across our front yard and into the street, walking behind the cab so that I can get a good look at the back seat. When I do, everything suddenly makes sense. Weston's cheeks are red, his eyes unsteady, and the second he opens his mouth I smell liquor.

He's drunk.

"Weston," I say calmly, placing a hand against the side of the car to peer inside and get his attention. When he looks over at me, I ask, "Hey, what's going on?"

The cab driver immediately starts yelling. "He's leaving me a two-dollar tip and it's Friday night, that ain't fucking right!"

"Shut up!" Weston shouts, his angry voice making me take a step back. "You drove me two miles, dipshit! And you're an asshole, so you don't even deserve the two dollars!"

Cursing silently to myself, I wrap a hand around Weston's bicep and pull him toward me, urging him, "Come on, you don't need to be doing this right now."

Weston's unfocused eyes meet mine and I swear I see them soften for just a moment, as if he wants to listen to me, but before he can slide out of the car the cab driver starts to protest his lack of a tip yet again.

Already having had enough, before Weston can chime in with anything too loud and threatening, I say to the driver, "It's nine thirty at night, I'm sure you weren't that busy, so stop acting like you did anything for him other than your damn job."

The driver turns to me, his unattractive face contorted and red from his anger. "Look, lady, I got kids I got to feed and child support I got to pay and—"

I cut him off angrily. "Then stop arguing with us and go get someone else to drive that'll pay you again! It's not that difficult to understand!"

"Get away from my car, bitch," the driver seethes. "And take this fucker with you."

"The fuck did you just say to her?" Weston shouts scarily loud, punching the passenger seat's headrest.

The situation starting to scare me, I squeeze my hand wrapped around Weston's arm and practically yank him out of the car, my breath catching when he stumbles against me. I get him settled on his feet, my arm wrapped around his trim waist, then slam the cab door and wince as the driver peels away.

Ignoring the screeching tires, I murmur, "Come on, West," and feel my skin electrify when he wraps an arm around my shoulders so I can help him walk.

I'm carefully leading him across the grass when he says lowly, "Of course you'd fucking be here for this."

Even though I know he's drunk and probably doesn't mean anything by it, I can't help but ask tightly, "Excuse me? What's that supposed to mean?"

"You're just... you're always around now. It's just.... It's like everywhere I go—*hey, there's Iris*! Every fucking time. It's so annoying."

The hurt is like a huge blow to the chest. I bite down on my lip and don't even bother to respond. Is he really that put out by my being around? At first I somewhat understood his hesitance toward liking me, but now... now that I've talked to him about my dad and Meg? Now that things haven't been quite so uncomfortable?

"God." He chuckles almost painfully, tilting his head back. "You've been here, like what, two months now, right? And already it's just like fucking high school all over again."

"Like high school?" I ask, confused.

"You wouldn't get it," he grumbles, looking down at me with shockingly sad eyes before shaking his head.

"Okay," I whisper, trying not to let my urge to cry win as I help him up the porch stairs and wait for him to fish his keys out of his pocket.

When he opens the door, my first instinct is to head home and just pretend tonight never happened, or to clean the shower or something, but then I see Thumper leap off his doggy bed in the corner of the living room and I realize he probably needs to be let out to use the bathroom.

Weston's not in the mindset to do anything but sleep, so I

follow him inside even though every ounce of my self-preservation is screaming at me to get away from him before he can hurt me even more.

Shutting the door behind us, I ask Weston, "Where's your Advil?"

"Cabinet above the stove," he answers gruffly, falling heavily onto the plush beige couch in the center of the room.

As I head into the kitchen to grab him some water and medicine, Thumper bounds over to me, his tail wagging impossibly fast and panting to let me know he's been inside far too long.

"Just a second, buddy," I murmur to the dog, patting him on the head before looking for the Advil bottle.

A groan sounds from the couch. "Thumper needs to... he needs to go out...."

"I'll bring him," I answer Weston, finding the medicine and emptying two pills onto my hand.

After grabbing a bottle of water from the fridge, I cross the wooden floors to where he's motionless on the couch, his eyes closed and his arms splayed over the armrest. Ignoring the somehow comforting look of him, I grab his shoulder and shake. "Come on, West, you got to drink some water and take these."

"Mmm...," he groans stubbornly, letting me know he's awake but refusing to open his eyes.

"Seriously," I urge, starting to get annoyed.

This man here has insulted me and treated me badly almost every time he's seen me this summer, and here I am breaking up fights and babying him when he's drunk.

"You're going to be miserable tomorrow," I say, and when he still refuses to comply I decide to take things one step further.

Dropping my hand from his shoulder, I reach toward his exposed ear and pull at it, something my mom used to do to me when I was young and wasn't listening.

"Ow!" Weston cries, his eyes shooting open before he gives me the nastiest glare. "Was that really necessary?"

"Yep," I say simply, depositing the pills in his hand and then handing him the bottle of water. "Drink it all," I inform him once he's tossed the pills into his booze-drenched mouth, and then as he starts on that I rise to my feet and call for Thumper.

He's at my side in a flash, so I lead him toward the back door, undo the locks, and pull it open, smiling a little bit to myself when Thumper leaps out of the house. Not wanting to be in the house with Weston any longer than I have to be, I shut the door behind me and sit on the edge of the back patio, watching as Thumper sniffs around the enclosed yard.

I'm trying my hardest not to think about what Weston said to me outside, about how annoying it is that he sees me around town a lot, but unfortunately the words have already etched their way onto my already bruised feelings. While I never really thought Weston and I would be the best of friends, I did think that maybe we were on our way to being friendly acquaintances, at least.

I guess I was wrong about that.

Once Thumper's done using the bathroom, I let him back into the house, locking the back door behind me, and then head to the couch to tell Weston I'm leaving. I can't do it, though, because he's now officially passed out on his sofa, light snores already sounding from his expansive chest.

Feeling some part of my hard feelings toward him chip away at the sight of him asleep, so vulnerable and groggy and problematically adorable, I look around the room for a blanket and then lay one from the recliner over his oversized frame.

I give Thumper a quick kiss on top of his head and then, after killing the lights, head back across the street.

Without my dad here and with Weston having just told me he wants nothing to do with me, the emptiness of the house feels painfully oppressive, claustrophobic almost. It's too small and too...

too damn empty. I lock the door, grab my blanket from the couch, and then head into my bedroom, tears crawling up my throat.

Not even bothering to wash my face or brush my teeth, I slide between my sheets, tears starting to leak out of my eyes the minute the side of my face hits the pillow.

I don't think I've ever felt this alone before, not since my mom left. It feels horrible, painful, and as I pull the top of my comforter up to my chin, I can't help but think that maybe I was wrong, that maybe I'm not as at home here as I felt.

Maybe I just don't belong here.

# Chapter Ten

To say I'm nervous for tonight is an understatement of the highest capacity.

I'm absolutely dreading the double date that Jenny was somehow able to trick me into agreeing to. Even though my relationship with Campbell has been smooth sailing over the past month, I'm still not ready to face Weston after what he drunkenly admitted to me.

I'm standing in front of my closet, trying my best not to panic as I figure out something to wear. It's just Buffalo Wild Wings, so it can't be too nice, but I also don't want to show up in something casual when it's a guaranteed fact Jenny will be dressed to kill.

Eventually I pick some dark wash skinny jeans with a couple of holes at the knees and a hunter green and gold tank top that makes my light brown eyes stand out. After I slide into all of that and match it with gold hoop earrings and black ankle boots, I quickly touch up my makeup and then head into the living room to wait for Campbell's call.

It takes two minutes, but it's not Campbell who lets me know they're here.

Jenny texts me.

**Jenny: Bitch! We be outside!**

My dad's at work late yet again, so I don't have to say bye to him, and instead just lock up the house and hurry on over to Campbell's familiar shiny black car. It's just him and me in the car, so after we greet each other, he's quick to take advantage of the privacy, his hands tangling into my shoulder-length hair and yanking my face to his for a few quick yet highly powerful kisses.

We pull away from each other and he's grinning as I hurriedly pull down the mirror to check my lipstick, when the back doors open and the other couple slides in, Jenny greeting me cheerily. "Hey, Iris!"

"Hey." I chuckle, craning my neck to look back at her. "Long time no see."

She and Campbell both laugh as Weston remains silent, of course, but so I'm not labeled as the rude one, I meet Weston's dark gaze and say, "Hey, Weston."

"Hey," he greets stiffly.

Forgetting about it and trying to concentrate on having a fun night with my best friend and my new boyfriend, I turn back around and, after giving Campbell a sly wink, I buckle in and brace myself for what's sure to be an interesting night.

The restaurant is pretty crowded for trivia night, but luckily we don't have to wait and are led over to a table off to the side of the restaurant. After we're all brought our beer and playing tablets for the game, we order our wings and then chat amongst ourselves for the ten minutes it takes for the last game to end.

Instead of playing as a team like Jenny thought when she first invited us, we actually play by ourselves, which quickly proves to be much more fun.

"Ha!" Jenny squeals a while later, slamming a hand down and pointing the other at her brother. "I told you that West Virginia was the mountain state! Who even thinks it's South Dakota?"

"You're still losing." Campbell laughs at her, Weston and I

joining in at the look of pure dissatisfaction on Jenny's face. She's doing the worst out of all of us, and she's down by a lot of points, which is so much fun to keep reminding her. Campbell is currently first, and I'm second, but Weston's a very close third, and every time a new question comes up he's quick to tell me that he's going to pass me this time.

Tonight has actually been going really well, and I'm enjoying myself far more than I thought I would. Despite Weston's cold greeting in the car, he's either warmed up to me for the night or has decided to be a good sport for the sake of his girlfriend, either of which I'm happy with.

"You want another beer, babe?" Campbell asks as the second round of the game ends for a five-minute break, his hand sliding out to rest on my thigh.

"Yeah, that sounds good." I nod, gripping his hand with my own and giving it a quick squeeze.

I watch as he waves the waitress over and orders my favorite beer for me as well as ordering another round for everyone else, and I realize with a jolt that I'm much happier with him than I thought I'd be.

He's so attentive and kind, and even when he's teasing me I know he doesn't have bad intentions. He just likes making me blush, something he's told me on multiple occasions now. He hasn't even been pushy about sex, something I know from experience is pretty rare from someone who's taken me on more than a couple of dates.

I stop thinking about Campbell, though, when the waitress brings us our next round and Jenny takes a large sip of her beer and comments, "This shit is so good, but I really didn't think it'd be this strong."

I say, "Well, you don't have to drive or anything, so what's the harm, really?"

"True." She smirks, taking another sip and then giggling. "I haven't gotten drunk in forever."

Campbell's arm threads around my shoulders as he pulls me in close and murmurs in my ear, "What about you, huh? You gotten drunk recently?"

I know better than to tell him about my night of degradation at the Boot a couple of months ago, and thankfully Weston and Jenny are too busy talking amongst themselves to hear him and rat me out.

I lift my eyes to meet the beautiful blue ones staring back into mine and I smirk. "Why? You want to get me drunk tonight?"

His free arm skates back toward my thigh, his hand once again resting against it, but this time much higher. "I don't think that'd be the worst idea."

I narrow my eyes playfully at him. "Are you trying to take advantage of me, Campbell Turner?"

He smiles mischievously, his fingers squeezing my thigh as he says, "I'd let you take advantage of me too, you know, to make things fair. Equality and all that."

I laugh out loud, shaking my head at him before turning back to face the table and enjoy the rest of the night.

Things are relatively quiet as Campbell drives us all home, Jenny and I having had enough to drink that we're now sleepy, and Weston being the quiet guy he always is.

When Campbell pulls onto Weston's and my street, he prompts, "Hey, West?"

"Yeah, man?" Weston's gruff voice replies.

"Would you mind bringing Jenny back to the apartment? I wanted to hang out here a little longer."

My eyes widen as I look over at Campbell, hating that he's putting Weston out so he and I can be alone. I feel a gaze hit the back of my skull as Weston answers with, "Uh, yeah... I can do that."

"Great," Campbell says, flashing me a smile, completely oblivious to the fact that I'm now faintly annoyed. "Thanks, man."

We all say our goodbyes after Campbell pulls into my driveway, and as soon as Jenny and Weston are out of the car, he asks, "Is your dad here? I don't see his car."

"Umm...." I trail off, looking out the window. For some reason, dread trickles into the pit of my stomach when I see that my dad's truck really isn't here despite it being late. "No, I guess not. He must be staying at Meg's or something."

"Well, how about I come in for a little while?" Campbell asks, his voice dropping an octave and his eyes flashing with something that has my nerves buzzing unpleasantly.

"I have work really early," I tell him, grasping for an excuse, as the thought of being at home alone with him doesn't sit well with me. "Maybe next time?"

"Really?" he asks, his voice slightly disbelieving. "It's not even midnight yet."

"And?" I say, my annoyance starting to burn. "I had, like, four beers at trivia. I'm tired."

"Come on," he whines with a playful smile, reaching out to drag me closer to him. "We never get time alone."

"Yes, we do," I remind him, still irritated. "We go on dates at least twice a week."

"But that's not alone alone," he says, pulling me closer as he dips his head into the crook of my neck and starts nuzzling.

"Campbell," I say uncomfortably, moving back. "I said another time, right? Just not tonight. I'm tired."

"I can make you not tired." He grins, leaning in and unbuckling my seat belt before grabbing my cheeks and pulling my lips to his.

I go along with him for a couple of minutes, not wanting to completely ruin tonight, but then he starts trying to take things further and I begin to panic. One of his hands grabs at my chest, lightly at first and then, after a few seconds, hard enough to hurt.

Yanking away from him, I attempt to end things by saying firmly, "I'm done for tonight, okay? That hurt."

"I'm sorry," he murmurs, sticking his bottom lip out while trying to lean into me again.

I back away to where he can't reach me, my heart beginning to pound and my adrenaline rising. "I'll see you later," I say, reaching down to grab my purse from the floorboard.

"This is so fucking stupid," he curses, his voice simmering with a barely repressed heat.

And it scares me.

"Campbell...." I trail off, not knowing what to say.

"I've taken you out like a hundred times now," he says, his jaw clenching, "and you still won't put out? Are you serious?"

My mouth opening in shock, I ask, "Are *you* serious? Do you even hear yourself?"

"I mean, I don't understand what's wrong with me coming in. You're not a virgin, are you?"

"No," I say through clenched teeth, "I'm not. But just because I've had sex before doesn't mean I'm automatically willing."

"What, so it's me then?" he demands in a shout, and when I see his fists clenching I know I need to get the hell out of this car.

"We're done," I say seriously, officially never wanting to see him again. "This is over."

"How is this over when it never fucking started?" he yells again, making my heart leap in my chest in fear. "This was a middle school relationship, Iris.... This is bullshit!"

Not wanting to hear any more, I hurriedly hop out of his car and slam my door shut, rushing up the stairs and feeling my heart race painfully until I have the front door open and I hear his car peel out of the driveway, spraying gravel.

Still panicked, I lock the front door behind me and lean my forehead against the old wood, trying to calm my nerves.

Completely unsure how our fun night turned into what it did, I dig the heels of my hands into my eyes, the oncoming tears burning, and try to stop them from falling. I don't want to cry over that, over what he just said to me. I don't want to give him that kind of satisfaction.

Taking a deep breath and eventually feeling the urge to cry starting to subside, I double-check the lock on the door and then head into my bedroom, eager to fall asleep and escape the steaming pile of dramatic crap that my life seems to have turned into.

# Chapter Eleven

Luckily for me, but not quite so much for Jenny, she gets sick that night and stays out of work for the rest of the week, which means that, as of now, I have still yet to talk to her about Campbell's and my less-than-great breakup.

The conversation needs to happen, I know that; I'm just in no hurry for it.

I'm also not in any great hurry to go to the party currently happening across the street, the Alcorns' annual dinner to honor Marcus's birthday. I'd completely forgotten about it even though my dad always has it marked on our fridge calendar, and I'd be lying if I said I was excited to go celebrate Weston's dead older brother's birthday.

Weston's parents, Carl and Patrice, have always been the sweetest people and the cutest little couple in town. When Marcus died his first year deployed overseas, the town wept right along with them. Their oldest son had been incredibly well-known and well-liked, as he'd been the kind of person who was always happy and willing to make new friends.

Which is why, the year after his passing, Carl and Patrice decided to celebrate his life on his birthday and not on the anniversary of his death.

I went to the party every year when I was still living at home, and even though I'd only been thirteen when he passed, I'd still known him as the cute older boy across the street who bought me a Bugs Bunny treat from the ice-cream truck one afternoon when neither of my parents were home to give me money.

"Iris!" my dad calls from the other side of my bedroom door, rapping his knuckles against the wood and breaking me out of my thoughts. "You ready yet? I don't want to be late!"

"Yeah!" I call back, slipping the second gold hoop earring in my ear. "Two minutes!"

I hear him walk away from the door, and then muffled speaking between him and Meg. The two of them going together is yet another reason I'm not all that thrilled about today. It's their first public outing as a couple, my dad having made it exclusive this past weekend when he took her to a fancy casino in Biloxi for a weekend away.

In the month since I first found out about the two of them, she's been over a lot more frequently and I've slowly warmed up to her being the new woman in my dad's life. It's still a bit strange at times, especially when I see him being affectionate toward her.

I do try my hardest not to think about it, though, and for the most part I'm just thrilled he's so happy.

After spritzing on some new perfume, I quickly slip on cute wedge booties and then head out into the living room, where I see Meg tenderly fixing my dad's hair.

"I'm ready," I announce to the loved-up couple, crossing to where they're standing. "Sorry I took so long."

"Nonsense," Meg says with a wave of her hand, stepping away from my dad. "It's not like we really can be late since it's across the street. Your dad's just too uptight."

My dad scoffs, "Please, I'm not the one who spent an hour just picking a dress out."

"Excuse you!" Meg squeals, sounding insulted as she smacks my dad's arm. "It was not an hour!"

"Fifty-nine minutes then," my dad says, playfully rolling his eyes and making me giggle. "Same difference."

"You're such an asshole." Meg laughs, shaking her head before looking at me. "I don't know where you came from, honey, 'cause you are just so much more charming than your father."

"Tell me something I don't know." I smirk, poking my tongue out at him.

Looking dramatically wounded, he says, "Well, since both my ladies are ganging up on me, let's get the hell out of here. I need some more testosterone around me."

Meg catches my eye and winks before responding with, "I always knew you and Paul had something going behind my back."

I laugh. "Really? I always thought it'd be Frankie."

Finally deciding to join in our teasing, he says, "Well, Paul *does* have a cabin in Grand Isle."

There are only a few other people besides the Alcorns across the street when we get there five minutes later, most of them being from the same crowd as the Fourth of July party. My dad, Meg, and I spend the first thirty minutes we're there giving everyone hugs hello and catching up on what we've all been up to this past month, and by the time we're done food is being served and I figure everyone who's coming is already here.

Jenny has yet to show up to be by Weston's side, and I feel pretty damn guilty about how relieved I am. I know she's sick and she's my best friend in town, but I'm still so torn about how to handle the Campbell situation.

After filling my plate with far too much food and grabbing a bottle of water from the cooler, my mind too full of incriminating things for alcohol, I find an empty seat at one of the three plastic tables they've set up in their living room.

They've pushed all the furniture to the walls to make room for the tables, but my eyes still find Thumper's doggie bed next to the back door and I smile when I see him contentedly chewing a large bone Weston probably got specifically to keep him occupied today.

My dad and Meg come and sit next to me after making their plates, and we spend the first half of the meal talking amongst ourselves and with friends of theirs.

I've finished my dinner and have moved on to the two cookies and chocolate cake I got for dessert when I hear a throat being cleared and look up to see Carl and Patrice standing in front of everyone.

"Hey, y'all," Carl starts, looking at the small crowd of people with fondness and graciousness in his eyes. "Patrice and I just want to say thanks for coming out again tonight, as I know we've done this for so long now—"

"Ten years," Patrice interrupts a bit sadly, stepping toward her incredibly tall husband and threading her arm around his waist.

My heart squeezes when I see Carl return the gesture, gripping his adorably short wife to his side and planting a comforting kiss on top of her head. He continues hoarsely, "Yeah, ten years. It's still so crazy to think that it's been a whole decade since that man showed up on our doorstep...."

As he trails off, woefully shaking his head, Patrice cuts in for him. "Y'all have been here for us since then, and we are so very lucky to have all y'all in our life. No parent ever thinks they'll outlive their child, even if that child decides to enlist in the Army, and for a short while there we didn't know how we'd cope."

My throat starts burning with emotion when I see Carl wipe a couple of tears from underneath his eye, and it's almost painful to keep listening to Weston's mom. "But we did cope, and we got through it, and it's mainly because we've had your love and support."

Her voice cracks at the end, and for some reason the sound of it makes my eyes immediately seek out the man sitting at the table in front of me, his bright green eyes intently trained on his plate.

Weston's always been so different from his family, choosing to withdraw when his parents and Marcus would reach out instead. And even though he's been so open with his dislike of me, it still breaks my heart when I see the look on his face and recognize it as the same look I get when I think about my mom leaving.

Even though he and his older brother were so different, they were still so very close. I'd always look out my bedroom window and see the two of them riding their bikes in the street, trying to beat each other in races and with the cool tricks they could do.

One afternoon in particular that I remember, I'd been sitting on our porch doing my homework, and they had been outside playing basketball with Marcus's friends. Weston and one of the friends, some jackass named Tommy who I think moved up north after high school, got into an argument and Marcus took up for his brother, making Tommy so pissed that he stormed off and left.

What I remember most, though, is the huge and breathtakingly happy smile Weston had on his face as Tommy left, just because his brother had picked him over his friend.

When Marcus died, I never really saw Weston playing outside again.

Weston's name catching my attention, I turn back to Patrice and hear her in the middle of saying, "...his big brother, but has still grown into the best man we could've ever hoped to raise. Carl and I know that Marcus is watching us from up in Heaven, despite those few nights we caught him sneaking in either drunk or stoned as hell"—she smiles fondly as we all laugh—"and he's so very happy with what he sees."

From the corner of my eye I see Meg lean into my dad, sparse tears running down her cheeks, and a bittersweet smile touches my lips when I see him whisper something comforting into her ear.

"Marcus would be twenty-nine today, and probably pissed as hell that he's almost thirty," Carl says. He raises his beer bottle. "So happy birthday, son. We miss you."

They end the night the same as they always used to, with them lighting nineteen candles on a funfetti cake, which was Marcus's favorite growing up, and then us singing Happy Birthday and Carl, Patrice, and Weston blowing out the candles.

Around nine o'clock everyone's saying their goodbyes, and as they do Meg walks over to me to ask, "You want to stay and help clean up?"

"Yeah, sure," I agree with a nod, standing and starting to collect the empty plates.

A few minutes later as I'm heading into the kitchen to toss out what all I could carry, Patrice crosses the now empty living room toward me and says, "Honey, you don't have to do that."

"Oh hush," I scold her playfully. "This is a party for y'all. It'd be awful if you had to clean up."

She smiles fondly, her bright green eyes, so much like Weston's, sparkling with emotion. "Well you are still just the nicest li'l thing, huh?"

My cheeks flush. "I wouldn't say the *nicest*."

She laughs at me, placing a hand on my shoulder before saying, "Well, just because you've taken the job upon yourself doesn't mean I won't help. And we can catch up, 'cause I haven't gotten the pleasure of talking to you yet."

I grin, once again hit in the gut by how genuinely good this woman is and how much she didn't deserve the tragedy she had to go through.

"So how've you been?" she asks, leaning over to grab some of the trash I wasn't able to carry. "How was school?"

"It was really good," I answer. "And I was sad to leave, but I am glad I'm here. I missed it here, missed my dad."

"Oh, and he missed you too, honey," she says, finishing up with her stack of trash and motioning for me to follow her into the kitchen. "When you first left, we had him over for dinner at least once a week, if not twice. It was clear as day how much that empty house was weighing on him."

Despite having been reassured multiple times by my dad that he's glad I left and that I should feel no remorse whatsoever, I still feel a shred of guilt squeeze my chest. I know how shitty it felt going back to an empty house that one night after seeing Weston drunk, how alone it felt, and that was just for a night.

My dad had to deal with that for four years, mere months after his wife left him.

"Yeah," I admit, my voice soft. "I hate that I had to leave him."

"It was for the best, though," she says, obviously picking up on the guilt in my voice. "If you hadn't left, you wouldn't have been able to really grow into the woman you are now, you know? And he wouldn't have let himself get close to Meg if you were here, which looks to be the best thing that's happened to him since your mom left."

"You're right. Thanks for pointing that out." I chuckle gratefully, dumping my trash into an empty bag she's holding out. "I hadn't thought about it that way."

"Of course, honey." She smiles at me. "It's the same kind of dilemma Carl and I went through when we were talking about moving. Didn't know if leaving Weston here would be the best thing."

"How is Florida, by the way? I'm so jealous."

"It's great," she says, before laughing. "No wonder old people like us move there. We found the best deal in Destin and were a bit worried about the tourists, but luckily the area we're in isn't too overrun."

Not too much later, after we head back into the living room to continue picking up, Weston and his dad walk in, both with empty bottles of beer in their hands and both looking emotionally drained.

Patrice seems to notice this as well, asking, "Y'all okay?"

"Yeah," Carl answers as Weston's gaze hits me, causing my nerve endings to crackle to life. "Just catching up."

"Good!" Patrice says happily. "Did you get him to tell you anything about this girl he's seeing?"

My stomach turning cold, I avert my eyes from the three of them and try to put my focus on cleaning up as fast as I can. "Only that her name's Jenny and she's from Houston."

"That's it?" Patrice basically whines, and even though I'm not watching them I know she's glaring at her son. "Weston, come on! A mother needs to know these things! Where'd y'all meet? How long has this been going on? Is it serious?"

"Is she hot?" Carl adds, making Patrice respond quickly with a dry, "Shut up, Carl."

The front door opens, Weston still declining to respond to anything, and as Meg and my dad come in from dragging the trash bins to the street, Patrice says, "I bet Steve knows."

*Oh shit.*

"Hey, Steve?" Patrice asks. "You know anything about this girl my son's seeing?"

"Jenny?" my dad says. "Yeah, I know her. She and Iris are good friends. She's been over for dinner a couple of times."

"Oh really?" Patrice directs toward where I'm hanging my head, this conversation being the last thing I want to do. "Iris? I trust you. Is Jenny worth my son's time?"

"Um, yeah," I say a bit uncomfortably, finally looking at her and cursing underneath my breath when I see everyone's but Weston's attention on me. "Jenny's great. She works at the same law firm I do."

"She's a lawyer?" Carl asks, almost sounding like he's choking. "Hell yeah, son!"

Weston finally decides to open his mouth and explains, "She's not a lawyer, Dad. She's the secretary."

"That's still real impressive," Carl says, reaching out to clap him on the back. "Why isn't she here tonight so we can meet her?"

"She's sick," Weston says, casting a quick glance over at me. "And it's really not that serious yet."

For some reason him saying this makes the stress in my chest deflate. I immediately berate myself. Jenny wants them to be serious, I remind myself, so I should be annoyed he hasn't committed to her yet.

"Well, if y'all are still seeing each other next time we come to town, I expect to get to meet her, okay? It's killing me that I'm so far away and can't keep tabs on you through the other women in town," his mom jokes.

"Yes, ma'am," Weston says, obviously deciding to placate her.

The conversation after that dwindles into something not nearly as interesting as Weston and Jenny's relationship, so I halfheartedly listen and keep on cleaning.

After the trash from the tables is picked up and my dad and Weston are folding the tables up and moving them into the shed out back, Meg, Patrice, and I are all in the kitchen picking up the uneaten food, saving it, and cleaning the dishes.

"So what about you, Iris?" Patrice asks as I'm scraping a piece of dried cheese off a pan with my thumbnail. "You seeing anyone?"

"Um, well, I was," I say reluctantly, my voice catching in my throat when I hear the back door open and Weston and my dad come back into the house and then, unfortunately, into the kitchen.

I keep quiet once they're in here, having not yet told my dad about Campbell's and my split and not really wanting to do so in front of Weston.

Unfortunately, Weston's mom doesn't let it slide even though the boys have joined us. "And?" she asks curiously. "You're not seeing this person anymore?"

I immediately feel two sets of eyes dart my way, my stomach dropping in humiliation as I am forced to say, "No, um, I'm not. We ended things a few days ago."

"Oh, I'm sorry," Patrice says. "That's rotten. He must've been an idiot to let you go."

Weston snorts after she says this, and at the sound of it I feel my fists clenching. His mom doesn't ignore it either, turning around from where she was stuffing baked mac and cheese into an empty old butter container. "Did you know him, Weston?"

"He's Jenny's brother," Weston answers, his voice dry. "And he is an idiot. But you can't really expect anything more from someone named after a brand of soup."

Instead of angering me further, the fact that Weston says this makes me feel a little better about the breakup. Although I know I was never obligated to have sex with Campbell despite us having passed that three-date mark, a part of me still felt at least a little responsible and thought that people might agree with him.

"Oh?" Patrice asks, looking over at me. "And you're sure Jenny's nothing like him?"

I nod, wanting to ease her worry. "She's great, I promise. I wouldn't lie to you."

"Hey, West?" Carl says, popping his head into the kitchen through the archway. "Can you come help me with this?"

"Sure," Weston says, his eyes falling on me once more before he heads out.

My dad eagerly follows the two guys, muttering something about being around enough girls at home, and I'm a little surprised he didn't say anything about my little announcement. Knowing him, though, he could tell I was uncomfortable talking about it and is waiting to bring it up until we're alone.

Once they're gone I focus once again on doing the dishes, now more than ever really just wanting to go home, but a minute or so later, Patrice asks, "Can I tell you something, Iris? I don't want to overstep any lines, but...."

"Yeah." I nod, dropping what I'm doing so I can look at her.

"It's just, I always...." She trails off, looking quickly at Meg, who seems to be watching our conversation with interest. "Well, a bunch of us actually always thought you and... you know, you and Weston would end up together."

Burning heat scorches its way to my cheeks. I nervously look between the two women before stammering, "I.... Well, we....."

Patrice cuts me off, her eyes compassionate. "I don't want to make you uncomfortable, Iris, but everyone kind of knows about you two at your graduation party and... and I don't know. Y'all just seem like such a good fit. Everyone's been kind of rooting for y'all since y'all were young."

"That's so embarrassing," I murmur, crossing my arms over my stomach and wanting to fold into myself and disappear. "I... I mean, it was one time and...."

"It was such a long time coming, though," Patrice says, looking to the side as if she's nervous one of the guys is out there listening. "Weston may not have been very open with me, but I'm still his mom. I still knew when he liked someone and... trust me, honey... he liked you. *A lot.*"

My skin prickles.

"That can't.... That's not true," I stammer. "He's.... Not trying to be rude or anything, Mrs. Patrice, but Weston hasn't really been too thrilled that I'm back in town. He's kind of made damn well sure that I know that."

She smiles sadly, placing her hand on my shoulder. "That's 'cause you broke his heart, honey. The morning after you moved, when he still didn't know, I hadn't seen him that happy about anything since before Marcus had passed. And then... when he came home after your dad told him, it was.... Iris, there's no doubt in my mind that that boy had it bad for you."

Guilt hits me like a wrecking ball, even though a large part of me is still reluctant to think that Weston Alcorn could have ever had a crush on me. I was the girl who sat in the front of the bus, busy listening to happy pop music and doing homework or flashcards, while he was the boy who sat in the back and was cool despite never talking.

Which is why, even though we're both older, I still can't wrap my head around what Patrice is saying.

So I try to deflect this ridiculous conversation by saying, "Well, he's with Jenny now, and they're both happy and... I don't know. If he did ever feel anything for me, I'm sure it's long gone by now, especially with how I handled things back then."

Patrice smiles and says, "I think, judging by how bad he had it back then, that it'd only take an apology or two for him to fall right back into it. I think, if he really felt serious for Jenny, he'd be more open with his father and me about her. When he gets excited about things, when he's passionate about something or someone, it's really not that hard to get him talking."

I open my mouth to say something, anything, to change the subject, but before I can Meg pipes up and says a bit mischievously, "And, Iris... you still have yet to say you don't like him like that. You've just been giving excuses as to why *he* wouldn't like *you*."

Starting to feel annoyed and incredibly pressured, I close my eyes, take a deep breath, and then look at the two of them as I try to say calmly, "Because what's the point of saying that, admitting that, if I know it'd never work?"

"So we'd know that we're right," Meg quips, making Patrice grin mischievously.

"Well, I'm not saying anything else about this," I tell them seriously. "If we keep talking about it, it's only going to start trouble."

"Fine," Patrice huffs, even though she still looks pleased with herself. "I just wanted you to know all that, okay? I had to get it off my chest, and I'm happy now even if it doesn't end up with y'all being together. Even though that'd be so great."

"*So* great," Meg emphasizes, making me roll my eyes.

But even as we all turn around and get back to work and the two of them start talking about these weight loss wraps their friend sells, I can't get my mind off what they've just told me. Whether or not I'd like to admit it to myself, this conversation and how I've reacted to every other Weston-involved thing since I've been back tell me that I'm still not over him.

I still have a major thing for Weston Alcorn, even though he's so cold to me the majority of the time and even though he's dating my best friend whose brother tried to pressure me into sex.

So much could go wrong, though, and that's why I know what's been spoken of here can never be spoken of again.

There's just too much to lose.

# Chapter Twelve

Jenny's back at work Monday morning, and the smile that she gives me when she walks through the lobby does nothing to quell the nerves in the pit of my stomach.

She has to know about Campbell and me splitting, as the two of them are living together and Campbell never struck me as the guy to keep quiet about relationship drama. So now it's just a guess of if he told her the exact reason why we split.

The morning passes by quickly, and when lunchtime rolls around and I haven't heard from her, I decide to bite the bullet and call her myself.

She answers her desk phone after the second ring. "Hey, Iris."

"Hey," I say, "Do you want to do lunch or...?"

"Oh, actually," she says, and although she sounds off, I can't figure out if it's because of anger toward me or because she's getting over a cold, "I'm going to go to lunch with Weston today, since I haven't seen him in a while."

"Oh, well okay!" I say, trying my best to sound normal. "Have fun."

"Will do," she says before hanging up and leaving me sitting at my desk wondering if we're going through our first rough patch.

As the next few days go by, nothing happens that makes me feel any better about Jenny and my friendship. After her lunch with Weston on Monday, she was too busy to take one on Tuesday. On Wednesday she said her stomach was feeling weird, and earlier today she said she'd brought leftovers that were going to go bad if she didn't eat them soon.

So by the time we're about close up on Thursday, I'm slowly giving up on my hope that our friendship is unscathed and preparing myself for yet another night of dinner and TV with my dad.

Which is why, when I see Jenny come out of the back hallway and not just give me a lame wave goodbye, instead turning and walking over to me, I can't help but feel a jolt of surprise.

"Hey," she says with a small smile, her usual enthusiasm for closing time not all that evident. "You have plans for tonight?"

"Nothing special," I answer. "Why?"

"You want to go grab some dinner and drinks? We need to talk."

My stomach lurching at the seriousness of her voice, I nod and say, "Okay. You want to meet up somewhere so you won't have to bring me back here?"

"Yeah, that sounds good. Ralph's sound okay?" she asks, referring to the local seafood place that has just about every beer known to man on tap.

"Perfect," I say. "Let me just close up my stuff and I'll meet you there."

"Okeydokey," she says with a small smile before turning and walking gracefully out of the lobby.

After a drive filled with adrenaline-pumping nerves, I pull into the crowded parking lot of Ralph's and head inside, Jenny having texted me saying she'd already gone in and gotten us a table in the back. I ignore the admiring looks of the few older guys in town I didn't grow up with, and then spot my beautiful blonde friend at a booth, already with two frosted glasses of beer in front of her.

"Hey," she says when I sit down, "I already went ahead and ordered you an Ultra since they're so busy. Is that okay?"

"Yeah, that's fine!" I exclaim, taking a sip of it and feeling my nerves ebb just a little bit. "Thanks. Have you ordered food yet?"

"Nah," she says, shaking her head. "He just brought these a minute or two ago."

"Oh, okay," I say, deciding to be a wimp and give my attention to my menu and not to her.

She goes along with me for a few minutes, remaining quiet as she too looks through a menu, but then the waiter comes and we place our orders and have no reason left to put off this conversation. Jenny still remains quiet though, and eventually the silence gets to me so much that words just start bubbling up in my throat.

"Look, I'm sorry if you're mad about the whole Campbell thing, but it's just.... I mean, we said a while ago that it wouldn't interfere with our friendship, and I don't want it to, and it's not like I hate your brother or anything, you know? We just didn't work out, and I wanted it to, I really did.... I mean, I liked the guy, you know? I don't—"

She cuts me off. "I'm not mad that y'all broke up, Iris. I knew the odds of y'all *actually* getting married were super low."

"Okay," I say slowly. "But—"

She dives in firmly. "There's two things that are kind of bothering me about this whole situation."

*Two?* Has something happened that I'm completely unaware of?

"Okay," I say, my nerves still pumping. "What, then?"

"Well, first, I just... I'm so sorry about what happened with you and Campbell. He told me everything."

I swallow. "Everything?"

Somehow that just doesn't seem plausible.

She nods, looking down at the table and tucking a piece of shiny blonde hair behind her pierced ear. "Campbell and I tell each other everything, Iris, no matter how shitty it is. And I'm sorry he pressured you. He had a few drinks at dinner. That probably had something to do with it, but that still doesn't excuse it, and I'm glad you called him out and ran off. If that had happened with me, I'd have ended things too."

"Thank God," I breathe, all the stress in my chest dissolving. "I'd been so worried and I really didn't want to bring up what actually happened 'cause I didn't want it to cause a strain between you and him since y'all are so close and everything, and I was just.... I was freaking out, Jen."

She giggles slightly, shaking her head but still not looking quite content. "No, I get that. Don't worry. And I smacked him around for a little while too when he told me."

"Good," I say before taking a quick sip of my beer. "Now what's—"

She cuts me off again, looking so determined to get the words out that she's not bothering to be her normal polite self. "But Campbell did say something that's had me freaked, and I really hope it's not true."

"Okay...?" I say, my brows furrowing. "What'd he say?"

"You and Weston," she starts, making my chest go cold. "Are y'all.... I mean, is there anything, like, between y'all?"

I shake my head in earnest, slightly panicked. "No! Why? What gave Campbell that idea? I mean, we never, Weston and I rarely ever talk, so I don't—"

"Campbell thinks y'all don't really talk and that things are always a little uncomfortable between you two because something is going on, and I don't want to believe it... but it does make sense, you know? Y'all have grown up near each other and... and I just.... And he still refuses to make anything serious with me, Iris. So I just.... I'm trying to figure out what's going on, or even if there is something going on."

*Shit, shit, shit*, is all I'm able to think, absolutely despising Weston and myself for not being able to be around each other normally. If we were actually the adults that our ages suggest, we'd be able to be fine around each other and not give any hints to someone who's only known us for a handful of weeks that something happened between us.

If Campbell was able to notice that with how far his head was shoved up his own ass, then apparently we're pretty obvious.

"Jenny—"

"Please don't lie to me," she interrupts, her blue eyes pleading. "I just.... I need to know if he's not getting serious because something with you is holding him back, or if it's just because of something with me. I mean, it's been like two months and... and I don't know, *he should want to have sex with me!*"

My mind starts painfully whirling, conflicted by her words, by that desperate look she's giving me.

Do I tell her that we kissed four years ago and that we still can't be normal with each other? Would that make her feel better or worse? It could be either, honestly, and that's what's killing me.

I don't want this to end badly; I want this to go back to how it was before Campbell moved here.

"Just...," I drag out, my mind still not completely set on what I'm going to say next. "Just listen to me, okay, and... and, Jenny, I don't want our friendship to be weird, okay? I just.... You may be mad, and I don't want you to be, but if you listen to the whole story and you—"

"Just fucking tell me!" she snaps, dramatically smacking her hand against the table.

I jolt at the loud noise, and when I feel the curious eyes of other patrons in the restaurant, I can't help the blush that spreads across my cheeks and the overwhelming need to hide underneath the table.

Staring at the table, I quickly run over my words in my head and then gulp back my nerves, looking back at her scowling and yet somehow terrified face.

"Four years—" My voice is so hoarse that I have to swallow

before continuing. "Four years ago, my mom left my dad and me. She just... she just walked out."

"You've told me this," she says, her lips pinched together.

"Yeah, I know," I say quietly, wishing I had a sweater on so that I could pull the sleeves over my fingertips and feel some kind of comfort. "But just.... I.... It fucked me up big-time, okay? There was no warning or anything, she just disappeared one day and left this note on the fridge that said that the town was too small and she was just sick of her life... of me and my dad... so she disappeared, and I don't... I still don't think I've actually recovered from that, Jen."

"Okay," she says dryly, her expression having not changed from that unpleasant scowl. "And what's that have to do with Weston?"

Pushing back the feelings of embarrassment and rejection at how easily she's able to dismiss my emotional trauma away in lieu of talking about her love life, I say, "The night before I left for college, we had this big graduation party at my dad's and it was just... just too much for me to handle, you know? So I went outside and I sat on the porch, and Weston.... He still... he still lived across the street from me, he always has, and I don't know, he came up and saw me crying and was trying to make me feel better and...."

When I trail off this time, not entirely able to finish the story, she snaps at me yet again, "And what, Iris? You're just.... You're doing that babbling you do all the time, and I'm trying to stay calm but this is so fucking long. Just tell me, did you and—"

I cut her off this time, anger and annoyance and this overpowering pressure rolling off her finally making me come loose.

"We kissed, okay?" I snap, easily seeing the pain that inflicts on her but for once not feeling guilty about it. "We kissed and that was it, and then some lady from the party came out and we stopped and Weston said we'd talk about it later, but there was no later because I moved four hours away the next morning. And still to this day we haven't brought it up, okay? That's all. That's all that's fucking happened. It's not like it's some huge conspiracy against you, Jen. It's just really damn awkward between us, that's all."

She's quiet for a long moment after my rant, her eyes trained on the tabletop in front of us. The longer she sits there, all self-pitying and quiet, the more my adrenaline wears off and the more I start to feel badly about how I handled things.

I shouldn't have yelled at her like that. I bite down on my bottom lip and feel tears start to burn at the base of my throat. Whether or not she handled this whole conversation the right way, whether or not she could've asked me in a much better way, I know that me telling her all this has hurt her.

And that's the last thing I wanted to do, especially knowing how sensitive she is about her love life and how she feels as if she's in this fast-moving time frame to settle down.

"I'm sorry," I say quietly after a few moments, and it's like a punch to my gut when I see that her eyes are rimmed in red. "I didn't... I didn't mean to snap like that. I just.... This whole awkwardness between us has had me so stressed out since I've been here, and you.... And I don't know.... I didn't know how to approach it with you, but I know yelling wasn't the best thing... so I'm sorry."

Her eyes remain trained on mine as if she's debating mentally what she's going to say, and then after a few tense moments she lets out a deep breath and says, "I'm sorry too. I just.... I guess I've just been stressed too. I don't know why this whole Weston thing is making me so crazy, but I just.... When Campbell told me that, I felt like it just all made sense and.... But I didn't want to end our friendship either. That's why I've waited this long. I needed to calm down before talking to you."

"Fat lot that did, huh?" I say, a lame attempt at a joke that thankfully makes her smile.

"Yeah." She chuckles slightly. "I guess you're right."

We both fall into silence again, this one still tense but much less

145

so than before, but I still can only handle it for a couple of seconds.

"So are we good?" I ask, feeling antsy.

She's about to answer when our food gets delivered, the waitress placing our plates in front of us and then telling us to enjoy before swaying off to her other tables.

I look down at my food and feel my stomach squirm unpleasantly, realizing that I'm far too worked up with jitters to have a decent appetite. Jenny seems to feel the same way, as I see her look down at her large chicken salad and make a face that is less than pleased.

She sighs and grabs her fork, beginning to pick around her food, but then she suddenly looks straight at me and asks point-blank, "How do you feel about Weston now, then?"

My chest tightens, and then I'm remembering Sunday night at Marcus's birthday party when I couldn't fight anything Patrice and Meg said because they were right, because I do still feel things for Weston.

But I can't exactly tell Jenny that, can I?

Especially when I know that nothing will ever come of my feelings for him. They're better dead and buried, where they're only my problem, than they are out in the open.

So I lie to her.

"That night," I say, not able to look her in the eye, "it was just.... I was just vulnerable, Jen. I was upset and emotional and I felt abandoned, and... he was there. Weston was just there, and I'm the one who initiated things, so I doubt he felt anything for me, okay? I think he was just reacting... just like any guy would've."

I can tell that she's so eager to believe me, but judging by the downturn of her lips and the wrinkles between her brows, she's finding it difficult to do so.

So I continue. "Jenny, all that's between us is awkwardness because we're both so reluctant to talk about it, okay? I hate awkward situations, and I know Weston does too. So that's it, that's all. There's nothing romantic or even lingering between us, okay?"

"You promise?" she asks meekly, the vulnerability gleaming in her eyes making me feel completely rotten.

But if I want all of this to go away, this is what I need to do.

So even though I feel a shred of my human decency chip away as I do so, I smile softly at her and lie, "I promise."

# Chapter Thirteen

I'd like to say that after our god-awful talk, everything between Jenny and me was just automatically solved.

But if I said that I'd be lying.

Things are still tense between us, and both of us are hesitant to bridge the gap even though we left things on somewhat decent terms that Thursday night. I don't know why she's still being distant with me, but since I still feel so guilty when I'm around her, I'm okay with it.

This is why I spend the majority of my weekend either by myself or with my dad and Meg. Since my nerves are still so wrung out from talking to Meg and Patrice, as well as Jenny, I need a weekend to myself with no drama and no thoughts of pressuring ex-boyfriends, dwindling friendships, or maddeningly potent feelings.

Which is exactly what I get.

That is, until I'm in the kitchen with Meg, who's chopping vegetables while I'm finishing up a romance novel I started a week or so ago, and she comments, "I think I'm making way too much."

"That's okay," I say, looking up from my book. "We can just

save the leftovers."

"Or...," she says with a guilty smile, trailing off when my dad enters the room. He's been outside mowing the lawn since the sun started setting, and the second he walks in the most ghastly smell hits my nose.

"Dad, you smell like shit," I say bluntly, covering my nose.

"Aw, thank you, honey," he says in a sugar-sweet voice, pulling open the fridge and grabbing a bottle of water.

Meg laughs before turning to face my dad, leaning against the counter. She says, "So, Steve, I was just telling Iris that I've made too much dinner and I think it'd be a great idea if we had Weston come over to help us eat. What do you think about that?"

Panic grips my stomach at her words, but the other two people in the room, the people who've just completely betrayed my trust, are smiling knowingly at each other. The two assholes know what they're doing; they know that having Weston here is going to make me a bundle of nerves, and yet they don't care.

They only care about their amusement.

The bastards.

My dad agrees wholeheartedly. "I think that's a great idea. And, Iris, since I smell so bad, how about you go across the street and invite him?"

My first instinct is to reply with "how about you go and put your head in a blender?" but I know that doing so will alert the two of them to how on edge Weston makes me.

So instead I push my homicidal tendencies away and close my book, placing it on the table before rising to my feet and saying as nonchalantly as I can, "Okay, I'll be right back, then."

I try to control myself as I walk across the street, but by the time I've knocked at the front door, I'm nearly shaking with angst. I haven't seen Weston since I admitted to myself I had feelings for him, and I haven't talked to him since the night of our double date.

So it's pretty safe to say I'm not all that eager for him to open the door.

When he does though, I try to appear as unshaken as I can.

"Iris?" he asks, and when the light hits his face and I see the reading glasses perched atop his nose, I almost lose my nerve.

It is *entirely* not fair for someone to look that good in glasses.

"Hey." I nearly have to cough, my hormones swirling in with my jitters and creating a lump in my throat. "Um... what's up?"

I curse myself when I hear how lame I sound, and when I see a slight teasing smirk grace Weston's pink mouth, I can't help but blush a little too. He is far too attractive. My gaze falls from his devilishly handsome smirk to the T-shirt he's wearing and the way it's hugging his chiseled biceps so well. I catch myself, and the blush on my cheeks deepens when I see that his smile has widened.

I've totally been caught.

Once our gazes meet, though, he says, "Nothing, really. Getting ready for work tomorrow, hanging with Thumper."

"Well, um...." I trail off, having become just a little bit delirious at the sight of his full lips moving. "Meg's at the house cooking, and uh... she said she made too much and her and my dad said I should come over here and invite you to help us eat it all."

"What's she cooking?" he asks casually, folding his arms across his chest and leaning his shoulder against the doorframe.

My mouth goes dry in response.

"I forgot to ask," I manage to say with a slight chuckle. "Something with vegetables. And bread. I don't know. I've been in there the whole time she's been cooking, and I'm sure she mentioned it, but I was reading so I was kind of spaced out and...."

The longer I babble, the more amused he becomes, his smirk from earlier now a beautiful smile with teeth and gums, his eyes green and bright and sparkling. As I realize he's teasing me, I quickly shut my mouth and have to bite down on my lip to keep from continuing.

His eyes drop to my mouth for a second and darken. My lower belly clenches in response, my hormones racing as I realize I'm not the only one affected, but then he snaps out of it and says a bit distractedly, "Yeah, I'll come. Let me just slip some shoes on."

"Okay." I nod, and right as I go to turn back to my house, he opens his door wider and ushers me in before him.

As he goes into his room, I look around and see that the house has been brought back to its original state since Marcus's birthday party, and that just like last time it's impeccably clean except for the two dog toys I see on the rug underneath the coffee table.

He comes back out and I watch as he locks up the house. Then we head across the street, him mentioning casually how ready he is for fall and how done he is with this heat. I'm in a bit of shock as we walk through my dad's front door. Weston being so friendly toward me is getting to me more than it should.

Before the front door can even close behind us, Meg calls out happily to Weston, "Come give me a hug, boy!"

He chuckles and I follow him to the kitchen, watching as he embraces the tiny woman. "Hey, Meg," I hear him tell her. "How've you been?"

"Excellent." She smiles at him as they pull away. "And I hope you're hungry. I cooked way too much food."

"I'm always hungry." He laughs. "Where's Mr. Steve?"

"Oh, he's in the shower," Meg says with a wave of her spatula. "According to his lovely little daughter here, he smelled like shit when he came in from cutting the grass."

Weston looks over at me with amusement his eyes, his brows raised, and I laugh before defending myself. "What? He did!"

"I'm sure it's not that bad," Weston says with a roll of his eyes, but for once I don't think there's actual malice behind it.

Meg seems to catch on to his good mood as well. I see the pleased gleam in her eyes as she glances between Weston and me, telling me she's as pleasantly surprised as I am.

"So what're you cooking, then?" Weston asks curiously, stepping further into the kitchen so he can peer over Meg's shoulder. "Iris couldn't remember."

"Stuffed bell peppers." She smiles. "And I'm pretty sure these are going to be the best ones I've made yet. I want to start selling them at the diner, but I want to perfect them first."

"I'm sure they will be," he says, "'cause they smell delicious."

"Weston, my man!" my dad calls, walking into the kitchen with wet hair. He pulls Weston into a hug. "How've you been? Haven't seen you since Marcus's party."

"That was only a week ago," I point out blithely.

My dad pulls away from Weston and stalks toward me, pointing and scolding me playfully. "You, little missy, need to chill on the sass. I've had enough of you today!"

I grin mischievously at him. "You're just mad 'cause I can dish it and you can't take it."

"You little punk." He laughs, flicking me on top of the head and only laughing harder when I shout in protest. "I should've put you up for adoption when I had the chance!"

"Children!" Meg calls, looking over at my dad and me with a fond smile on her face. "I'm trying to cook here!"

We fall into a conversation about the upcoming hurricane season and if we think we'll get one this year. After that, dinner is ready and we all settle into our food and wine, Weston and I sitting next to each other while my dad and Meg are on the opposite side of the table.

The whole time we're eating I try to fight how much this feels like a double date, and how uncomfortable yet somehow content that makes me. Weston's good mood from earlier has yet to dissipate, and he's even gone out of his way to make conversation with me.

It feels so damn good too, his good mood, that I have to remind myself that just because Weston's being nice to me now doesn't necessarily mean it'll last.

When the conversation falls into a lull a while later, as I'm scooping my last bite into my mouth, Meg shoots me a quick wink across the table and then turns to Weston.

My stomach's churning before she even opens her mouth.

"So, West, how are you and Jen? Is she still not feeling well?"

"Um no," Weston says, visibly tense. "She's fine now. Just a little cold."

"Well not too little, huh?" my dad inquires, his brows raised. "Iris said she was out of work three days."

"Yeah." Weston nods. "It wasn't too pretty, that's for sure. But it wasn't anything serious."

"Good." Meg smiles, but for some reason I know it's not genuine. "So the two of you are good, then? Still going strong?"

Weston shifts a bit in his chair, making me wonder if talking about Jenny is uncomfortable for him. "Yeah, we're good. Still nothing too serious, just casual."

Even though that should be the end of the topic, Meg decides to press. "It's been a while though, hasn't it? You think y'all will ever make it serious?"

Luckily my dad cuts in before Weston can answer. "Meg, the guy's twenty-five years old. He doesn't have to settle down until he wants to."

"I know, I know," Meg says defensively, holding her hands up in front of her. She gives me yet another sly look as she puts them down. "I'm just curious. I've known Weston since he was a baby. I'm protective. Especially now that his parents aren't in town."

"Thanks, Meg. That means a lot, but Jenny's not going to corrupt me or anything," Weston says, still sounding uncomfortable.

The topic thankfully changes, Meg asking, "How'd your parents enjoy the trip back home? I didn't get to talk to them much at Marcus's party. Were they here long?"

The relief rolling off him nearly palpable, Weston chuckles. "Long enough that I wasn't too disappointed when they left. But yeah, they had a really good trip. They love Destin and everything and they've made new friends, but I know they miss everyone here. It's just different breeds of people, you know?"

"Tell me about it," my dad agrees. "That trip I took not too long ago to Georgia... even the people there are so different. I have some coming up soon that are further north, and I'm not even that excited to go."

"Where are they to?" I ask curiously, not at all thrilled that I'm going to have the house to myself again.

"Around mid-October I'm going to Tennessee, then in December I'm going to Arkansas. The Tennessee one's pretty major, actually."

"Really?" Meg asks. "How long will you be gone?"

"Two weeks, I think," he says, and I can tell by the look on Meg's face that she's not pleased either.

"When did you find out about this?" she asks tersely.

My dad's confused at her change of tone, his eyebrows creasing together as he answers her, "This past Monday. I was going to tell you when everything was finalized."

"Okay then," she says, sounding a little less tight but still not like her normal self.

My dad looks at me, his eyes wide in question, but even I don't know what to do, so I just shrug. He sighs and I see him lean in close to her, his voice lowering as he says something in her ear.

Figuring that this will probably cause the easygoing atmosphere of tonight to disintegrate, I lean in and tell Weston, "You can go if you want. I know this is kind of awkward."

He looks away from where he's been picking at his green beans and leans into me as well, his warm, spicy cologne washing over me like a comforting blanket. My breath catches in my throat as a lock of his blond hair nearly brushes against my forehead, and I find it incredibly difficult to pay attention as he tells me, "I can help clean, if you want? If I leave now it'll just be awkward next time I see them."

A bit taken aback at his offer, I breathlessly nod. "Okay, yeah. Thanks, West."

My dad and Meg don't say a word as we silently start collecting the dirty plates, my dad still quietly trying to talk that scowl off her face. Since there's only four plates and four glasses, Weston and I only have to make one trip, and even though the kitchen is open to the dining table, it still feels much more comfortable being away from the two of them.

Weston and I decide that he'll rinse the dishes and I'll load them into the dishwasher, and after a few silent moments of us doing that, I say randomly, "I'm sorry about that, by the way. We invited you and then it got uncomfortable."

"It's not your fault," he says simply, running a plate under the stream of water.

"I know, I just—"

"Parents fight, Iris. It's fine."

His words knock the wind out of me, and I guess I don't do as good a job of hiding it as I think. Weston immediately whips his head around to face me, and I see his widened green eyes, his lips parted as he realizes what he's said. "Oh no, Iris, I'm so—"

"It's okay," I say hoarsely, willing to play off how bad him calling Meg my parent felt so that we don't have to talk about it.

I can't look at him, though, so I try my hardest to keep my emotions at bay as I grab a dish and shove it into the dishwasher. His eyes are on me the entire time, and for once it doesn't have my hormones playing keep-away with my rational thought.

Chairs scrape behind us, and then footsteps retreat in the direction of my dad's room and his door shuts, leaving Weston and me entirely alone.

The moment that door shuts, he grabs my forearm and pulls me so that I'm forced to face him. His green eyes are dark, almost hazel, and they're boring into mine so hard I'm not sure whether I should be scared or turned on.

My thighs make that decision for me, though, as they clench together on the warm pressure starting to build between them.

"I'm sorry," he urges, him having pulled me so close that his breath hits my face. "I didn't.... I wasn't.... I wasn't thinking, okay? I know how touchy a subject that is and—"

"You didn't mean to," I say softly, still looking away from him, the urgency in his voice rattling every nerve ending I possess. "It was a mistake. It—"

"*Damn it, Iris*," he hisses, squeezing tighter at my arm and forcing my chin up with his other hand. "Could you please fucking look at me?"

For some reason the intensity rolling off him has tears clawing their way up my throat, and before I can even register what's happening, they're building up in my eyes and Weston's noticed them, his tense face falling and his mouth opening with unspoken words.

Humiliation washes over me as I realize that Weston now knows he's made me cry. I avert my eyes yet again, gnawing on my bottom lip as I look down at the floor.

He's silent for a moment, but when I go to pull away from him so I can run off to my room and forget he's ever seen how he affects me, one of his hands curls around my waist, pulling me in so close that I'm physically unable to walk away.

"Why do you always do that?" he demands softly, his voice close to my ear. "Why do you run away anytime you need to have a real conversation with someone?"

Absolutely hating that he's called me out, that he's said out loud that I'm the coward I know I am, I hang my head. "I don't know. I just.... I get so panicked every time there's a hint of confrontation, and all I can think about is running away, getting far away."

"That's not healthy, you know?" he murmurs, his free hand gently grasping my chin and pulling my face just a breath shy of meeting his.

My heart practically stops beating inside my chest at the look he's giving me, that same empathetic yet somehow strengthening look he gave me the night of my graduation party.

*He's so beautiful.*

"I know," I admit shamefully, my voice scratchy with tears. "But I don't really understand what that has to do with you. I said I wasn't mad about you calling Meg my parent. Why do you...?"

"Why do I care?" he finishes for me with a tensed jaw and narrowed eyes.

I solemnly nod, my heart once again going wild at his closeness and the care for me in his eyes.

"Because if you...," he starts, trailing off when I switch my weight from foot to foot and my waist brushes against his. He swallows. "Because if you hadn't run that night.... If you...."

He's bringing it up?

Oh my God, no, I'm not.... I'm not prepared for this. I'm not prepared for him to lessen the significance of it, to make it something any less beautiful than what I've always thought. I can't....

Panic surges and I go to pull away, but once again he jerks me back and makes me look at him. My heart is beating so fast that my head's spinning. "Weston, I—"

"You let me leave," he whispers brokenly, hurt weighing his voice down, and his grip on my waist tightening almost painfully. "You let me leave that night thinking we could talk about it, about the kiss, and then... and then you...."

"I'm sorry," I breathe, my voice shaky with years' worth of repressed emotion. "I know... what I did was awful and you deserved so much more, and I just.... I couldn't be here anymore, okay? This town, this house... it was so toxic for me after my mom left, and I just.... No matter how I felt for you, no matter.... *I just had to get away.*"

My hands start trembling after I quit talking, a couple of tears trickling over the edge and leaving their warm wake down my cheeks. I didn't know it had affected him this much; I didn't know kissing him just once would lead to him holding a grudge for four years.

How was I supposed to know that?

How was I supposed to know he cared for me as much as he's showing me right now?

*Because he kissed you like his life depended on it*, my subconscious reminds me in a whisper, making my guilt even heavier.

"You ran," he says seriously, pushing me back a bit so he can look directly at me. "You ran back then, and you just tried running again."

"I had to," I practically cry. "I couldn't.... It was so—"

He cuts me off angrily. "You could have at least fucking told me, Iris! If you'd had the decency to tell me you were leaving before... before you kissed me like that. But you didn't say anything! You just fucking left like it was nothing!"

"I'm sorry." I practically grovel, more tears falling hot and fast. "I'm so sorry. I thought.... I just.... I don't know. I don't know what I thought. I was so scared that...."

"Scared that what?" he nearly yells, his fingertips digging into my waist. "Of me? What the hell could—"

"I was scared you'd say it didn't mean anything!" I throw back at him, pushing against his chest so that his fingers won't leave bruises. "I was terrified that to you it'd just be this nothing kiss with a girl who needed comfort and that the next day you'd be walking around like nothing happened! I couldn't.... I couldn't have it mean nothing to you when it.... Not when it...."

"When it what?" he croaks, his voice so much gentler now.

I look back down at the floor, more tears falling from my eyes, guilt and hurt squeezing my heart so tight that I don't want to breathe.

"No you don't," he growls, stepping close to me once more and placing his warm, rough palm against my cheek, holding my blurry gaze to his. "Look at me, Iris. Talk to me. What did that... what did that kiss mean to you?"

I squeeze my eyes shut, the vulnerability and years' worth of anguish in his eyes nearly killing me. I did this to him, I hurt him like this, and for some reason that hurts me more than any sarcastic remark he's hurled my way since I've been home.

How much he's hurting now proves to me that he cares far more than I ever thought he would, and instead of that thrilling me, it terrifies me. I'm not going to trick myself into thinking that the two of us will get that happily ever after I've been dreaming of. No, I'm not that naïve.

I know that the most life-altering pain stems from abandonment, from someone all of a sudden deciding they don't care, and I can't risk that happening to me again. Not with Weston.

Not when.... Not when I feel for him like I do.

Not when one soulful look from him can steal every breath from my body.

Not when I think I'm absolutely, painfully in love with him.

My heart breaking, I tilt my head against his hand, giving myself just a moment to love the way it cradles me and the way his fingertips are brushing softly against my skin.

When I open my eyes and he slowly comes into view through my tear-blurred vision, I smile sadly and say earnestly, "It meant *everything* to me, Weston."

I vaguely register a smile on his face, a strong arm reaching out toward me, but everything in my body, every single self-preserving cell, is screaming at me to back away and run.

No matter how much Weston may think that kiss meant to him, it'll ruin it for me. That kiss saved my life that night; it kept me from thinking it'd never get better.

That kiss was my lifeline.

And I refuse to let it be turned into anything less than that.

"Go back to Jenny," I tell him, my voice cracking. "She loves you, Weston. She...."

He's adamantly shaking his head, reaching out for me again, but every time he steps forward, I just take another step back.

"Iris, *stop*," he begs, the broken sound in his voice nearly killing me.

But this is what's best for him, I remind myself. He doesn't need a coward like me, someone who can't face emotional issues and who runs away anytime things get hard. He needs Jenny. He needs strong, beautiful, mature Jenny.

He doesn't need me.

"I'm so sorry, okay?" I cry, wiping a fist over my eyes. "I'm so sorry."

"Iris, I—" he starts, but before he can finish, I've turned and run into my bedroom.

I slam and lock the door behind me.

And then, two minutes later, I hear the front door being thrown open and slammed shut, the heavy footsteps pounding down the porch stairs.

All the while, all I can think of is that I'm running away.

Because I'm so damn scared of being hurt, of being abandoned, I'm running away.

Just like I'm so damn good at.

# Chapter Fourteen

Thursday afternoon, I'm at work and that heart-wrenching look Weston gave me the other night is still haunting me every damn minute. The guilt of running from him has subsided a bit, mainly because I've assured myself he'll be so much happier with Jenny in the long run. He can hate me all he wants, but as long as he ends up happy I'm okay.

That doesn't mean I'm not miserable, though, because in all honesty I am.

I haven't been able to sleep since Sunday night. That crack in his voice when he'd begged me to stay kept me up until the wee hours of the morning.

The phone ringing snaps me out of my thoughts, and I quickly lean forward to pick it up. "Yeah?" I ask, knowing from the ring that the call's coming from inside the office.

"Hey," Jenny says, "Chet just cut his finger pretty badly and we're out of Band-Aids, so do you think you could run to the CVS around the corner to get some?"

"Yeah," I say. "I'll leave right now."

"Thanks!" she says before hanging up.

I quickly set up automatic voice mail and then lock up my computer, hurriedly grabbing my purse and heading outside. I'm at the CVS at the corner in just three minutes, and I'm standing at the checkout watching the cashier ring my things up after another four.

After he hands me my change and I thank him, I walk back out in the blisteringly hot afternoon and start toward my car.

That is until I see a somehow incredibly familiar silhouette just a few yards from me. Squinting against the sun, I pull the sunglasses from the top of my head so that they cover my eyes, and what I see has the world stop spinning.

The brown curly hair and light brown eyes so much like my own, the slim angle of the neck, the large curve of the chest.

It's my mom.

Four years and some odd months later, my mom is here, and she's standing right in front of me.

At a *fucking* CVS.

I see her start to approach me, my mind still spinning in every which way, and once she's close I open my mouth to try and say something, but my throat seems to have stopped working. Nothing but air comes out, and I snap it right back shut.

"Iris?" she asks, and it's the sound of her voice that makes me snap.

The voice that I've heard so many nights in my sleep, in memories of my dad being sick and her singing him to sleep.

"What?" I say slowly, my mind still not having caught up with my vocal chords. "What are you doing here? Are you...? What...?"

She smiles sadly, her thin lips stretching across her aged face, before she says, "I'll answer any questions you have, honey, but can I please get a hug first?"

"What?" I say for the third time, starting to feel a little bit dizzy. "You want...? You want what? What are you...? Why are you here? Why are you at CVS, Mom?"

I'm on the verge of hysterics, my voice growing shrill and loud even though we're in the middle of a public parking lot.

"Iris," she says seriously, taking a few steps toward me and grabbing my arm, which I immediately rip from her grasp.

The hurt in her eyes does nothing to me, absolutely nothing.

This woman ruined me.

She ruined any shred of trust I ever had, any sense of self-worth.

And she ruined my dad.

"What the fuck are you doing here, Mom?" I demand harshly, watching her nearly crumble at the venom in my words.

I watch as she pulls the edges of her thin cardigan over her fingertips, her bottom lip trembling as she says, "I... I've been here a couple of days, honey. I was going to wait until tomorrow to try and talk to you, to apologize for leaving, to.... I don't know, to make up for everything I did."

"Really?" I ask coldly, folding my arms over my chest and refusing to let my emotions get the best of me in front of her. After what she did to me, she doesn't deserve to see how much she hurt me. "And how long are you in town for? Were you going to try to fix everything in just one afternoon?"

"No," she says shamefully, shaking her head. "I'm here indefinitely. I... I don't know. I didn't have a plan when I came here. All I knew was that I wanted to see you, and I figured everything would fall into place after that."

"Well, I have to get back to work," I say, praising all that is holy that I have an excuse to get away from this parking lot, from her. "Do you still have our number or did you throw that away too?"

"No, I...." She shakes her head again. "I still have it."

"Then use it, I guess," I say. "That is, if you don't run off again before then."

"I will," she says, her voice gaining an ounce of strength. Even though there's guilt etched into every line of her face and tears in her eyes, she meets my gaze steadily and says in a strong voice, "I will call you, Iris. We will talk."

"Okay, then," I say, heading in the direction of my car.

Before I'm too far, though, I feel her hand on my wrist again, and then she's pulling me into an unanswered hug and whispering frantically in my ear, "I love you, baby. I love you so much."

My hard shell nearly cracks at that, but somehow or another I'm able to keep up the cold front, and when she pulls away and looks at me expectantly, like I'm going to say it back to her and everything's going to be okay, I say simply, "See you, Mom."

And then I walk away.

---

By the time five o'clock rolls around, I feel as if I've only been at work for a few minutes.

My mom showing up has rocked me to my very core, and I have yet to wrap my head around it. It's like I'm trapped in this fog, as I can't admit to myself that I really did see her, but I also can't go back to pretending nothing happened either.

Not only that, but I'm not even sure how I want to feel.

Should I be happy that she's back, or terrified? Should I feel content now that I may finally get some answers, or should I feel insulted that she thinks I even want answers? How do I treat her? How do I talk to her?

But despite my stunned-into-numbness limbs and my head that can't decide between shutting down or running a marathon, I still clock out of work and pack my things up like normal. Jenny gives me a half-hearted wave as she exits through the front doors, but I can't find the energy to try and return it.

Instead I just sling my purse over my shoulder and head out as well, my phone starting to vibrate as I slide into my car.

I don't recognize the number.

"Hello?"

There's a silence over the line for a split second, and then, "Iris, honey? It's me.... It's Mom."

"Oh," I respond, my voice hollow. "Hey."

"You off work yet?" she asks, the question partially distorting my sense of reality.

It's such a normal question, one that I'm sure gets asked by mothers to daughters all the time, but for some reason it has my world spinning on its axis. Nothing outside of my car feels real; everything feels as if it's been muddled out of focus.

"Um, yeah," I say, feeling like I'm talking incredibly loudly. "Just walked out, actually."

"Well...." She clears her throat. "Well, if you don't have plans tonight, would you want to come grab dinner? I was going to ask you tomorrow for some time this weekend, but since we saw each other today, we can—"

I cut her off, almost wanting to laugh at how perfectly this all works out. Just this morning as my dad and I were sitting at the kitchen table before work, he mentioned that he was taking Meg out tonight and that he probably wouldn't make it home.

"That's fine," I say, not realizing how dry my throat's gone until I have to cough after speaking. "Where do you... um... where do you want to meet?"

"I'm staying at the Radisson," she explains, referring to the more expensive of the two hotels around here. "I was thinking we could just sit in my room, order room service? This talk isn't exactly one for public eyes, so...."

"That sounds good," I tell her. "I'll just head straight there from here, I guess?"

"No rush," she says. "Just drive safe."

I almost roll my eyes at the sentiment.

"See you in a few," I respond, vaguely hearing her tell me she loves me before I hang the phone up and toss it back into my purse.

All of a sudden, everything hits me. No longer do I feel like I'm simultaneously floating away and being weighed down by a bag of bricks. No longer does my mind feel like it's been emptied out and filled with sand.

All at once the emotions of the past four years... the tears, the feelings of inadequacy, the painful jealousy I felt every time I saw a girl with her mother... it all hits me.

I'm gasping for breath before I even know it, memories surging through every inch of my skin, my body humming with that feeling I used to get any time she'd come lie with me before bed and talk to me about the universe. Everything I've pushed into the deepest holes, everything I've locked away just because it was too hard to think about it, it's all here and laughing at me and making me feel like my subconscious is running at a speed I'll never be able to catch up to.

I have no idea how much time passes before I feel everything come to a screeching halt inside me, my breathing still more labored than usual but no longer painful.

Luckily no one is around, I see, the world seemingly the same as it was before I left it a good five minutes ago. I take meticulously deep breaths for the next few minutes, calming myself as much as possible before operating a car, and then finally pull out of my parking spot and head toward the hotel.

I haven't been to the Radisson since my thirteenth birthday, when my parents splurged on a room for me and three of my best friends, and as I pull in I'm just a little bit surprised that this is where she's staying and not at the cheaper Red Roof Inn a few miles down the highway.

After I pull into the first spot I see, I text the number she called me from, asking for a room number, and just a second later my phone is dinging with her reply.

Before I go in I make sure my nerves have stilled as much as possible, and as I grab my things and head through the lavish lobby, past the bar, and up in the elevator, I give myself a much needed pep talk.

But as soon as I'm knocking and she's pulling the door open, it's like I'm standing in the hot sun at that CVS parking lot all over again.

"Iris, hey," she says, not immediately going in for the hug like I thought she would.

Instead she just stands there and looks me over, her large honey-colored eyes taking in my appearance for the first time since I was an awkward teenager.

I do the same, taking in her long, skinny legs enclosed in light-wash jeans, her thin torso and chest wrapped in a thick Gap sweatshirt, and her brown curly hair tucked back with an elastic headband. Except for the more pronounced age lines etched at the corner of her eyes, she looks no different from the last time I saw her.

She's beautiful.

She's my mom.

After a few moments of appraisal, she takes a step back and waves me in. It's a stereotypical hotel room inside, a large queen bed with pristine white sheets that have been rumpled by my mom, a flat-screen TV on a dark wood dresser, and two plush chairs situated in front of the large window, the blinds open to give the room a beautiful view of the Mississippi river.

Feeling awkward and not knowing what to do, I decide to sit in one of the chairs and fold my legs up underneath me, still wholly aware of my mom sitting at the edge of the bed and staring at me like she's afraid I'll disappear.

"How was work?" she asks me once I'm situated, her voice meek and tentative.

"It was okay," I answer, looking down to pick at a spare thread on the chair. "I just answer phones and do the schedule and stuff, so it's nothing too exciting."

"I'm still so proud of you," she says softly. "Landing a job after graduation is pretty special nowadays."

I shrug. "It's just temporary, so it's not like I'm set for my future or anything. Just for the next few months."

"Do you know what you're going to do after?"

I shake my head. "No idea. My major is in business, though, so I have options."

For the next half hour or so, we cautiously discuss what I was up to after she left without explicitly mentioning that she did, in fact, leave.

We quickly run out of things to talk about, though, and even though the thought of talking to her about why she left terrifies me, I won't be content until we do. We're both quiet for a while, me trying to work up the nerve to actually bring it up, and her most likely doing the same.

She beats me to it.

"I'm so sorry, Iris, for leaving... for... for everything. I know that a sorry isn't going to begin to make up for it, but—"

"You're right," I say firmly, surprising myself. Feeling some strange kind of confidence wash over me, I look at her and continue. "You're right, you.... What you did.... I don't know if I'm ever going to be able to forgive you for that. Not only just leaving, but the way you did it. I...."

"I'm so sorry," she reiterates, her voice cracking a bit. "I don't.... I can't...."

The back of my throat is burning with tears, but I'm on some kind of roll here. Having her here to look at, having her say she's sorry... it's everything I thought it would be, but also not at all what I expected.

I always thought that if my mom came back, it'd be this huge emotional thing and I'd have no choice but to forgive her and we'd immediately become close again. Right here, though, being here right now shows me I'm never going to get back what my mom and I used to have.

No matter how silly and unrealistic a dream that may have been, I still believed it and it still hurts that this is where she and I stand now.

It *hurts* that eighteen years of the best mother-daughter relationship can boil down to an awkward conversation in a hotel room.

"Why did you leave?" I ask despondently, my depressing thoughts taking a toll on my strength for just a second. I catch it, though, and ask again, "Why did you leave, Mom? And don't spew some shit about being sick of the town. That's not a reason to leave your husband and your kid."

"Oh, honey," she cries, tears falling down her cheeks. "I just.... Back then, honey, I.... I just.... I would look at you and you were about to go do such great things for yourself, graduating top of your class, going to college on a full scholarship. I... I was just.... I was so incredibly jealous, honey, and of my teenage daughter no less! Knowing that you were about to leave, knowing that you wouldn't need me anymore, I.... I don't know, Iris.... I just snapped. I couldn't do it anymore. I felt like staying would kill me, would throw all my failures in my face."

"What failures?" I ask. "What failures did you have, Mom? You had me, you had Dad, you had—"

"*I had nothing!*" she nearly screams, her eyes going wide the moment she realizes she's raised her voice at me.

Slowly, brokenly, she raises her hand and covers her open mouth, my heart giving a dull thud at the sight. She looks down at the floor, taking in deep, labored breaths, and her thin frame is trembling.

Speechless, I sink further back into my chair, refolding my legs so that my knees are now at my chin.

I'm silent until she looks back over at me, her eyes rimmed in red and her face looking so, *so* tired, before saying, "I had nothing, Iris.

I.... You were leaving and your dad...."

She trails off, looking to the side, so I ask her timidly, "Did you even love him, Mom?"

"Of course I did!" she responds instantly, sounding aghast. "I loved him more than anything, Iris, except for you."

"So why'd you leave? Why? I just don't get it."

"All I had in this world was you and your father. I was... I was nothing, Iris. You went to school, your dad went to work, and I just.... I cleaned the house and cooked the food and waited for y'all to come home. I wasn't.... I was never me. I never had the opportunity to be me, Iris. I met your dad when I was so young, and then I was his girlfriend, and then I was your mother and his wife."

"You could've been everything," I point out, thinking that her reasons were, and still are, ridiculous.

This heartbreak could have all been avoided if she had just said something. I know my dad well enough to know that he'd never be okay if he knew my mom felt that way, and that he'd go to the ends of the earth to make her feel better about herself.

My mom robbed him of that chance.

She was a coward.

She opens her mouth to say something, but I cut her off, my bravado blazing. "You could've gone to school. You could've gotten a job. We weren't forcing you to stay home and just *be there*! You could have been yourself *and* a wife *and* a mother, but you robbed yourself of that chance when you decided to be a fucking coward and skip out of town. So don't blame anything or anyone but yourself. This, all of this shit, is all on you."

She's openly sobbing now, her cheeks pink while the rest of her face is pale. I know I'm being harsh on her, I know that there're probably better and more mature ways to handle this, but at this point I just don't care.

She hurt me.

*Back to You*

She's been hurting me every day since she left, and I'd be lying if I said it didn't feel good to make her hurt too.

"You had *so much*, Mom, we all did," I cry, my strength from earlier having wilted away into this god-awful mix of fury and sorrow. "And you ruined all that when you left."

"I know," she croaks. "I know. I ruined our little family, and I hate myself for it, Iris, I do. You have no idea how much."

I go quiet after that, my emotions having got the best of me, so I just bury my chin into the crease between my knees and close my eyes.

"You were my only accomplishment," she says brokenheartedly, my eyes lifting at the sound of her voice. Our gazes meet, and my heart squeezes in pain when she says, "But you were also *the best accomplishment* I could have ever asked for. I'll never forgive myself for hurting you like I did."

"I don't know if I can forgive you," I say meekly. "I just... maybe, after some time, I—"

She cuts me off with a sad shake of her head. "Honey, I'm not here to ask your forgiveness. I don't deserve that."

"Then why are you here?"

Her gaze trails off to the side for a second, something dark entering her expression, but she quickly shakes it away and turns her attention back to me. "I'm just here to see you, to see your dad, to... to talk things through. That's all I want."

"Are you staying?" I ask. "Are you.... Or is this just...."

"I'm here indefinitely," she answers. "I... I'm not sure just what my plans are yet, but I have the means to stay here until I figure it out."

"In this hotel?" I ask, my eyes trailing around the room. "Isn't that expensive?"

"It's nothing for you to worry about, sweetie," she answers vaguely, reaching up and wiping a clenched fist across her still damp cheeks. "I just.... Please know that I'm here whenever you need, if you ever want to... I don't know... catch up, go get our nails done." She giggles before continuing. "I know we'll never be as close as we were, but I want back into your life, Iris. There's nothing I want more."

"What about Dad?" I ask curiously, the thought of him just having hit me. "Have you seen him, have you tried to talk to him?"

"I wanted to see you first," she answers. "But I'll be calling him or stopping by the house sometime soon. Whenever I recover from this conversation, I'll be there."

I give a small laugh and then immediately stop myself, not wanting to get too comfortable. "So should I...." I trail off, tightening my arms around my knees. "Should I tell him you're here? I don't want to lie to him and not say anything."

"That's up to you." She shrugs. "I don't.... I'm not here to get back with him or anything, Iris. I know that ship has long sailed. I just really want to make my peace with him. I don't want him to think I've been here all this time and avoided him, which he'll probably think knowing that me and you talked first, but I also don't want to drive a wedge between the two of y'all. So it's entirely up to you. Just let me know which you choose so I'm prepared when I go to talk to him."

"Okay," I answer, glad she's putting my best interests first but also a bit miffed that this is just another weight added to my shoulders.

The large hotel room suddenly feeling smaller, and a prickly, uncomfortable heat starting to spread across my limbs, I ad-lib, "I'll have to think about it. I'm in a bit of overload right now."

Her lips purse in guilt. "I know. I knew coming here would be a lot for you, and I'm sorry about that. I just.... It'd already been too long, and I couldn't let it go on any longer."

After another few moments of pensive silence, she lets out a random hoarse-sounding chuckle. "I just realized that I invited you for dinner and never even asked if you were hungry."

I can't find the will in me to laugh along with her, so I just say, "It's okay, I probably couldn't eat anything if I tried right now."

*Back to You*

Her features pinch in a barely there wince, as if maybe she thought there'd be a chance that I'd hang out longer.

She asks after a couple of seconds, "Well, I... I mean, do you have any questions for me? Is there anything else you want to know?"

Of course there is, but right now I'm a little bit more preoccupied with self-preservation. Remembering how I felt four years ago isn't going to help my current mental state.

I can wait to get my answers.

That is, if she's still here when I feel up to asking them.

"I can wait," I tell her honestly. "I think I've had enough reminiscing for today."

"Okay, honey," she says, her voice as down as the frown on her mouth. "I understand. I'll be here whenever you need to talk. I'm just a phone call away."

I nod, trying to make that sentiment stick but finding it incredibly hard. She keeps saying that she'll be here when I need her, that she'll stick around for me, but with her track record, how can I *truly* believe her?

If I were stronger, I'd take advantage of her being here right now, but sadly I'm not and right now, I'm teetering on the verge of an emotional breakdown. Staying here will only make it worse.

"All right," I say after a while, finding the strength to leave for the night. Placing my hands on the armrest of the chair I've been sitting in, I push myself up and say, "I'm going to head out, then."

"Okay," she says, standing up as well.

Once again I'm floored by her presence here, so different from four years ago yet so completely the same.

I deeply inhale to steady myself as she wraps her arms around me in another unreturned hug, and don't exhale until she's pulling away and saying, "I'll see you soon, honey."

I can't find the words to say anything back, so I just murmur some incoherent agreement and quickly step away from her, grabbing my purse from where I'd deposited it then all but running to the door.

As I open it I know I should look back at my mom, say *something* to her after all these years, give her some kind of goodbye, but I just can't.

So, just like that, I step out of the room and shut the heavy door behind me, my mind in such a deep haze that I don't realize until I'm in the elevator that I've just walked out of a room that my mother was in.

That I just spoke to Mom for the first time in *years*.

That I'm finally starting to get answers.

Once again everything hits me incredibly fast and I feel myself about to fall into that same stress-induced hysteria I felt in the parking lot a couple of hours ago. I can feel the pressure in my chest building with every step I take through the hotel lobby, and right before I step out into the parking lot, I see the hotel bar out of the corner of my eye.

My feet stop of their own accord, my gaze switching from the door that'll only lead me to having to address the dilemma of if I should tell my dad or not, to the empty yet inviting-looking set of barstools that I know will temporarily ease my worries.

The answer is so very simple.

# Chapter Fifteen

Turning, I walk through the lobby and step onto the dark, glossy floors of the bar.

I know that being alone and a relatively long drive from home probably isn't the best environment for me to abandon my woes in intoxication, but all rational thought fled my mind the *second* I laid eyes on my mom at a damn CVS.

As time goes on, one drink quickly turns into two, and two into three. Time passes and more patrons come into the bar, and I find myself feeling light-years better as I socialize with two middle-aged women here for business.

I'm too conscientious to mention anything to them about my mom, as it's probably too heavy of a conversation for a Thursday night at a hotel bar, so instead I just tell them all about my drama with Weston, Jenny, and her asshole of a brother.

The two of them provide hilarious commentary on my problems, both of them agreeing that I should just jump Weston's bones to get the tension out of the way and then do the talking after that.

If I were sober, it'd be something I'd never want to talk about, but since I'm entirely *not* sober and because my number-one priority is to not think of my mother in her room only five floors away from me, I'm enjoying the hell out of talking about it, giggling with Helena and Delia about things that I've been so torn on for weeks now.

It's a nice step away from reality, but by the time the two of them are looking at their watches and saying they need to get to bed, I'm at a complete standstill. After they give me hugs goodbye and wish me luck with my whole situation, I sloppily plop down back onto my barstool and take another swig of my drink.

I know it's getting late, and since it's a Thursday night, I desperately need to sober up and get to bed so that I can make it to work on time tomorrow morning. But the more I think about it, the more I realize that going into work tomorrow means seeing Jenny, which is just another drama to add to the pile.

*Maybe I can call in sick tomorrow?* I reach into my purse and drag my cell phone out.

I haven't missed a day yet, so it shouldn't be that big of a deal. And if anyone deserves it, it's someone who's recently broken up with a boyfriend, is in an awful situation with their best friend, in love with the guy who's *with* said best friend, and whose absentee mother just catapulted into their life.

I deserve a day in bed to feel bad for myself, right?

My mind immediately made up, I set an alarm on my phone so that I can wake up in time to call in with a lame excuse like a cold or something, and then I wave the bartender over and order another whiskey and Sprite.

If I'm going to get drunk and miss work tomorrow, I damn well better do it right.

------------

It's an hour later when my happy tipsy becomes sleepy-almost-drunk, so after I tell the very kind bartender that I'm done and in need of my tab, I pull my phone out and attempt to weigh my options.

There's no way in hell I can drive home, obviously, and since the town is so small, the only cab driver is that asshole who drove Weston home that night.

I know my dad and Meg wouldn't think twice about interrupting their night to come out here for me, but I'd probably drunkenly mention Mom being in town, and that should wait until they're not on a date.

Realizing who the only other person I'd be comfortable asking is, my fingertips start tingling in excitement as I bring up my contact list and press Weston's name. Pulling the phone to my ear, I grin as I hear it ring.

"Hello?" he answers after two rings, his gruff voice turning my body even mushier than the alcohol's made it. "Iris?"

"Heyyy, West," I drag out, my grin stretching further. "Whatcha up to?"

"Have you been drinking?"

"Yes." I giggle, placing my elbow on the bar to steady the hand holding my phone. "But I have a *really* good reason, promise."

"Where are you?" he asks seriously, not bothering to join in on my good mood. "And why, of all people, did you decide to call me?"

"I'm at a hotel up the interstate," I tell him, my attention swaying when I see the bartender make his way toward me. As he hands me my bill, I coo graciously, "Thank you, this was great!"

The bartender just smiles at me. "Stay safe, all right?"

"Will do, captain." I giggle, using my free hand to salute him before looking down at how much I owe.

"Iris?" a loud voice blasts through my phone, reminding me that I've completely forgotten about Weston.

"Oh, I'm sorry!" I chuckle, tucking my phone between my ear and shoulder so that I can dig my wallet out of my purse. "I'm paying my bill and I was thanking the guy and I *completely* forgot I was talking to you, which is *so* weird 'cause usually I have the opposite problem and—"

"Iris," he interrupts me, his voice so firm that I feel everything south of my waist clench.

"Yes?" I breathe.

"I'm going to come get you, okay?" he says, my grasp on my phone tightening at the thought. "Now can you please tell me where you are?"

"The Radisson," I say softly, my giggly, silly mood from mere moments ago having fled the building. "I'm at the bar."

"Okay," he says with an audibly defeated sigh. "I'll be there in fifteen."

"All right," I say meekly before hanging up and dropping my phone back into my purse.

As I wait for him to show up, I fill out the bill for all my drinks, incredibly fortunate that I'm not sober enough to be freaking out about the fact I've spent almost eighty dollars on whiskey Sprites and shots with those women from earlier. I'm sure I'll panic tomorrow, about the bill, about my mom, about Weston, but right now... right now I'm going to appreciate the little bit of fun I've had here tonight while I still can.

I seriously doubt it's even been fifteen minutes when I feel the air in the bar shift, a chilling tingle of pleasure shooting up my spine. Looking over my shoulder, the persistent goofy smile I've been wearing for the past hour widens when I see the mouthwatering sight that is Weston Alcorn making his way over to me.

"Hey!" I exclaim, my gaze not knowing where to rest as I take in his beautifully scruffy jawline, his intense green eyes, his mussed dirty-blond hair, and the somewhat tight T-shirt he's wearing.

How I was able to make out with this guy, I'll never know.

"Iris," he says once he reaches my stool, his eyes flitting around the room before he turns to face me. "What exactly is this? What're you doing here?"

"Long story," I say nonchalantly with a wave of my hand, too caught up in my whiskey-induced good mood and the sight of him to let any thoughts of my mom ruin it. "Maybe I'll tell you later."

"Okay," he says, thankfully not pushing it. "You ready to go?"

"Yes, please," I say with a chuckle, sliding my bill closer to the other side of the bar and then moving to hop off my barstool.

Before I can, though, Weston grabs my forearm and says, "Steady, Iris, come on."

My breath is caught in my throat at the feel of his fingers on my skin, and once my feet are on the ground, I realize just how incredibly close we are. Our noses are almost brushing. In an uncharacteristically bold move, I slowly lift my eyes so that they can look into his.

They don't disappoint either. His bright emerald-green gaze is unrelenting, tight and intense, and absolutely mouthwatering. I vaguely feel his fingers clench my forearm tighter. I'm too caught up in how he's looking at me, how I've been *dying* for him to look at me recently, to notice much else.

Swallowing down my last shred of inhibition, I lean in closer to him, my torso delicately brushing his, and just as I'm relishing the little catch of breath the movement evokes from him, he's pulling away and tensing up like nothing's happened.

"Did you pay?" he asks coldly, looking away from me.

"Yes," I murmur, disappointment burning hot and bright. "I'm good to go."

His jaw tightens briefly. "Good, then, let's go."

He heads out of the bar without even checking that I'm behind him, his steps long and determined. I immediately pick up my pace, my feet scurrying across the hard floors as quickly as my three-inch heels will allow.

Letting out a loud huff, I call, "West, hey... wait!"

He doesn't listen, keeping up his furious pace the entire walk to his truck. By the time I slide into the passenger seat with no help from him, I'm huffing and tearing my shoes off. The truck smells incredible, though, just like he always smells, so I sigh in contentment, pull on my seat belt, and then fall back comfortably against the seat.

As he pulls out of the parking lot and starts toward the interstate, he remains quiet and stoic. The longer he doesn't talk, the more I feel like I *have* to.

"Thank you," I start, noticing his hand flinch slightly at the sound of my voice. "For coming to get me. It was irresponsible of me to drink that much without a ride home already planned out."

"It's fine," he says curtly, his eyes remaining trained on the road in front of him.

"It doesn't seem like it's fine," I point out simply, the whiskey bringing out my brusqueness. "You seem really angry with me."

"Dammit, I...," he curses, his hands on the wheel clenching so hard his knuckles turn white. After shaking his head, he says, "Iris, I'm not really.... I don't want to have this conversation with you, okay? You needed a ride home. I'm giving you a ride home. That's all this is."

My body deflates as hurt and rejection pulse through me, my eyes starting to burn. I knew that Weston and I weren't on good terms anymore after I rejected him in my dad's kitchen, but it still doesn't make him treating me like this any easier.

I fall into a depressed silence as I gaze out my window, and hate that the urge to cry doesn't lessen any as the ride home wears on. And just a minute or so later, the palpable tension in the silence only having made it worse, I'm silently cursing because I've made the most obvious about-to-cry sniffle.

I pray that he somehow didn't hear it, even though the radio's not on and the only noise is literally the sound of the road beneath his tires. Of course he did, though. He exhales deeply. "Iris, I—"

"No," I quickly cut in, shaking my head as I look over at him. "It's okay, I... I get it. This is all my fault. I know I.... It's...."

He's quiet for a long moment, completely focused on driving, but then I feel him look over at me. "I don't know what it is that you're trying to do here, what you want... between us. I... you've made it so damn confusing, Iris, and I'm sorry you're upset, but I really have no other idea how to treat you."

"I know," I answer, my voice cracking. "I know this is all on me, but I just.... Does it have to be so black and white? You're either so nice to me or the complete opposite—"

"Pot, kettle, Iris," he interrupts, his voice tight. "I don't know how you're looking at things here, but you've been more indecisive than I have."

"That's not true!" I exclaim, my eyes widening at him. "I'm not the one.... I'm not.... West, you're either insulting me or you're talking me through finding out my dad and Meg are together. You've given me no middle ground to work with, so how the hell am I—"

He cuts me off again, his voice elevated and much angrier. "And you're either throwing yourself at me or completely avoiding me! Where's the middle ground in that?"

Shock ricochets through me at his words, utter humiliation quickly flooding my face with redness and shame. What he's said has reduced me to silence, and I attempt to grasp at memories to prove him wrong, but the effort is futile since I can't seem to think of anything but him yelling that at me.

"See?" he says matter-of-factly, as if he thinks my quietness is a testament to him being right. "You can't get upset for how I've treated you when you've treated me—"

"It's not the same!" I wail, my words and voice apparently finding themselves all at once. "It's *so* not the same, Weston. I've been nice to you. I've tried being cordial and—"

"So have I!" he exclaims angrily, slamming one of his hands against the steering wheel.

"Oh really?" I say, a dry laugh coming out of my throat. "When at all have you been cordial to me? When you brushed me off at

Walmart, when you made fun of me that one time you were at dinner with me and my dad—"

"I had to get back to work and you were spaced out!" he argues. "And not only that, but let's not forget how fucking horrified you were when you found out I'd be working on the porch."

"Of course I was horrified!" I yell. "You'd been nothing but an asshole to me!"

"Oh don't be a baby!" he shouts back, looking over at me with blazing eyes. "I'm sorry big ole bad me hurt your feelings, but—"

"Come off it, West!" I explode. "Don't pretend I'm reading too much into nothing. You know what you were doing."

"Oh do I?" He laughs loudly, sarcastically. "Please tell me what I was doing then, Iris, since you're such an expert."

"You're such an asshole!" I yell, my anger running away with itself. "God, I don't even know why I—"

Luckily I manage to cut myself off, my heart stopping as I realize what I've almost just let slip. I don't think I've ever in my life argued with someone like this, so it's no wonder I almost lost control of my words, but thank God I didn't. If I'd... if I'd let it slip that I was in love with him, I'd never be able to live with myself.

He's with Jenny. He's *so* right for Jenny, and I need to remember that.

I need to remember to stay in my space, to not overstep anything.

When my mind stops spinning in horror at what *almost* came out of my mouth, I realize he's pulling off the interstate at our exit. The truck comes to a stop at the red light, and we fall into a dense, edgy silence.

"What were you going to say?" he asks, his voice low.

"What?" I ask, my heart pounding as I feign stupidity. "What was I about to say?"

His jaw clicks in annoyance, and he takes a deep breath before he turns to look at me, his eyes hard emeralds. "Iris, don't.... I'm done arguing with you, okay? You were about to say something. You said 'I don't even know why' and then just stopped yelling."

"I...." I start, but my mind is a complete and utter blank. "I don't...."

He cuts me off with a humorless, almost taunting laugh, shaking his head.

"What?" I ask, dread filling me.

The light turns green and he presses on the gas, urging us toward our town's main road, staying quiet and not answering my question.

"Why were you laughing, Weston?" I ask indignantly as we come to stop at another light, my need to know trumping the hurt I know will come from his answer.

"This," he says, waving his hand between the two of us. "Just this whole fucking situation."

"What about it?" I ask slowly, full of dread.

"It's just fucking ridiculous!" he exclaims, whipping his head sideways to look at me. "This whole thing, it's just.... Why? Why is it like this? Because of that kiss four years ago? So what?"

My heart squeezes at the detachment in his voice. I brace my eyes shut for a moment and then ask brokenly, "What do you mean, so what?"

This light turns green, and he steps on the gas again before he answers, "So what if we made out that night? What's it matter? Why the fuck is it making us so crazy around each other now?"

"I mean...." I trail off, trying to figure out how best to salvage my dignity. "It was a pretty intense—"

"It was just a kiss, Iris," he says drolly, casting me a quick side glance. "It's not like it means anything now. We both know I'm with Jenny."

Even though I feel as if I've just been punched in the stomach, breathless, unable to think clearly, I'm somehow able to say, "Yeah, you're right."

183

I look down at the floor, tears burning the corners of my eyes, and pray I have the strength to keep them at bay until I get home.

I've had my heart broken once, when my mom left, and I thought that I'd never be able to feel that kind of pain again. But now, now I know that, deep down, I'm experiencing another heartbreak.

A different kind, of course, but still just as painful.

That kiss that meant so much to me, that kiss that was a damn lifeline for me that night... he's just told me it meant nothing to him.

It saved me, while he didn't feel anything.

And even though I knew this rejection was coming, it hurts more than I ever imagined it would.

"Iris?" he says a couple of silent minutes later.

I lift my head. "Hmm?"

"We're here," he tells me, and when I look forward and see his house standing in front of us, relief washes over me.

I hurriedly unbuckle my seat belt and hop out of his truck, grabbing my purse, and then turn to head toward my house.

Before I can take a step, though, Weston grabs me by my elbow. I can't look him in the eye, not after he's just hurt me like that, but unfortunately I don't have a choice because he slides his rough fingers underneath my chin and tilts upward so that I have to lock eyes with him.

The second I see him looking back at me, those tears start trickling down my cheeks, hot and slow and completely humiliating. His gaze falls to the tear tracks and his mouth drops open, as if he's shocked I have anything to be upset about.

"What's wrong?" he asks, his voice so much softer than it was in the truck.

"Nothing," I say with an unconvincing sniffle, pulling away from him. "I'm fine."

"Iris...." He trails off doubtfully, his concerned eyes raking over my face, looking me up and down, as if he'll somehow be able to see what's wrong.

"I'm fine," I whisper brokenly, shaking my head and stepping away from him, *needing* to be away from him. "Don't worry about me."

He takes a step toward me, but I just take another back.

"Iris, I always wor—"

I cut him off with the best smile I can muster, even though I know it's a sad attempt. "Thank you for tonight, okay?"

He's staring at me in a way that makes me think he's pleading, but I remind myself that that can't be the case, not after what he told me in the car. The way he yelled at me, the way he brushed off our kiss, it all spoke volumes. He's never cared for me, not in the same way I care for him.

He's just the boy across the street, the boy who's too handsome *not* to hurt me, the boy who needs to be with Jenny instead of me.

No matter how many times I tell myself this, though, it doesn't make the hurt lessen any.

He doesn't say anything in return, so I just turn and hurry across the street, desperate to be alone.

I'm already sobbing by the time I manage to get my key in the doorknob, my heart feeling like it's been ripped to absolute shreds, and once I get it open I find myself stumbling through the house, my breath coming out in loud gasps, tears pooling into the corners of my mouth, dripping onto the wooden floors.

I'm such a fucking mess.

Thank God my dad's out with Meg and not here to see me like this, collapsing into myself, becoming a shell of a person.

But it's all I have the power to do.

---

I don't get out of bed all day Friday.

I stay huddled underneath my covers, in the quiet security of my childhood bed, pretending that the outside world doesn't exist.

I think I owe myself at least that.

The only time I ever emerged was to text Jenny and e-mail Chet and David my reason for missing today, and that was at six this morning when I was still downright delirious from my lack of a stable sleep.

It's around three in the afternoon when I finally decide to emerge from my room for a reason other than using the bathroom or getting a drink of water, and even though the late summer sun is beaming in through our front windows, I still can't grasp that there's a world outside and that life is even going on.

My empty and angrily growling stomach tells me otherwise though, that time has indeed passed, so I busy myself with making a grilled cheese to tide it over until my dad gets home for dinner.

As I cook, my thoughts turn to telling my dad about Mom, when I should do it, *how* I should do it, and I realize with a heavy heart that I need to tell him today.

My decision is emphasized about half an hour later when, as I'm tucked into the couch and gnawing on the remaining crust of my sandwich, my cell phone goes off. Figuring it's probably my dad checking dinner, I lean forward and grab it off the coffee table.

But the phone isn't flashing my dad's name and picture; no, instead it's flashing Weston's name and causing a cold panic to grip at my nerves. Weston doesn't call me... ever, and he'd *especially* never call me after a confrontation like the one we had last night. It has to be a butt dial or something, I assure myself.

I press the ignore button and then set the phone aside, and when I hear the beep as it goes to voice mail, my chest deflates and some sense of stillness fills me.

Just three seconds later, it goes off again, though, and once again I start to panic. The cowardly part of me, that dominant part I hate so much, is screaming at me not to answer, but every other ounce of my being is telling me that I have to. Weston never calls me, and if he's calling me after last night, then something serious may be going on.

I can't just ignore that.

"Hello?" I say hoarsely after picking up the phone, my heart beating painfully fast. "West?"

"Hey," he greets quickly, and even over the phone I can hear the distress in his voice. "I... I know this is a little bit weird, and I don't want to freak you out or anything, but... but I'm pretty sure I remember what your mom looks like and...."

He trails off, obviously not knowing how to continue, and when I finally catch up to his quickly paced words, I understand what's going on. He's seen her. Weston's seen her in town, he knows she's back, and it sounds like he's really shaken up by it.

"I know," I say, wanting to calm him down. "I know she's here in town, Weston. *I know.*"

He's quiet for a long while, the sound of his breathing almost soothing me when I know it should be doing the opposite. "I... when, Iris? I mean, how long has she been...? Does Steve know? 'Cause I just had lunch with him at Meg's place today and he didn't seem like he knew...."

"He doesn't know," I respond with a sigh. "She... she just showed up yesterday, and it was a complete accident that I even saw her. I had to run to CVS for work and she was in the parking lot and I just...."

I trail off, not knowing what else to say, and he quickly picks up on it. "Jesus," he breathes out. "Did you talk to her? I mean, is she in town for good or what...? What's she even doing here?"

Starting to pick at a bare thread of the woven blanket draped across my thighs, I answer him honestly. "I talked to her, yeah, in the parking lot there, and then I went and met her at her hotel. She's... she says she's here indefinitely, that she doesn't know her plans yet, but that she wants to make amends with my dad and me."

"So *that's* why you were all the way out at the Radisson?"

"Yeah," I say uncomfortably, not at all wanting to discuss the events of last night. "Where'd you see her?"

"The bank," he answers. "I was there for work and she was in the lane next to me. Took me forever to realize how I knew her."

"Yeah, it's been a while," I muse. "I can't believe you remembered what she looked like. It's not like you saw her all the time."

"She came over to hang out with my mom occasionally," he tells me. "And then when she left, she sort of became that infamous face no one could ever forget, you know?"

"Yeah," I breathe, not knowing what else to say.

He seems to feel the same way, his side of the line silent as well, but thankfully he eventually asks, "So, uh... you're going to tell your dad, right? That she's here? I know it's personal and everything and I—"

I cut him off, finding his awkward rambling and fear of offending me kind of adorable. "It's fine, West... and yes, I do plan on telling him. Today, actually, when he gets off work."

He's silent again, but somehow or another I can feel him nodding against the phone, and I know that he's doing his best to try and comfort me. "Are you...?" He trails off. "Are you okay? That's got to be a terrifying conversation to think about having."

"A little bit, yeah," I say through a chuckle. "I'm definitely not looking forward to it. But he needs to hear it from me first, not her."

"You're right," he says immediately, his voice coming through strong. "And that's really good of you to know."

"Thanks," I say shyly.

I think it's absolutely crazy that we're talking about something so uncomfortable so comfortably, even after what happened last night, and a part of me starts to wonder if I'll ever *truly* be able to dislike Weston.

Despite how rude he can be, despite his ridiculous mood swings, he's still so nice to talk to about things like this. He can make me feel so on edge at times, so antsy, but other times, like right now, he makes me feel so comfortable, so warm.

He's able to make me feel like I'm safe, like nothing could ever hurt me.

And it's that thought that has everything in my body screaming at me to end this phone call.

I can't keep romanticizing Weston.

Not when he's romanticizing someone else.

Now desperate to hang up the call, I say, "So now you know what the cause of last night was, and I'm sorry. It shouldn't have happened."

He says quietly, "Iris, it's okay. This... this is major. Anyone would have needed a few drinks."

"Yeah," I say quickly, hating that he's being understanding and kind about it. "But still, I shouldn't have called you. I made a mistake and I'm sorry."

"Iris...." He sighs. "You don't need to apologize to me."

I don't know what it is, whether it's the gentleness of his voice or the emotional toll of the past two days, or even some sick combo of the two, but as soon as he says that, I feel yet more tears starting to come up. I've cried so outrageously much recently, and unfortunately most of those tears have started in front of the one person I don't want seeing them.

"Well, I am," I say, cringing when I hear my voice break. "So just accept it, okay?"

"*Okay*, okay. I accept."

"Thank you. I'll see you around, Weston."

"Iris—" he starts, but I quickly cut him off.

"Say hi to Jenny for me."

And then I hang up.

I don't know if I sounded as bitter as I felt saying it, but it just had to come out. Maybe it's because he threw Jenny in my face last night, so now I feel the need to return the favor, or maybe it's because I'm subconsciously reminding myself that there even *is* a Jenny. I don't know.

All I know is that, even though Weston and I have spent the past two months avoiding each other, arguing, and basically being as awkward as possible, I've still fallen for him.

And no matter how hard I've been trying, how much I've reminded myself that he's with someone else and obviously doesn't feel the same way, I can't seem to fall out of love with him.

After the call, I attempt to lose my nerves and emotions in TV, and it helps for a little while. But the second I hear gravel crunching underneath a car outside, I retreat back into being a ball of nerves.

My dad walks in then, red-cheeked from the heat outside. He immediately spots me perched on the couch and gives me a broad grin. "Hey, honey."

"Hey, Dad," I greet, reluctantly pulling myself into an upright sitting position so I can face him. "Good day?"

"It was all right." He shrugs, tossing his keys and wallet onto the kitchen table and then joining me at the other side of the couch. "You? You look like you didn't go to work."

"That's 'cause I didn't," I explain, figuring that this is the best entrance I'm going to get into the upcoming heartbreaking conversation.

His brows furrow. "What? Are you sick?"

"Dad, I...." I trail off with a huge gulp, my heart already squeezing painfully at what I'm going to have to tell him. It's going to mess with him so badly, and that's the last thing in this world I want. "I have something to tell you."

# Chapter Sixteen

The next couple of weeks go by agonizingly slowly. After my horrible conversation with my dad about Mom's return, it's been hard for the two of us to get back to normal.

The night I told him, he went back to Meg's because he knew he had to tell her before anyone else did, and when I asked him about how it went the next time I saw him, all he could do was shake his head. Turns out they didn't break up, though, as they went out that following weekend and he seemed happy about the outcome, but I can tell it's put an extra weight on both of their shoulders, and that's something that no new relationship needs.

He and my mother have spoken once, over coffee at Meg's diner, and I still haven't asked him about it.

He's seemed so reluctant to let this affect him and our renewed relationship, but in that reluctance, he's kind of been achieving it anyway. With his efforts to focus on the positive, the two of us haven't talked about anything real since I told him she was back. It's all been so fake, and I've hated every second of it.

But I still have no earthly idea how to go about fixing it.

As for Mom and me, I've seen her twice since that first meeting at her hotel. The first time we went and got lunch, and I was still so wrung with unpleasantness that I could barely eat. The second time I went back to her hotel and was finally able to eat around her, and after that we silently watched some romantic comedy before I left. Nothing has been talked about, no answers have been given, and I'm starting to wonder if her being back will actually change anything.

Today is the first day since her return that I have something to do to take my mind off her, and that's the Labor Day end of the crawfish season boil. While I'm dreading it since Jenny is actually able to make it as Weston's date, all of which she cooed to me over lunch this past week, I'm still glad it's something getting me out of the house and out of my own head.

"Iris, you ready?" my dad calls from his room, resulting in me laughing my way out of my thoughts and shouting back at him, "Already by the door!"

He emerges from his bedroom, clad in khaki shorts and a red button-down shirt that's very holiday appropriate. As he walks over, he looks at me and says, "You look nice, honey."

"Thanks." I smile, looking down at my jean cut-off shorts, white billowy tank top, and wedge ankle boots. With all the negativity that's been surrounding us of late, I need to feel good today, even going as far as touching my natural curls up with a curling iron and using some of my more expensive perfume.

"Meg's already there, then?" I ask.

"Been there since six this morning," he answers. "I offered to go out and help, but she said she had it all. Her brother and his family are in from out of town, so I think she just wanted time alone with them."

"Well that's good," I muse, grabbing my purse from the floor and following him outside as he opens the door. "Have you met him yet?"

"I've met him before in past years, but not since we've been dating," he explains, locking the door behind us and then leading me to his car. "He's a cool guy, though. Weird laugh."

I giggle. "Seriously?"

He winks at me across the top of his car. "Just wait till you hear it." We both slide into the steaming hot interior.

Blasting the air conditioning as soon as the engine's started, he asks, "What about you? Any new guys since that soup boy?"

"Soup boy?" I ask, narrowing my eyes at him.

He gives me that mischievous, completely immature grin of his before he says, "Oh, it's just a little nickname West and I came up with for him."

"But soup boy?" I reiterate. "That sounds like some bad kid's superhero."

"His name's Campbell!" my dad exclaims, blue eyes wide as he looks at me. "What'd you expect?"

"Good Lord," I groan, leaning my head back against the seat as my dad backs out of the gravel driveway. Without even thinking about it, I open my eyes and find the empty driveway across the street, and my stomach is quickly churning as I realize Weston and Jenny are probably already at Meg's.

I don't have long to think about it, though, because my dad's asking me again, "So? Any new boys that I need to be warned of?"

"No, Dad," I say with a sigh. "I'm still single as a Pringle."

"A Pringle?" he asks, and when I look I see that he's wrinkled his nose in confusion. "But those come all stacked together? How's that singl—"

I cut him off with a roll of my eyes. "It's an expression, geez!"

He chuckles at me. "You need to get some beer in ya, honey. You are way too tense."

"It's been a rough couple weeks," I point out. "I don't know how you're so chipper."

"There may've been more Baileys than coffee in my coffee this morning," he says meekly, attempting to sound guilty but really just sounding like he's on the verge of laughing at himself.

"Dad!" I squeal, completely appalled.

"What?" He roars with laughter, finding my disapproval hilarious. "It's a holiday!"

"But we had coffee at, like, eight thirty! That's so early!"

"That's how early we're out tailgating during football season," he points out matter-of-factly. "And everyone's drinking there."

"Whatever, Dad," I say, attempting to be disappointed but not completely able to hold back a little laughter. "If I have to drive your drunk ass home, I'm not going to be happy."

"Oh, we'll be fine," he says with a wave of his hand. "I took care of Meg last time, so she owes me a favor."

Meg doesn't quite seem to agree with that statement though, because as soon as we walk in and she takes one look at my pink-cheeked dad, she shakes her head and says, "Oh uh-uh, mister. It's not even noon yet."

"Geez, would y'all lighten up?" My dad chuckles. "I'm fine. And I'll be more fine once the day wears on and I get some food in me."

Meg looks to me for agreement on that, and when I just shrug and tell her, "I'll keep an eye out," she seems a little more at ease.

"Good," she says before pulling me into a hug and then whispering in my ear, "You doing okay?"

I know she's referring to my mom's reappearance, since I haven't really had a chance to talk to her since, so when I pull away from her I say, "As okay as I can be, I guess."

"You're a tough cookie," she says fondly, squeezing my upper arm before grabbing my dad and quietly berating him as she leads him away.

The first part of the day goes by quickly, albeit it's pretty damn awkward since everyone has now heard of my mom being back and either asks me straight up about it, or just gives me that sympathetic look telling me they know. Both are driving me absolutely crazy, so by the time the afternoon rolls around and people are crowding around different folding tables to dig into their trays of crawfish, I'm finishing off my fourth beer.

Somehow I've been able to avoid speaking with Weston and Jenny except for the hug I gave her when they first arrived, but it's still painful to see them walk around together like the perfect couple they are and hear people fawn over how good they look together.

Right now they're at a table two down from ours, and I'm too busy joking along with my dad, Meg, and two of his friends to worry about how Jenny's loud laugh keeps twinkling over the crowd of people.

It's only when I hear her squeal and shout, "Campbell!" that their table truly gets my attention.

My heart falling into my stomach, I whip around in the direction of her voice and my worries are proven true when I see her enveloping her tall, still charming-as-ever-looking brother. The same brother who tried to feel me up in his car.

Why didn't she tell me he was coming?

Why didn't she warn me?

Hell, why didn't Weston warn me?

As Jenny pulls Campbell inside, most likely to get him a drink, my eyes seek out Weston's, desperate to shoot him the glare of a lifetime for not telling me.

He looks just as confused as I do, though, his bright green eyes wide and his lips slightly parted, and the moment we lock eyes and I start to glare at him, he shakes his head and shrugs, mouthing to me, "No idea."

So this was all just Jenny, then?

Feeling utterly betrayed and positively livid, I let my eyes fall from Weston's and instead focus on taking an obnoxiously large swig of my beer. Campbell and Jenny come back out, both with a drink in hand and charming smiles on their faces, but it's me that has the undivided attention of Meg and my dad.

"What?" I demand harshly, my annoyance completely misdirected.

"Soup boy?" my dad asks, causing Meg to give him a weird look.

"Yep," I answer dryly, feeling my anger surge when I hear Campbell laugh loudly at something.

"Did you know he was...?" Dad trails off, only for me to answer, "Nope. Not at all."

"Goddammit," he curses, Meg squeezing his arm in an attempt to calm him down.

The afternoon continues without incident, but my anger only grows more intense.

Once the crawfish has all been eaten, everyone heads inside to cool down, groups of people dividing off to play cards or drinking games or just stand in a circle gossiping.

Somehow I end up amongst a group of middle-aged women that I knew from church when we used to go, and listening to them talk is making me feel like more of a sinner than I've ever thought I was. So I excuse myself to go to the bathroom.

Once I'm done washing my hands and checking my reflection in the mirror, my lips undeniably red thanks to the spice from the crawfish, I head back out into the small, darkened hallway that leads into the main dining room.

But a cold hand grasping my elbow stops me.

"What the hell?" I gasp, pivoting around and feeling a hollow beat in my chest when I see Campbell standing before me.

"What do you want, Campbell?" I ask, taking a step back when I realize just how close he is to me and how glazed over his eyes are.

"I just wanted to talk to ya, Iris," he says with a shit-eating grin, one of his arms extending out to rest against the paneled wall beside us. "It's been a while."

"Yeah," I say dryly with a nod. "It has. With good reason."

"You miss me?" He smirks as he looms in even closer, keeping his balance with the hand braced against the wall.

"Campbell." My discomfort intensifies when his blue eyes trail down to look at my mouth. "We broke up for a reason, remember? You—"

"Yeah, I remember," he says, his voice sounding distant. "You wouldn't give it up."

"That's not...." I trail off in a slight panic when he comes in so close to me that I have to back up, my back hitting the wall behind me and rendering me unable to move. Swallowing back the lump of fear in my throat, I start again. "That's not why we broke up."

"No, I'm pretty sure that's exactly why it happened." He chuckles, bringing his other arm up and settling it beside my head so that I'm now pinned between him and the wall. "After all those dates... all those kisses...."

"Campbell, come on," I urge, standing up straighter. "Let's not do this right now."

"When else, then?" he asks. "You won't answer any of my texts, any of my calls...."

"You've only texted twice," I point out.

"But you didn't respond to either." He pouts, readjusting his weight. "Why don't you like me, Iris? I'm a good-looking dude, right?"

"Well, yeah...," I stammer out, "but I—"

"Iris! Hey!" My heart leaps to my chest in liberation.

Whether or not I'm pissed at Jenny for not telling me about Campbell coming today, she just made up for it by interrupting whatever this could've turned into.

"Hey, Jen," I greet graciously, stepping around Campbell and ignoring the pointed look she's giving us. "I can't believe I haven't seen you more today."

"Right?" She giggles, obviously feeling the beer I've seen her drinking. "I've missed you, Iris! Being with Weston is just so time-consuming."

She tries to look and sound sincerely exasperated, but there's a look on her face telling me that's not exactly the case. Even though the two of us have gotten relatively back to normal, I guess she's still unsettled about Weston and my brief history, and she's making it damn well known to me that she's the one who has him now.

As if I'd be able to forget that, anyway.

"I'm sure." I laugh, trying my hardest to be civil. "Well, I'm going to go grab another drink, okay? I'll talk to y'all later."

"Okeydokey," Jenny says with a grin, that bright white smile of hers stretching across her face with an almost baleful enthusiasm. "Don't leave without coming to talk to me for real!"

"Okay," I say with a slight smile, ignoring the piercing glower Campbell's sending my way.

As I walk off, I see her grab his arm and pull him close so they can talk, their hushed voices echoing throughout the hallway and only going away once I'm back in the dining room. My pulse is still running wild, that scarily tense confrontation between Campbell and me making me near desperate for a beer.

I'm heading into the kitchen when I see Weston coming over to me, his painfully handsome face not helping my throbbing pulse. He stops in front of me. "Hey, Iris?"

"Yeah?" I respond, crossing my arms over my chest.

My heart completely stops when he reaches out to grab my forearm, a delicious buzz traveling over my skin at the contact. He pulls me off to the side, a small space away from where everyone else is.

His face is mere inches from mine, his eyes dark and firm. I'm completely transfixed as I wait for him to say something. I'd be completely intimidated if I weren't already losing myself in a haze due to his proximity, and I only lose myself further as he reaches a hand up to push through his overgrown hair.

"Did you know?" he asks lowly, his voice gruff.

Despite the sound of his voice making me want to sink even further, I snap out of my lust-filled smog at the question and clarify, "Know what?"

"That Soupy was coming." His nickname for Campbell makes me grin since it's so close to the one my dad mentioned in the car earlier. "Did Jen tell you?"

Overcoming the red-hot jealousy that hearing him affectionately shorten her name causes, I tighten my arms across my chest and ask, "Why?"

"Just tell me," he urges, leaning in a little bit more. "You looked surprised when he got here, but I just want to make sure I read you right."

"You read me right," I tell him through a sigh, ignoring how good it feels to say that. "I had no idea he was going to show up."

"Goddammit," he curses underneath his breath, pulling away from me with a newly clenched jaw.

"What, why?" I ask.

Completely ignoring me, he asks pointedly, "You were just with her, right? In the bathroom hallway?"

"Yeah, but...." I trail off when he pushes past me and stalks toward the hallway.

Once again I'm overcome with the need for a beer, so I push away from the second wall I've been backed into in the past five minutes and start back toward the kitchen.

The only other person in the stainless steel room is one of my dad's best friends. "Hey, Paul."

"Hey, shortcake," he says, calling me the same thing he's called me since I was four years old. "You want another beer?"

"Yes, please." I grin sheepishly, reaching out and grasping the cold bottle he hands over. He murmurs something about finding a bottle opener, and it's right as he's reaching out to pop the lid off my beer that a loud commotion sounds from the main dining room.

199

"Hey, hey, stop that!" someone shouts, and that's quickly followed up by more yelling that swiftly turns into indiscernible hysteria.

Paul hurriedly looks over at me and we run into the dining room. My eyes widen and panic grips my chest when I see where the turmoil is coming from. Most of the women and kids have moved to the far side of the room while the majority of the guys have converged into that small, dark hallway I left Campbell and Jenny in just a few minutes ago.

The same one Weston just angrily stomped into.

A loud crash echoes across the diner, and as women start ushering the kids outside, away from the craziness, I feel my legs pulling me in the direction of that hallway regardless of the logic screaming at me to leave it alone.

The closer I get, the more I'm able to make out what people are saying, and the first thing my mind clenches on is, "Weston, let him go!"

My adrenaline comes roaring to life at that, causing me to push harder through the teenage guys in the back of the crowd trying to get a glimpse of the action.

"Stop!" I hear Jenny scream. "West, stop! Please!"

I'm almost to the front of the crowd when my dad commands everyone, "Get the hell out of the way! Move!"

I can't find the willpower to listen to him, though, and as soon as I make it to the front of the crowd, I seek out Weston, knowing that my heart won't stop pounding until I know he's okay. When I see that he's been pushed against the wall, my dad holding him there by his shoulders, a large breath of relief empties my chest.

The sound of hiccups and crying coming from the corner pulling my attention elsewhere, I see Campbell sitting on the ground just feet away from Weston and my dad, his legs stretched in front of him and his head leaning back against the wall.

It doesn't take me long to notice the thin flow of crimson running

*Back to You*

down his chin, over his jaw, and dripping onto his neck. Jenny is right there by his side to catch it though, running a wet wad of paper towels over the blood.

I'm silent for a while, lost in my hectic thoughts, and I'm only snapped out of it when my dad says, "Iris?"

"Yeah?" I answer, realizing that everyone in the hallway is now staring at me.

"You don't need to be back here," Dad says, sounding completely exasperated. "Why don't you go back out front until this is all settled?"

"Because she's as guilty as anyone else?" Jenny pipes up coldly, causing my jaw to slacken in shock. "Hell, she belongs in this more than I do."

"Shut the fuck up, Jenny," Weston growls, looking ready to charge toward the Turner siblings, and my dad has to push him back even harder.

I'm staring at Weston in shock when I hear a pained-sounding laugh and Campbell says, "See, Jen? I told you they were fucking."

"You want to say that again?" my dad bellows, taking his eyes off Weston and piercing my ex with his fiercest glare.

Campbell chuckles again, infuriating me with his nonchalance, and says, "Chill, dude. Weston here's already rendered me helpless."

"I'll render you fucking mute if you keep talking," Weston barks, causing my dad to slam him into the wall for a third time.

"West," my dad urges, "you need to chill out. You're going to land yourself in jail if you keep this up."

Weston's clearly reluctant to listen to him, anger still pulsating off his chest, but soon enough he slumps against the wall in agreement. My dad looks over his shoulder and asks Jenny, "Is he good to walk yet? Y'all need to get out of here."

"Of course," Jenny says with a dry chuckle, her thin fingers reaching up to brush away tears and smudges of mascara. "Because we're dealing with the prince and princess of town here, we're the

201

ones being punished for Weston turning into the fucking Hulk, right?"

"Jenny, that's enough," I say in my firmest voice, not wanting to add myself to the equation but having had enough. Although it's clear Weston was the winner of whatever fight was going on, Jenny and Campbell have no room to play the victims here.

"Excuse me?" she says, standing up and crossing the floor over to me. "The hell did you just say to me?"

"I said that's enough," I reiterate, so entirely thankful that my voice isn't shaking like my nerve is. "This isn't anything to do with how Weston and I are treated here. Your brother was being an ass the second he cornered me, so y'all are the ones that should leave. It's as simple as that."

Campbell coughs out a laugh, and I see the anger in Jenny's eyes only harden at the sound of it. "This isn't fair to me, Iris, you know that," she says. "I know what my brother did to you was shit, but he's still my brother."

"I get that," I say softly, trying to be rational and sympathize with her. "But you still gave me no warning he was going to show, and you know how things ended between us. You're my friend, Jen. You should've said something."

"I didn't know for sure he was coming," she says as an excuse, her blue eyes starting to water. "I invited him, but he said he'd probably have to work."

"You still should've mentioned it," I say, not able to relent. "But whatever. It's done now."

"Obviously it isn't to some people," Campbell taunts, throwing a look over at a still infuriated Weston.

"Man," my dad says to Campbell, looking at him over his shoulder and sounding even more exhausted, "you really just need to shut the fuck up."

Campbell laughs in response, causing the red he already had me seeing to get even more vibrant. How the hell did I date this asshole for a month? Was I that ignorant?

Jenny looks back to me and says, "I'm sorry for this, for all of this, okay? I hate it, having to choose between my brother and my boyfriend."

"Oh, you don't need to worry about that," Weston pipes up. I look that way and my gaze instantly meets his. His expression is calmer than it has been this whole time, and when he moves his eyes off me and onto Jenny, I see absolutely no emotion on his face. "'Cause we're over, Jenny."

A barely audible gasp leaves her lips as she takes a baby step toward him. "What?" she croaks, her voice only a squeak.

"I'm breaking up with you," he says, his voice still as calm as ever. "The shit you knew, the stuff you let him get away with, that's not.... I don't want to be with anyone who's okay with that kind of stuff."

"It wasn't like it was that serious!" she argues. "They got into a stupid fight and, yeah, Campbell was an ass, but it's not like you've never been an ass!"

"I'd never fucking do what he tried to pull, though," Weston says, his eyes clouding over and that calm starting to fade. "And you lied to me about it, too. I never would've known if I hadn't heard y'all today."

"Well, I'm sorry we can't all be perfect like you," Jenny seethes. "And the fact that you're breaking up with me over something my brother did just proves you were never really in this."

"Think what you want," he says, briefly glancing at me before moving back to her. "But I'm done."

"Fine," she says after a moment's hesitation, and the next moment she's turning on her heel and rushing out of the hallway.

My heart squeezes painfully for her. I know she must be devastated. Despite how much I want Weston for myself, he did make her happy and I know she was starting to fall for him. Not only that, but our conversation from the night of her first date with Weston is ringing guiltily in my ears, reminding me of how truly insecure she is.

I never wanted this for her, even though I wanted what she had for myself.

"I guess that means I have to help myself up?" Campbell grumbles childishly, reaching out to press against the floor to push himself up.

He looks miserable, and even though he's been a top-tier asshole today, I can't just stand there and watch him struggle. I walk over and extend my hand to him, fighting the urge to snap at him when he doesn't immediately say thank you. After I help him up, he turns to face me and takes a step closer, giving me a told-you-so grin when we both hear Weston make some type of grunting noise.

"Don't miss me too much, babe," he says with a wink, brushing his knuckles over my cheek before finally deciding to leave the hallway.

Once he's gone, my dad cautiously releases his grip on Weston and asks sharply, "You good?"

"Yeah," Weston says, and from my stance a few feet away I can see that he's having a hard time looking my dad in the eye. "I'm sorry 'bout that, Mr. Tilley."

"Jesus Christ," my dad says in a falsely angry tone, "I've told you a million and five times to call me Steve, have I not?"

I crack a grin, my love for my goofball of a dad warming my chest. The grin stretches even further, too, when I see a shy smile touch Weston's pink lips as he looks down at the floor and says, "Yes, sir, you have."

"Then call me Steve, son," my dad says fondly, stepping away from him and coming over to me. My dad threads a strong arm over my shoulders and squeezes me to his side, pressing a kiss to the top of my head before telling Weston, "Besides, there is no reason to apologize. Hell, if I'd heard what made you so angry, I would've punched him myself. And you're in better with the police, so...."

I can't help but giggle despite my nerves still being shot. "And thank you, by the way." My voice comes out much shyer than I originally intended. "I don't know what they were saying, but I'm glad you dealt with it and not me."

"You're welcome," he says, his eyes piercing mine for a brief second and sending bone-melting warmth down my veins.

"Well," my dad cuts in after a moment of almost awkward silence. He clears his throat. "Let's go let everyone know we're not dead, all right?"

# Chapter Seventeen

"Hey, Mom," I greet the thin-framed woman the next weekend, awkwardly returning her hug before stepping past her into the hotel room she's still using as a temporary home.

Despite having been here for three weeks now, the room still looks completely unlived in, no dirty laundry on the floor, no clutter on the nightstand. This is my fourth trip into the room, and I still feel as if it's part of some alternate world.

After we ask each other how we've been, she's grabbing her large purse and leading me out of the hotel and down to where her rental car's parked in the lot.

Once I've shut the passenger door, I adjust my seat belt and reach forward to put the radio on, a soft hum to fill what's most likely going to be unnerving silence. A part of me is terrified that our relationship is now always going to be awkward and riddled with tension, while another part of me is equally as terrified that it won't be and I'll get comfortable only for her to leave again.

Either way, thinking about it for too long leaves me feeling miserable.

I'm quiet as she drives us out to Baton Rouge, her having told me on the phone that there's some new boutique out there she wants to try out. She also mentioned wanting to drop some cash on me since she hasn't been able to for a while, but I doubt I'm going to allow her to do that.

She's pulling into a parking spot in a crowded lot a good thirty minutes later, and as I go to unbuckle my belt, I look over and ask her curiously, "How'd you hear about this place again?"

I can't help but question it. The girly and nearly over-the-stop storefront wedged in between two others in the strip mall doesn't seem like her type of place, even with her Tory Burch bag.

"One of my friends on Facebook liked their page," she explains, lifting her arm to shift the car into park, her cardigan sleeve falling and exposing a thin forearm.

My eyes widen and my eardrums start thumping, the large yellow bruise marring my mom's wrist causing a tense pulsating noise that blots out her voice as she keeps talking. The longer I look at it, the more it occurs to me that the massive bruise with several smaller, fingertip-sized bruises around it looks like a mark a strong hand would leave.

It looks like someone grabbed her wrist and tried to squeeze the life out of it.

As she finishes what she's saying and realizes I haven't responded, she glances over. When she sees the surely horrified expression on my face, she looks back at herself and tenses as she sees what's stunned me into silence.

"Iris...." She sighs, looking like a kicked puppy as she tugs her sleeve back down.

"Mom," I croak out, my voice shaken as the huge discoloration wrapped around her skin won't leave my mind. "Is that...? Who...? Is that why you're back?"

"Iris," she says as my mind trips over itself. "Honey, it's okay.

I'm... I'm fine. This is old news, okay? It's—"

"That," I say harshly, pointing at the skin she just covered, "cannot be old news, not when it looks like that! That's.... Mom, I mean, you've been here, like, three weeks and it's still...?"

"It's fine," she urges, unbuckling her seat belt and adjusting herself in her seat. "I've been to the doctor. It's not broken. It's just a bad—"

"Okay," I interrupt, newly angry because she's trying to make this into a nonissue. "Okay, but... but who the hell did that to you? I mean... was it intentional, or.... I mean, it looks like a handprint, Mom!"

"It's a long story," she says, her voice straining to remain calm. "But it's over now, so it's nothing for you to worry about, okay? Let's just go inside and look at—"

"No!" I shout at her, my terrified fury bubbling. "No, it's not okay, Mom! Who the fuck did that to you?"

"Iris!" she exclaims, her face pale, making the frustration in her tawny eyes stand out. "I don't want to—"

"You don't want to talk about anything!" I protest. "You've been gone four years and all you want to talk about is what you missed with me, what I've been up to, and you haven't spoken a damn word about where you ran off to! How's that fair to me, huh? You're not the only one who missed four years, Mom!"

"Honey, don't—"

"No, Mom," I say a moment later, my voice coming out in pants. "No. You're not.... I'm calling the shots today, now, after that... that *thing* I just saw. It's my turn to get some damn answers."

Panic slowly starts to mar her pretty yet exhausted-looking features, and when she says, "You don't want to—" I cut her off with a firm shake of my head.

"No, I don't want to go in that damn store."

------------

By the time my mom leaves Dad's and my house, I'm entirely drained of emotion.

Since Dad's out of town on business, we decided to bring me to my car at the hotel and then just drive out there separately so she could tell me what caused that bruise, because she knew it'd upset me and didn't want me to drive afterward.

And she was completely right.

When she ran away four years ago, it was into the arms of some guy she'd met through a mutual friend on Facebook. His name was Tim and he was a wealthy investment banker with gorgeous eyes and a full head of hair. She knew she liked him the day they started talking, and was in love with him the first time she laid eyes on him in person.

The first two years were a fucking fairy tale apparently, full of expensive vacations, lavish gifts, and a circle of friends that were fancier than anyone my mom had ever met.

She was starstruck.

But after a while he started to become possessive, she said, telling her she couldn't hang out with her friends because he needed to know she'd be home, beating up some random guy at a bar who politely asked to get her a drink, or screaming at her when she put on too much makeup.

She sobbed to me as she spoke of the first time he hit her, which was when she bought a beautiful designer dress for their three-year anniversary and he decided it was too slutty. He said he didn't want any other guys to see her in a dress like that, and when she argued with him, he smacked her across the face.

After that, the abuse only got worse.

She was a prisoner in that house, she said, a slave to his every demand. She lost all of her new friends because he wouldn't let her see them, and then smacked her around after they went to an event because she complained of having no one to talk to. She said it was when the sexual abuse, the rape, started that she knew she had to get away.

So she started plotting, and eventually was able to figure out how much money she'd need to hole up in a hotel for a couple of months and recover. She was able to steal a blank check from his checkbook, forge his signature, and then use the hundred thousand dollars she made the check for to open her own bank account. Then, one day while he was out at work, she caught a cab to the airport, paid for a flight with cash, and flew directly down here.

The memories she spoke of, the pain that speaking them inflicted upon her, has my heart in unspeakable turmoil, pain and anger dueling for power as I watch her climb into her rental car through the open window in the living room. My eyes don't stray from her as she starts the engine and adjusts her mirrors, as now, after learning all of this, she no longer seems like the same person she was this morning.

She's stronger, more resilient, a lion where I first saw a mouse.

For once I'm not angry at her for leaving, not hurt that she picked someone over us. I'm sure it'll come back eventually, once all of this has worn off, but for now... now I'm internally crying out for my mind to turn my image of her back into the flighty, selfish woman I initially thought she was.

This? This horrible, gut-wrenching pain I feel knowing someone hurt her as badly as that guy did... I hate it.

I want it gone.

I'd give anything for it to go away.

Which is why when my first attempt at ridding myself of it, a scalding-hot shower, fails, I'm throwing on a sweatshirt and some ripped jeans and driving to the one place I know I'll never be alone.

Meg's diner isn't that crowded since it's only four thirty, and that makes finding her when I walk in incredibly easy. She's hovering over a table and talking to the family there, the one belonging to the local Baptist church's pastor, but when she sees me she quickly bids them goodbye.

She stands straighter, an excited grin touching her lips as she calls out, "Iris! Hey, sweetie!"

Gripping the strap of my purse tighter, I watch through tired eyes as she starts toward where I'm standing at the little hostess's podium. That initial smile starts to fade the closer to me she gets, and I'm sure it has everything to do with the fact that I look like I just crawled out of the nearest sewer.

"Hon?" she asks, the corners of her mouth turning down in concern as she gives me a maternal once-over. "What's wrong? Everything okay? It's not your dad, is it?"

"No," I answer, my voice coming out much softer than I intended. "No, last time I talked to him he was enjoying the buffet at his hotel just a little too much."

"Then what is it?" she asks quietly, intensely, stepping closer to me.

"It'll be fine," I assure her, wishing the sentiment would resonate with my worries as well but knowing better. "I just... the house was too quiet, you know? So I decided to come out here."

She doesn't look convinced, but she thankfully lets it go.

"All right then," she says, her short blonde curls bouncing around her face as she nods strongly. "Just go sit wherever you'd like."

I look around to see which tables have already been taken, and the first one I notice is populated by my painfully handsome neighbor who, judging by the scowl on his lips and the empty beer glass in front of him, is having as great a day as I am.

"He's been here over an hour," Meg says, apparently having caught where my gaze fell.

"Do you know what's wrong with him?" I ask, my internal pain over my mom disappearing only to make room for the haunted darkness in his expression.

"It's the thirteenth," she says, in a way that has me thinking I should know what it means.

"The thirteenth?" My eyebrows furrow as I glance back over at Weston.

And it only takes that one look for me to know exactly what that means. That sadness overshadowing his handsome features is an exact replica of how he looked at his brother's birthday party.

It's September thirteenth.

The day that Marcus died exactly ten years ago.

Shit.

I feel the warm touch of Meg's dainty hand on my shoulder as she says to me softly, "Why don't you go sit with him, huh? Maybe each other's company will get those horrible looks on y'all's faces off."

I turn to look at her, her attempt to set the two of us up at a time like this striking some chord. "Meg...."

She shakes her head, knowing what I'm insinuating. "Nothing silly this time from me, I promise. Y'all are both just going through some rough stuff. Nothing makes anyone feel better like knowing you're not alone."

*She's right*, I think with a sigh. I know she is.

"I'll bring you a beer over, okay?" she continues with a smile. "And if neither of y'all can drive home, I can always leave the place to Hank for a little while."

"You're incredible," I tell her in all honesty.

"Remind your dad of that every once in a while." She grins, flashing me a wink. "Now go, little lady."

I chuckle. "Okay, okay."

I know I should be nervous as I walk over to Weston's table, his eyes so focused on his hands as he picks his nails that he doesn't see me coming over, but for some reason I'm not. I don't know if it's because I'm so emotionally drained from my talk with my mom earlier, or if... or if I just *know* that this is inherently the right thing to do.

Judging by how natural it feels to just slide into the booth across from him, I know deep down that it's the latter.

"Hey," I manage to say, my heart giving a dull little thud when he looks up from his nearly bleeding nail beds.

"What're you doing here?" he asks a moment later, his normally piercing gaze significantly dulled.

"Same as you," I say honestly, placing my bag down to the left of my thigh. "Not wanting to be alone... but at the same time wanting to be alone."

"If you know I want to be alone," he asks gruffly, his voice not giving any of his feelings away, "then why're you sitting with me?"

"Because you sat with me on the porch that night. Just returning the favor."

The statement brings just a little flicker of light into his eyes, and when I see the corner of his mouth twitch, I know that sitting here with him was *definitely* the right thing to do.

He opens his mouth to say something, but is interrupted by Meg. "Here ya go, hon," she says, placing a chilled glass of beer in front of me.

"Thanks."

"What 'bout you, West? Another?"

He gives her a slow nod. "Thanks, Meg."

"Sure thing." She grins, giving his large shoulder a squeeze before walking away.

We're both silent for the next couple of moments, me sipping at my drink and him choosing not to continue with what he was going to say earlier. Thankfully I don't feel that restless energy in me I usually feel with prolonged silences, which is something this situation definitely doesn't need.

"What about you?" he asks after I've taken my fourth sip, causing me to meet his eyes across the table and arch my brows in question.

"You said you were here for the same reason as me. Unless I've been completely out of it the past twenty years, you don't have a brother, alive or dead."

"You sure you want to know?" I ask dryly, not wanting to unload any of my heavy issues onto his already jam-packed shoulders. "I don't want to burden you."

"It'll get my mind off my own shit, so hell yeah I want to know. If you're okay telling me."

"Okay, well," I say, maneuvering my weight in my seat to make myself comfortable. "I found out the reason my mom's been wearing long sleeves in this heat isn't because she's batshit crazy."

When I don't immediately continue, I see an adorable crinkle appear on his nose right before he says, "I'm confused."

Somehow managing to smile at his cuteness, I say, "She has bruises. On her arms. And I'm sure in some other places too."

"Wha...?" he trails off, his eyes falling to the table.

For some ungodly reason I can't seem to say straight out that my mom was abused, that the guy she ditched us for developed a liking of beating the shit out of her, but after the gears in Weston's mind start to move, his head snaps up and I know just by looking at him that he knows exactly what I'm insinuating.

"What? Are you serious?"

I nod even though I wish I didn't have to. "Yeah. His name was Tim. An investment banker who had a shit ton of money, apparently."

"Good Lord," he says quietly, shaking his head. "Is she...? Is that why she's back? Is she in hiding or is he in prison, or...?"

"He's not," I answer. "I don't know why, though, I didn't even think to ask about that."

He's quiet for a long while, looking like he's trying to process everything, and then he asks softly, "When did you find all this out?"

"'Bout an hour ago," I say as nonchalantly as I can. "I was home, but my dad's out of town again, and it was just so damn quiet that...."

"Did I ever tell you why Thumper is named Thumper?" he randomly asks, the question jutting into the sentence I couldn't finish forming.

I slowly shake my head.

He takes a sip of the new beer Meg must've slipped onto the table while we weren't paying attention, and then says, "It's 'cause his tail is so big that when he wags it, it thumps really loudly."

I grin, my affection for this man growing tenfold. "That's adorable, West."

Even as the lightest shade of pink flushes over his face at my words, he decides to keep talking. "I adopted him when my parents left, and he was grown enough for his tail to be that loud. And I knew he'd be perfect 'cause...."

Understanding immediately, I finish for him, "'Cause the sound made you know you were never alone."

"Bingo," he says with an embarrassed smile, one he quickly covers with his glass as he takes a large gulp of his beer. As he puts it down, he continues, "Sometimes it's not enough though, like today, so that's why I'm here."

"Yeah, today's a pretty shitty one for you, isn't it?"

He barks out a laugh, shaking his head before saying sarcastically, "Just a little bit."

I smile at him, loving how I've been able to make him laugh. His eyes meet mine and I'm truly struck by how much I love this man. I've known him for over two decades; I've watched as he dealt with the tragedy of his brother's death.

He's always been such a huge part of my life, whether or not I was aware of it at the time.

And that's why seeing him hurt, seeing him upset, *kills* me on the inside even when I have my own demons to be battling.

Which is why I find myself speaking far more boldly than I ever would've thought possible.

"I am here for you too, you know. Just across the street and everything. I get how the alone thing—"

I'm cut off midsentence by the jarring sound of rowdy laughter, and when I look over my shoulder to see what's going on, I see a group of about five young guys walking through the front door, one of them with a neon-yellow shirt that says "Show me your boobs! (I get married tomorrow)."

I roll my eyes and go to look back at Weston, but one of the guys, a dark-haired one that looks vaguely familiar, catches my eye. His eyes widen as he sees Weston as well, but soon after he's being nudged by one of his friends as Meg leads them to a table.

Turning back to Weston, I see that his face has gone completely rigid, his eyes trailing the group of guys.

Utterly bewildered, I ask, "West, do you know him?"

His stare doesn't waver from the guys until they're all seated and talking loudly amongst themselves, and then he looks back at me and says, "Yeah. He's that dipshit from the Boot."

My eyes widen. "The guy you punched 'cause of me?"

"Mhmm...," he grates roughly, picking up his glass and finishing the beer left inside.

"Jesus." I groan, rolling my eyes as I look at the ceiling. "What else could go wrong today?"

"Isn't it, like, bad luck if you say that kind of thing?" he asks with just a smidgen of humor.

"Fuck if I know," I curse, looking back at him and seeing that my dramatics have eased some of the tension on his handsome face.

We both quiet for a little while, my attention wholly on that bachelor party. I don't remember anything from that night, but according to Jenny, that curly-haired guy and I got *very* familiar with each other before he and Weston got into it.

It's the strangest feeling, knowing you've been semi-intimate with someone and yet not being able to remember, but a very immature part of me can't help but be a little bit proud. As much of an asshole as that guy may have been, it can't be denied that he's cute.

Just moments later, my focus is averted as Meg walks over to us and sets down two new beers and two shots of what smells like Fireball. "What's...?" I start, looking over at Meg with a raised eyebrow.

There's no way she's going to be *that* transparent about trying to hook us up, right?

"Not from me," she immediately claims, leaning forward to grab our empty glasses. "From one of the guys over at that table."

"The fuck?" Weston grumbles as both of us turn our attention to the table in question.

The guy from the Boot promptly meets our gazes and gives us a guilty smile, tipping his frosted beer glass in our direction as a sign of apology.

I, of course, smile back and nod as if accepting, but when I glance over to see what Weston's chosen to do, I see the end of an eye roll.

"West," I scold.

Meg asks, "What's all of this about?"

"A guy got too friendly—" I start to explain right before Weston rudely talks over me.

"Douche bag over there tried taking advantage of Iris a while back."

"What?" Meg gasps as she looks at him over her shoulder. "Really? Does your dad know?"

"I don't think so," I tell her. "It really wasn't that big a deal anyway."

"Sure sounds like it was...." Meg trails off, looking interestedly between Weston and me.

When neither of us offer anything else up, instead just staring at each other as if trying to provoke the other to say something, she clicks her tongue and says, "*Anyway,* I'll be over there if y'all need anything. West, try not to start any more fights in my diner."

"I'll do my best," he huffs immaturely.

Right as I start sinking into thoughts about the fight he started over me just last weekend, Weston's pulling my attention away by grabbing a shot glass and pushing the other toward me.

"You in?" he asks, eyebrows furrowed. Something in his eyes tells me that this shot may lead to all kinds of trouble, but that it's totally fine with him.

And without a doubt in my mind, I know that it's totally fine with me too.

Picking up the shot glass and looking him dead in the eye, I agree.

"I'm in."

# Chapter Eighteen

"So," Alex, the guy from the Boot, says firmly, his arm over my shoulders tightening as he looks between me and Weston. "You two banging yet?"

"What?" I gasp, my mouth dropping open as I look to the curly-headed cutie Weston and I dubbed as our new best friend sometime during the past couple of hours.

He laughs boisterously at my shock. "Yeah! I mean, I know I lost my chance with you and everything, and that's cool 'cause I've got my eye on someone else, no offense, but I figured you two would be a thing by now."

"And why'd you think that?" Weston asks, the almost insulting composure in his voice making me look over at him.

I've quickly come to learn over the span of the evening that, despite Weston's size, it doesn't take too much alcohol for him to start feeling good. He still has the same adorable pink tinge to his cheeks that's been there since our second round of shots, his eyes are still shimmering with the temporary relinquishment of his grief over Marcus, and there's still a happy almost-smile on his lips.

The hostility he felt for Alex when they initially got here has long since disappeared, the two of them and some of the other guys giggling like old friends a short while ago. In fact, even I have developed a bit of a soft spot for the guy I made out with months ago.

That night at the Boot must've just been a drunken fluke, a normally dormant asshole trait making itself known for the night, and now we're quickly learning that while he's still as brazen as ever, he wants nothing but for everyone around him to have fun.

Which, honestly, is probably the best thing for both Weston and me right now.

"Well, you know," Alex says mischievously, wiggling his eyebrows. "It was just obvious! Right? Wasn't it obvious?"

His voice starts getting higher and higher, as if he's desperate for either one of us to tell him that he's right. I meet eyes with a smirking Weston, who winks at me as if saying we should mess with Alex as much as we can.

"I don't know what you're talking about," I say with a shrug, tearing my gaze from Weston.

"Yeah, man," Weston agrees. "I think maybe you were just imagining things."

Alex huffs impatiently. "I definitely *was not*! I know for damn sure I didn't imagine that black eye you gave me!"

Weston chuckles. "That's 'cause you were trying to take advantage! Not 'cause I was jealous."

"Yeah, right," Alex huffs. "I know I wasn't totally in the right, but no one would've reacted the way you did unless they were emotionally invested. I know that much."

"Oh yeah?" I laugh. "How do you know that? You some kind of relationship guru?"

"*'Cause it was obvious!*" he cries, throwing his arms up in exasperation.

"Alex, dude!" a deep voice suddenly calls out from behind our seat, making me jump.

"Yeah, man?" he responds, both he and I craning our necks back so that we can face the rest of the bachelor party sitting in the booth behind us.

Directly behind us is the groom, whose name I don't remember, a blond guy on the shorter side, and a tall, lanky guy that I don't think I was ever actually introduced to.

He seems to be the most drunk out of the four at the table, so when his gaze meets mine and he says, "You're hot, dude," I can't help but giggle.

"Thanks, hon," I say with a sweet smile, patting him on the shoulder.

Turning my attention to the blond guy talking with Alex, I hear him in the middle of saying, "...need to get on the road soon. It's a Saturday, so parking's going to be a bitch."

"Where are we going?" the groom asks, sounding just a tad bit apprehensive.

"None ya business, Holmes," the lanky guy who called me hot says, pushing lightly against his friend's shoulder.

Alex says, "Let me go pay and then we can head out."

The three guys other than the groom voice their approval at the plan, and Alex turns back to Weston and me. Placing his hands on the tabletop crowded with empty beer bottles and shot glasses, he whispers to us, "Going to Bourbon. Y'all in?"

My eyes widen in surprise that he's even thought to invite us along, but when I look over to Weston to gauge his reaction, he's already answering, "Nah, man, we don't want to intrude."

"No intrusion!" he insists. "Seriously. It'd be fun! We have a room down there, and since it's not a holiday or anything y'all could probably get one at the same hotel."

Having to completely focus on putting my attention toward giving a reason as to why I'm opposed to going to one of the most fun streets in the country *and* sharing a hotel room with the guy I'm slightly obsessed with, I shake my head and say, "It's totally fine. Besides, I'd feel weird being the only girl."

"But you're a *cool* girl," Alex emphasizes, before saying deviously, "and since you and Weston have absolutely nothing going on between y'all, I could hook you up with Mark. Nice guy."

"Go pay the fucking bill, Alex," Weston cuts in, and when I see the slightly possessive glint in his expression, I can't help but feel immeasurable contentment.

Alex shoots me a quick wink before he climbs out of the table and heads across the now empty diner to where Meg's standing at the podium.

Biting down on my bottom lip to keep from grinning too hard, I look down at the checkered tabletop and then think to say, "You can go if you want, you know. You don't have to feel bad about leaving me."

He shrugs, saying matter-of-factly, "I'd rather hang with you."

"Really?" I blurt, my heart skipping a beat.

"Why do you sound so surprised?" he asks after taking a swig of his beer. "I've made it clear that I don't hate you."

"Well yeah," I say dumbly, adrenaline pumping as I try to fathom something to say. "But I just.... Even if you don't hate me, I still didn't think you'd choose me over going to party on Bourbon Street."

"Do you want me to go?" he asks after a moment, his voice sharp as he finally looks me in the eye.

I nearly roll my eyes. "Of course not! I just.... I mean...."

I'm cut off midbabble by Alex, his voice booming across the room as he asks, "Y'all ready to go get fucked up?"

The three groomsmen cheer together in response, the groom giving a much less convincing "woohoo" instead. His innocent reluctance makes me grin, and is probably well deserved if Alex is one of the guys in charge of his night.

As all of them move to get out of the booth, Alex sidesteps toward our table and looks between us. "Last chance, guys."

"Y'all have fun," I say as an answer, not even the thrill of New Orleans making me regret my choice to hang out with Weston instead.

The five of them then tell us goodbye, Alex pressing a friendly kiss to the top of my head and assuring me he'll keep in touch, while Weston and I tell them all to stay safe and to not corrupt the poor little groom too much.

Once they're gone, the atmosphere of the diner does a complete one-eighty, a peaceful yet somehow still loaded air taking over. I reach forward and take a sip of my lukewarm beer, nerves settling in my stomach even though I've had enough to drink this evening to keep them gone.

I must make a face at the warmth of it, though, as Weston asks, "You want another?"

"No, I think I'm good," I answer, despite knowing that it'd probably make hanging out with him easier. "If I have too many it upsets my stomach."

"You think food might help?" he asks. "You haven't really eaten since you got here."

He's right, seeing as how I only had a small handful of the fries the groom got for their table, and the concern he has over it has me eagerly wanting to say yes. "Yeah, that's probably a good idea."

"Hey, Meg!" he calls, waving her over.

She's been uncharacteristically noninvasive since I got here, so busy with other patrons that she hasn't given us any attention, which, of course, is more than fine with me.

"You guys doing okay?" she asks, reaching forward to pick up the empty glasses.

"Yeah, but I think we're going to get some burgers to go, if that's cool?" he asks, casting a quick glance over at me as if checking that that's okay.

I give him a slight smile, nodding my approval.

"'Course," she answers. "Y'all going somewhere?"

"Yeah," Weston answers, drumming his thick fingertips against the table. "We've been here so long I think my ass has made a permanent impression."

"At least it's a cute ass," she jokes, and then follows that up by asking us what we want on our burgers.

She makes her way back toward the kitchen, and I look over at Weston and ask curiously, "Where are we going?"

"My front porch," he says. "I thought it was going to rain today so I left Thumper inside, and the poor dude's probably cursing me right now. That okay?"

"Yeah, that's fine," I answer wholeheartedly, the idea of being away from the town's curious eyes already relieving some of the pressure in my gut. "Are you okay to drive, you think?"

"Mhmm." He nods, and then after a couple of seconds of pondering, he says, "Well, maybe you should drive."

"I can do that." I smile.

"I'm sorry 'bout this," he says, a slight blush caressing his cheeks. "I'd get us a cab, but I don't want it to be that asshole from before. 'Member him?"

"Oh my gosh, yes!" I laugh, clapping my hands. "That was so crazy! I don't think I've ever told someone off like I did that night. And I don't think I've ever seen you that mad either. Except for Labor Day, maybe."

I add in the Labor Day comment selfishly, wondering if he'll bring up what happened. Despite how their fight escalated and the complaints from patrons, I'm still pretty smug that Weston got that overwrought over me.

"Yeah, Labor Day was bad," he says, lifting his hand to pick at a peeling nail bed.

"Everyone said he deserved it," I tell him, wanting to ease his apparent guilt. "Hell, my dad still talks about how awesome it was."

"That's 'cause it's you," he points out. "Which automatically means Meg, your dad, and half the town are on our side."

Fighting the urge to bask in how damn delicious "our" sounds coming from his mouth, I say, "Exactly. The other half can either get the fuck over it or go eat at Denny's."

He laughs, the light filtering back into his expression, but right as I see it, it starts to fade again. Solemnly, he asks, "How're things with you and Jenny, by the way? I've been meaning to ask."

"We haven't really talked," I tell him truthfully, hating how disappointed that makes him look. "But I blame 100 percent of that on her, West. Technically, I didn't do anything wrong, so the fact that she's acting as if I did just proves maybe she wasn't as good a friend as I thought. Yeah, Campbell is her brother and I get her loyalty there, but she didn't have to let that interfere with our friendship."

"Y'all were close, though," he says.

"At first, yeah, but... but not recently, okay? And none of that's your fault. Hell, that's probably more my fault than yours—"

"What?" he asks, sounding confused. "Why?"

"I don't... I don't know if she told you any of this, but... but after Campbell and I split, he told her that he thought there was something between you and me, West."

"What? Seriously?" he asks, the gears in his mind evidently going to work to put the pieces all together.

Sometimes I forget that even though he was front and center in a lot of my recent issues, he wasn't aware. He had no idea how torn I was between my feelings for him and my friendship with Jenny. He didn't know that I spent every minute I was with Campbell combating thoughts of what it'd be like to be with him instead, and he didn't know that Jenny blamed her insecurities on me.

Then it hits me.

If he didn't know all of this stuff, if he didn't know how much

I put myself through just *thinking* about how much I liked him, then maybe he hasn't been as bad to me as I've thought all this time.

Deciding to comb through all of that later, though, not wanting to jeopardize the time I actually have with him, I nod and say, "Yeah. She ignored me for a little while there after we broke up, and I thought it was because of that, but then she told me it was actually 'cause Campbell put the idea in her head that we had something going on."

"Damn," he breathes, placing an elbow on the table and resting his chin in his work-blistered palm. "I mean, it makes sense and everything what with how she was so eager for double dates, and then all of a sudden your name got brought up and it was like I'd said Voldemort or something."

"Are you kidding?"

"Nope." He shakes his head. "And the timeline fits 'cause it was right after you and Campbell split."

After a silent moment, he asks, "What'd you tell her, when she asked that?"

"I didn't want to tell her at first," I respond, thinking about how conflicted I'd been. "But, I mean, she was flipping out so I kind of just blurted it out. I told her about four years ago, but then I said that nothing else had happened and she had nothing to be worried about."

He nods. "Yeah, she was really good at making you say stuff you didn't want to."

Not knowing if I should feel guilty or not with the way we're talking about her, I add, "She did really like you, though. That's why I always brought her up, just 'cause... I don't know. She was my friend, I thought it was the right thing to do."

"Yeah, I know," he says. "She was way more invested in the whole thing than I was, and at first it didn't get to me, but then... then I don't know. She got really territorial, almost kind of desperate. I felt bad, dumping her like I did, but I just.... I'd been looking for a way out for a while and it just felt like the right time."

"Yeah, you punching the lights out of her brother definitely made for a good opportunity," I say sarcastically, a huge smile stretching across my mouth when resounding laughter spills out of him.

The sound of the kitchen door swinging open cuts through his laughter, and when I see the two brown paper bags already stained with grease in Meg's hands, my stomach lets out a huge gurgle.

"Here you babes go," she says once she gets closer to the table, placing the bags down in front of us. "It's on the house, 'kay?"

"Meg, no," Weston immediately protests, shifting in his seat so he can grab the wallet out of his back pocket. "All those drinks, I can't—"

"Oh, those drinks were paid for," Meg says with a wave of her hand. "So it's just two burgers, and next time you can leave me a kick-ass tip if you want."

"All those drinks?" I ask, my eyes wide in shock. "Seriously?"

"Yeah." She nods. "That guy who was sitting with y'all paid for them. Told me to tell y'all not to make the black eye you gave him worthless. Had no idea what he meant by that."

"We do," Weston and I say at the exact same time, and give each other impish smiles.

"Yeah, well...." Meg trails off, looking between us with the brightest of grins on her face. "You two just leave, okay? If you leave any money on this table, I'm putting it in your burger next time you're here."

Weston chuckles. "Okay, okay. Thanks, Meg."

"Anytime, sweetie," she says, and then after she tells me she's cooking for my dad and me tomorrow night and invites Weston along as well, she's giving us hugs and disappearing back into the kitchen.

Weston hitches an eyebrow at me and I rise to my feet, then try not to blush when he yanks my to-go bag out of my hands.

Biting down on my lip yet again to keep from smiling at the gesture, I follow him out of the diner and can't seem to take my eyes off him, off his deliciously strong arms that were probably made for wrapping around a girl, off his wide shoulders and trim waist, off the soft blond hair curled up right at the base of his neck.

It feels just so *fucking* right to be doing this with him, to be leaving the diner with him, to be going back to his house to hang out and eat drunk food.

And it's not just his looks that get to me either, even though that's a very happy bonus.

It's the way he calls my dad "sir" no matter how many times he tells him not to, the way he rushed over without hesitation that day I fell through the porch, the way he called me the second he saw my mom just to check on me.

It's everything he does.

It's *him*.

We're out in the parking lot as they wash over me, the feelings I have for him, have had for him for years, and they hit me harder than the palpably oppressive evening humidity.

I've been pushing them down, quelling them to the best of my ability all summer, and it's been one of the hardest things I've ever had to do.

Ever since my mom left, it became second nature to me to keep people at arm's length, to keep them from infiltrating that spot in my heart she'd shattered. I never wanted to be hurt like that ever again, I never wanted to feel so unwanted and utterly worthless.

Since seeing him again this summer, hell since that kiss four years ago, I knew that Weston Alcorn would be the one to make me want to open that part again, and these past few hours here at the diner have only reiterated that.

Which is why, as I step toward the driver door of my car, the one that Weston's already pulled open for me, I can't bring myself to climb inside.

Instead I just stop moving, my feet firmly planted on the gravel

*Back to You*

lot beneath my Converse, and attempt to figure out what it is that I'm trying to accomplish here. I know I can't climb into my car with him like this evening didn't happen, like we didn't just act as if we were in an almost-relationship for the past few hours, but what do I... what do I do now?

"Iris?" he asks, the deepness of his voice making me snap my gaze up to his. His eyes are so firmly focused on me, the green in them completely unreadable, and it makes me start to shake.

"Yeah?" I barely manage to respond, my voice coming out hoarse and hardly audible.

Tonight *did* mean something to him too, right?

I roll my bottom lip into my mouth as we keep looking at each other, his eyes darkening and making me shake so much more that it looks like I'm shivering.

"You okay?" He takes a concerned step toward me.

And suddenly, just like that, my nerves are gone.

I'm completely still.

I can feel my heart pounding inside my chest, but other than that, all I'm conscious of is the man standing in front of me, the man I grew up only platonically aware of but still somehow became enraptured with.

"I just...," I start unsurely, my eyes flickering between his eyes and his mouth. "I really just want to...."

Without even realizing, I've reached out and grabbed his shirt, my grip so tight that I can feel my short fingernails through the cotton.

And then I'm shoving myself up on my tiptoes and yanking his chest toward me, everything I've felt, come to terms with, about him tonight swirling around me in a dense and insuppressible cloud.

There are no pleasantries once our lips meet, no hesitancies.

It's wild, rough, all at once, and so damn staggering that, mere moments into it, I feel my balance wavering and know it has absolutely nothing to do with the handful of drinks I've had tonight.

229

Weston must feel it too, the delirium our kiss is putting me under, and instead of releasing me from it, he just wraps his arms tight around me, his clenched fists digging into the small of my back to keep me steady, and then kisses me that much harder.

His breath is hot, wet, and as the kiss goes on it becomes even crazier, less thought-out, our tongues curling against each other, our teeth clashing, and our lips pressing together so hard that it turns into this strange and beautiful kind of almost pain.

I can't bring myself to drop my tight grip on his shirt, terrified it'll cause him to pull away, so instead I use my free hand to wrap around his neck and bring me upward, closer to him, and a rough groan escapes his throat as he bends down to keep his unyielding possession of my mouth.

It's four years ago all over again, but this time just *so* much better.

"West...." I pant for the split second our mouths are separated, him having pulled away and his swollen lips now hovering so close to mine that I can't stand it. I can feel the gears in his head moving, the rational part of him trying to make sense of all of this, but I can't wait for that.

I need to be kissing him again, to be an indiscernible part of him, so I thrust back upward and kiss him once more, my tongue wasting no time in pushing through his lips. He reacts immediately, the breath he'd gathered in that brief moment apart escaping into my mouth and making my hold on sanity falter so intensely that my grip around his neck becomes almost too severe.

"Iris," he grouses as he disentangles our mouths, his hands moving to my hips yet staying as bruisingly tight as they were moments ago. "I...."

"What?" I breathe out unsteadily, my eyes falling on his lips and finding the wetness on them, the pinkness, far too enticing.

"We just.... What is...?"

Completely abandoning any hold on self-control that I have, I boldly push my hips into his and whisper, "*Please* finish what you're going to say."

A nervous yet devious smile stretching that mouth of his, he says, "Before this goes any further, as much as I don't want to say it, I need to just... We need to make sure we're on the same page. I don't.... If you pull away from me again like you have this *adorable* little habit of doing, I don't think I'll be able to handle it."

Despite how blindly eager I am to continue what we were just doing, to abandon all rational thought and my overwhelming fear of not being enough, I find my chest warming at how cute it is that he's so unsure.

That self-doubt I've had around him all summer now momentarily diminished, I rise back up on my toes so that we're as eye to eye as his ridiculously tall frame allows, and then slide my palms across the rough sides of his neck and up to his cheeks before saying wholeheartedly, "I'm *so* all into this, West. No more running away."

"Thank fucking God," he groans right as he surges into me with another kiss.

Our mouths instinctively entangle together and the take-out bags he'd somehow managed to keep a hold on until now fall to the ground behind me, his fingertips digging in my back instead.

If he'd been at all irresolute about this before, he's making it entirely clear now that he's *all* into this as well. He's become the instigator, making the kisses hotter, deeper, the kind of kisses that aren't complete until they've ended in the bedroom.

But instead we're outdoors, in public, in our town which boasts absolutely zero privacy, so when we hear someone say, "Well, well, well... this looks quite familiar," we shouldn't be at all surprised.

We are though, springing apart like someone just tossed a hand grenade between us, and when I manage to overcome my shame to open my eyes, I see Mrs. Frederickson, the town gossip and the *same damn lady* to catch us on the front porch four years ago, standing across the parking lot in front of her navy blue Subaru.

Thank God it's just her, but the look she's giving me, that coy little smile that means this will be all around town by midnight tonight, has my cheeks blazing almost painfully.

We hadn't even heard her pull in, and the lot is loose gravel.

*Loud* loose gravel.

Good Lord.

"Mrs. Frederickson," Weston pipes up, and by his tone I know he's as embarrassed about this as I am. "How're you doing? Haven't seen you since Labor Day."

"That was just last week," she points out with a teasing smile, knowing he's trying to divert her attention. "But I've been doing pretty well, thanks for asking. Although we did just have to get Dixie treated for heartworm."

"I'm sorry to hear that," he says, taking a step closer to me, the heat rolling off his body somehow managing to calm me down.

"Yeah," she says. "But enough about me and more about this little show I just saw. I'm guessing that Jenny girl is out of the picture, Weston?"

"Uh, yes, ma'am," he answers uncomfortably.

"Good. As much as I…." She trails off, the sound of her car's passenger door slamming shut interrupting and making my heart drop.

Her best friend, one of the teachers from the high school, walks around the car and then stops when she sees us all talking, her eyes flickering between Weston and me as she gauges what's going on.

"Hey, Mrs. Jenkins," I greet her, not wanting any silence left open for Mrs. Frederickson to fill.

"Hey, Iris, honey." She smiles, stepping forward to give me a hug and then greeting Weston the exact same way. "Y'all leaving or staying? We're just 'bout to get a table."

"Leaving," I answer. "We've been in there for a while."

"Aww, that's too bad," she responds. "I miss hanging out with young people."

Weston and I laugh at that, coming off far more awkward than we'd like. My mind is racing to come up with something to say to get us out of here, but before I can figure something out, Weston says, "Well, we've got to get going. My dog's been locked up too long today."

"Bye, y'all," the two women say in sync, then giggle at each other.

They go to head inside and I'm just about to comment to Weston how direly mortified I am, but before I can Mrs. Frederickson decides to point out, "Hey, are those y'all's take-out bags on the ground?"

She's barely managing to contain her laughter, and I feel my cheeks burning even hotter as Weston calls out, "Nope, were here when we came out!"

"Okay then," she responds dubiously, the two of them pushing through the diner's front door and *finally* leaving us alone.

"Oh my God," I groan, pressing my palms against my cheeks as if it'll calm the redness. "That was so horrible."

"Um, yeah," Weston says dryly, leaning down and grabbing the still-closed take-out bags from the ground. "Let's get the hell out of here."

"Yes, please," I agree before letting him help me into my car.

My heart pounding, hormones surging, and my annual quota of humiliation having been met, I realize it may take me a while to get back to the semi-levelheaded state I was in earlier in the diner.

It only worsens when Weston slides into the passenger seat and shuts us inside my car, the smell of his cologne, deodorant, or whatever the hell he wears to make him smell so good filling the space.

It seems so much more real now, the weight of what just happened out there and what it may mean for us now. Now that Mrs. Frederickson has squashed the rush of things yet *again,* and now that we're in my car to head to our empty homes, all the baggage that could

233

accompany this thing with Weston hits me.

Like the fact that if this ends up badly I may never recover.

Or the fact that I have so much else going on in my life right now that adding anything else on, especially something like a new relationship, may be too much.

But then I look over at him and find him already looking at me, a soft smile touching his kiss-swollen lips and his eyes such a beautiful, compassionate light green, and realize that I don't care about any of that.

I don't fucking care.

All I need is him, that's it, and all the baggage that may come along, all the issues that may arise... none of it matters.

I need him.

It's as simple as that.

"You okay?" he asks, a little wrinkle etching itself above his nose as if he's worried I'm overthinking things.

My whole body deflates, the stress that my overthinking caused escaping as naturally as an exhale, and I give him a reassuring smile back. "I'm perfect, West."

# Chapter Nineteen

Thumper is understandably pissed at Weston when we walk into his house.

The second after Weston unlocked his door, the large golden retriever bounded over to us and instead of jumping up and attacking us with hugs like I've seen him do, he just sat in front of us with the most serious expression on his face and let out a loud, "how dare you?" bark.

"I know, man," Weston tells Thumper like he's talking to another human, kneeling in front of the dog and reaching up to pet his face. "I'm sorry."

At first Thumper turns his face away, but after a few more minutes of Weston petting him and whispering to him how sorry he is, Thumper apparently forgives him and leaps onto his bent, outstretched thighs and starts licking his face.

Weston chuckles before straightening and grabbing my wrist, saying softly, "I'm going to take him out then I'll be right back. There's drinks in the fridge."

"Okay," I say, feeling almost shy.

Just under half an hour ago I was throwing myself at him like someone with no inhibitions, but now that we're here at his house, alone, I'm feeling strangely domestic and loving it more than I care to admit to myself. I can't seem to bring back that bold girl from before.

He gives me a small smile before turning away, calling out excitedly to Thumper, "You wanna go outside, boy?"

Once they let themselves out and after I grab a bottle of water from his nearly empty fridge, I look around the generously sized living room. The past few times I've been here I haven't really had the chance.

Despite this house having belonged to his parents first, everything in here just screams Weston.

Strong hardwood floors, a light shade of hunter green on the walls, a matching set of a beige loveseat and sofa with a striped recliner in the corner by the fireplace. Other than a framed picture of Weston and Marcus when they were little on the mantle and the dog bed with a little crate of chew toys next to it by the back door, there's nothing really that personal or ornamental.

The house is tidy, durable, with no frills.

Just like Weston.

When he walks back in, a much more content-looking Thumper trotting behind him, I curiously ask, "Was all the stuff in here from your parents? Or did you get it after they left? I can't really remember from before."

He furrows his brows at me, probably confused at the randomness of the question, but nonetheless he answers, "No, it's mostly mine. They brought most of the old stuff with them to Florida."

As I nod, he asks, "Why do you ask?"

I shrug, trying not to be embarrassed. "I don't know, I was thinking that this house just kind of *looks* like it belongs to you, you know?"

"Yeah?" He grabs himself a bottle of water and crosses the floor to me. "What's that look like, then?"

Seeing the amusement twinkling in his eyes has my cheeks burning. "I don't know! It just does, I guess. Clean, sturdy looking...."

"Wow." He chuckles, taking a sip of his water and looking me dead in the eye. "I'm almost a bit insulted if that's all you can think of to describe me."

My cheeks flushing even harder, I roll my eyes and say, "Shut up, West, you know what I mean. It was a compliment. I like it here."

"I like *you* here," he responds softly, and my heart gives a solid, heavy thump in my chest.

"Yeah?" I manage to croak out.

He sets his bottle of water down on the countertop and then takes the few steps to me, reaching out to jerk me forward so that our bodies are pressed up against each other.

"After what you just pulled in the parking lot," he starts, his eyes lit up with amusement as he tucks a piece of my hair behind my ear, "you can still stand here and be awkward with me?"

My gaze ducking down in shame, I almost whine, "I'm not *trying* to—"

"Iris." He laughs, his rough fingertips grazing my skin as he lifts my chin up. "What's—"

His eyes intent on me, I admit quietly, "*You.* West, this, this whole thing... it's terrif—"

Cutting me off, he murmurs, "C'mere," and before I know it, my eyes are closed and he's kissing me and it's just as incredible as it was before. It's soft and comforting, slow and reassuring, and when his mouth opens to deepen it, my inhibitions are nowhere to be found.

Instead, my hands are coming up and gripping his shoulders, my feet straining my weight upward so that I'm as close to his mouth as I can be. His tongue brushes along my bottom lip and I let out a breathy sigh, his arms tightening around me.

Moments later when he pulls away, he says, "I'm done with

the shit we've been pulling all summer, Iris. You've been tiptoeing around me, I've been doing the same thing, and I'm sick of it. One conversation could have made this happen the day you got back in town."

His aggressive tone, the boldness, and the fire in his eyes have my lower stomach clenching in the most pleasurable of ways.

"Really?" I manage to breathe, most of my functioning self still lost swimming in that kiss he just laid on me. "That very day?"

"If you had been wearing those cut-off shorts you like to run around in, you're damn right that very day."

I can't help but giggle. "Yeah, right. You nearly ran away from me that day at Walmart."

"'Cause you were wearing those damn shorts!" he argues playfully, his grip on me tightening. "And don't even get me started on when you started working and wearing those heels."

"Really?" I grin even harder. "The heels did it for you, huh?"

"*You* do it for me," he admits, the humor in his voice calming down and making my heart squeeze. "Even when it pissed me off to no end that I did, I always had a thing for you, Iris. That never went away."

"I'm sorry that liking me pissed you off," I say, grabbing his forearms. "I should've told you I was leaving that next day. I just.... It never really occurred to me that you could actually like me, you know?"

"Hey," he whispers, catching on to my serious tone. "Let's not hash all this out tonight, okay? It's been a long day."

"Okay," I agree, my hands squeezing his arms. "But I just... I really liked you, West. I don't think I was ever actually aware of it, but I did.... I always liked you. I... I still like you."

"Yeah?" he asks quietly. His face is still so close to mine that when he smiles, this huge beaming smile that warms me to my core, I can practically feel it.

"Mhmm." I gulp. "That's why... it's why I'm so weird around you."

"You must like me *a lot* then," he teases.

My earlier desire to talk everything out having evaporated the minute his lips came within an inch of my own, I'm now focused only on him as I reach up to trail my fingers across his stubbly jawline, his eyes darkening to a near black.

I nod. "A lot, a lot."

And then his lips are back on mine, soft, tentative, everything that our earlier kiss in the parking lot wasn't, but still just as beautiful. It's so natural, so effortless, to fade into him and his kisses, his warmth.

He pulls away just a second later and the whimper it tugs from me is humiliating, but it only makes his lazy smile stretch further.

His palm coming up to cup my cheek, he asks jokingly, "Are we done talking for tonight?"

I smile. "I really fucking hope so."

------------

And true to both our wishes, no more serious talking was done for the rest of the night.

Well, the rest of the night being the one hour that we managed to stay awake after we'd agreed to leave the tiring conversations for another time.

After trying to make up for more than four years of missed kissing opportunities, we cuddled up on the couch with the intention to watch a few episodes of *The Office* on Netflix, and then passed out on a blanket pallet on the living room floor just ten minutes into the first episode.

It was a completely innocent night since we both knew how much we still needed to talk over everything, but being with him like that, actually acting on the feelings we have for each other, was better and more natural than I ever thought it'd be.

Which is why, when I wake up the next morning, my stomach

pressed to the floor and my cheek to a pillow, Weston's arm draped low over the small of my back and his nose buried in my hair, I don't feel like I shouldn't be here. Instead I feel comfortable, at home, and incredibly warm.

Weston must still be sleeping, his breath steadily blowing against the back of my ear, but as I go to adjust more comfortably against him, Thumper's big brown eyes meet mine from across the room and he lets out a small whine.

Biting down on my bottom lip to contain the giant smile the past two minutes of consciousness have brought me, I uselessly mouth at Thumper, "I'm coming, I'm coming."

After moving carefully so as to not wake Weston up, I tiptoe over to where Thumper's in his bed and pat my thigh, whispering, "Come on, boy."

He understands, quietly following me outside.

I watch as he uses the bathroom and then decide to prolong our time out here so that he doesn't go back in and wake up Weston.

So instead of going back indoors, I take advantage of an orange rubber ball I find in the middle of the grass and play fetch with him, the whole thing making me feel strangely content. I feel at peace, domesticated, and yet exuberantly happy, and the fact that I know the hot guy I'm in love with is asleep just one wall away has no comparison.

I love it.

"Hey," a deep, almost hoarse voice sounds from behind me, causing me to jump.

When I turn around I see Weston standing there, adorable sleep lines etched into his face, hair mussed in every direction, and lips curved into a smile as he laughs at me.

I swat his taut stomach with the back of my hand and scold, "Don't sneak up on me like that!"

"I'm sorry, I'm sorry." He grins, but I know by the sparkling in his eyes that he's not being truthful. "I figured you would've heard the door."

"Well, you figured *wrong*," I say, trying my best to sound mad but failing the second he darts his hands out to my waist and yanks me toward him.

Once I'm pressed against him and feeling *very* awake, he reaches out and fingers a piece of my hair that's escaped my bun. His eyes, somehow managing to be bright and sparkling mere moments after waking up, meet mine as he says, "You look good out here."

"Yeah?" I ask with a smile, leaning into his touch.

"Mhmm." He nods, his face a soft kind of serious. "You fit."

I smile in agreement, the comfort I feel such a dramatic change from before, and then thread my arms around his waist so I can slip my hand up the back of his shirt. "We didn't wake you up, did we?"

"Nah, you didn't," he replies. "I'm usually up by six in the morning anyway."

"What time is it now? I didn't even think to look."

"Around nine or so," he answers, stroking his thumb across my jawline. "What time does your dad get back?"

"Plane lands at two," I tell him, recalling the texts I exchanged with my dad yesterday morning before I saw my mom and everything went to shit. "Meg's going to try to get out of the diner to go pick him up, but if she can't I'm going to."

"You can stay here till then?" he asks, sounding strangely vulnerable, as if maybe last night's sleep made me change my mind about everything.

I give him a ridiculously wide smile in response, hopefully easing his worries. "If you want me to."

"Damn right I want you to," he murmurs, yanking me even closer to him so he can close the gap between our mouths.

Immediately he's swiping his tongue across my lower lip, and the second I open my mouth to him, he's showing me just *how much* he wants me to stay. I can barely keep up with him, my toes digging into the damp grass to keep my mouth level with his, and my hands retreating to his front to fist his shirt tightly.

Needing to breathe, I pull back and ask through panting breath, "Are you always this... *lively* in the morning?"

"Aww, babe," he coos patronizingly, his breathing seeming completely unaffected and his grin stretching incredibly hard. "Can you not keep up, little Iris?" he teases, his fingers brushing the fabric of my shirt up so that he can trail them along the skin right above my waistline. "It's okay... we can practice."

"Shut the fuck up!" I argue playfully, shoving on his shoulder and causing him to lean back a little bit.

He's chuckling when he takes that little step toward me, and once he's back against me, I smile deviously at the feel of him. Slyly rolling my hips, I can feel his not-so-slight excitement brush against me and, hearing the slight catch of his breath, I meet his gaze and grin. "What was that, *babe*?"

His cheeks turn the lightest shade of pink as he dips his head down, his lips pressing to mine just a handful of times before he pulls back to whisper in my ear, "Shhhhh, don't be mean."

Then he releases his tight hold on me, steps back, and asks, "You hungry?"

"Depends," I say, "I'm not cooking, am I?"

He rolls his eyes at me, but then presses a kiss to the top of my head. "I wouldn't offer, then make you cook. Give me some credit here, Iris."

"Sorry! I didn't see any food in your fridge last night, so I just assumed you didn't cook."

"I really only keep breakfast food here," he says, extending a hand to lead me back inside.

Once Thumper trots in behind us, Weston shuts the door and explains, "There's a little sandwich place next door to my work that we're doing small renovations on, so they're paying us in lunches. And by the time I get off it's late and I'm too tired to cook, so I just grab takeout."

"Oh," I muse, following him into the kitchen and feeling my heart jump in excitement when I see his coffee machine. Instead of sitting at the dining table, I cross the kitchen and ask, "Can I make a cup of coffee? I'll make you one too."

"Duh, of course you can," he scoffs, as if that should be obvious. "And yes, please."

We both go quiet as he starts on the food and I start on the coffee machine, and after asking how he likes his and fixing up each of our respective cups, I take a seat at the table and fold my legs underneath me.

After my first few sips, when I feel an actual energy start to bubble inside me, I ask, "So how'd you get to be the boss where you are? With you being so young and all that."

"I started working there part-time during high school, so when I started looking for full-time after graduation, they offered me a spot already pretty high up so I wouldn't leave and they wouldn't have to train someone else. I was in really well with the previous owner, but he eventually wanted to retire and a larger company wanted to buy us out. He sold it to them with the catch that they had to keep me on as a project manager, which is a pretty up-there position."

Swallowing a large gulp of coffee, I ask, "Wouldn't that annoy the new people?"

"Oh yeah." He nods with a chuckle. "That and the fact that I hate being stuck at a desk so I'm not always reachable by phone. But, you know, fuck them."

I giggle. "So can they, like, not fire you or anything? Since having you as project manager was in the contract when they bought y'all out?"

"They can only fire me if I do something illegal," he explains.

"Or if something I do causes a minimum of a fifteen-thousand-dollar loss. So as long as I'm not a total dipshit, I have my job."

"That's awesome, West, and so damn lucky. Do you still talk to the old owner? Since y'all were so close?"

"He died three months after the purchase went through. It was so shitty. He... he'd just moved to North Carolina, I think, 'cause his grandkids were there and everything. He'd just gotten settled in his house there when he had a heart attack, killed him instantly."

"West...," I breathe, hating that he's had to go through so much pain. Twice.

"Iris, it's fine," he tells me reassuringly, giving me a small smile over from where he's stirring egg goop in a frying pan. "That was years ago. I've made peace with it."

"Yeah, I get that." I relent, not wanting to talk about it anymore if it's going to upset him. After a couple of silent moments, I ask, "You need any help with food?"

Lips pursed, he looks over at me and teases, "I thought you didn't want to cook?"

"Well, I didn't," I say, "but now I have coffee in me and feel useless."

"You can grab some plates for us?" he offers, pointing the spatula to a cabinet to the left of the stove. "The food's done for the most part. You like cheese on your eggs?"

As I give him a wholehearted yes as my answer, I go to find two paper plates so no one will have to do the dishes, put them on the table, and then see that Weston is already walking over to put food on them.

When we're about halfway through and have made enough conversation about food for a morning, Weston randomly asks me, "So are you still okay if I come to dinner at y'all's tonight?"

"Yeah," I answer dumbly, having forgotten the invitation Meg extended to him last night. "Why wouldn't I be?"

"Well... 'cause your dad's going to be there," he starts off before taking a sip of his coffee. "And I think we need to figure out what... what *this* is before we bring it around him, you know?"

"Oh yeah," I say, feeling my nerves start to churn my newly eaten food at the thought of having to define our relationship right here and now, mere hours after we'd only kissed each other. "Yeah... you're right."

I can feel him looking intently at me, as if he's trying to read my mind when, in all honesty, I don't even know how I feel about all of this.

"I'm *in* this, Iris," he says quietly, as if he knew I needed to hear it, and when I'm able to look at him, I see his cheeks blushing just the slightest shade of pink. "I just... you know how the people here are. I don't want to give them the chance to ruin this before it's even really started, to scare you off."

"*West.*" I sigh, feeling guilt hit the bottom of my stomach like an anchor.

Without thinking, I rise out of my chair and go around to the other side of the table, Weston already reading me and scooting his chair back to offer up his lap.

I slide onto him, the heat that always seems to radiate off him warming me to the bone, and before I can say anything, he speaks up. "I'm not bitter about it, Iris. Looking back at it, I get why you left and why you were the way you were this summer. And we're here now, okay? No harm, no foul."

"Do you really get it, though?" I ask, my hesitance at opening up to him now deep and unreachable.

If I want him like this forever, if I want to keep having mornings waking up next to him and playing fetch with Thumper and making us coffee while he cooks breakfast, I have to stop being such a fucking coward. In these past few hours, he's opened up to me, showed his vulnerabilities more than I ever thought he would, and I have to reciprocate.

Fingering the short sleeve of his worn shirt, I say, "I'm not going to go into it all this morning, 'cause Lord knows how long that'd take, but... I just... I'm.... You *have* to know why I acted the way I did."

After tightening an arm around my waist to keep me on his lap and pressing a comforting kiss to the top of my head, he urges softly into my ear, "Tell me, then."

Looking down at his floor, I start, "That kiss, West, when we were on the porch, when you came up and comforted me, no questions asked, even though we'd barely ever spoken in our lives—I just, something hit me, then. It should've been the most awkward thing in the world and it wasn't... it just wasn't, and it wasn't until months later that I realized why.

"You just... I think...." I giggle nervously, not knowing how to put density of my feelings for him into words without coming off as too pathetic.

"I get it, Iris," he assures me, his rough fingers grasping at my jawline so that I'll look at him. "It's... it's hard to explain." He chuckles, his eyes so soft that it has me feeling like maybe I'm not this crazy, emotional mess. Like maybe he feels as strongly as I do. "But I get what you mean."

"Yeah." I'm so damn glad that I don't have to try and make sense of it, of the feeling that we should've been like this, together, long, long ago.

"So while I was gone, West, while I was at school, that kiss became this huge thing in my head. I mean, obviously it'd been a huge thing to me when it happened, but then as I thought more about it, I... I realized how much it *helped* me through everything I was going through with my mom. It got my mind off it. It.... I don't know, it helped me *breathe,* if that makes any sense."

"It does." He smiles, his lips so soft as they press a kiss to the spot right below my ear. "Keep talking. I like this story."

Not even bothering to fight the grin his words coax out of me,

I continue, "So, anyway, I'd built it into this huge thing and yadda yadda yadda... and, I don't know, when I saw you on your porch that first day I was back and realized I was still affected, I was... terrified, naturally. I think I mentioned that yesterday."

He chuckles at my newfound humor of the whole situation. "You did."

"And, you know, because I'm this huge coward and all that stuff, and was scared you and I'd get to talking and I'd realize that kiss didn't mean as much to you as it did to me, I just.... I avoided talking to you, being around you. Which, apparently, I'm really super good at."

"You're a pro, sweetie," he teases.

When those words come out of his mouth, that sweet little name he's never called me, I can't help but look him in the eye and smile, a smile so damn big and cheesy that I'd be embarrassed if he weren't mirroring it right back at me.

Suddenly wanting to get this conversation over and kiss the hell out of him, I look away from his gaze so I can focus. "So that's why... it's why I was so damn spastic around you. It's why I could never look you in the eye, and why I ran that night in my dad's kitchen, and... and why in your driveway that night when you asked me if I was okay, I straight-out lied to you, because if I said how *not* okay I was with the whole you and Jenny thing, it'd all come out. And you'd know everything. And then... I don't know... and then you'd be able to hurt me."

"Hurt you?" he asks after a silent few moments, raising my face to his once more.

His strong dirty-blond brows furrowed, his eyes narrowed at me in a soft sort of way, he asks, "What're you...? Iris, if there's one thing I've made clear this summer, it's that I'd never go out of my way to hurt you."

"I know that now," I attest, hoping that he believes me. "Looking back at it now, you were always there. When I fell through the porch and I made you leave the hospital 'cause I'm a raging bitch, when you... when you talked me through the Dad and Meg thing, when you punched Alex, when you punched Campbell, I...." I trail off and cast a teasing look his way. "You start a lot of fights over me, mister."

He chuckles, not even looking slightly embarrassed when he defends himself. "I'm not the most rational person when it comes to you, okay?"

"I'm cool with that," I assure him, squeezing his arm. "*Very* cool with that. Although you never did tell me what you walked in on Campbell and Jenny talking about that made you so mad."

He groans, tipping his head back. "*No*, Iris, I really don't want to bring that up. It'll only upset you."

"No it won't," I urge, my curiosity over the whole thing having been killing me since it happened. "How could I possibly be unhappy right now, West? I never really liked Campbell, if I'm being honest, and Jenny's already on my shit list, so...."

His head pops back up at my words, his eyes pinning me with a glare. "You never liked him?"

Feeling a bit confused by his sudden animosity, I say slowly, "No....?"

"I had to put up with the shit of y'all being together and you didn't even *like* him?"

"Wouldn't that make it better for you, though, now? Knowing it wasn't real?"

"No!" he argues, laughter slowly starting to spill out of him. "I didn't know that when it was happening, so I had to watch that—"

I cut him off. "Hey, hey! I had to watch you and Jenny for so much longer than you had to watch me with Campbell. And I was friends with her, so I had to constantly hear about it!"

He playfully rolls his eyes at me, shaking his head as he says, "Nope, no way, not the same. I had it so much worse."

"Bullshit!" I yelp, smacking his arm. "I know for damn sure Campbell didn't come to you for sex advice like Jenny did to me, so, you know, just for that I win!"

"She did what now?" He gapes, a blush appearing in splotches across his neck.

"Yes!" I bellow, loving that I'm getting to throw the hell I went through in his face. "She'd come to me whining about how you wouldn't have sex with her and asking what she could do to convince you and all this stuff, and it... it was terrible, Weston! You don't even know the shit I went through when y'all were together!"

"Okay, okay," he says, his voice giving away his defeat. "You had it worse. But still, that soup asshole pissed me off to no end."

"Yeah, well," I say, feeling almost ashamed about dating the guy even if it was just for a handful of weeks. "I learned my mistake, okay? So, as a present, you should *totally* tell me what they were talking about."

"Okay, I'll tell you, but just... just don't let it get to you, okay? I'm done with the drama. I just want.... I just want to be me and you. No bullshit."

The smile I've had on my face for about ten minutes now stretching even wider, I say, "Deal. No bullshit."

"Okay, so," he starts, tightening his arm around me so he can adjust himself in the wooden chair. "When I walked back there, it was honestly just to ask Jenny why the hell she didn't at least warn you that Soupy would be there. But then I see the two of them talking and their sides are to me so they can't see me. Jenny was actually standing up for you, and getting onto him for having you cornered?"

"Yeah," I clarify with a nod, answering his unspoken question. "He came up to me when I was leaving the bathroom and backed me against a wall. He was just being a stupid drunk, but it... I don't know, it was really uncomfortable. Thank God Jenny walked in."

His expression darkens severely at my words, and I feel his

fingertips press harder into the skin of my hip.

"So, uh," he continues after a tense moment, having to clear his throat, "he started defending himself for having cornered you and then... and then he brought up having pressured you in his car, and that that's why you ended things?"

"Yeah." I nod, the hesitancy in his words confusing me a little bit. "Didn't you... didn't you already know that? Jenny told you, huh?"

"No, she didn't," he says grimly. "Which.... I mean, I get that that's something strange to bring up to the guy you're dating, but it just... knowing that she knew and didn't tell me *lit me up*, Iris. Yeah, maybe she was insecure about your and my friendship, but... but still. She saw me that night at the Boot, she knew I was protective of you, and she should've—"

"She probably knew you'd kill her brother," I tell him. "And she's... I don't have siblings so I'm not too sure, but I know how I am with my dad, and they're super close in age, so it's probably crazy strong how protective she gets over him. Even if he *is* an ass."

"Yeah, but still," he says, still seeming angry. "In my head she was throwing you under the bus and sticking up for the guy who would've taken advantage of you if he'd had the chance."

"I get it." I smile, finding his blind savior-like mindset toward me incredibly attractive. "But, anyway, finish the story."

"Long story short," he says, "he was defending what he did, saying that you wanted it but were just scared, saying that you owed it to him, that... that he just had to get you a little more warmed up to him. And then Jenny, she... she was saying the right shit, telling him how wrong it was that he thought that way. Then... then she completely ruined it 'cause she said you weren't worth it and then called you frigid and immature. *Because you wouldn't fuck her brother.* How fucked-up is that?"

The hostility in his voice grows with every word that comes out of his mouth, and by the time he's done talking, I can't even find my own anger at what the Turner siblings said about me. Instead I only feel this overwhelming need to calm him down, to make him see that I'm entirely okay.

So that's why I don't think twice when I sling my left leg over his lap and turn so that I'm straddling him, my face a hair's breadth from his own. After sliding my arms over his shoulders, I press a lingering kiss to his mouth to prove to him how utterly *okay* I am with how everything's turned out.

If he hadn't overheard them that day, then maybe he wouldn't have broken up with Jenny and we wouldn't be where we are right now, with his arms tight around me and his fingertips hot on my bare skin.

So I pull away from him and say brazenly, "I'm glad they said that, and I'm glad you heard them. Without the two of them, you and I may never have grown the nerve or gotten the opportunity to end up here. Like this."

"Really?" he asks, seemingly a little concerned. "You don't think this ever would've happened if not for them?"

I smirk at him. "I'm just trying to turn the whole situation into a positive, okay? You should do the same before you end up punching someone else and end up in jail."

His expression lightening up considerably, he grins and says, "I'm friends with half the police force, Iris. I'm not going to jail, trust me."

"Well, whatever," I say carelessly. "No matter how hot it is, I don't like you getting in fights over me. Too much drama. And we promised no more of that, right?"

"You think I'm hot?"

I roll my eyes at him. "I don't consider myself a shallow person, West, but trust me when I say I'm *very* okay with your looks."

"I think you're pretty hot too," he says with a teasing smile that's entirely too large. "If it makes you feel any better."

I laugh loudly, happily, my arms around his neck tightening as I say, "It does."

We're both silent for a good while, soaking up how it feels to be with each other like this and giving our minds a chance to process everything that's just been talked about. It's not even halfway into the day yet and I'm already mentally spent and thinking about my need for another cup of coffee, but I know that this conversation just opened a world of opportunity for the two of us.

"Hey," he says softly, cutting into the silence and making my eyes snap up. Soft green vulnerability looking back at me, he questions, "We're good, right? All of this means we're okay?"

To answer him, I just lean my head against his shoulder, his hand immediately coming up to stroke my back.

Smiling against him, I say, "We're so good, West."

# Chapter Twenty

"Oh God," my dad's voice announces into his living room later that afternoon, when he and Meg walk through the front door and he spots me sitting on the couch. "You're still here?"

Rolling my eyes at his need to make an entrance, I climb off the couch and hurry over to him, wrapping the tall, slender man in a hug.

Ignoring his dig at me, I just whisper into his shirt, "Hey, Dad."

"Hey, booger," he greets back, this time much more affectionately. "I missed you."

Pulling away from him, I say back, "I missed you too. Although the quiet here when you're gone can spoil a girl."

"Oh hush." He laughs, his eyes lighting up with sass now that our affectionate moment is over. "You hate the quiet."

"Yeah, you're right." I laugh too, stepping to the side so he and Meg can walk further into the house. "Where are your bags?"

"Still in the car," he answers, tugging his things out of the pocket of his jeans and setting them on the end table beside me. "It's raining now, so we'll get 'em when it stops."

"Really?" I ask. "I didn't even notice."

"Yeah, I was surprised not to see you on the porch," Meg points out. "Your dad mentioned how much you love going to sit out there when it rains."

"Oh, it's my favorite." I grin, purposely leaving out that the reason I didn't notice was because I was too busy thinking about Weston pressing me against his truck after I brought him back to the diner to pick it up.

Luckily no one got an eyeful of us this time.

When my dad announces, "I'm going to go shower real quick, get the plane off me," I have to force myself to rid the delicious memory of Weston's near-bruising kisses so that I can pay attention to Meg.

And the minute the door to the bathroom shuts, she says, "All right, little missy. What happened after you and West left last night?"

*Shit.*

I completely forgot that Meg was there the entirety of yesterday to watch Weston and me get along, almost flirt, and then leave together.

And obviously she's not in the same giving mood as yesterday, when she left her interference and commentary at the door.

"Uh, Meg, I—"

"Nope, no babbling today," she scolds me, taking a step closer so she doesn't have to talk as loud. "Your dad's not in here. I won't tell him anything until you want me to, but Lord have mercy, child, you're going to give me something to live with after what you put me through yesterday."

"Put you through?" I gape.

"I had to watch you and Weston, when I've been gunning for y'all for months now, sitting in that booth and talking like you've been dating for years, grinning at each other when you thought no one else was looking, which, newsflash, I totally was, and then *leaving* together. It's been killing me all day not knowing, and now you're here and I gave y'all free food, so *you're going to tell me!*"

I can't decide if I'm irritated with her for being so pushy or loving how much she cares and how entertainingly crazy that's making her.

"Okay," I concede with a deep sigh. "But if I tell you, you have to promise not to make things weird when West is around, okay? I do enough of that on my own."

"So...." She trails off, her eyes sparkling. "Something did happen, then?"

I take a deep breath and brace myself. "Yes."

"Oh, thank God!" she exclaims, before catching herself and whispering, "Sorry, sorry. So... what're y'all going to...?"

"Nothing's defined," I tell her, "but I know we're both serious about it. We just... haven't had *that* conversation yet."

"See? I *knew* that boy was serious boyfriend material and that Jenny was just not the girl for him and that's why he refused to settle. Justine was convinced he was not the settling type and we'd all just read him wrong, but I knew it!"

Discomfort squeezes my stomach. "You talked to Mrs. Frederickson about us?"

Her blatant excitement softening a bit, she steps forward and places her hand on my shoulder before saying, "It's nothing bad or anything, I promise, but for all of us 'round here, watching y'all has been the best entertainment we've had in years. But rest assured, we've all been rooting for you and Weston."

"It's not that," I say, my good mood from earlier finally starting to waver. "I just... what if it doesn't work out, you know? It's a small town and seeing him everywhere would be hard enough, but knowing everyone wanted us together and hearing the endless questions, it—"

"Honey, you don't need to worry about that," she says, cutting my nervous ramblings off. "You and that boy, Iris, y'all were.... It's not going to end that way, not badly. Not you and him. I promise you that much."

"Really? And how do you know that?"

"'Cause y'all just... I don't know how to explain it, Iris, but you know what I mean. Y'all... you two click, make sense. It's not the kind of thing where you see two people together and have to squint your eyes and tilt your head to the right to understand. It's just... there."

The more she talks, the more I know exactly what she's talking about.

It's that feeling Weston and I talked about this morning.

But it's just... how do I know that one little feeling will keep us together?

"I'm not trying to freak you out here, hon, okay? That's the last thing I want. I'm just... I'm letting you know that obviously you and that boy have something major if this whole redneck hillbilly town can see it."

*That* gets a laugh out of me and quickly has my good mood filtering back in.

Meg's right, I know she is. She's so kind and has such a strong intuition and, knowing my past bad decisions, I really should trust her more than I trust myself.

I forced myself earlier today to be strong enough to tell Weston everything I felt, and if those kisses he laid on me afterward are anything to go by, the strength was well received.

So that's just what I need to do now, right?

"Thanks, Meg. And maybe you can help me, 'cause I have no earthly idea how to tell my dad."

"Oh, don't you worry about that," she says, waving a hand carelessly. "I've got that covered."

------------

It turns out that Weston had it covered as well because, ten minutes into him being over, he asks my dad to go talk to him on the porch.

The entirety of the time they're out there, the whole half hour it takes, I'm sitting at the kitchen table staring into my glass of white wine while Meg cooks spaghetti a few feet away.

A part of me is absolutely thrilled that I won't have to be there when my dad initially finds out about Weston and me, but another part of me is dying to know how it's going. This is the part we were most worried about, as I wouldn't put it past Weston to stop our relationship if my dad didn't approve.

Luckily, I know that all my dad wants is for the people he cares about to be happy, and if Weston can convince him that us being together will accomplish that, my dad will be more than supportive.

When the front door squeaks, I'm already leaping off my chair and hurrying to where my dad and Weston are stepping inside.

"Everything good?" I ask, and their eyes snap over to me.

Weston's eyes immediately fasten onto the bareness of my legs and the shorts he claimed tortured him all summer; the decision to change into them when I got home earlier was the easiest I've ever made. He must've been too nervous about talking to my dad to notice when he first got here, but now, judging by the darkening of his eyes, he definitely notices.

But I push the heat his gaze has coursing through my bloodstream to the side, knowing that it's highly inappropriate to be thinking those things around my dad, especially when he hasn't even told me if he approves or not.

"He makes you happy?" Dad asks simply, making my already nervous stomach clench even harder.

I answer with no hesitation, "Yes."

"Then we're all good, honey," he says nonchalantly as he comes over, pats my head, then brushes past me and into the kitchen.

My eyes, widened by shock, follow my dad for a few moments. I can hardly allow myself to accept that it really was just that easy. He doesn't turn to reassure me, so I look at Weston instead and see the huge grin stretching his lips as he comes toward me.

"Wha—" Weston's arms thread around my waist and he presses a kiss to the tip of my nose.

"It was seriously that easy."

257

"But... but how?" I stammer, shifting my weight back so that I can look up at him. "What'd he say?"

"A little more to me than what he said to you." He chuckles. "But it's pretty much what I expected. The rational part of me, anyway."

"Will you tell me everything later?"

"That depends," he says. "Are you coming back over tonight?"

The deep timbre of his voice has me thinking that me going back over is exactly what he wants so, my confidence boosted, I slide my hands up his chest and respond slyly, "Well, only if I'm invited."

"You're *totally* invited." He smirks, pressing a quick kiss against my mouth and then dropping his hold on me.

He steps out of the privacy of the wall and starts moving into the kitchen, his fingers lightly grabbing my wrist so I'm dragged along. To announce our entrance, Weston comments, "It smells delicious in here, Meg."

"Of course it does," she jokes, setting a glass lid on the sauce pot. After taking a long sip of her wine, she asks Weston, "So I'm assuming that since you're still here everything's okay?"

My dad cuts in from where he's sitting at the table and scrolling through his phone. "I'm not some kind of barbarian, Meg. Give me some credit!"

"I only give credit where credit is due," she teases him, leaning against the counter near the stove. She then looks at us and says, "This is what y'all have to look forward to now, you know."

"I think we'll be able to handle it," Weston says, giving my wrist a squeeze before heading to the table where Dad has placed a new beer bottle for him. He takes a sip of it and then starts asking him if he's looking at sports scores or something, but since I have nothing else to do, I decide to join them as well.

It's after I'm taking a sip of my wine and putting my glass down that Weston's large, warm hand takes my own, turning it over so that it's palm up and he can intertwine our fingers. My heart leaps in response, and I slide my gaze over to him as slyly as possible. When I see the slight grin touching his lips, I can't help but feel my mouth stretch into a mirroring one.

I give his fingers a squeeze and then listen as my dad says, "Yeah, they beat the shit out of 'em, actually."

I'm sure he's talking about some sports game or something, but the second I hear those words my mind immediately flashes back to yesterday morning when I found out everything about my mom. When I found out about Tim and how he liked to beat the shit out of *her*.

In all of my being caught up with Weston, I'd completely forgotten about the horror my mom went through.

I'd completely forgotten about *her*.

Maybe that'd been my initial plan when I went to the diner after I found out, but now that it's been a whole twenty-four hours without thinking about her, I feel almost as bad as I did when she initially told me.

Guilt overcoming me in the most powerful of tidal waves, I try to take in a deep breath to calm myself. I cannot believe I let her pain slide to the back of my mind like it never happened. No matter how much she hurt me, no matter what she did, I never should've treated it like that.

I'm so caught up in mentally berating myself, hating myself, that I don't even notice when my dad stands and leaves Weston and me alone at the table. That is, until Weston tugs my hand and lays it on his thigh so that I have to look at him.

"Iris," he says, his eyes filled with worry as they flutter over me. "What's going on? What's wrong?"

"I... I...." I stammer, hating that I have to admit this out loud. "I... forgot, West. About my mom. I forgot."

Saying it, actually tasting the words as they fall off my tongue, makes it feel so much more real, and suddenly the urge to burst into tears is burning my throat.

"Hey, hey...," Weston coos softly to me, his eyes flicking over my shoulder as he probably checks to make sure my dad and Meg can't hear us. "It's okay. It's not.... Baby, it's not your fault. You've had a lot on your plate. Things are going to fall through the cracks."

"But it shouldn't be that," I urge. "I mean, God, how could I...?"

"It's not something you choose," he reassures me, reaching out and grabbing my other hand so that now he's holding both. "Look, I know you, and I know you don't want to tell your dad about it tonight, right?"

I adamantly shake my head.

"Okay, so, just... just drink your wine until you feel a little better about the whole situation, and then when we go back to my place later, you can yell at me for charming you so much that it made you forget."

A snort of laughter comes out of me at that, the mischievous twinkle in his eyes already making me feel a little better. Running my thumb over the back of his hand, I whisper, "I'm glad I like you."

He winks at me. "I'm glad you like me too."

------------

"West...?" I croak, my random spurt of sleep having turned my voice into something akin to crumpled paper.

"We were on the couch and you fell asleep on me." He chuckles, his arms tightening under my legs and making me realize he's carrying me across my dad's living room. "You okay?"

"Yeah, I'm fine," I assure him, burying my face into his arm. "Where's my dad and Meg?"

"They're going to stay at her house, she had medicine there she had to take or something like that," he says, nudging my bedroom door open with the toe of his shoe. "They left a few minutes ago."

"Oh," I say. "I can't believe I slept through all that."

"You've had a crazy few days," he replies before reaching the bed, sitting down on the mattress so that I can stay curled up in his arms. "Although your dad did get a little bit worried."

"Yeah?" I ask, removing my face from his warm skin so I can look up at him.

He nods. "Just said it was weird for you to be able to sleep with all of us talking."

I sigh, curling up even more in his arms and trying to forget my parental worries by basking in how comfortingly small and secure he makes me feel.

"Should I tell my dad?" I murmur.

His arms tighten around me. "Don't worry about it tonight, okay? Why don't you just go back to sleep?"

"Here?"

He smirks at my confusion. "You were dead asleep just five minutes ago, Iris. I figured you wouldn't want me carrying you all the way across the street."

"Well, you figured *wrong*," I grumble, reaching out and touching the sleeve of his T-shirt. "I liked waking up to you this morning. I want to do it again."

His cheeks turn the slightest, most adorable shade of pink at my words, and I'm almost shocked it's not the other way around. My sleepy haze must be making me bolder than normal, because I know if it were any other time, saying something like that would mortify me.

"Okay," he whispers. "Let's go then."

He keeps a protective arm over my shoulders as we head out of the house, me making sure to turn out all the lights and lock up first, before we travel across the street and through his front door. After he flips on the lights in the living room, he says, "Let me let Thumper in and get him some food, and then we can go to bed, okay?"

"Okay." I smile, my love of our sudden domesticity overwhelming the nerves I should have about us going to bed.

As Weston works on grabbing the dog food from the cabinet, he calls out to me, "There's some sweatpants in my bottom drawer if you want to borrow them to sleep in."

"Okay, thanks," I call back.

Despite having slept here last night, I still have yet to lay eyes on his bedroom, so when I walk in and turn the light on, I can't help but let my curiosity get the best of me and look around. The room, just like the rest of the house, is clean and simple, and has just the right amount of manly sturdiness to remind me exactly whose house this is.

There's a king bed dominating the center of the room, a plush hunter-green duvet covering the striped white-and-cream sheets I see peeking out underneath the matching pillows at the head of the bed. A dark wood dresser that matches the headboard and end table stands directly across from the footboard, the top of it ornamented only with a complex-looking sound system, some jam-packed manila folders I assume contain things from his work, and a small stack of folded clothes.

After I let myself look around just a little bit more, I decide to do what I came in here for and open the bottom drawer of his large dresser, grabbing a pair of neatly folded Nike sweatpants. I also take it upon myself to grab a clean T-shirt from the clothes on top of his dresser, knowing the shirt I'm wearing won't be comfortable to sleep in.

The door to his en suite bathroom is open already, so I head in there and quickly change into his clothes, folding my dirty ones and placing them on the counter next to his sink.

Once I'm changed, my eyes find my reflection in the large mirror dominating the wall behind the clean white countertop, and I can't help but notice the sparkle in my caramel-colored eyes that virtually overwhelms the bruise-like bags beneath them.

No matter how much shit I've been through these past few weeks, no matter how much I've cried or how much sleep I've lost, being with Weston at his house and wearing his clothes has me feeling like the luckiest girl in the world.

Before I let myself think too much about it, though, I brush the tangles out of my wavy hair with my fingers and then head out of the bathroom.

Weston's sitting on the edge of his bed, his fingers scrolling over the screen of his phone, but at the sound of the bathroom door opening, his head snaps up and his eyes find mine. As hastily as his gaze found my own, it's leaving and trailing over my body instead, taking in the sight of me in his overwhelmingly large and comfortable clothes.

As much as I want to be embarrassed, as much as I feel like I should be cowering away at the dark heat encompassing his expression, I just don't have it in me. Instead I'm taking the few steps forward needed to reach him, him instinctively reaching out and pulling me in so that I can slide onto his lap.

His strong arms twine around my waist to keep me anchored on his thighs, and mine slide over his shoulders. I say, "I hope you don't mind, but I stole one of your shirts too."

"Believe me," he murmurs, his normally strong voice coming out slightly hoarse, "I *do not* mind. Not even a little bit."

"Yeah?" I smirk, the obvious effect I have on him releasing something bravely sensual inside of me. Lifting one of my hands from the back of his neck so that my fingers can tangle in his hair, I ask, "What's your favorite, then? My shorts, the heels, or this?"

"Really?" He groans, his fingertips pressing into the skin right above the waistband of my pants. "You want to make me play that game?"

"Aww, come on," I tease, leaning in and pressing a lingering kiss against the corner of his mouth. "I need to know these things so I can have you wrapped around my finger."

"*Baby*," he breathes out, his hot hand slipping underneath my shirt. "As much as I hate to admit this, I'm already there."

If him calling me baby didn't already have a smile on my face, admitting to that would definitely have done it.

"I don't know if I believe you," I muse, my smile morphing into a smirk as I tighten my grip in his hair and see the resulting darkening of his pupils.

"I'd have done anything for you the second you got back to town, and now that... now that we're doing this and I know how *fucking* good it is, it's not even fair for me at this point."

My mind is wholly encompassed by what he's just said, by how overwhelmingly sweet he can be even when we're on his bed and I'm acting like a horny teenager.

I've never felt this before, nothing that even came close to it.

Not with the small handful of guys I was with in college, not in the daydreams I had about the cute guys I saw around campus.

No, the only time I felt anything even remotely like what I'm feeling now was four years ago on my front porch stairs.

Never in my life have I felt intimate in both senses of the word. When I was with those guys, it was only pure lust and that reckless sort of abandonment people feel when they've moved away for college. I was physically intimate with them, yes, but there was never this warmth that only comes with *truly* trusting a person, a sort of soul connection instead of just a physical one.

And that's exactly what I feel with Weston.

"West...," I croak out, suddenly feeling like I'm getting buckled into the scariest roller coaster.

"Yeah, babe?" he asks, the concern in his voice telling me he's picked up on my sudden change in mood.

"You...," I start, my hand falling from his hair so that it can squeeze the juncture of his neck and shoulders. "You... you scare the hell out of me. You know that?"

"You don't need to be, I—"

"I know," I tell him, for some reason feeling emboldened staring into his bright green gaze, instead of wrecked with nerves. "I have no reason to be, but... but I am. And it's not 'cause I don't trust you, because, West, I don't know if I trust anyone more, really... but I just...

the fact that I feel this much when we've only been together a day...."

"But doesn't that tell you it's something worth keeping?" he asks. "That it's this good this early on?"

"That's exactly what it tells me," I whisper. "Which means that if you leave, it'll just hurt—"

"I'm not going to leave, baby," he reassures me, his throat sounding tight. His fingers touching underneath my bottom lip, he says, "I get why you're paranoid about me leaving, okay, what with everything with your mom, but I'm... I'm not like that, Iris. When I'm into something, I'm all-in. No secrets, no nothing. If anything is worth living through, it's not as good as it can possibly be if everything's not out in the open."

Despite the multitude of amazing things his little speech has just made me feel, the only thing I can come up with in response is narrowing my eyes and asking him, "Are you sure you want to settle with me? You're such a better person than I am."

He chuckles, the concern that'd been etched into his face now swept aside by that soft, affectionate look that's already become my favorite. As soon as I register his eyes closing and his face leaning in, I'm feeling his plush, slightly chapped lips on mine and I'm quickly falling into the sensation.

All of my ridiculous worries make way for the delicious spell his kiss always puts me under. I let my eyes flutter closed. It's tame, effortless, and something you'd see at the end of a Disney movie, but it still has my toes curling and my common sense fogging with warmth.

When it gets to where I can no longer handle the shallow kisses, though, I'm nipping his bottom lip to get him to open his mouth and then sliding my tongue in to meet his. The moment they touch, a thick groan escapes his throat and sets off the slightest vibrations against my mouth, my arms tightening around his neck in reaction.

His hands slide down from where they'd been resting against my back, moving to tilt my hips so they're pressed firmly against his.

He's pressing hard into my upper thigh, the passing seconds making it just that much more noticeable, and it has me reacting to each kiss with more and more frenzy.

Of their own accord, my hips slowly start to rock into his, my hold on sanity faltering. His hold seems to be fading fast as well, his fingers now tightly gripping my ass and his kiss becoming harder and more demanding.

It's when he tightly sucks my bottom lip into his mouth that I realize all sanity is lost for good, my hands dropping from around his neck and falling instead to the bottom hem of his shirt. I wrench my mouth away from his, the guttural noise of protest Weston makes when I do so making my thighs clench together.

But when I tug upward on the bottom of his shirt and he opens his eyes and lifts his arms, realizing what it is I want, his lips curve into the most sinful and delicious-looking smirk I've ever seen.

Once I've got his shirt off him and I practically leap back into kissing him, the sight of his bare chest only adding to my dazed euphoria, his arms brace me a couple of inches away from him and his eyes fall to the shirt I still have covering me. A blush tinges my cheeks when he gives me a teasing smile that says it's my turn now. I hesitantly pull the large cotton shirt off, tossing it onto the floor behind me.

No matter how comfortable I may normally feel with Weston, the bareness of my skin has me unable to look him in the eye, the wide expanse and strong, visible muscles of his chest making for a very happy distraction. He doesn't let me enjoy them too long, though, his fingers coming underneath my chin and forcing my gaze to his.

"You okay?" he asks, his voice husky with need and quickly bringing up that tension low in my stomach from before. "You want to stop?"

I adamantly shake my head. "No...."

Seemingly picking up on just the smallest bunch of nerves I still have lingering, he brushes my hair back from my face and then cups my cheeks, his palms hot against my already burning skin. "Iris?"

"Mhmm?" I ask, the intense stare he's hitting me with overwhelming me in the scariest, most beautiful way ever.

"You're fucking breathtaking, okay? Please don't be shy with me."

The second I nod, his tongue is delving into my mouth, his kiss tight and powerful as he grabs my waist and stands, my legs holding me tightly to him as he turns around and gently tosses me onto the bed. I giggle at the surprise of it, but it's immediately silenced when he crawls on top of me and grips at my hair, delivering another near-bruising kiss to my mouth.

And just like that, we've succumbed once again to whatever's been building up between us for four years, the kisses from earlier today and yesterday apparently having not made a dent in our need to be together. I feel like I can't get close enough to him, that warmth in my lower stomach from before having turned into a raging fire that's causing me to be as rough as he is.

I'm gripping his shoulders, his back, any part of him I can hold on to, with a ferocity that I know will leave bruises tomorrow, and just the thought of my mark on him has me aching for him even more. I've never been a rough person, but for some reason, with Weston, I feel comfortable enough to be as crazy possessive and desperate as I want.

His lips are on my neck now, his teeth randomly biting and then his tongue coasting over the same spot in the most seductive of apologies. My lower body is throbbing with a pleasurable kind of torture, and it's as his lips travel down and press onto the swell of my breast not contained by my bra, that the words, "Weston, please," are thoughtlessly escaping my mouth.

"Shhh, baby," he whispers against my damp skin, his hand clenching tight at my waist as he moves his mouth over to my other breast and kisses it just the same.

Some kind of whimper spills out of my mouth, and as his other hand grips the other side of my waist, I feel his lips curve into a smile against my skin right before he starts to move lower.

My eyes spring open as he presses a kiss against my belly button, and, if it all possible, my eyes get even bigger when Weston whispers against my waistline, "Can I touch you?"

It's not even a complete thought when I press my head into the pillow beneath me and answer, "Yes, God, *please*," giving him myself to take complete control over.

He's slow at first, his removal of my sweatpants agonizingly slow, and his fingers' journey to the center of my thighs only a heartbeat quicker. I'm holding my breath in a tight little ball in my chest the entire time he's teasing me, his fingers not venturing through the barrier of my underwear for the first few moments, but when he slides in the first one, it all comes out in a heady moan.

It's only uphill from there, my body heating up and going crazier with every passing second, my hips bucking into the air with an almost humiliating urgency, my fists so tight on his duvet that it'll probably leave everlasting wrinkles.

"Iris?" he says, his voice barely audible.

"Mmmm?" I groan.

"Come for me," he says lowly, and before I can even make sense of what he's said, I feel his hot mouth descend on me, his tongue pinpointing the bundle of nerves he only let his fingers tease over.

A hoarse scream escaping my throat, I dig my fingers into his hair with an almost punishing grip, my hips surging up with need and Weston only forcing them back down with his free hand.

It takes me less than twenty seconds to come spiraling down, one of my arms thrown over my face as I return back to earth, my breath coming out in pants and my skin, I'm sure, flushed. I'm barely aware of it as Weston presses a final kiss right at the top of one of my thighs, and it's not until he's removing my arm from my face that I realize he's climbed back up to the head of the bed.

When he does though, I let my eyes flutter open and meet his, the almost boyish sparkle I see making my heart squeeze in my chest. "Hey," he greets simply, his lips in a wide grin as he hovers his face over mine and brushes some of my sweat-dampened hair out of the way.

"Hi," I greet lamely.

"You good?" he asks, and before I can answer, he adds, "And please think carefully before you answer. My pride's at stake here."

I giggle, reaching up and trailing my fingers over his lips. "I'm *so* good, West."

"Yeah, I figured as much," he teases with a wink, leaning down and pressing a quick kiss to my mouth. "What with you screaming like that—"

"Weston!" I squeal, absolutely appalled.

He chuckles, pecking me with another kiss before rolling sideways so he's lying at my side. He turns, propping his head up with his hand before asking, "You still as tired as before, then?"

I shake my head. "No, the nap definitely gave me some energy. Are you tired, though? You didn't...."

He smirks. "How bad of a host would I be if I went to sleep when you weren't ready to?"

"Just a host?" I tease, sliding my hand under a pillow and resting my cheek on top. "Is that all you are to me now?"

He shakes his head. "Never."

I purse my lips, his sudden seriousness taking me aback. "Never?"

"You're never going to be 'just' something to me, Iris. Even when we didn't speak to each other in school, you were always still so much more to me than 'just' my neighbor."

He says it so simply, so effortlessly, like what he's saying is just as unimportant as his McDonalds drive-thru order, when really those words have hit me straight in the heart.

"West," I croak, my eyes filling with tears.

"Hey, hey," he says, immediately spotting them and then tossing an arm over my bare skin so he can scoot his body close. "I didn't want to—"

"Don't take it back," I beg. "*Please*."

To know that he's always thought so much of me, to hear that I was never invisible to him when I thought I was, means so much to my past insecure self. Sure I'm nowhere near as self-critical as I was back then, but still to this day I always thought that my going to school there didn't mean anything to any of the other students.

So to hear that Weston, this beautiful boy with this beautiful heart, cared for me when I thought no one else did, when I thought maybe I was unlovable, fills a gaping void in me.

After a few moments of me trying to rein back tears, Weston tightens his arm around my waist and leans in to give my forehead a gentle kiss before saying, "You're worth other people's love, Iris. I hate that you think you aren't."

And just like that the tears are back, but this time they're rolling down my face. Humiliated that Weston's been able to figure me out so easily, that he's been able to reach that deeply inside me so quickly, I lean in and bury my head against his chest. I know he can feel my tears since he's still sans shirt, but I'm so overwhelmed that I can't be bothered to care.

Weston doesn't try to move away from me, doesn't try to say anything, instead playing with my hair and making soothing noises anytime I make a crying sound. I know that tomorrow I'll be completely ashamed of letting our night end like this, but right now... right now I feel too comfortable to even think of moving.

So that's why, sometime later, when I feel his hand stop moving in my hair and hear the slightest of snores come out of him, I just deepen my cuddle against him and let myself fall asleep too.

# Chapter Twenty-One

"Hey, Jen?" I manage to say, looking up at the blonde bombshell who just dropped meeting notes to type up on my desk.

"Yeah?" she responds, halting her trek out of the lobby.

She looks the same as she always has; her blonde hair curled and worthy of a Pantene commercial, her bright blue eyes highlighted by gorgeous eye shadow and perfect lashes, and her body perfectly sculpted by her biweekly spinning classes.

If you'd told me she was dumped just a week or so ago, I never would've believed you. There's no sign of exhaustion or sadness on her. But for some reason, even though the two of us were close only for a handful of weeks, I still know she's wounded over the way things ended between her and Weston.

Which just makes the conversation I need to have with her even harder.

I've been forcing this responsibility to the side for three days now. It's the Thursday morning after Weston and I got together, and I've seen her at work every day since then. Weston and I had a talk about this Monday night when I stayed over at his house for the third night in a row, and we both agreed that the two of us, no matter how

Jenny may have treated us lately, needed to keep things hidden from the town until we told her.

It'd be completely unfair for us to just let her hear it from someone other than us.

"Do you...," I start, my courage wavering the longer I look at her. "Do you want to grab lunch today or something? I need to... to talk to you about something."

She adjusts her stance and crosses her arms underneath her chest, making the fabric of her teal-blue peplum dress crease. "About you and West being together?"

"Wha...?" I gape, my mouth dropping open unattractively. "How did you...?"

Jenny says breezily, "Iris, there's like thirty people that live around here and they all gossip like bored old ladies. I heard the day after it happened."

Immediately feeling terrible, I start to apologize. "Jen, I'm... I'm so sorry. I...."

She rolls her eyes at me, and when she speaks it's with a quiet sort of venom tainting her voice. "It's fine, girl. Not like I'm surprised or anything."

"I know, I'm just.... We both really wanted to tell you before you heard about it. We weren't trying to hurt you keeping it quiet these past few days."

She nods, a darkness in her expression I hadn't even noticed starting to soften. Tucking a blonde wave of her hair behind her ear, she says, "I figured as much. Y'all are both too good of people to just never tell me. It's what pisses me off."

"Wait, what?" I ask, trying to decipher if I need to be offended.

She looks around the room quickly and lets out an audible sigh before she crosses the few feet between her and my desk and comes to lean on it, her strong and beautiful floral perfume caressing my senses.

"Look," she starts out simply, a vulnerability in her eyes that I've only ever seen that one time. "I know things got way out of hand on Labor Day and some really harsh things were said, but pretty much all of them came from my jealousy, so it's not like you should *actually* be offended."

My heart beginning to pound, I say, "Jen, there's no reason to be jealous, seriously. It's—"

"No, just listen," she interjects with a shake of her head. "You didn't really do anything wrong, Iris, okay? As much as I hate saying that. That first night at the Boot, I should've realized there was something between you and West no one could get between, but I chose to ignore it, and I ignored it for the entire time we were together because I stupidly thought there was a chance for me and 'cause I was terrified of being single again. So that's all on me. Yes, I do hate how much everyone in this damn town loves you and Weston and how, even though everyone was so nice to my face, I just knew it was *you* they wanted him with and not me."

She goes silent for a little while after that, and feeling overwhelming compassion for her, I know I have to say something to make her feel better. "If it makes you feel any better, Jen, I've been so jealous of you the entire summer, and not just because of some guy. I'm jealous of *you* as your own person, and you being with West just made it that much harder."

When she scoffs and I see that vulnerability digging even deeper into her self-esteem, I decide to hell with being corny and keep on talking. "I'm serious! You're hot as hell, obviously, and you even go to the gym, which just drives me up the damn wall. You're outgoing and—"

"Iris," she says, and when I look her in the eye and see tears building up there, I can't decide if I made the right decision by talking her up like that.

But I just couldn't help it, honestly.

I know everything she's done to me this summer has stemmed

from a place of insecurity, and I hate that for her. I know how shitty it is to be that down on yourself and feel that hopeless, but even for me, I never let it get to the point where I was consciously hurting other people.

Jen knew what she was doing to me, though, and as bitter as that may make me toward her, I still can't find the will to hate her for it.

"Just shut up, okay?" she says, reaching up to swipe underneath her eyes. "I'm torn between loving you and hating you because you're still so fucking nice after everything my brother and I have done these past few weeks. But, just know, it's heavily leaning toward hating you."

I chuckle, feeling a little bit better that she's starting to find some humor in everything. "Sorry."

She's quiet for a long moment, her fingernails tapping against her toned arm, and when she speaks again, she says, "I am too. Really sorry. You and West deserve to be happy together."

"You think?" I ask, not wanting to make it worse for her but not being able to fight the small smile stretching my lips.

She rolls her eyes at me yet again, and she sounds so tired of the conversation as she says, "Yeah, although it won't stop me from being a little happy if it ever doesn't work out."

My stomach clenches at the mere thought, my heart already having gotten accustomed to him being mine the past few days. "Well, let's hope it never comes to that."

She purses her lips. "Yeah, sure."

We both fall quiet after that, as I have no idea how to respond, but the longer she doesn't talk the more awkward I start to feel, so I ask a bit uneasily, "So are we okay, then? No more drama?"

She nods. "No more drama. But... Iris, I'm not going to lie to you though, okay? I'm not going to be okay with being that close again for a while. I don't know if ever. As much as I can rationally say my being hurt is pretty much my own doing, it still hurts like a bitch to be around you."

It's a bit hurtful to hear, but I get what she's saying.

So I have to agree with her.

---

"So that's it?" Weston asks later that night. "Y'all just aren't friends anymore?"

I place my empty dinner bowl onto the end table next to his couch and stretch my body even further, my feet ending up on his lap. "Yeah... but, I mean, we pretty much stopped being friends a while ago. We just never finalized it, is all."

"Are you upset about it?" he asks with furrowed brows, picking up one of my sock-encased feet and starting to rub.

I shrug. "I mean it sucks, yeah, but no matter how insecure she was, it didn't give her any right to treat me like she has been recently. I'll take no friends over a friend like that."

"So what, then?" Weston asks, teasing humor in his voice. "I'm not your friend?"

"Aww, West." I giggle, seeing the adorable pout on his lips. "Of *course* you're my friend."

He grumbles, "I better be."

I'm still laughing when I take my foot out of his lap and replace it with the rest of my body, my knees resting on either side of his thighs and my arms draping over his broad shoulders. Placing a corny kiss to the tip of his nose, I whisper, "You're my *best* friend."

When I pull away, I see that the dramatic pout has now been replaced with the softest, most handsome of little smiles. His eyes are full of something I can't read, and the sight of it does something to me. I squeeze the crook of his neck before asking jokingly, "I'm your friend too, right?"

A quiet nod is his only response, and when I go to lean back so I can get a better look at him, he stops me by squeezing tightly at my hips. I ask him softly, "West, what's wrong?"

His eyes run fleetingly over my face, the tightness of his fingers not budging, before he says painfully, "I don't want to trap you, Iris."

Something inside my stomach squeezing at how guilty he sounds, I wrinkle my nose at him and ask, "What?"

"You don't have Jenny anymore 'cause of me, and I know your relationship with the people here isn't the greatest because of how they were four years ago, and I just don't want you to think of our relationship as a tie-down to stop you from moving somewhere bigger or better."

"West, stop," I insist urgently, hating that my simple joke has upset him like this. Sliding my hands over the roughness of his cheeks, I say, "You're not trapping me, okay? Jenny and I would still be friends if not for *her* issues, not mine and not yours. And the work thing is on me, okay? It's my choice what I do with my time, and if I wanted to not see you to look for jobs, I would. And I know you'd be okay with that."

"I just...." The lightest little blush graces his thick neck. "You just... you could do anything in the world you wanted to, Iris, and I don't want to keep you from that."

Some type of breathtaking emotion wraps around my heart and squeezes it like a vice. I dig my fingers into his hair and scold, "Whether or not that's true, you're not keeping me from anything I want. Right now and probably for the longest, most embarrassing amount of time, you're the only guy I see myself wanting. And it's crazy that I'm actually admitting to that out loud, but I just... you *have* to know that you're not making anything worse or harder for me. You're making everything better, West. *So* much better."

The most beautiful light spreads across his face. "The *only* guy?"

It's my turn to blush, and I feel the blood scorching my cheeks as I say humiliatingly, "Don't make me feel like some crazy clingy girlfriend for saying that. *Please.*"

"Oh, I won't." He chuckles, his hands coming up to lightly grip my jaw. "Because then I'd be saying the same fucking thing about myself."

"Yeah?"

"Damn straight." Before I can even take a breath, he's swooping in and stealing my lips for a strong and deliciously possessive kiss.

The surprise of it causes a gasp to escape my throat and into his mouth. I feel his smile stretch both of our lips before he's dropping his arms so they can brace around my waist and pull my hips even tighter against his. Letting myself sink down onto him, my hips cradling his building excitement and letting the heat of it spread throughout me, we both open our mouths to let everything deepen.

The softest of groans vibrates his throat when I let my tongue rub against his, which has me doing it even more, slowly, deliberately, trying to tease him. It only takes him a few seconds to be done with that, choosing to retaliate by sliding his hand up the front of my shirt and grasping one of my breasts, a breathy sigh filtering out of my mouth when he pushes the bra down and lets his thumb flick over the hardened peak.

Biting down roughly on his bottom lip, I move from kneeling over him and instead wrap my legs around his waist, my heels pushing into his lower back so that his erection is firmly fitted between my thighs. As the hand up my shirt moves to the other breast, his other hand grips tightly at my jaw, and that newly familiar loss of bodily control starts to take over my limbs.

My hips start rocking against him with no rhyme or rhythm, just a desperate need for him to rid my body of this highly uncomfortable yet insanely pleasurable throbbing between my legs. He must start to feel it too, as his hands move to my ass and his hips lift every time my core brushes over him.

It doesn't take long for that to be too much, as he wrenches his mouth away from mine, leaving my wet lips just a hair away from his. "Iris," he gasps.

"Mmmm?"

"Can we...? I mean, if it's too fast... it's... I don't want to...."

Instantly knowing what he wants, as it's the same exact thing my body is in complete agony for, I give him my answer silently, tugging my shirt over my head. After tossing it behind me, I slowly meet his gaze and squeeze my thighs together in response to the intense need burning his stare.

When he doesn't make any moves, his eyes just taking in my bareness and casting a burning warmth on my skin, I reach down again but this time take the fabric of his white undershirt into my hands, tugging gently upward. He lifts his arms so I can slide it up and off him.

I toss it back as well, letting it meet mine on the living room's hardwood floor, not once breaking the heated trance between us. My eyes fall to the tanned, hard skin showcased in front of me, and I reach up to press a hand against his sternum, the heat coming off him nearly scorching my palm. I let my fingers trace over the warm skin.

I can feel his stare still firmly on me, his breathing even and steady in the same oddly subdued way mine is, and it only urges me further as I keep drawing over the lines etched onto him, the scar right above his left nipple, the birthmark located in the exact center of his chest.

The lower I go, the more his breath picks up, and by the time my hand's reached his jeans, I can tell by the throbbing excitement constrained beneath them that this tense little moment is just about over. My eyes lifting to meet Weston's, I blindly undo the button and zipper of his loose-fitting Levi's.

His eyes are scorching mine as I let my hand slide underneath the hem of his jeans and boxers, and when my fingers come into contact with his hardened length, I see the black in his gaze fully take over.

His mouth comes down hard on mine just a second later, all that breath I'd gained while we weren't kissing leaving my body in one elongated sigh. My free hand wraps around his neck, and as soon as it does, Weston's using my anchor against him so that he can pull me up by my hips and lay me down on the couch without separating our mouths.

He crawls on top of me and wastes no time in letting his weight fall onto mine, and then I'm back to madly urging my hips upward to meet his.

"West," I whimper against his damp lips, begging him to do *something*, right before surging my mouth back onto his and letting my tongue wrap around his.

He answers by undoing the button of the jean shorts I changed into after work today, and then finally rips them partly down my legs.

His lips come off mine with a wet smack, and before I can protest, he's kissing down the column of my neck and length of my chest, leaving open-mouthed kisses and little nips of the teeth wherever he can. Once he's down between my legs, he rips my shorts off the rest of the way and throws them to the side, and it takes no time whatsoever for him to do the same with my underwear.

I throw my head back and clench my eyes shut, waiting for him to fix the painful throb between my thighs, but then I hear him say, "No... no, I don't want to do this...."

I open my eyes and immediately push up on my arms to look at him. "Weston, what...? Do you... do you not want to anymore?"

His eyes bug open. "No! Iris, I just... not *here*. Not on my couch."

I furrow my brows. "So... your room, then?"

"Yes." He nods fervently. "I want you in my bed."

With no warning, he's standing and scooping me into his arms, crossing the floor quickly and then, once we're in his darkened bedroom, laying me gently on the mattress and sliding back on top of me. His arms are braced on either side of my head, that darkness in his eyes now mixed with a certain type of softness.

Looking up at him, I lick my lips and ask, "This better?"

"God, yes," he answers in a breathy groan, right before leaning down and tangling our mouths together once again. My arms are wrapping around his neck and tangling in his hair as he wastes no time, one of his hands going underneath me to undo my bra and the other skating down to torture the sensitive nerves between my thighs.

We become a mess of desperate mouths and frantic limbs, both of us now completely shed of our clothes and learning each other's bodies in the most mouthwatering of ways. We're groaning and whimpering and whispering each other's names, and he's telling me I'm beautiful and I'm begging him to finish me off.

"West, please, baby... oh my God... yes, oh wait, West!" I'm nearly screaming, my fingers tangled tight in his hair as he moves his face away, yet again, from where it's been pressed between my thighs.

Moving upward, his lips find mine for a moment, the saltiness of his kiss leaving me feeling so dirty in the best way. When he pulls away from me, though, I cup his jaw with my palm and nearly cry, "You're killing me here, West."

"I know, baby, I know...," he soothes, one of his hands reaching down to grab the foil packet he'd at some point tossed next to us. "I have a reason."

"Yeah, and what's that? 'Cause you hate me?"

"Not at all, baby." He chuckles, pressing a kiss to my forehead before ripping the packet open and quickly sliding the condom on. "Because I want to be inside you for that."

And it's then, before I can even respond to those sinful words of his, that I feel him push his way between my thighs and inside of me. Anything I could've said is lost as my body arches into him and he starts his thrusts, a loud mix between a sigh and cry sounding from my throat as he buries his head against my shoulder.

With every movement as we lose ourselves in each other, I climb higher and higher, reaching a feeling that's almost otherworldly, like I'm not even a part of myself. It has me clinging to him roughly, digging my heels into the small of his back, my fingers keeping his bicep in a tight grasp.

I cry out when he takes it deeper, rougher, but before I can let him think it's because I don't like it, I'm tightening my legs around his waist and thrusting my hips into his even harder, the new wildness of it causing my high to become shaky.

He grunts into my neck as I force him into me, my thrusts almost matching his in ferocity, and it's not until he pulls his face away from my neck and whispers into my ear "My baby" that I *finally* fall over the edge. I feel his high hit at the same time, his body becoming a tight line above mine until he winces and falls back down onto me after pulling out.

We're both silent for a while, his head burrowing back in the crook of my neck and his skin slick with sweat. I lift a hand and let my fingers run through his damp hair, nowhere near in a hurry to get him off me.

Not after that. Not after we were just that close.

This... *that*... with Weston... it's just so perfect.

"I think I like you in my bed a little too much," he whispers, the words a spoken warmth against my neck.

"Yeah?" I smile, tightening my hold in his hair.

"Mmm," he murmurs, which I think is his way of saying "yes."

"You just need to stay here forever."

I laugh. "What? And be your sex slave?"

"Well, yeah!" He chuckles, finally pulling his head up so that I can see the huge smile on his face. "What else would I want you here for?"

"You jackass." I giggle loudly, pushing on his shoulder.

"Nah, I'm just kidding," he says, his voice dropping an octave or two as he dips his face down to meet mine. "Although, believe me when I say I'd *never* be opposed to that."

He presses his lips to mine, the intimacy established within the past half hour transferring into it as neither of us waste any time in wrapping our tongues together in that sloppy kind of amazing way. My arms instinctively lift to wrap around him, to pull him into me, and judging by the newfound hardness already poking at my thigh, Weston doesn't mind at all.

I pull away from him, just for a moment, to tell him, "This doesn't mean I'm agreeing to be your sex slave!"

He laughs. "Okay, okay... I'll agree with that. For now," and then he pulls me right back into him.

# Chapter Twenty-Two

"Iris," my dad says, sounding just a bit confused, "what is all of this?"

He just got home from the accounting firm to find me hard at work in the kitchen; well, as hard at work as baking a frozen lasagna and packet of garlic bread is, anyway.

I haven't had the chance to cook for him in quite some time, but tonight I'm going to tell him about my mom, and I feel like easing into it with his favorite meal and a fifteen-dollar bottle of Sauvignon Blanc can't really hurt.

Last night, after a little liquid courage in the form of a beer, I called my mom. Ever since she told me what happened to her during her time away, I've been conflicted about whether to tell my dad. On one hand, they were together for so long and she was such a crucial part of his life that I felt he *had* to know. But on the other hand, it wasn't my abuse, my story to tell.

Despite how much closer I am to my dad, how much more I respect him, I realized how utterly wrong it'd be of me to share Mom's trauma.

The plan was simply to ask when she was going to tell him, but instead, it turned into her sobbing that she couldn't admit to his face what horrors her leaving him turned into. So eventually, after she stopped crying and I tried to fight back irritation, she decided that Dad did need to know, but that she wasn't going to be the one to tell him.

No, she appointed that fun job to me.

Which is why I'm in this situation now.

"I got off a little bit early," I explain to him, closing the oven and turning to look at him. "Well, I left kind of early anyway, and thought I'd cook dinner. It's been a while since I have."

"Well thanks, booger," he says with a gentle smile, coming over and pressing a kiss to the top of my head. "It smells delicious."

"It's Marie Callender." I chuckle. "Your favorite."

"Ooooh," he coos, pulling away from me and then quipping, "I knew having kids had to pay off sometime."

I roll my eyes at him. "Whatever, you loser. I got wine too. It's in the fridge. You want me to open it?"

"I got it," he offers, heading over to the fridge. "That boyfriend of yours across the street joining us?"

"Nope," I say, the mention of Weston bringing a stupid grin to my lips. "Thought it'd just be me and you, Daddy-O."

"Hmm," he muses, popping the cork out of the top of the wine bottle. "Do you need money or something, Iris?"

"Hey, I take offense at that!" I argue, taking a ratty dish towel off the counter so I can smack him with it. "You know I have no problem asking you directly for money."

He laughs loudly, his eyes crinkling at the corners and making my heart blissfully happy for a fleeting moment.

About fifteen minutes later, the lasagna is done and I'm pulling it out of the oven while my dad is setting the table for us, paper plates and napkins along with fancy wine glasses filled more than enough. It's as Tilley a night as possible, and even though I know our conversation is going to be about as emotionally brutal as I can take, it still makes me happy.

We make normal father-daughter talk for a little while, him asking me about work and me asking him about his upcoming trip to Tennessee. By the time that small talk has dwindled down, I'm halfway done with my food and more than two-thirds done with my wine, so I know it's the ideal time to bring up my mother.

As much as I don't want to.

"So...." My nerves momentarily getting the best of me, I stop midsentence to swallow. "I um, I saw Mom the other day... Saturday."

"Yeah, you mentioned she was taking you shopping or something when we talked on the phone. Was everything okay? Is she doing all right?"

My dad still cares deeply for my mom, no matter how much her leaving hurt and humiliated him. But even though I know her being back is hard on him, I know he's also glad she didn't leave us confused for the rest of our lives.

But that still doesn't mean I'm not terrified to tell him what all I found out Saturday.

"Well, not really...." I trail off, my chest clenching. I take a huge gulp of my wine, and once I feel its warmth loosen my nerves, I explain, "I mean, she's fine now, I think. But she told me what all happened while she was gone and, Dad, I don't... you're not... you're not going to like it."

His hand stops, the forkful of lasagna he was about to eat now hovering midair, and when his eyes meet mine, I can see the worry I've struck in him. He slowly places the fork down onto his plate and then asks, "What do you mean, Iris? What'd she tell you?"

"I...," I start breathlessly, my heart pounding. "I.... We'd just gotten to the store and she was putting the car in park, which made her sleeve fall down. And I.... There was... there was this huge old bruise on her wrist, Dad. I mean, like really huge. It wrapped all the way around."

I see his throat move as he swallows hard, painful confusion flashing across his face. He opens his mouth to say something, but stops when just a breath of air escapes his lips, his jaw clamping shut in response and his eyes falling to the table.

Guilt wraps around me, squeezing me like a vine. I take yet another sip of my drink, hating that I'm hurting him and wondering for the umpteenth time if telling him is actually a good idea.

"And I... I should've known something was up 'cause every time we were outside she was wearing long sleeves and it's been over a hundred degrees like every day since she's been back, and I should've known that wasn't normal, and I should've asked her earlier why she was back, but I was scared. I was scared she'd say she was back to make amends and then leave again, and that was selfish of me 'cause maybe if I'd asked and she'd told me, she wouldn't have been suffering alone these past few weeks."

"Iris, stop." Dad pushes his plate forward so he can put his elbows on the table and rest his face between his palms. "You never could've really known. I mean.... That's just not something someone thinks of automatically."

"Yeah, I know," I admit, sinking a bit into my chair. "I just... even though she left and she hurt us so badly and everything, I just... I hate that she had to go through that, I guess."

"What did she...?" He stops so he can take a large gulp of his drink. "You don't have to tell me if you don't want to, hon, but I just.... What all did she tell you?"

So I launch into the story, telling him what my mom told me, and watch that light in his eyes he'd had the second he found out I was making dinner slowly start to diminish. By the time I'm done, he looks like he's in outright pain, which has the same damn effect on me, and I feel like I should almost hate myself for telling him.

"Have you seen her since?" he asks.

I shake my head. "No. I.... When I found out and she left, I... I went to Meg's. I couldn't be here alone, you know, the quiet was just...

just too much, I guess. And when I got there, West was there and it was the anniversary of his brother's death, so we... we got to talking, and yeah. He helped a lot."

"Is that how y'all got together? Meg told me the gist of it, but she didn't go into much detail."

"Yeah, it is," I respond, a small smile gracing my lips no matter how agonizingly painful this conversation is. "We were both upset, and so we had some beers and, funny story, but this guy he punched a while back that night I went to the Boot showed up and apologized via shots so... so, yeah. The alcohol opened us up for sure, got us saying stuff we were both too scared to say, and once everything was out there, we realized how stupid we've both been all summer."

"Amen to that," he says, a bit of happiness seeping into his voice. "It's been killing me all summer, knowing how good y'all would be for each other and watching y'all be like freaking awkward thirteen-year-olds around each other. Was terrible."

"Oh hush." I giggle. "We're good now, so you, Meg, and the rest of the freaking town just need to back off. It's weird knowing y'all were watching."

"It was like something you'd see on TV," he teases, almost sounding back to normal. "And I had prime seating the whole time. It was so great. I'd never been so popular when I went and ate by myself at Meg's."

"Oh my God, stop!" I exclaim, ripping a piece of garlic bread off and chucking it at him.

Even though he and I are so alike in the fact that we both avoid awkwardness and things we know will hurt like the plague—him deflecting it with humor and me just running away at any sign of it—I still love that when we *have* to deal with it, I never truly have to worry about it affecting our relationship. We'll talk about whatever we have to, we'll both hate it, but by the end of it, we'll both feel better.

Which is why, for the rest of the time we're at the table, joking around while we get our appetites back and then finishing up our food, everything feels perfect.

---

The next two weeks pass relatively quickly and quietly and, before I know it, it's the end of the first week in October and I realize I've been back in town for nearly five months. It's taken only five months for my entire world to be turned sideways, both in good ways and bad, but as I let myself through Weston's unlocked-just-for-me front door on a Monday evening, I know that I'll take the bad moments time and time again if it means Weston and I can be like this.

I shut the door softly behind me and am immediately greeted by Thumper rushing over so I can rub him behind the ears. I hear the soft murmur of Weston's voice, and so I leave the large dog with a kiss to the top of his head before seeking out my irresistible boyfriend.

I find him seated at the dining room table, empty take-out containers in front of him and his cell phone pressed to his ear, and when he sees me, he smiles and scoots his chair back so I can join him. A ridiculous childlike grin on my face, I nearly skip over to him and then slide onto his lap, and as his arm wraps around my back, I faintly hear a masculine voice speaking to him over the phone.

"Mmm, yeah I saw that on the news this morning," Weston says in response to whoever's on the phone. "But they said it's supposed to completely bypass us and just get Texas."

Figuring he's talking about the small tropical storm out in the Gulf that my dad and I were just discussing over burgers and cheese fries at Meg's, I nuzzle my face into Weston's chest and let his delicious, purely masculine scent overcome me and send me to that warm, safe, happy place in my mind.

His arm tightens around me and I feel him smile against the top of my head, but he pulls away after a moment so he can talk. "Yeah,

Dad, of course I'll keep my eye on it. I'm the one who makes the final call at work about if we close for the day, so I kind of have to anyway."

After a moment of his dad talking, Weston says, "Mhmm, yeah she's good. She just got here, actually... yeah, I'll tell her... love you too, and Mom... yeah, yeah, okay... bye, Dad."

Once he's done and places his phone on the table, I remove my face from his chest so I can look at him. "Hey, you," I greet with a grin, lifting my hands to slide them over his rough cheeks.

His lips part ever so slightly, and just when I think he's going to greet me in return, he leans forward and captures my mouth with his own, his hands sliding up the back of my blouse and caressing the base of my spine. His tongue flickers over my top lip and immediately I'm dropping my hands from his face and twining them around his neck, my fingers clenching the blond hair curled there.

A gruff noise vibrates through his mouth at my slight roughness, and then his tongue is shoving through my lips and he's devouring my mouth in a way that only he can. Not knowing what's gotten into him but not being able to stop to ask since he's already rendered me helpless, I just kiss him back as possessively and forcefully as I know how.

He pulls away a couple minutes later, my lips feeling exquisitely swollen and my head in complete disarray. Brushing a few pieces of my hair back, he smiles almost shyly at me and says, "Hey, baby."

"Not that I mind at all or anything," I say lightly, a small grin on my still-wet lips, "but what was that all about? You okay?"

"Of course I'm okay," he answers, his cheeks turning just a little bit pink. "You just.... I couldn't kiss you when you first got here and you were on my lap all like that, so I... I lost it for a second."

I giggle, every sweet and shy word coming out of this man's mouth making me love him even more. "Oh," I say, rubbing the pad of my thumb over his bottom lip and feeling so incredibly warm when I see his pupils dilate in response. "Well, I guess that's okay, then."

"You *guess*?"

I roll my eyes at him. "West, we both know how entirely and pathetically *okay* I am when it comes to you kissing me, okay? Let's not tease me for it."

He grins widely at that, the blush on his cheeks fading away as he leans in and kisses me again, this one sweet and soft and gentle. We pull away at the same time, both smiling at each other, and then he says, "Let's go sit on the couch or something. This chair gets really uncomfortable after a while."

"Why didn't you just eat on the couch?" I ask, climbing out of his lap. "That's what we do whenever I'm here."

"Yeah, but I got Greek food," he says, grabbing my hand and towing me into the living room and to the couch, "which is Thumper's favorite. So whenever I get it, I have to sit at the table so it's harder for him to steal it from me."

I laugh as I take the seat next to Weston on the couch and waste no time in curling up next to him, my head resting on his chest and his hands reaching down to slip my legs over his thighs.

After a little while of the two of us just sitting there in each other's company, his hand stroking my hair and my eyes closed, he asks me softly, "How was dinner with your dad?"

"It was good," I say, catching sight of one of his hands and reaching out so my fingers can tangle with his. "We just talked about his trip and stuff, and he mentioned the storm out there you and your dad were talking 'bout."

"He leaves Friday morning, right?"

"Mhmm."

He smooths the hair back on top of my head and then rests his chin there. "You bringing him to the airport?"

"No, Meg is," I answer. "His flight's at like ten in the morning or something, so I'll be at work."

"This one's the big one, huh? The two-weeker?"

"Yeah." I sigh, curling up tighter against him. "But after that, I think he has one more small one and then he's done for the year, thank God."

He's quiet for a long while, his fingers playing with mine and his breath warming the top of my head. He says softly, "You can come stay here, you know... while he's gone. I know you hate being home alone."

"What, really?" I ask, my voice breathless.

Removing my head from his chest so I can peer into his eyes, I'm taken aback by the vulnerability there, the softness amongst the green. He's worried, obviously, that I'm going to say no or be scared off by how quickly the suggestion says our relationship is moving.

His eyes anxiously flick between my own, checking to make sure I'm not panicking, and it's so cute that it has my heart squeezing almost painfully.

"I'd love to, West."

Immediately the tension in his expression melts away, the rigidness of his jaw slackening and some light filtering back into his eyes, and before I can say anything else, he asks, "Really? That didn't send you running for the hills?"

Feeling a bit saddened that he's still so unsure of my feelings toward him, I raise my free hand not encased in his own and graze my fingertips across the stubble on his jaw. "Of course not. I've told you I'm in this for the long haul, West. Do you still not believe me?"

He sighs, obviously seeing that he's hurt my feelings. "It's not that I don't believe you, I just... I keep remembering those times I came on too strong and you got freaked and ran away. It's kind of hard for me to believe it can go from being that difficult with you to this easy."

I'm silent for a moment, thinking hard over how to approach this with him, and then I say, a bit jokingly, "You talk such a big talk, Mr. Alcorn. You know that?"

His brows furrow. "What do you mean?"

I giggle, shaking my head and coming up with the best way to put this. "You just, you know... those times we fought and everything, you said that I couldn't make my mind up. That I was either throwing myself at you or running away, remember?"

"Yeah...?"

"Well, I'm here now, West, aren't I? I'm here and I've thrown myself at you more times than I can count since we've been together, and yet you still think I'm going to run?"

The whole time I'm talking, I'm wondering where my embarrassment is, my anxiety over spilling to him just how much I care, because it's nowhere to be found. Instead I feel emboldened by my feelings for him, by his obvious feelings for me, and by the time I'm done with my little spiel, I'm crawling into his lap and wrapping my legs around his waist so I know he has to look at me.

He's stunned into silence, I think, so I keep talking, the two beers I had at dinner with my dad helping my nerve. "And, back then, West, I was a coward. A *fucking* coward. I refused to admit to myself how good I knew it'd be once we got together so I wouldn't hate myself for not trying, but... but now I know how good it is. It's incredible and you make me happier than I ever thought I could be, and... and I don't know. I'm done running from you. Hell, I don't think I have it in me *to* run."

He's laughing at me by the end of my little speech, and then he's sliding a hand up my neck so he can cup my cheek, and as I rest my face against his palm, he says, "You're anything but a coward, baby. And you're right, we are incredible. *You're* incredible."

"I do try," I tease.

"So," he says after a minute or two of just blindly smiling back at me, "it's settled, then. You're staying here while your dad's gone."

"Yes, it's settled." I nod firmly. "Although I've stayed here pretty much every night since we've been together, so I don't really get the difference."

"The difference, Iris," he says, brushing his thumb across my lips, "is that when you've been here, it's been on borrowed time. I've had to ask, you've had to ask, and it's been a conversation. I don't want to have that conversation while you stay here. I just want to know that I'm going to come home to you, go to bed with you, and wake up with you. No questions. *That's* the difference."

His words have every inch of my body swimming in love for him, dying to reach out and be with him, touch him, be a part of him, and I can tell by the darkening of his eyes that he feels the same way. His hand squeezes mine tightly, pulling it to rest on his thigh, and before I let my logical thought be clouded over by my desperation to be with him, I whisper, "That sounds perfect."

# Chapter Twenty-Three

It's the Monday after my dad left for his two-week trip and I'm currently sitting at my desk at work and flipping through the appointment book when one of my two bosses, David Poole, sticks his head out from the door leading to the office's main hallway.

"Hey, Iris?"

I jump a little bit in my seat in surprise, not used to my bosses really talking to me except for the morning "hello."

Swinging around in my chair so I can face him, I ask, "Yes, sir?"

"Can I talk to you about something? In the conference room?"

Something heavy plops down in the pit of my stomach, my heart knowing that those words can never mean anything good. I swallow the hard lump in my throat and nod. "Sure thing. Now?"

He nods, his expression not showing any hint as to what this could possibly be about. "If that's all right. Jen said she'd cover the phones."

"Okay," I manage to say, my knees a little bit shaky as I rise to my feet and smooth out wrinkles on my pencil skirt that probably aren't even there.

The conference room is dark and empty when he opens the door, but he flips on the lights and immediately goes to sit in one of the leather chairs on the far side of the long, dark wood table.

"Do you want me to shut the door?" I'm not sure if I'm going to want whoever's in listening distance of this room to hear me cry if I end up losing my job.

"Yeah, that's fine," he agrees, so I do just that, the sound of the door closing striking a painful chord in my chest.

I then sit down across from him and feel myself torn between wanting to stare down at my skirt or look straight at him to get a read of his mood. David's always been the more subdued of the bosses, Chet being the boisterous one, but something about Mr. Poole has always put me at ease.

But unfortunately that usual comfort is nowhere to be found at the moment.

"Now I know you haven't been here very long," he starts, "and that Miranda isn't due back for another seven or eight months, but there's something I'd feel very wrong for if I didn't speak to you about it."

"Oh?" I ask, an immense frustration shooting through my mind at the ambiguity of his words. "What's that, then?"

He places his folded arms on the edge of the table, his demeanor that same sort of calm that I'm, for once, finding very irritating, and then says, "One of the guys that Chet and I play with in a volleyball league runs the Budweiser factory right outside of Baton Rouge, and he mentioned they're about to start looking for a couple new people to work there in Human Resources. Now I'm not exactly sure of what you're looking to do career-wise, but the second he mentioned it, Chet and I immediately thought of you."

My eyes are bulging in shock, I'm sure, this lead possibly able to stop the few nights I've spent this summer researching job opportunities on the Internet. "Are you—are you serious?"

He grins at me, obviously pleased by my reaction, and nods. "Yes, ma'am, I am. We're all very impressed by what you've added here since you started working, but unfortunately this job *is* Miranda's and it's against many laws and pretty much every shred of humanity I have to take it away from her because of her new baby. But Chet and I think a lot of you, Iris, and we know how difficult the post-college job search can be. If there's any way we can help out, we'd love to."

"Thank you so much," I breathe, my heart still pounding but now for a much, *much* better reason. "I can't.... I mean, I don't even know how to thank you for this. I've been on *such* a hunt for something to do when my time is up here, but it's *so* hard to find anything near here and that'd be so perfect."

"Great!" he exclaims, a beaming smile stretching across his face. "He e-mailed me all the details so I can forward it to you when I get back to my desk, but I do know it's positions they want filled as soon as possible, so it'd be a pretty hasty thing."

"But that wouldn't leave y'all in a bind, would it? Y'all have done so much for me here, I don't want to—"

He shakes his head, cutting me off. "We can find a temporary receptionist pretty much anywhere, so it wouldn't be a big ordeal for us, no offense to you. It'd be far harder for you to find something than it would be for us to find someone."

I giggle. "Yeah, I guess that's true."

He smiles. "Well, I'm glad you love the idea and that we could help you out."

"Thank you so much, Mr. Poole."

---

After that the rest of the workday passes quickly, my usual attention to my work set aside as I eagerly comb over the job details David sent me and then get to work figuring out life changes I'd have to make if I got it.

The job sounds perfect for me, as it's a nine-to-five entry-level human resources position with good pay, benefits, and a ton of room for growth.

The only issue is that the factory's on the other side of Baton Rouge, and the commute could end up being close to an hour due to all the traffic. Of course, if I got it and had the steady income, I'd be able to move out of my dad's house and closer to the factory, but it also means I'd be further away from Weston than I'd really like to be.

I've gotten spoiled the past few weeks we've been together, living across from him and all, and I've always known that I can't just live with my dad forever to reap those benefits, but still, it'd be harder for me to see him every night, and that's something I've really grown to love.

It's a talk we're going to have to have, but I don't want to bring it up if I don't get the job. Me moving is already a touchy subject with Weston, as he's got a deep-rooted fear that I'm too good for this town, for him, and will leave once I have a solidified offer. But on the other hand, he's mentioned before that he doesn't want me to feel trapped by our relationship, and that I should go anywhere I feel is right.

But still, even with that slight stressor on my shoulders, I'm overly cheerful when the workday comes to a close and I'm starting to get ready to leave. I've already called the Budweiser people and sent them my resume as well as scheduled my initial interview for Wednesday afternoon, and even though I've decided not to tell Weston unless my chances of getting the job increase, I still can't wait to go to his place and build on this good mood of mine.

I'm shoving my phone in my purse when I hear the door from the parking lot open, and when I look up I see an unfamiliar middle-aged man walking over to me.

"Hi," I greet in my formal-yet-friendly work voice. "Can I help you with something?"

"Yes, actually," he says, his vibrant blue eyes meeting mine. "I'm in from out of town and meeting some friends at a bar called

Murphy's, but for some reason the GPS on my phone can't find it. You wouldn't happen to be able to give me directions, would you?"

I chuckle. "Yeah, it's so far from actual city limits out here that GPSs usually don't work. But to get to Murphy's you just need to take a left out of this lot, drive down about two miles until you hit the highway, take a right at that light, and then go until you hit the only stretch of road with restaurants and stuff. It's right after the Walmart."

"Okay, great." He smiles. "Thank you so much...?"

"Iris," I finish, reaching forward and shaking his hand when he extends his as an invitation. "I'm glad I can help. Oh, and just so you know, the fried pickles there are legendary."

He laughs. "Oh, okay, great. Thanks! You have a good one, Iris."

"You too," I tell him, watching him as he walks out, and then finish packing up all of my things.

I'm out the door right at five and I head straight to Weston's house, where I've already brought two weeks' worth of my stuff over.

He isn't home when I get there, as he's usually stuck at work until six or so, so after I take Thumper out and give him a good five minutes of petting since he's been alone all day, I quickly change into some comfortable cotton shorts and one of Weston's old, worn-in T-shirts.

Since I know he'll be starving once he gets home, I go ahead and order a large meat-lovers pizza, something I love knowing is his favorite, and then sink down onto the couch with a hearty glass of red wine before turning the TV on to check on the storm in the Gulf that's still projected to completely bypass us and only hit Texas.

One of the meteorologists is busy talking when I hear the front door open and see the deliciously large form of my boyfriend step through.

"Hey, babe," I greet him, pushing off the couch and hurrying over so he can give me my daily greeting kiss. He places his keys and wallet onto the shelf by the front door and then pulls me to him, his arms tight around my waist as his lips meet mine and his tongue pushes into my mouth.

After a few moments of deep, heart-pounding kisses, he pulls away and says, "Remind me to never shower at night again."

I wrinkle my nose in confusion. "What?"

"When I do that it means I still smell like you while at work, and it's incredibly distracting."

My chest tightening in warmth, I bite down on my lip and give him a small smile, placing my hand on his sternum and saying, "I like that, though, lets me know you're always thinking about me."

He blushes ever so slightly. "I'm already always thinking about you, you dork. This is... it's *really* distracting."

I laugh. "Well, that just means I'm going to try and persuade you to shower at night even more."

"'Cause you're evil," he groans, leaning in and kissing my forehead before pulling away from me. "I'm going to go change. How long have you been here?"

"About half an hour," I answer, heading back over to the couch. "I already let Thumper out and ordered dinner."

"God, I'm glad I'm dating you," he says right before disappearing into his bedroom. A stupid grin stretches my lips as I reach for my glass of wine and sit back down on the couch.

About half an hour later, I'm signing for the pizza despite Weston's protests to let him pay, and then crossing the floor back toward the couch where Weston's sipping on a beer, distractingly shirtless. At the smell of the food, Thumper leaps off his bed and hurries over to us, his big brown eyes begging.

Weston scolds him. "No, man, no pizza for you. You almost had a whole steak last night."

Thumper, almost as if he understands, makes a soft whining noise and plops his chin on the edge of couch right between us.

"Awww," I say.

Weston opens the box, pulls out a piece of pepperoni and a small piece of sausage, and lets Thumper eat them out of his hand. "That's it though, boy."

A few minutes later, when I finish my first slice of pizza and eagerly reach for a second, I ask, "You think if I got a dog, Thumper would like him? I'd want them to be friends and Thumper to not resent it for stealing his thunder or anything."

"You want a dog?" Weston asks with raised eyebrows, rubbing his greasy fingers on his plaid pajama pants as he finishes his second slice of pizza.

"I think so," I answer, curling my legs underneath me. "Like, I've always wanted one but just seeing you with Thumper makes me *really* want one, you know? I'd wait until I moved out of my dad's, of course, 'cause neither of us are really there anymore, but whenever I get my own place I'd love one so I'm not there alone."

He nods, his eyes falling from my face, and after a silent few moments, he says softly, "I keep forgetting you're not going to be across the street forever. I've gotten so used to you being *just right there*."

"I know," I agree just a little bit sadly. "I was thinking about that at work today, you not always being just an arm's stretch away from me. I'm sure I'll be over so much you'll get sick of me, though."

"Have you been looking at all?"

I shrug. "Here and there. More so at the beginning of the summer when I didn't have so much going on, but I've been thinking about it more often lately, since I have a pretty nice chunk of change saved up from the law firm."

"What about jobs?" he asks, making my heart throb a little bit. "Have you found anything around here?"

Seeing how much this kind of talk is already putting a damper on our night together, on our two-week living together binge, I decide once more to not bring up the Budweiser job unless it becomes more of a possibility. I don't want to lie to him, though, so I say, "I've found a few things and sent in applications. I'm just, you know, waiting to hear back. Nothing I'm setting my hopes up for too much. I still have more than half a year at the firm anyway, so I'm not too panicked."

"I've been looking around too," he mentions, and when he sees the shock on my face he explains, "Not for me, for you! I have an alert on my phone for when new jobs are posted and everything. It's pathetic."

"That's incredible," I correct him. He no longer has food in his hand, so I scoot over to him and rub my palm over his stubbly cheek. "The fact that you care so much kills me, I swear."

He rolls his eyes at me. "Of course I care, dummy. New jobs are so rare around here, you know, so I'm trying to make sure you don't go anywhere too far. Not that I'd hold you back if you did, but—"

"*West.*" I use my free hand to squeeze reassuringly at his thigh. "My plan is to stay as close to here, to you, to my dad, as possible. My first choice is definitely *not* to go to some big city or something. I'd get swallowed up."

He shakes his head, his eyes softening as he looks on at me. "No you wouldn't, Iris. You'd be incredible in that kind of environment, in any kind of environment, which is why I'm so dead set on finding you the perfect job here. Close to me. If it's perfect, then I won't feel bad for holding you back."

I groan. "West, if you think one more time that I've ever thought you'd hold me back, I'm going to scream. Never in my life will I think that, okay? If anything, you make me a better worker, and I'd be an idiot to give that up. You—you give me confidence, you make me happy, and I don't care if I had the best job in the world, if I didn't have those things with you, I'd feel useless." Before the moment gets too serious, I joke, "And you're pretty fucking fantastic at the sex thing too."

That gets a loud laugh out of him, and once he's done and looking at me with this soft kind of vibrancy, this glimmer that has my heart fluttering almost painfully, I know I've calmed his nerves.

I'm in complete shock that he feels that deeply about me moving far away, but I absolutely love it, and if I have to reassure him a million times to know he cares that much about me, I will.

I love him.

I'm in love with him.

And, when he looks at me like he is right now, I feel like maybe, just maybe, he loves me too.

# Twenty-Four

"Thanks for this, Mom," I tell the smiling woman walking beside me. Her face has been lit up with happiness since I met her for dinner at the only Italian restaurant in town.

With all the craziness surrounding Weston and my new relationship, I feel as if I've been neglecting her lately. It's just the day after I spent the majority of my night reassuring Weston of my seriousness about staying near him, and even though a part of me feels like I should be extra clingy for the next few days to drive the point home, I can't abandon my mom when she's dealing with all the things she is.

I'm the only person she has right now, since the entire town has stigmatized her for leaving my dad and me, and I know being with me is crucial for the improvement of her mental state.

Not only that, but I know the odds of her leaving again are pretty damn high and, when she's gone, I don't want to regret not spending enough time with her.

"You're welcome, honey," she says, stepping in front of me so she can unlock her rental car for us. "I've really been needing to get out of that hotel room."

"Have you been doing anything?" I ask her, my voice cut off by the sounds of us opening our car doors and sliding into the clean interior. "I hate to think you've just been holed up in there."

"I've been getting out, don't worry," she says, starting the car and looking over her shoulder to back out. "There's a support group near here I've been going to twice a week that's really helping, and me and some of the other women from there will sometimes go for drinks or dinner or something. They're all so nice."

"That's great, Mom," I respond, some deep-rooted anxiety coming out of me in a big sigh. "Support groups are pretty much the best things for people going through stuff. We had this whole chapter about it in one of my sociology classes at school."

"I do feel much better since I've been going," she says. "I've put on a little weight, thank God, because the last time I went to the doctor she got onto me for being so thin, and I've been sleeping through the night, which hasn't happened in ages."

"I'm so happy for you, Mom," I say honestly. "I know I don't come see you as much as I should, but I am constantly worried about you."

She waves a hand nonchalantly. "You're twenty-three, honey, you have your own life and you shouldn't have to abandon it for someone who... someone who abandoned you. Just the fact that you see me occasionally makes me feel better than I have in years. I don't deserve your forgiveness, I know that much, so I'm going to take advantage of whatever you give me."

I'm quiet for a long while after that, and before I've even come to terms with what I'm going to say, my mouth takes over.

"I don't think I'm ever going to be able to truly forgive you, Mom, not after everything, but that doesn't mean I don't want you in my life. I'd rather have you around and part of me resent you than you just not be around at all. I hope that's okay."

"Of course that's okay," she murmurs, turning her head for a brief moment to give me a small smile. "Like I said, whatever I can get."

I don't have time to think of anything else to say, as my purse on the floor starts vibrating against my feet. After apologizing to my mom for the interruption, I lean down to extract the phone from the outside pocket of my purse.

Weston's name is flashing on the screen and, since he knew I was going to be at dinner with my mom and is still calling, I figure it must be important. "West?"

"Hey," he says, his voice sounding different than normal, tense where it's usually soft. "You're coming to stay tonight, right?"

He doesn't sound right.

"Yes, of course," I say, my stomach churning with nerves.

"Why wouldn't I be?" I ask him, before adding the lame attempt at joking, "You're stuck with me for another week and a half."

"Just checking," he responds slowly. "How much longer you think you'll be with your mom?"

"We'll be back at the hotel in about twenty minutes, and then I'll be there."

"Okay," he says, and before I can respond with anything else, he's hanging up and I'm feeling incredibly rejected just by the sound of a click.

"Everything okay?" my mom asks, obviously picking up on the oddness of the phone call.

"I'm not sure, actually," I admit. "That was West, and he... I don't know, he sounded weird."

As I already told her all about my new relationship over our calamari appetizer at the restaurant, she assures me, "I'm sure it's fine, Iris. Men, I swear to you, can be so much moodier than we girls can. We just get the bad rep for it."

I make some kind of incomprehensible noise in response, already feeling partly guilty about dismissing our meaningful conversation so quickly, but unable to push aside this nervous anxiety blooming in the pit of my stomach.

We get back to the hotel pretty quickly, and the entire ride there my mom just hums along softly to the radio so that I'm able to lose myself in my thoughts. I'm not sure if I'm pleased by her choice to leave me alone, as by the time we're back I've thought myself into a near frenzy, but I still give her a tight hug goodbye right before she heads inside her hotel.

I blare my radio on the way to Weston's house, desperate to alleviate this most likely unneeded alarm, and as I'm pulling into his gravel driveway some euphoric Calvin Harris song is nearly shaking my car.

I cut the engine immediately but remain buckled in my seat, my eyes focused on Weston's front door. The small rational part of me is telling me that I'm making a huge deal out of nothing, and that Weston's probably just sitting on his couch waiting for me with Thumper at his feet.

But the larger part of me, the part driven by my immense gut-wrenching fear at not being enough, at abandonment, is screaming that I should just disappear into my dad's house only twenty feet away, so that there's no chance of me being hurt.

I can't let myself do that though, not anymore.

I refuse to hide, to resort to cowardice in order to save myself from hurt at the expense of being close to someone.

If anyone is worth me being heartbroken, it's Weston.

Which is the only reason I'm climbing out of my car and heading up the porch stairs to the front door, pausing only briefly to wonder if I should knock. I don't though, not wanting to make this evening anything unlike the past few if unnecessary, and right as the squeak of the screen door announces my arrival, I spot the large frame of the man I'm in love with, sitting on the couch with the remote pointed at the television.

"Hey, West." I give him my best attempt at a normal smile.

Thumper pops up quickly and contentedly trots over to me, and just for the briefest moment, as I'm scratching my nails against his head and seeing his large tail wag in response, I feel at home. But then Thumper decides he's done with me and heads back over to Weston's feet and I'm forced to look up, the expression on my boyfriend's face enough to make me seriously regret that I didn't run home to my dad's.

He looks equal parts disappointed and angry, his jaw clenched and his back rigid.

"What's going on?" I ask, slowly stepping further into the house. "What's wrong?"

"I'm just trying to decide if I should congratulate you or ask what the *fuck* is wrong with you."

Something sharp pierces my chest at the stabbing hurt in his voice, and so it's incredibly difficult for me to get out the words, "What're you talking about, West? I don't—"

"Jenny texted me earlier," he says, cutting me off. "She wanted me to extend her congrats to you on the new job. She said since y'all weren't talking much anymore she thought it'd be better for you to hear it from me, but that she had to say something because it was such an incredible offer."

"*West.*" Panic slowly starts to consume me as I realize what he's saying, what he actually thinks is going on. Jenny must've made the tip on the Budweiser job seem like an actual job offer, and Weston's insecurities most likely turned the text from her into an even bigger deal.

He shakes his head, standing and walking over to me in determined strides. "And I just think it's kind of funny how she thought it'd be better coming from me when, really, I didn't even have a clue you'd gotten a job."

"I didn't get the job!" I exclaim, sounding out of breath. "I just got an interview, that's all, which I haven't even had yet. I was going to tell you once I figured my chances were better, that's all!"

"Your boss practically handed you a job, Iris. That sounds like your chances are pretty damn good!"

I'm fervently shaking my head, stepping forward and grabbing at his arm as if it'll make him *really* listen to me. "West, you know me. You know I don't get my hopes up for anything, especially something that seems as easy as this does! I thought I'd have to take an unpaid internship somewhere, or get something with no benefits or... or *I don't know!* I was in complete shock when he told me about it, I still am, and I still think my chances are pretty low and that's why—"

His booming voice cuts me off. "But you know how I feel about all this job stuff, Iris! You know how paranoid I've been about you leaving town for a job, and it's just really fucking suspicious that you get this incredible offer and don't tell me about it, especially when *yes*, I do know you, and I know how much you love running off when things get a little too personal."

The insult ricochets through my chest, and suddenly I'm more angry than I am guilty.

"That's not fair," I respond, bristling. "I've told you a couple times now that I'm working on that, and throwing it in my face is really fucking not okay, West. I kept this from you because I knew it'd turn into a conversation kind of like this, yes, and that you'd get spooked, and I—I didn't want to put a damper on our time staying together."

"And you didn't think lying to me would put a damper on things?" he asks, his voice sarcastic and patronizing.

"I didn't lie to you!" I cry. "God! I told you last night I'd sent in applications to a few places and was waiting to hear back but that I wasn't getting my hopes up. That's exactly what this is!"

"You have an interview, for Christ's sake! The job was practically handed to you on a silver platter, so obviously—"

This time, I take my long overdue turn at cutting *him* off. "West, I don't know what all Jenny told you, but apparently she made it into a much bigger deal than it needed to be."

"But at least she told me *something*," he emphasizes, taking a step back from me and crossing his arms tight across his chest. "You... you just... you left me out, Iris, after everything I've told you and admitted to."

Tears burn my throat at how utterly rejected he looks, a guilty sort of distress taking over me as I say, "That's not at all what I was trying to do, and I'm sorry if it came off that way. If the interview went well, I was going to tell you right after. I promise. I just didn't want to worry you by telling. Things were going so well and I just... I didn't want to put a damper on that."

He's quiet, the steady thump of Thumper's tail the only sound, and after a few moments of him staying that way and my anxiety intensifying because of it, I add, "You have to *trust* me, West. I'm.... I've told you a million times that I'm in this for the long haul, so I don't... I don't get where all of this comes from with you."

"Really?" he scoffs, finally looking up from the floor and meeting my gaze. His eyes are bright, but not in that beautiful, happy way I've come to love so much. Instead they're almost taunting. "You don't get how you not telling me you were leaving town, or all the shit you pulled this summer with you running away the second anything important got brought up could've made me feel that way? Hell, it wouldn't surprise me if you randomly decided to run off like your mom did!"

The most excruciating kind of shock hits me the second the words are out of his mouth, a squeaking, tearful gasp coming from my throat. My body goes cold, still, the only thing working the part of my mind that processes pain.

Those tears from before return with a vengeance. I say in a hoarse, wounded voice, "I can't... I just... I can't believe you'd even.... You know how I.... *God*...."

My stammering trails off into tear-filled hiccups, my hand coming to cover my mouth as I see that hardness in his eyes telling me he's not going to take his words back.

He really means it.

He really thinks I could do to him what my mom did to me.

He thinks that lowly of me.

And all this time... all this time I truly thought he believed in me, *trusted* me.

"Do you—" I gasp, my chest heaving with labored breaths, gasping for air because, for some reason, I kind of feel like I'm drowning. "Do you.... I mean, if you think that I'd do that, even if—if for a... for a second, then why'd you ever get with me? Obviously you don't... you don't trust me."

His eyes are boring into mine, and the intensity I see reflected in them would remind me of his feelings for me if his body weren't so tense, if he were actually reacting to the state of pain I'm in. But no, right now he's just standing feet away from me, and the only sign that he feels something other than anger toward me is his frantic breathing.

"I thought something would change," he admits. "This whole... this whole thing has been based on a kiss over four fucking years ago, and I thought that if it went further, if we... you know, actually tried, then maybe my confidence in you would change. But, but... I don't know... it never did, Iris. Sometimes I still think you're seconds from leaving me some bullshit note and then skipping town."

I shake my head, the callousness of his words and the lack of faith he has in me just stirring my tears even further.

"I'd never...." I croak, in complete disbelief over what he actually thinks of me, of the piece of shit he must think I am. "I'd never do that to you, West. Not to you, not to my dad, not to Meg. Not in a million years."

"Yeah?" he murmurs, uncertainty in his voice for the first time tonight as he tightens his arms across his chest and shifts the weight on his feet. "And how am I supposed to be sure of that?"

"Because," I sob, my hand in a small, clenched fist as I reach up to swipe away the hot tears from my face.

And that's when I realize it.

I realize that I'm standing in front of a man who's made it very clear how little he thinks of me. And as he's done all this, as he's doubted me, I've just fallen more and more in love with him.

He doesn't even trust me, while I'm in love with him.

And it's the most painful, gut-wrenching thing.

But still, somehow or another, even with everything he's confessed to me tonight, the words I've been holding back for months now finally decide to be spoken.

"Because I'm in love with you, you asshole."

I can tell he wasn't expecting that, because his lips snap together. His eyes grow large, larger than normal, and I see all the tension in his chest deflate in one long exhale.

I have no earthly idea why, but the fact that I've finally said the words leaves me feeling emboldened, at least momentarily. Which is why, as I see his head spinning, I decide to bite the bullet so he doesn't have to respond.

"And obviously you don't love me back."

The words taste like poison because never in my wildest dreams would I have imagined actually saying them, but they fulfill their purpose. His eyes stop frantically moving and he just stares at me, making it clear that he has no idea what to do.

So once again, I do it for him.

"I know I've given you reasons not to trust me, I do, and maybe I still have a fleeting urge to run and hide, but since we've gotten together, I haven't run. Because I've been conquering this huge fucking fear to be with you, because I've been fighting against every fiber of fear in my body to not be a coward again. But obviously that means nothing to you, and I can't be with someone who doesn't trust me, West, who's always waiting for me to leave. That's not a relationship and... and even though that's what I thought we had, I guess I was wrong."

"I...," he stammers, his expression lost, confounded. "I don't...."

Tears once again trickle down my cheeks as I shake my head to get him to stop trying to talk. "No, West, it's—it's fine, okay? I get it. I'll go."

He takes a step toward me, and his mouth opens and moves as if he's saying something, but whatever it is I can't hear it.

I stare at him a moment longer, my heart begging for him to say something to make this at all better, but the more seconds that pass in silence the more I realize I'm never going to get the ending I want. He's never going to trust me, and if he can't give me that, then he can't give me anything.

Releasing my bottom lip from where I've been gnawing it so hard that I taste blood, I manage to say, "I'll come get my stuff tomorrow morning after you leave for work. Just leave the spare where it always is and... and I'll take care of it."

His eyes squeeze shut for the briefest of moments, and right then and there I allow myself the fleeting comfort of thinking he's as heartbroken over this as I am. But then he opens them and says, "Tell Steve I'm sorry, all right?"

I scoff, feeling the millionth stab to my heart since I stepped foot in this house less than half an hour ago at the fact he's apologizing to my dad, and not the girl whose heart he just mutilated.

"Whatever, West."

I turn toward the front door, dying to get into the comfort of my dad's home where I can scream into a pillow until I pass out, and it's then that I realize something.

No matter what he's said to me today, no matter how many times I may have run in the past, he's the one doing it now.

He's the one stopping something that could've been forever.

He's the coward.

I'm not even completely aware of myself as I turn to face him again, my hand still hovering in midair from where it'd been reaching for the doorknob, and say, "Just know that you're the one running this time, okay? This is all on you. Not me."

His expression hardens, the muscle right above his strong jawline twitching, and for the first time in ten minutes, he gets out a full sentence.

"Feels pretty shitty on the other end, doesn't it?"

And just like that, whatever grasp I have on sanity is relinquished.

I rip the front door open and sprint across the road to my dad's house, sobs pouring out of me in painful, chest-ripping gasps. My mind is in a dark, dense fog, both hysterical and painfully calm, and I don't know how much time passes before I realize that I'm in my bed, buried underneath the covers with a mascara-stained pillow under my cheek.

And all I can think of, the only thing that I'm capable of processing, is that, once again, I'm completely and entirely alone.

# Chapter Twenty-Five

I roughly respond, "Dad, it's going to be fine," to his hysterics into the phone sometime the next day, my vocal chords in near pieces after all the crying I went through yesterday.

I was in shock that I was able to call in to work today, and I was even more surprised when David told me they were closing for half a day anyway to prepare for the storm that's supposed to hit late tomorrow night.

Apparently the tropical storm that's been out in the Gulf and aiming for Texas has decided last minute to turn toward Louisiana's coastline and intensify as much as possible. According to the alert I got on my phone earlier this morning, due to the hotter-than-normal summer having the Gulf's temperature at a freakish high, the storm is supposed to become at least a category three hurricane by the time it hits.

If this were any other time, I'd feel that slightly sadistic kind of excitement I get for hurricanes and have the Weather Channel on for the next twenty-four hours, but instead, when I saw the alert, I didn't even blink an eye.

As pathetic as it is to admit, the end of my barely month-long relationship has rendered me completely nonfunctional.

But since my dad got the same phone alert about the storm and is now officially freaking out about me being home alone for it, I know I have to suck it up to at least quell his nerves.

"God, I just... even if I wanted to get home I couldn't! I have that meeting tomorrow morning. I'll lose my job if I don't go, and I've already checked with the airlines about flights after that, and they're planning them to be cancelled by then. Iris, I'm so sorry, honey. I hate that I can't be there."

"Dad, calm down," I murmur, sitting up in my bed to see if maybe it'll ease the frog in my voice. "I've been through hurricanes before, right? I know how to handle it."

"I know, I know," he says, not sounding at all appeased. "I'm more worried about the tornadoes, you know? We have that big tree out front and—"

"Dad, that tree's been through more storms than I have."

"Well, I just—hey, wait, aren't you just going to go stay with West anyway? I didn't even think about y'all being together now."

Knowing far better than to inform him of our less-than-graceful breakup yesterday, as it'll send him even further into hysteria, I decide to lie for now and say, "Exactly! See, Dad? It'll all be fine and I won't even be alone. So don't worry, all right? Enjoy your trip."

"You're batshit crazy if you think I'm not going to worry, Iris," he says dryly.

And for the next half hour my dad nearly shouts instructions at me, stuff I've known since before puberty, but I just listen quietly and tell him I'm taking notes to reassure him as much as I can.

When he hangs up, it's so he has enough time to call Meg before his meeting tonight, and as soon as his voice is gone, I'm wishing he were back and yelling at me about canned goods and radio stations again.

This silence is just too damn much. It's painful and awful and it has this mocking kind of feel to it, like a constant reminder that no matter how much I put into a person, I'm still not going to be enough.

I can't cry anymore, that's for damn sure, my body immensely dehydrated and my eyes probably bruised from all the rubbing. I need to.... God, I don't even know. I have to get my mind off this; I just have to.

Just like that, I'm flashing back to when my mom left and later on when Weston was working on the porch and driving me crazy, images of rubber gloves and blistered fingers shooting across my mind.

It takes me just five seconds to be out of bed, hauling myself to the cleaning cabinet in the kitchen and my head spinning with all I can get accomplished before I'm likely to pass out from exhaustion.

And, for the rest of the day, I feel just that much better.

------------

The wind is howling outside, causing the sounds of scratching branches and pelting raindrops to ricochet off the windows and overshadow the meteorologist's voice currently blasting from the television.

It's now Thursday, the storm having made landfall early this morning, and the entire state of Louisiana has been shut down to brace for Hurricane Maia, the category four storm that wasn't even supposed to hit here just three days ago.

I've been up since around four thirty this morning, unable to sleep due to nerves and the omnipresent thoughts of the man who broke my heart just a few yards away. The power hasn't gone out yet, just the outer edges of the storm having hit us so far, but judging by the radar I've had my eyes glued on for about eight hours now, I won't have the luxury of electricity for much longer.

The only good thing about not having slept well is that I've had pretty much all morning to get the house prepared. I went to the store last night after reducing my fingertips to raw skin from cleaning so hard, and even though most of the shelves were completely empty, I was still able to get some of the essentials.

I doubt I'll have to use half the stuff I got, but my dad was adamant about sending him photographic evidence that I'm actually prepared.

*"Grand Isle is already getting smashed by ten-foot storm surges. The owners of the campgrounds along the coast praying, I'm sure, that it doesn't get much...."*

The Weather Channel is drowned out by the sudden loud banging on the front door, which causes me to nearly leap off the couch in surprise and confusion as to why someone's out in all this.

I have to shove the door open due to the crazed winds, and it's as I'm in the middle of jokingly commenting, "Good Lord, that was difficult," that I see just who's crazy enough to be out in this weather.

My eyes flit hurriedly between my terrified, rain-soaked mother and the hand that's holding on to her forearm so tightly that the knuckles are white. Bewilderment induces my body into a state of near paralysis.

"What's...?" I choke out, having no earthly idea as to what's happening but knowing by the look on my mother's face that it's entirely *not okay*.

"Mom." I step forward and extend my arm to pull her inside, to get her safe, to... I don't know, to just... have her and know she's okay.

The second I touch her, though, my hand is slapped away and a voice is demanding harshly, "Don't you fucking touch her."

My eyes bulging at the threat, I look away from the thin, terrified face of my mom and let myself get a good look at who else is here, at who's brought her here, and my mouth drops open in shock as I see the same dark-haired man who came into work the other day asking for directions.

"You," I gasp, looking between the two of them frantically before concentrating just on him, the charm that'd been on his face Monday completely overshadowed by burning fury. "What're you.... *Who the fuck are you?* Why do you—"

"Stop talking!" he shouts, and when he moves forward, I

317

instinctively block his access. His free hand then comes barreling toward me, the edge of my shoulder taking the brunt of the force as I fail to jump out of the way in time.

I cry out in pain, grasping my shoulder as he forces his way through the door, never once dropping his hold on my mom, and it's as he shuts the door behind him and flicks the lock that the horror starts to creep over me.

He forces my mom across the wooden floor and then shoves her onto the couch, her head bouncing back from the strength of the push, and I'm already hurrying over to check on her when he demands, "On the couch, Iris."

I stop midstride, something inside me stirred by my name on his tongue, and boldly lock eyes with him from across the room. "Who the fuck do you think you are? You can't just barge your way in here and—"

"Enough!" he screams, his face burning red as he reaches into his jacket pocket and pulls out a black handgun. My heart plummets to the floor, my eyes seeking my mother's out in panic, and my hopes at anything being okay dashed when I see her cowering in the corner of the couch. "On the couch, Iris!"

My body completely rigid, I follow his order, coming around the side of the couch and sitting down next to my mom. Hysteria rolls off her in vibrantly terrifying waves. She quickly seeks my hand out with her own, her fingers folding over mine in what's most likely a useless form of comfort.

She says, "Tim, you don't have to do this. I'll come back with you, just... just leave my daughter out of this. Iris had nothing to do...."

And then everything hits me.

*Tim.*

The handsome rich guy from hundreds of miles away who charmed my mother into leaving us, the guy who treated her like royalty until the day she tried to be her own person, the guy who beat her so badly her only choice was to run away.

This is the guy she left my dad and me for, the guy who abused her, and... and he's found her.

He's found us.

"She has had *everything* to do with this, Barb! Fucking everything! She's the reason you left me, left our home together! She made you feel guilty, forced you into coming back here and that's—"

"She didn't do anything!" my mom cries, her grip on my hand tightening. "I left on my own, Tim, just like I told you on the way here! She didn't know how to contact me. I left her with—with *nothing*, so how could she have—"

"No you didn't!" he roars, his body palpably shaking. "You didn't leave me! She *made* you, she made you leave me!"

"She left because you beat her!" I scream, my adrenaline pumping so fast that it has my rational thought in a storm-induced puddle on the floor. "She left because you're a piece of shit who thinks 'cause he's rich and—"

"You shut the fuck up, you bitch!" he bellows, taking a few steps toward me and getting so close I can almost feel him shaking, can see what's either leftover rain or sweat trickling down his clenched forehead. "You don't know anything about your mom and me.... She loved me. She—"

My mom cuts him off, her voice the strongest and most rigid I've ever heard, "You back away from my daughter, Tim. Or else I'm never coming back."

He listens to her by backing away the few steps, but the slight relief of the movement proves useless when he starts laughing. My stomach churning at the sound, I watch as he settles down and then says breezily, "Oh you're coming back, honey. That's not up to you."

"You're not touching her," I seethe, the arrogance of this man pushing every single one of my buttons. I don't care how upset or traumatized he is over my mom leaving him, there isn't any way in hell I'm letting him hurt her.

There's no way in hell I'm letting him touch her *at all*.

He smirks, the sight of it twisting my stomach. "Well, why do you think I came here, Iris? It wasn't just to properly meet you."

"What're you talking about?"

"I'd already found your mom 'cause she's stupid enough to go to the first place anyone would look for her." He chuckles, starting to pace. "But unfortunately I was never at the hotel at the same time as you, so I had to seek you out elsewhere. I was at that diner in town when, lucky enough, one of the tables by me started talking with some woman who works there about you and your new little job. So I swung by, made sure it was you, and then followed you home."

"But I...," I stammer, "I didn't go home that night. I went to—"

"Your little boyfriend's house, right? I overheard them talk about that too. But I saw you in your car, and when I came here today, your car was parked here. Just works out in my favor that you live right across the street."

"What do you want from me?" I dare to ask, no longer wanting to hear about how easy tracking us down was for him. "You're the one... you're the one who stole my mom from me. If anything, you should be apologizing."

He cracks out another maniacal laugh. "*Apologize*? You and your dad had each other when she left you. When she left me I had no one! Not one person!"

"Okay, well, that..." I hesitate. "That doesn't answer my question. Why are you here? Why am I even involved in this?"

"It's a simple solution, really," he says, stopping his pacing so he can perch on the armrest of the recliner. "I'm here for a little insurance."

"Insurance?"

"Yes," he says simply. "So that when I bring her home with me, there's nothing left for her here."

"Wha...?" I trail off, my chest clenching deathly tight when I see his fingers flex around the handle of the gun. "No, you don't—"

"If it makes you feel any better," he says, his lips twitching with the beginnings of a smile. "This only has to happen because she loves you so much. At least you have that, right?"

"Tim," my mom says, her voice a scary calm. "If you do this, if you hurt her, I'll never forgive you. If you leave her be, if you just take me back home right now, I'll come back willingly and forgive you for everything."

"Mom, no," I urge desperately, my head whipping around to face her. "Don't... don't do that. You're going to.... He's going to kill you eventually, Mom."

She faces me, her face flooded with tears and immense guilt, and after she gives my hand another squeeze, she says, "He'd never hurt me that bad, honey. He loves me. He just... he just has a very bad way of showing it."

Her voice so soft, her expression so full of love for me, I feel tears of my own start to build up.

I shake my head. "No, Mom, I can't let you—"

I'm cut off by a huge crash of thunder outside, the windows vibrating in response, and once the shock wears off, I'm reminded that not only is there a crazy man in here threatening to kill me, there's also a major hurricane going on outside.

Tim seems to be reminded of this as well, and before I know it, he's crossing the floor to us and grabbing at my arm to jerk me to him.

I struggle against him, digging my heels into the floor, attempting to elbow him, anything to give me a split second to run the *fuck* away, but then I hear the click of the gun's safety being released and his voice saying sternly, "You move one more time and I won't give you the satisfaction of doing this away from your mother."

Knowing it's my only chance to prove to him my compliance so he doesn't shoot me, I nod and let him grab my arm. "Now which is your room?" he muses. "I wouldn't want your dad to have to live with knowing his daughter was killed in his bedroom."

As he talks to himself and lightly pulls me away from the living room, I realize it's my only chance, the only opportunity I have to make sure I get out of this alive, and so before I have the time to second-guess myself, I'm slamming my foot down on his and catapulting my head back as hard as it can go.

He screams, and I take off, screaming at my mom to follow me and trying to get to the front door as quickly as possible.

It's then that I hear the earsplitting, heart-stopping sound of gunfire and my feet just stop.

My mind at a complete and utter standstill, it takes me far longer than it should to realize that I'm not hurt, that there's no bullet in me, and as soon as I figure that out, I whip my head around to make *damn* sure it didn't hit my mom.

What I find instead is a furious man with a gun aimed toward the sky and a trembling woman half his size yelling at him that she ran over to mess up his shot, and that she'd do it again. There's water trickling down from the ceiling, the bullet seemingly having pierced through the structure, and for some reason, my reality becomes muddled the longer I stare at it.

It's like I'm not real, like this whole situation is just some out-of-this-world nightmare my fucked-up head produced.

Where I should be panicked, where I should be feeling that bone-shaking fear from mere seconds ago, I now feel absolutely nothing.

Not a thing.

Even though I know my life depends on it, it's like I just can't snap out of the daze.

It's then that the room is suddenly clouded in darkness, the electricity falling out with a stomach-hollowing purr, and the only light in the living room is in gray, pulsating shadows coming from the windows.

My consciousness slowly starts filtering back in, the hysterical pleas of my mom brushing across my ears and the muffled expletives from Tim sickening me to my core.

"No, Barb! She deserves this! She stole you from me, *do you not get that?*"

What my mom says in response is lost on me as I slowly let my gaze fall from the ceiling and back to them, but the second I register the back of his hand violently striking her already fragile cheek and my mom stumbling from the impact, I'm bursting out of my dangerous stupor and rushing back over to them.

I barely have time to slow down when Tim's wild eyes meet mine, and even less when his arm comes up and the barrel of a gun replaces his pinched face in my line of sight.

My body comes to an exhausted, hopeless standstill as I realize what's happening, that I can't stop what's happening, that no matter how hard I run back to where *I just was* I can't stop the split-second decision that he's going to make to kill me.

My eyes desperately seek out my mom's, the big, light brown eyes so similar to my own, and as I let myself just bask in the image of her, a picture of reality I never once thought I'd get back, a morbid peace settles in my stomach.

There's a second blistering crack of gunfire just moments later and my eyes squeeze closed, my body bracing for the burning, pulling-apart sensation I assume comes along with being shot.

But nothing comes.

Initially I don't let myself believe that he didn't hit me, that I got that lucky. Maybe the spiral of insanity my body's being ripped through just numbed the pain.

It's not until I hear a hoarse masculine cry that I let my eyes open and come back to the present, to a moment I never could have imagined, and what I see there in front of me has panic scorching my throat.

"Mom, no!" I scream wildly, my knees buckling as I leap over to where her crumpled body is sprawled out across the wooden floor, a gaping hole in her chest spilling blood.

My sanity, the part of me screaming that I don't need to get any closer to Tim, all but disappears as I fall beside her, just feet away from where he's sunk to the floor and is sobbing brokenly. I can hear his voice, soft and tortured, as he berates himself for hitting her, *for hitting my mother*, and it's only then that the idea hits me to take his gun while he's too overcome to notice.

My body shaking so hard that my fingers are almost a blur, I twist around and lean forward, grasping at the gun and pulling it to me almost too easily.

I flick the safety back on and then cradle it to my chest, turning back to face my mom as the worst burning I've ever felt starts scalding deep within my throat and rages up into my tear ducts.

Her eyes are open and, as I look more carefully at her, there's a strange sense of peace as she gazes at me.

"*Mommy*," I cry, my head bowing as my free hand forlornly seeks hers out.

She gives me the weakest squeeze in response, her hands already too cold to be normal, and it sends the most heartbreaking trigger of love through my veins. "I don't... I can't...."

"Iris, honey," she breathes, and I can tell she's trying her hardest to keep the pain she's feeling out of her voice to make me feel better. "It's okay, my baby. It's okay."

"No, it's not," I sob, shaking my head and unwillingly letting my eyes fall to the gaping, bleeding hole in her chest. "You're.... You just came back and—"

"I'm still here," she assures me, "but... but, honey, I need you to call an ambulance, okay? Use your cell and get some help out here."

"Oh God," I whimper, automatically hating myself for not having thought of that first and instead just letting her lie here bleeding out so that I can selfishly, pathetically cry over her. "I'm so sorry," I urge, fumbling around in my pockets for the cool metal of my iPhone. "I... I didn't even...."

My fingers are still nearly impossible to use, but thankfully enough I'm able to dial 911 and breathlessly explain the situation. The operator assures me that an ambulance and cop car will be here as soon as possible with the storm outside, and for me to stay on the line with her. But as I look back down at my mom and see her blue-tinged eyelids drooping, the operator's voice fades into the background.

"It's okay, Mom," I whisper painfully, my hand reaching out and smoothing the hair that's gotten stuck on her sweat-covered forehead. "It's going to be o—"

My words are cut off when I hear the sound of the front door being forced open and slammed into the wall behind it. Numbed to the point of not caring what else happens to me here, I reluctantly look up, wondering if it's some other man on a murderous rage here to kill me.

But when I see Weston there instead, his face pale and terror etched deep into his features, that fear turns into overwhelming relief.

"*West,*" I croak. "I... I need—"

He's immediately rushing over to me, his eyes frantically darting between my mom, me, and the crumpled man still sobbing in the corner. "What... what's going on? Neighbors... called... gunshots.... Thought it might be storm but saw the weird car in the driveway." His words are coming out in frantic pants, but I know exactly what he's trying to say.

"My mom's ex," I start, but then I hear my mom make a little gasp of pain next to me.

A soft cry escapes my throat and I put my focus back onto her, onto my mom, onto the woman who's currently bleeding out in front of me and may be seconds away from leaving me again, this time for good.

I squeeze her hand tightly and say vehemently, "It's okay, Mom,

I promise.... I won't.... You're not leaving me again. I won't let you."

"Iris," Weston whispers beside me, and when I tear away from my mom and look up at him, I see that he's extending his T-shirt to me. I grab at it, momentarily confused, but then understand as he says, "Put pressure on the wound. It'll help the bleeding. Like I did with your leg, remember?"

I slowly nod and then reluctantly turn back to my mom, my queasiness with blood nonexistent as I push the balled-up T-shirt onto the wound. My mom groans in pain, her eyes squeezing shut, and the sound of it makes hot tears trickle onto my cheeks.

"That's good, Iris, that's good," Weston assures me, squeezing my shoulder before he says, "I'm gonna go make sure this guy doesn't move, okay? You've called 911, right?"

"Yes," I murmur painfully. "They're on their way."

# Chapter Twenty-Six

And just a few minutes later, despite the storm raging outside and the roads most likely being a mess, we're being joined by two police officers and a paramedic.

A huge sigh of relief escapes me at the sight of them, their uniforms and badges making me think that maybe this whole nightmare is over. I don't get up to greet them, so intensely resolute on holding this shirt to my mom, but I am quick to tell them, "She needs to be taken in like right now. She.... He shot her in the chest and she's been bleeding for a while and—"

"We got her, ma'am," the EMT assures me, hurrying over to assess my mom while two more come in wheeling a stretcher. I shakily rise to my feet once he reaches her and I feel it's okay to let go, and the moment my hands are free Weston's grabbing on.

One of the cops, a middle-aged lady with a long blonde ponytail frizzed out by the weather, catches my eye and nods to Tim while asking, "This the shooter?"

"Yes." I nod. "He's her ex. He... he abused her and she ran away here, but he found her. Blamed me for her running."

Tim must hear me, as his cries turn from being muffled into his bent knees to hysterical shouts of, "She loved me! I know she did! We were soul mates and she loved me, and I... I shot her!"

When he sloppily stands up, my nerves surge with fear and I back as far away from him as I can.

"Hey, hey," Weston urges into my ear with a comforting voice, his arms wrapping around my waist. "They have him, Iris. You don't need to be scared anymore."

I sink into his hold and watch, completely stupefied, as the second cop puts a still rambling Tim into handcuffs and, after taking his gun from my outstretched hand, leads him out of the house.

Once they're gone and a part of me feels somewhat secure, I move my attention to where the paramedics are hurriedly strapping my mom onto the stretcher, two of them buckling her in while the other sets up an oxygen mask for her.

"Is she going to be okay?"

Not looking up from where he's helping my mom, the first paramedic says, "Due to the amount of blood, I think it's safe to say all major arteries were missed, but there's no way to tell for certain. Once we have her in the truck we'll have a better idea of the damage."

"O-okay," I stammer. "I–I can come, right? With her? To the hospital?"

He answers, "Unfortunately no, ma'am. Because of the storm and all, we're trying to keep the hospital as uncrowded as possible in case there are a lot of injuries. In situations like this, it's impossible to know how crowded it's going to get and it's better to be safe than sorry."

"But—" I start to argue, feeling pulsating irritation.

Another paramedic, this one a bit older and with more of a stoic face, cuts me off. "It's protocol, ma'am. I'm sorry. We can't make any exceptions. Once the storm passes you'll be able to see her."

"Well how am I supposed to know if she's okay?" I demand

angrily, Weston's hold on me tightening as I try to take a step forward. "She's my mom, and if she's on the brink of dying, I think—"

"One of her nurses will call you with any details once we have them. None of us like doing this, I assure you, but it's the rule for when hurricanes hit."

"Fine." I figure that the longer I argue the longer they'll be *not* working on my mom. "Where do I give you my number?"

The cop that stayed inside after her partner led Tim outside answers, "You'll give it to me during your statement and I'll bring it to her room when I go to assess her injuries for the shooter's charges, which will be right after this. We've done it this way quite a few times when we've had to keep family out of the hospital, and it works very well. I promise you that."

"Okay," I agree. "As long as I hear something by today. I won't be able to sleep tonight if—"

She assures me with a smile, "I'll make damn sure they've contacted you before I leave there, okay?"

I relent and allow the paramedics to wheel my mother away, part of my heart splintering open the moment she's out the door and out of my sight. Once they're gone, Weston walks me to one of the chairs at the dining room table and then fixes the cop and me some glasses of water while she gets ready to take my statement.

Since the kitchen only has one window, it's so dark she has to take her phone out and use its flashlight, her left hand holding it over her notepad after she places her voice recorder in the center of the table and gets a pen out.

"Okay, first I'm just going to get some basic info from you, all right?" she prompts, and after I nod my agreement, I answer all the questions she asks about me that she says have to go in the case file.

Once that's done and I've downed two glasses of water from Weston, she starts, "Now, focusing on today. You said the shooter was your mom's ex-boyfriend?"

"Yes," I answer. "She left my dad and me a little over four years ago and immediately went to him. Just this past summer she came back to town and we reconnected, and she explained to me how he'd started to abuse her and how it was crucial that she get away."

"Okay." She nods, scribbling a few things onto the pad. "And how did he get here? Did he track her with a phone or...?"

"He didn't mention exactly how he found her," I explain. "Just that she made it easy because she came back to the most obvious place."

"And how did he know where you lived?"

"He overheard a conversation at my dad's girlfriend's diner about where I was working, came in one day as a stranger asking for directions to make sure it was me, and then followed me home that night. That was earlier this week. I don't know why he decided to do all of this today."

"Most likely because the storm outside would make it hard for you or your mom to escape. Now, what happened when he got inside?"

As I tell her the rest of what happened, the details of earlier today that I'm sure will be etched into my mind like an unshakable Etch A Sketch for the rest of my life, she continues taking notes and making me feel as comfortable as possible.

She leaves about an hour later on the promise that she'll make sure I'm contacted about my mom sooner rather than later, and the second she's out the door, I'm burying my face into my clammy, cold hands and indulging myself in the dry heaves I've been putting off this whole time.

I'm not crying anymore, as I'm either in too much shock or because I've dried myself of tears over the past few days, but instead I'm overcome with painful gasps of breath, a pounding chest, and a horridly hollow and sick-feeling stomach.

And to think that I originally believed my mom leaving us was the worst thing that could ever happen to me, to our little family.

It's almost laughable now, now that my life was threatened and my mom's blood is spilled across the floor.

That one thought makes my head snap up, the thought of the actual evidence soiling a house designated as my safe place, and within a second I'm getting out of my chair and heading toward the cabinets to grab some bleach, heavy-duty gloves, and a sponge.

I have to clean it up, I have to.

I *have* to.

I'm harshly digging through the cabinet when I hear footsteps come up behind me, and it's then that I remember that Weston didn't leave when the cop did.

"Iris," he breathes, grabbing my elbow and pulling me up from where I'm squatting in front of the cabinet. His eyes are dangerously soft, filled with empathy and pity, things that make me more than a little angry, and when he says, "You don't have to clean it. I'll do it. You've been through enough today," that anger only intensifies.

"I got it," I assure him tightly, hating that he thinks it's okay to be here for me. "You can go now. I'm fine on my own."

He sighs, his eyes squeezing shut for a moment but his hand on my elbow not dropping contact. I'm rigid in front of him, annoyance lighting my every fuse, and it's not made any better when he opens his eyes and says, "Look... I don't want to have this talk right now, okay? Just let me... just let me be here for you. No one should have to be alone after all that."

"No," I urge, shaking my head and ripping my arm away from him. "If I let you stay, if I let you be here for me, it's just going to hurt worse when you leave. I know you're trying to be a good person and all, but I don't want that from you. Not anymore."

"Iris," he croaks out, the corners of his eyes twitching at my words. "Please. I...."

The soft, vulnerable sound of his voice, his pleading, has tears I didn't think were possible anymore clawing up my throat. I thought

331

that today could emotionally exhaust me to the point of being numb to anything else. Leave it to Weston to prove me wrong.

No matter how much bad stuff I have going on, no matter how much I've been through or the current load on my shoulders, anything with Weston can make me feel like rock bottom was nothing but a slight pothole.

And it pisses me the *fuck* off.

I wipe away a couple of trickling tears and say, "West, I'm serious. You... you broke my heart. I thought we were on the same page, but then because I didn't tell you one thing, you all of a sudden decided I wasn't worth your trust or the risk. You made me feel like an absolute piece of shit for things I've already apologized to you over and over for. I get that what I did four years ago and earlier this summer was wrong, but what you did was worse. You intentionally hurt me, and that's something I'd never, not *ever,* be able to do to you."

His eyes are rimmed in red, I realize. I hate to see him upset. I don't think anything could change that, but I can't let myself do anything about it. I need distance from him.

"I'm so sorry," he says, his voice cracking. "You didn't deserve how I treated you that day. You didn't... you didn't deserve one thing I said. I–It... you know, when Jenny told me before you did, I just jumped to the conclusion that you were hiding it from me and.... Iris, you know, as pathetic as it is, my biggest fear was you leaving. *Is* you leaving."

"I know that," I whisper, crossing my arms over my chest. "I didn't tell you because I knew that, and I didn't want to give you any reason to worry if it wasn't certain. I should have told you, and I was wrong, but you were wrong to doubt me as much as you did. Not after I poured my *fucking* heart out to you, multiple times. West, you don't even... you don't even know what me saying all that stuff meant. I was guarded before my mom left, and then... and then she ran and it only got worse."

"I know," he says, guilt turning his eyes downward. "Baby, I know that. I know how lucky I am, how rare it is for you to open yourself like that."

Swiping away more warm tears, I say, "And yet you still threw the entire thing with my mom in my face. I could've... I could've taken anything but that, West, anything but you comparing me to her."

He bows his head in shame, shifting his weight as I hope guilt makes him feel even half as shitty as he made me feel that day.

"I...," he starts, his voice muted as he continues staring at the floor. "I still cannot believe I said that. I can't.... I knew how much it'd hurt you, and I–I can't really tell you exactly why I said it except that I thought you were leaving and I was... I was trying to make it better for myself. Comparing you to her, no matter how not true it was, made me feel like, just for one second, I wasn't losing someone so good."

"Hurting me like that shouldn't have made you feel better," I say tersely, hating myself for starting to understand the mindset he was in that day.

After a long, drawn-out moment, he lifts his eyes to meet mine and says, "And that's why I felt like shit literally five seconds after you walked out that door."

Tightening my arms across my chest, I say sourly, "Good."

He scoffs a laugh, the smallest of smiles touching his lips, before he says, "I didn't mean anything I said that day, Iris. I promise you. What I said was based off my own insecurities and not anything you'd done wrong. Since we got together, you've been nothing short of perfect, and I–I hate myself for letting that be ruined by what I *thought* was going to happen, and not by what was actually happening."

I'm quiet for a long moment, my mind racing with everything he's just told me and what exactly I should do about it. Yes, what he said that day killed me, but I still understand why he did it.

He has worries too, insecurities that keep him from believing that things can be good for him, an affliction I share.

"So... so what, then?" I ask. "Are you... are you just apologizing for hurting my feelings or are you trying to get back—"

He shakes his head to cut me off, stepping forward and wrapping his arms around my waist in such a beautifully familiar way that I can't refuse it.

His eyes boring into mine, the green in them as sharp as diamonds and as vibrant as a flame, he says lowly, "What I'm trying to do here, Iris, is.... I'm... I'm telling you that I love you. I'm telling you that I should have said it back when you said it to me, and that I'll do anything you want to make up for how mean I was. I'm telling you that you... that you have me. Whatever way, shape, or form, I'm yours. It's all up to you, Iris. I–I love you. That's where I stand. And if... if you don't love me anymore, then I understand. You deserved my utmost trust, and I didn't give it to you, but you have it now, okay? If that's enough—if *I'm* enough—then I really would like to forget that the other night happened and have you come back to me."

Tears are trickling down my cheeks, muggy drops of water meeting the dried tear tracks from earlier, and I can't decide if I want to kiss the life out of him or *slap* the life out of him. I'm still in shock from what's happened with my mom and Tim, so much so that I can feel my heartbeat in my toes, and I think it's only that allowing me to not crumple into his arms and accept his love like the affection-deprived girl I am.

"*God,* you're such an asshole" is what finally comes out of my mouth. I shake my head in disbelief as I fist away the tears on my face. "You break my heart, literally just stomp on it like some sick son of a bitch, and then you wait until a fucking hurricane is going on outside and my mom's almost *just been killed in front of me* to apologize? What the fuck, West?"

I can tell by the look in his eye that he's confused about if he should be amused or upset by my reaction, but he still takes a step toward me. "I know. I didn't want to have this talk now, it needed to wait until this has all been figured out, but... but you were trying to make me leave you here alone! I didn't know how else to have you let me stay, so that's why I'm saying this now and—"

I cut him off, nearly flinching away from him as he takes another step closer to me. My words are dripping with venom as I say, "Oh? So that whole little declaration of love was just a ploy to let you stay so you could feel better about yourself? Great, West, thanks so much for that."

Frustration flashes across his face, and before I can register the movement in time to avoid it, he's leapt across the few feet between us and cupped my jaw just firmly enough to keep me from moving.

"Just listen to me, okay? I've been thinking that *little declaration* since the day you kissed me in Meg's parking lot. You've owned me since that *fucking* second, Iris, and I'm sorry about not saying that stuff earlier. But don't you even dare, for one second, think that I'm lying when I tell you I love you. I know what I said the other day was horrible and I'm so, *so* sorry for that and I'll spend the rest of my life apologizing for letting you walk out like that. And for telling you this, putting this on you now of all times, but... but, I can't leave you, okay? Not right now, not later on today. I'm not going to be able to breathe unless you're in my sight, Iris, not—"

The longer he babbles the more panic I see rippling across his face, and despite what he's put me through, despite him telling me all of this now when I can't truly enjoy it, I can't let him keep rambling himself into lunacy. So I lift my ice-cold hand to his face and lightly press my fingertips against his full bottom lip.

It shuts him up immediately, his frantic green eyes searching my face for any sign of forgiveness, and before he has the chance to say, to confess, anything else to me, I let out a loud exhale and say, "Later, West. We'll talk about this all later, okay?"

He weakly nods, his haunted eyes still plundering my own, and as a faint mist of tears begins to coat his pupils, he opens his mouth and nearly begs, "Can I please hold you now?"

I sadly smile at him, my heart giving the most painfully bittersweet tug, and then take that last step to him. His strong arms instantaneously surround me, digging into my back so hard I can feel it in my ribs, but it's the most comforting type of discomfort, and I know that if it lessens, it'll only allow my anxiety more room to run.

I'm not exactly sure how much time passes while I'm in his arms, Weston seemingly needing the embrace more than I do, but when a particularly loud crash of thunder has the wooden floors beneath us shaking, I slowly pull away.

Weston's voice is quiet, unsure, as he takes the tiniest of steps away from me and asks, "What can I do, Iris? How can I help?"

My eyes flicker over to the window facing the front yard, my heart no longer able to stand the sight of Weston's tortured face, and when I realize I can barely see his house across the street due to the sideways rain, I say, "I–I want Thumper, I think."

"Yeah? You want to go over to my house?"

My eyes glazing over the longer I stare out the window, I slowly turn back to face him and shake my head. "No, I–I feel like if I go anywhere else, the cop and my mom's nurses won't be able to find me."

"You gave them your cell, though, right? Do y'all even have a house phone here?"

I shake my head, suddenly feeling smaller and more childish than normal. "No, we don't, but I just.... It's kind of like when you're a kid and you go on vacation during Christmas or when you just lost a tooth and you're scared Santa or the tooth fairy won't be able to find you. You know what I mean?"

A small, heartbreaking smile stretches Weston's pink lips as he says, "Yeah, baby, I do."

He eventually calms me down enough to persuade me to take a bath while he hurries across the street to fetch Thumper, assuring me that he'll only be a second and that he won't be out of my sight again once he's back.

It doesn't take me long to get everything ready in the bathtub, and as soon as the water's reached the edge and I've mentally prepared myself to strip and get in, I hear the front door opening and Weston calling, "It's just me! I'm back!"

After I poke my head around the door to tell him I'm getting in and then answer his question of if I want him in there with me with a resounding "no," I cautiously slide into the water.

The hot water feels incredible against my skin, and at first I'm so unbelievably glad that Weston knew the power hadn't been off long enough to rid the house of heated water and came up with this idea. But as more and more time passes and the hot water and lavender bubble bath no longer has me in a lethargic daze, the screen behind my eyes seems to decide it's a good idea to replay all the horror from earlier today. Its favorite image is the one of my mom on the floor with a huge hole in her chest and that damn comforting smile on her mouth.

By just the third minute of that, I'm jumping out of the bath and dressing in the cotton shorts and oversized long-sleeved shirt I brought in here. My heart is pounding uncomfortably the entire time I dress and, for some reason, when I'm done and nearly leap out of the room, I'm shocked into relief when I see Weston on the couch scrolling through his phone.

I have no idea what made me think he wouldn't be here anymore, but whatever it was is probably the same thing that has tears filling my eyes when I spot Thumper across the room in front of the window. The large dog is most likely keeping an eye on the rain, but when he hears my footsteps his ears perk up and he lets out a friendly bark. He trots over to me, and the second I see those brown eyes of his, I'm plummeting to the floor.

Thumper is quick to push his way onto my outstretched thighs, and tears slowly fall down my cheeks as he smothers me in kisses. But before I can lose myself and just bury my face into his soft fur, strong arms come up behind me and pull me to my feet.

I'm not completely conscious of what's happening, only that I'm now pressed against a hard chest and that a soothing voice is whispering incoherent words of comfort into my ear. I clench my fists on the softest of cotton shirts right as my body completely shuts down, the events of today once again proving their hold over me.

------------

It takes quite some time for me to hiccup my way back into sanity, although I'm not entirely sure how long, but once I feel like I have a somewhat solidified hold on myself, I open my crusted-over eyes and pull away from what I'm most certain is Weston's chest.

"You're okay," he urgently whispers, reaching up to smooth away the stray baby hairs hanging across my sweat-slicked forehead. "You just.... You lost yourself for a little bit, but you're okay."

"Has—" I have to clear my throat. "Has anyone called yet? What time is it?"

"It's just now three," he answers. "And yes, Officer Harmon called about a half hour ago."

My fear taking off full throttle, I jump back so I'm resting on the bottoms of his thighs and look at him with wide eyes. "And? What'd she say?"

He smiles softly at me. "Your mom is going to be perfectly fine, Iris. It missed all major arteries, and since the shot was a wild one, it's not nearly as deep as it could've been. They brought her into surgery as soon as they got there, got the bullet out in less than an hour, and she's already in the recovery room."

Although I know I should be feeling some type of overwhelming relief that she's not in danger of dying, anxiety is still pulsating through me as I ask, "Has she woken up yet? Is she alone? Does she want to see me?"

Weston reaches out and smooths his thumb across my forehead.

"She's not up quite yet. She was just put in recovery like an hour ago so it might be a little while before she's up, especially with everything she went through today. But Officer Harmon assured me that a nurse would let your mom call you as soon as she's up to it."

My lips turn downward as I realize what that means. "So we still can't go there?"

"No, baby, I'm sorry," he says, sounding wholeheartedly disappointed to tell me. "We still haven't gone through the far side of the storm yet. We're in the middle of it now."

I look out the window to see if what he's saying is true, and sure enough the entire view of outside is cast in that creepy yellow-gray light that, even though it's an effect of the eye's calmness, promises a whole new oncoming onslaught of chaos.

Weston adds, "But the weather's saying it should be over by tomorrow morning and, if there's not too much flooding or debris, we should be good to go."

"Yeah, okay," I murmur in response, trying not to feel too guilty about her waking up with no one around.

"Iris," he says quietly, and when I don't immediately look up he's lightly touching his fingertips to the underside of my chin to make me do so. "This is a good thing, okay? Your mom is fine. Tim is gone and no longer a threat. And if we survive the rest of this storm, then eventually, you're going to have one badass story to tell at dinner parties."

I snort a laugh and then tears bubble up again, his evident care for me only adding to the multiple emotional whirlpools inside me.

I don't say anything in response, as I can see in Weston's eyes that he knows I need silence. Instead I grab his forearm, give it a little squeeze, and then curl into a ball on his chest as I think of how the storm outside has absolutely nothing on the storm raging inside me.

When I wake up, it's dark and the rain outside is just a soft patter against the window. I'm in bed, the soft cotton sheets beneath me telling me that I'm still at my dad's house, and it takes me only a moment after seeing the wrinkled sheets next to me to realize that Weston was in here with me as well.

He's not here anymore, though, the space next to me now an uninviting lukewarm temperature, and since the clock on my phone is showing well past eleven, I realize that I've been asleep for a good eight hours. Although the emotional drain is still a heavy cloud in my mind, my body is now too wired to even think of sleeping more, so after a few minutes I'm sliding out of my bed and heading into the living room.

Despite the darkness of the house, my eyes immediately find Weston, his back tense as he leans over the kitchen counter, his forearms pressed into the cheap tile. He's speaking softly into his cell phone, I realize, and when I hear my name I stop.

"...I just, I've never been that freaked in my life. I mean... not only am I worried about her being alone during the storm, but then I get that *fucking* phone call from the neighbors saying they may have heard a gunshot and.... No, I know her being alone is my fault.... Yeah, I just... if I think that way for too long, I'll want to put a bullet through my own skull."

"No, Mom, not literally. I just... I didn't think I could hate myself more than after I yelled at her over the job thing, but then... then I get here and she's sobbing over her bleeding mother and this guy *I don't fucking know* is in the corner and I–I could've stopped that from happening. I could've.... No, I know he had a gun, but even if I couldn't have stopped it, I could've jumped in front of the bullet instead of Ms. Barb and *then* maybe I'd feel like I deserve getting her back."

My heart is squeezing itself tight inside my chest, so tight I feel like I can't breathe, and so when a loud gasp for air escapes my throat, Weston pivots to face me, his lips dropping open in shock.

"Iris, I...," he breathes, the top of his bare chest and his neck turning a light shade of pink. "You're awake."

I swallow a hard lump in my throat. "Yeah."

All of a sudden his eyes snap away from me, like he's just remembered that his mom is still on the phone, and I can't seem to tear my eyes away from him as he finishes off their conversation with a promise that we'll be careful and that he'll call again in the morning.

Once he ends the call and places the phone on the counter, I see the four empty beer bottles lined up behind him. My eyes widen at the sight, and when I look back at him, I ask, "Were those even cold?"

He purses his lips. "They did the job."

A little unsettled by the hostility in his voice, I cross my arms over my chest and ask, "And what job was that?"

"To make me feel a little less like a piece of shit. Didn't help too much, you know, but I'll take what I can get."

And suddenly my annoyance is gone, emotion burning the back of my throat as I realize just how tortured he is. While he may not have been there for the main show, I know the panic he felt because I felt it the entire time Tim was here, and just one shred of that panic would be life altering.

Not only that, but the guilt that's radiating off him right now is nearly tangible.

"*West*," I urge, taking a step toward him and resting an open palm against the center of his chest. He won't meet my eyes, looking down at the floor like he's flooded with shame. "Please don't... don't do this right now. We're both exhausted, we're both drained, and the fact that you feel even a shred of guilt over what happened here today is ludicrous. So just stop that train of thought before it takes off."

"It's not ludicrous, Iris," he retorts sadly, running his fingers through his messy hair. "If I... if I hadn't let you leave the other day, if I'd just stopped being stubborn and an insecure little fuck for just five seconds and come over here, then I could've stopped it. I could've stopped him, Iris, and then your mom wouldn't be in the hospital and you wouldn't be here passing out from crying. I—"

I cut him off, shaking my head earnestly. "Yes, you letting me leave the other day was pure evil, West, and yes, maybe you should've apologized sooner so it didn't have to be while a huge puddle of my mom's blood was next to us, but those things did not, *at all*, cause Tim to bust in here with my mom and with a gun."

He opens his mouth to add something, but I keep going. "And besides, you saying that your being here could've stopped it is a bit insulting, okay? No, I don't have a gun like you do, but I tried as hard as I could to get my mom and me the fuck out of here. The man was deranged, and I don't think anything, not even you, Mr. Muscles with a gun, could've made him do anything differently."

After that he finally looks up at me, his green eyes filled with a guilt that's painful to see. His strong jaw, coated with stubble that's overgrown even for him, is tensed to the point it's probably grating his teeth, and it doesn't soften when he responds to me.

"I'm not trying to... to insult you, but I–I just, I don't know... I feel like I'm getting off too easy with all of this. And not only that, but even that you're just letting me be here, with you, so I can keep you in my sight and know you're not hurt, I–I don't deserve that, Iris. I should be helping you after what just happened."

I smile at him, what he's said proving to me for what's hopefully the last time that he's just as hopelessly into this, into me, into our relationship, as I am.

"West," I murmur, slithering close to him and twining my arms around his neck. "No matter what you may or may not deserve, this, you and me, is right now about what I deserve, okay? So I'm going to be selfish, and if that means being stupid too, then so fucking be it. I've been through enough today to last me a lifetime, and if there's one thing I think I deserve, it's being with you because, usually, you make me happy. Yes, what we both did was shitty, but everyone has their moments of weakness, and you've forgiven me after all of mine so... this is just me returning the favor."

He's stonily quiet the entire time I talk, and I can see in his expression the internal war he's having with himself over if he should relent his guilt, but luckily it doesn't take too long for him to give up the fight.

He anchors his arms around my waist, his forearms tensing around me so tight that I can feel the muscles flex against me. My heart is pounding in my chest when he leans down, his forehead delicately resting against my own, and not even the slight hint of warm beer on his breath can distract me when he murmurs, "I love you."

He's said it before, earlier today when he was apologizing, but hearing it now, hearing it now that things have been talked through, hearing it when I've been through hell and my appearance definitely holds proof of that, hearing it through Weston's lips when he's not distraught... it's the most incredible feeling.

So as I reach up on my tiptoes, curl my fingertips into his hair, and whisper those three beautiful words back to him, not a damn thing from today can ruin it.

# Chapter Twenty-Seven

"You're grounded, little missy. Two weeks!"

"Dad," I groan. "I'm twenty-three, you can't ground me."

His eyes widen and flash with anger. "Oh, I can and you damn bet I will! What you pulled, lying to me like that, I just can't—"

"I did it for you, though, you loser!" I argue, still not able to believe we're having this dumb of an argument. It's only been twelve hours since my dad's got back in town, and despite the stress still lingering from Tim's introduction to us four days ago, my dad's dead set on making up for lost time. It took a long while for his relief and shock to wither to anger, but now that it's been unleashed, I don't think there is any stopping his yelling. "I didn't want you to panic about me being alone, and you'd already told me there was nothing you could do to get back earlier!"

I can tell by that damn tweak of his lips that that means absolutely nothing to him, and I'm proven right when he retorts, "Well, I could've known what was going on, Iris! I could've known more and been more prepared for the *wonderful* phone call I got from the guys down at the station telling me I'd probably want to know that my daughter and my ex-wife had been involved in a shooting *during a fucking hurricane*!"

The hysteria in his voice and the fact that he's dropping the f-bomb in front of me, something he never does unless he's actually panicking, has my heart squeezing in pain for him. So instead of arguing, I stand and head over to him.

"Dad," I say softly, calmly, my arms extending to wrap around his thin waist so that I can give him the hug he desperately needs.

And just like that he's letting out the largest breath of relief, his arms wrapping around me and squeezing me so tight that if he weren't so distraught, I'd call him out for choking me. His chin buries into the hair on top of my head, hair that seriously needs to be washed, and I can feel the thumping pulse of his heart reverberating through my emotionally exhausted body.

Knowing he needs to hear it even though I've already told him the same thing a million times since that day, I promise him, "I'm fine, Dad. I'm safe and I'm good. You need to stop this panicking, okay? It's long overdue now, and you're going to give yourself a heart attack. I can only handle one parent's almost-death this week."

As soon as I say that he's pulling away from me and giving me a pointed stare, so I wince in response, saying meekly, "Sorry, bad joke." I continue, "And I'm so sorry I lied to you that day, but I was only looking out for your sanity, okay? It may have been wrong, yes, but I didn't know that all hell would break loose later on."

He nods. "I know, you just.... You're such a stubbornly selfless person and it pisses me off sometimes."

"Dad! Isn't that supposed to be a good thing?"

He yells at me with comically wide eyes, "Not when it means your safety and my sanity is on the line!"

I roll my eyes at him. "Oh my God, Dad, you're being ridiculous! Did you really just want me to tell you that Weston and I had gotten in a fight so I was at home alone and heartbroken for an impending hurricane? No! You would've tried to drive home and risked your job and your damn life!"

"No, what I could've done is called up Weston and told him to get his head out of his ass and to trek it on over here!"

The brief moment of peace is over. "I was just as capable being here by myself as I would've been with him here. I don't know why you and he think that him being here could've prevented anything. I'm a grown-ass adult just like he is!"

He runs his hands through his dark, gray-speckled hair, and with his jaw clenching in frustration, he says, "That's not what I'm getting at here, Iris! This isn't about you being a girl or anything like that. It's about you being my *damn daughter*! You're all I got, Iris. You're my girl, and knowing you're home alone during a normal day is one thing, but knowing you're alone during a hurricane is completely another."

"*Dad*," I croak out, the overwhelming fear tingeing his voice making my anger from earlier dissipate. "I'm sorry, okay? I'm so, so sorry for lying to you. I just.... I know you're always worried about me and I didn't want you to worry even more and risk your job. That's all."

His body seems to deflate after I say this, and he quietly responds with, "I know, and I get it. I probably would've done the same thing with you."

I pointedly glare at him. "See?"

He's immediately on the defensive. "But I can do that! I'm the dad. I get to pick and choose how all rules are applied in this house."

I roll my eyes at him and head back to the couch, eager to bury my body and my anxiety in my fuzziest blanket and my ongoing *Jane the Virgin* marathon. "Whatever, Dad."

Once I'm sitting down and settled, he remains standing in the middle of the rug, blocking my view of the television, and as the seconds tick by, I raise my brows at him and ask, "Thought you were going to the hospital?"

"I am." He nods. "I'm just... just trying to calm myself first."

"Well, can you calm yourself not in front of the television, please?

I have some serious reality-escaping to do."

"You're sure you don't want to come with me?"

Knowing he wants me to come just so I can alleviate the awkwardness between him and his injured wife, I shake my head and say firmly, "Nope. I've been there enough the past two days, and Mom said she'd refuse to see me if I go again."

"Ugh," he groans childishly. "Fine."

With that he stalks over to the front door and, as he's grabbing his things, he says, "I'll call you on my way back and we can figure out dinner. Sound good?"

"Yep," I say, slightly distracted by the TV.

Which is why, when he comes up behind the sofa and presses a kiss to the top of my head and whispers, "I love you," I'm a little taken aback.

I angle my body to face him. "Love you too, Daddy-O."

He gives me a small smile and then heads out of the house, but right before the door closes behind him, I yell out quickly, "And I'm not grounded!"

------------

A text vibrates my phone later that night, after my dad's already come home with pizza, watched a couple hours of TV with me, and then gone to bed claiming mental exhaustion. I'm still curled up on the couch, my body having refused to move unless for food or bathroom needs, but at the sound of it, I waste no time in stretching forward to grab the phone off the coffee table.

**Weston: Can you come outside?**

Seeing that the message is from Weston and knowing it means he's already here, I text back, **Sure, gimme a sec.**

After getting off the couch and stretching my tense muscles, I quickly grab a sweatshirt from my bedroom, the mid-October night air now having a slight chill to it, and then make my way out onto the front porch.

My eyes immediately fall on Weston's back, the muscles of it clearly visible through his cotton T-shirt, but at the sound of my feet on the wooden planks, he's turning around. "Hey, Iris."

"Hey," I greet back, pulling the sleeves of my sweatshirt over my fingers and digging my nails into the fabric as I sit down next to him.

In the couple of days since the shooting, things have been understandably weird between Weston and me. Even though we admitted we loved each other late that night, things are still a bit on edge as we try to get back to where we were before our fight. He did stay with me the nights my dad was unable to get back into town, but since my dad returned and found out everything, he hasn't been the friendliest person toward him.

But Weston is taking it in stride, I will give him that much. He apologized to my dad almost as fervently as he did to me, and has even agreed to no nights spent together even though I know it's putting a damper on how well he sleeps. But he's trying to earn my forgiveness, I'm trying to earn his, and us being around each other may still be a little raw, but it's something we have to do to fix the damage we both caused.

"I got you something," he says after a brief period of silence, reaching down to grab a manila envelope off the step below us.

His eyes are sparkling despite his obvious nerves when he hands it to me, so I give him a soft smile and place it on my lap so I can look through it.

My eyes widen in surprise as I read through the paper in the folder, the recommendation letter that, as I read it, is practically glowing with love for me. It's written as a personal reference as if I'm a close family friend of the author, and once I'm done I turn to look at Weston with an expression practically screaming for an explanation.

"It's from my CEO," he explains, "who just so happened to be the project manager on the Budweiser factory when it was being built. He said that if this letter can't get you in, then the people hiring are idiots and you don't want to work for them anyway."

"*West*," I breathe in disbelief, my gaze falling back to the letter.

"Iris, I just... I did this because I just have to know that you know I'm always fighting for you, that I'll always want what's best for you. I know the things I said that day were the complete opposite of that, but I–I was just in a dark place thinking that you were going to leave town. That's no excuse, I know it's not, and I know now that if your career ever does take you out of town or out of state or where-the-fuck-ever, I need to realize that that's what's best for you. One of the main things I love about you, Iris, is that your top priority has always been your education, your career, and that is just so freaking badass. And I know that you can get any job you want without this letter, but I just... I figured it was the least I could do to show you that I'm *actually* going to support you in whatever you do."

I'm nearly in tears by the time he's done talking, the pleading for me to trust him that's in his voice making my heart hurt, but there's one thing I don't understand. "But I–I thought the higher-up guys didn't like you? What with you not being a desk person and being practically unfireable...."

There's a teasing smile on his mouth. "I may have had to promise some office overtime for the next couple of months, but it's really not a big deal."

"It *is* a big deal," I urge, sliding the letter back into the folder and then setting it down behind me. "The fact that you did this, that you—"

He cuts me off, leaning forward and lightly tucking a stray greasy strand of my hair behind my ear. "I had to, Iris. You not trusting my feelings for you, not trusting that I trust you... it kills me, baby, and knowing that I'm the reason just makes it that much worse."

"Well, this definitely helps." I grin, grabbing his hand and intertwining our fingers. "And I do trust you, West. With everything I got, I trust you. And I hope you trust me too. I know I wasn't at all innocent in all of this."

He gives me a soft little smile that I know, without a doubt, means I have his trust. "I miss you. I miss being us."

"I do too," I respond. "I'm sure once all of this craziness dies down everything will get back to normal. As normal as it can be around here, anyway."

He chuckles. "How is everything, by the way? Since I talked to you this morning? How's your dad?"

I wince, thinking back to my dad and my intense conversation earlier today. "He's struggling, I guess. He's mad at me for not telling him I'd be alone, he's mad that he wasn't able to be here, he's mad that he had to go to the hospital to visit the woman who left him."

Obviously seeing the torment on my face from thinking about all of it, he wraps his free arm around my shoulder and pulls me in tight, my cheek resting against his chest. He says, "He's going to be fine eventually, Iris. I know he is. Just like you are and just like your mom is. It's just going to take some time."

"I know," I muse. "I'm just impatient, is all. You better than anyone know how I am when things are so emotional."

His chest vibrates in laughter. "Yes, I'm very well aware."

We fall silent for a couple of minutes, leaning on each other for the support that's so direly needed, and enjoying the fresh air. Now that the hurricane's long gone, our little town's weather has been uncharacteristically pleasant, and right now, tonight, is no exception. There's very little humidity in the air, there's a light breeze tickling my skin, and the usual mosquitos seem to have fled.

It's beautiful, it's relaxing, and Weston's here.

It's exactly what I need.

Weston's the first to break the silence, asking me quietly, "And how're you doing? With everything?"

For the first time since the shooting, I don't wince at the question. "I'm... I'm okay, I think. It's still pretty damn surreal to think about, honestly. Like I can't even believe it happened, you know?"

His large fingers slip underneath the hem of my sweatshirt, the warmth from his skin sending the most comforting of comforts through my veins. "I know. It's the craziest thing to think something like that could happen to you."

I nod, my cheek brushing against his solid chest. "Exactly. So it's really hard for me to even think about how it affected me, you know? After that night when it happened, when you were here, I haven't been all that sad or anything. Just... just confused. Like my head's kind of fuzzy."

"You think maybe it's 'cause it was with your mom? And you and she were on such uncertain terms before?"

The question shoots through me, and it takes only a half second for me to realize that he's exactly right. If it had been my dad, or him, or someone I was so certain of my feelings for, I think it would be so much easier for me to process.

But it happened to my mom, and even though our relationship since she'd been back had been steadily growing, a part of me still thought of her as a stranger. Then Tim arrived and I saw his hands on her and.... And I don't know. It was like she wasn't some stranger to me anymore, like she wasn't just some hazy version of the mom I used to know.

"Yeah, West," I answer, sounding a bit confounded. Lifting my head up from his chest so I can meet his eyes, the green in his caring, unwavering gaze making me feel even more sure of myself, I say, "I think you're exactly right. I think maybe that's what's making this so weird for me."

He doesn't say anything in response, his steady gaze just fixed on my face, so I keep speaking my way through figuring all of this out.

"When the whole thing with Tim was going down, she basically offered herself to him on a silver platter so he wouldn't shoot me. And, I don't know, anytime he touched her I just... I just saw red. I've never been so angry, never wanted to actually, like, kill a person. But, I don't know. So I guess maybe that showed me that, no matter what all's happened, I still think of her as my mom and I'd still do anything for her."

"Of course you would, Iris. No matter what you may think of yourself, once someone's weaseled their way into that steel-caged little heart of yours, they're there for good. No matter what they've done. I mean, after everything with Campbell you still helped him up when no one else would, you still tried to make amends with Jenny... you just, you do a lot for other people, and I really don't think you see that."

My moment of self-reflection shattered, I narrow my eyes teasingly at him and say, "West, you know I love you. You don't need to keep sucking up."

He rolls his eyes but laughs anyway. Brushing the pad of his thumb over my forehead, he says, "Yeah, I do. But that's not what I was doing. Just stating facts, you know? You're a pretty kick-ass person, baby."

"And you're incredibly cheesy." I grin, my entire body thrumming with warmth.

"But you love me." He smiles, although somewhere deep down in those bright green eyes of his, I can see the question mark he wants to put behind those words.

My heart breaking at his insecurity, I untangle our fingers and then run mine through his hair, pulling his head down to meet mine.

"Yeah, West, I love you."

# AFTER

"*West*," I exhale breathily, my fingers clenching his dirty-blond hair.

It's early in the morning on a Saturday, the light coming through the windows still a hazy orange, and Weston's face is currently buried between my legs and turning me completely inside out. I woke up a little while ago to an incredibly excited body part pushing into my lower back, and within my first minute of consciousness I was already draped over his naked body and kissing him in that lazy, sloppy, and completely intoxicating sort of way that only comes with true intimacy.

But now it's been quite some time and things have very quickly escalated, and the beautiful boy, with his fingers and his tongue, is proving to me for the millionth time in just five short months how lucky I am to be with him.

As he pushes a second finger into me, his mouth still suckling ever so lightly on my center, a loud, tortured groan escapes my throat and my head presses into the pillow beneath it, my back arching off the mattress.

Weston pulls his head away, and right before I scream at him in protest, he's nipping at the soft flesh of my upper thigh with his teeth and scolding me, "You gotta be quiet, baby."

My eyes open at the sound of his voice and quickly meet his dark, gleaming gaze, his chin now hovering over my belly button and his lips sinfully wet.

"It's a little hard to be quiet, West, when you're doing that shit to me!"

He chuckles low in his throat, the enticing sound of it making my core clench even tighter. He presses an open-mouthed kiss to my stomach and then slowly starts to make his way upward, pushing his large shirt I'm wearing all the way up to the bottom of my breasts. My skin is pebbling underneath the skimming, barely there touch, and the scratchy feel of his stubble is only making it beautifully worse.

After he plants a final kiss on the tip of my chin, I can see on his face that he's about to say something to me so, unable to help myself, I stop him by grabbing roughly at his jaw and yanking his mouth toward mine.

My tongue forces its way through his kiss-plumped lips, entangling immediately with his own, and when I feel his chest deflate and his strong arms wrap around my waist to force my lower body into his, I know that conversation is lost for now.

It's as easy as breathing, I've come to learn, being with him like this. Kissing him like this, feeling him, having him inside of me, it's all just... it's all so natural to me now.

It's home.

It's everything.

And it's so, so easy to get lost in.

Unless, of course, you start to smell the strong scent of bacon and realize that your mother is still under the same roof.

It's not until the sound of the TV in the living room mixes in with the smell of breakfast that Weston and I have to pull away from each other, him cursing under his breath in frustration.

Sighing, I reach up and delve my fingertips into the wild hair on the sides of his head. His eyes close as I start to massage his scalp with my fingernails, and then I point out teasingly, "You're the one who offered to let her stay here."

His eyes quickly open at that, the glittering green still there even as he narrows them at me. "I know, I know, and I don't regret it at all, don't think I do, but it's just...."

"Keeping you from acting on your caveman tendencies with me?"

"*Yes*," he nearly cries in exasperation, making a silly, high-pitched giggle escape my throat.

He's such a boy.

"It's killing me, Iris. When she wasn't here, I could come stay at your apartment during the week, but now I feel bad leaving her alone, so the weekends when you come here are the only time I can see you, and even then *she's still here*."

"I know, baby," I say gently, coddling him with only a slight hint of teasing. "But she closes on her house Tuesday, so she'll be gone by then. And then I'll owe you big time."

His eyes light up. "Really now?"

"Mhmm," I coo while batting my eyelashes at him, my hips tilting upward and a groan escaping me when I feel the hard bulk meet them. "In fact," I continue, my body pulsating with that familiarly hot sort of desperation as I slide my hand down his taut chest and underneath the band of his boxers, "We still have about ten minutes until she realizes we should be up."

His eyes nearly roll backward as my hand grips him lightly, and it's just as I'm getting into a rhythm that he grabs my wrist. I look up at him, my brows raised in question, so he explains through gritted teeth, "I need.... I need to be inside you, Iris. This just.... I'm...."

My heart squeezing in my chest at the desperation in his voice, I remove my hand from his boxers and then place my other lightly on his cheek. His eyes meet mine, his intense stare dark and hooded, and

355

after a brief breathless moment, I prompt, "Shower?"

His nod is immediate.

"Shower."

---

Thirty minutes later, I'm completely sated, my hair is dripping wet, and I'm happily munching on a slice of crispy bacon. I'm sitting across the table from my mom, who thinks Weston is taking a shower of his own when, really, he's just sitting in his room and passing the time so she doesn't realize we just spent the last half hour indulging ourselves in each other for the first time in the three weeks she's been staying here.

After she was released from the hospital, it only took her a week to decide what she wanted to do with her new life away from Tim. With my encouragement, of course, since Tim is in prison until trial with no option for bail, my mom decided to withdraw a good bit of their joint bank account and use it to pay for a nice condo just minutes away from one of her best friends from her support group.

Once that is done and purchased, which should be in just three days if everything goes according to plan, after testifying in Tim's trial in April, she will be free of the man who caused her so much pain.

And free from my dad too, since their divorce will be finalized not long after that.

But because of this plan, and the fact that the hotel she was paying for was starting to cost more than a mortgage, nearly a month ago Weston offered up one of the two spare rooms at his house. She has to be in town for physical rehab and counseling, so her staying at my new apartment forty minutes away would have been less than ideal.

I was shocked when Weston made the suggestion, of course, but as time has gone on and I realize how much less I've been worrying about her since I know she's here, I know that this was the best thing to do. Sure it puts a damper on our sex life, and I'm still a bit nervous about what they talk about when I'm not here, but mornings like this, when she's sitting across from me in a fluffy pink robe while sipping coffee from one of Weston's mugs, I feel completely at peace.

"How's the new job going, Iris?" she asks after she swallows a sip of coffee. "You getting settled in okay? It's at Budweiser, right?"

"Yeah!" I say, my mood brightening in pride. "I think everyone there is starting to no longer see me as the new girl, so thank God on that. And everyone's so nice, but there's this one guy there that loves to pick on me and, I swear to you, for the first two months I was there, he got everyone in the office to call me meaty."

"Meaty?" she asks.

"Like fresh meat," I explain, rolling my eyes. "It was funny at first, but then when I started getting like actual, important things to do, it got really old really fast."

Her eyes dart over my shoulder toward the hallway, and then she asks, "And this guy who started that? You think he may have a crush on you?"

I giggle. "Well, for my sake and his boyfriend's, I surely hope not."

"Good." She laughs. "I'm so happy that you like it there, especially this quickly. It usually takes people about a year to truly get settled in."

"Yeah." I nod, stopping as soon as I hear the opening of Weston's door so I can look over my shoulder at him. He gives me a quick, sneaky little smile that has my toes curling, so before I get too caught up, I turn back to my mom and continue. "Most people there haven't been there long, so I think they're all pretty welcoming of meaties like myself."

As Weston enters the kitchen and goes to pour himself a cup of coffee, he adds, "I still think Meaty is the dumbest nickname ever."

As my mom laughs, her susceptibility to his charm as powerful as ever, I taunt in response, "Says the guy who called a guy I was dating Soupy for months."

He settles the coffeepot back in its place and then narrows his eyes at me. "That's different. That's 'cause the guy was an asshole. You're not an asshole... not all the time, anyway."

I roll my eyes at him. "Thanks, babe, you're so sweet."

He lifts his steaming cup of black coffee to his lips and winks at me. "I know."

"Soupy?" my mom asks as Weston makes his way over to the chair next to mine.

"His name was Campbell," I explain, "and West was *very* jealous and *very* petty."

Weston gulps his current mouthful of coffee and shoots me a look. "Really, honey? You want to go there? You want to talk about how much you loved Jenny and me together?"

My chest tensing at even the thought of when they were together, I slyly slide my palm over his thigh underneath the table and say, "Yeah, let's not take that trip down memory lane."

He smirks. "That's what I thought."

For the next few minutes, the three of us just make random, typical breakfast-time talk, me continuing on about my new job and apartment, Weston making random jabs at me here and there, and my mom laughing along with him. Thumper sits on the floor next to Weston's chair and stares longingly at each piece of bacon he eats, my new little rescue dog, a pug mix I dubbed Smusher, watching in earnest and most likely internalizing the annoying little habit.

It's completely domestic, intimate, and I'm almost sad when my mom announces that she has plans to meet one of her friends for lunch and needs to get ready.

Weston and I, though, have no plans whatsoever today, just catching up on all the time together we miss with me no longer living

*Back to You*

just across the street. So when my mom disappears to get ready, Weston and I and our second cups of coffee just trickle into the living room and onto the couch. He sits down first and then pats the spot right next to him, as if I'd sit anywhere else, so I scoot in and grab a blanket to drape over us.

For the two hours it takes my mom to get ready and leave, promising us that she'll be back by dinner, Weston and I just silently enjoy being together and stay curled up watching reruns of *Modern Family*.

When she leaves, though, something in Weston quickly shifts.

My chest pinches in anxiety, and when he reaches over to the end table to grab the remote and put the television on mute, it only gets worse.

"West?" I start, turning my body to face his. "What's—"

"I want to talk to you about something," he says firmly, and even though there's an air of sureness in his voice, I can see the worry twinkling in his eyes.

"Okay?"

Underneath our blanket, he grabs both of my legs, pulling me in as close as possible and then draping them over the bottoms of his thighs. The contact puts me at ease. He says, "I realized something this morning."

"What's that?" I ask, lifting one of my hands and tracing my thumb over the sharpness of his jaw.

He looks at me and gives me a sad little smile. "I really freaking hate not sleeping next to you every night, not having mornings like we did today. I know I got spoiled with you living across the street and being able to stay the night every night, but... but, Iris, now, with you a little bit away and my access limited, I just... I realize me feeling this way isn't just 'cause I was spoiled."

My heartbeat picking up pace, I respond, "I know this is hard and everything, and I hate not seeing you too, I hate it so much, but I just....

Right now, at work, I can't take chances of staying here and getting caught up with you every morning and being late. I get there early, I leave late, and I'm doing it to prove I'm dedicated so I won't have to do this forever, not when I'm truly established, but—"

"No, Iris," he urges, shaking his head. "Stop. That's not what I'm trying to say. I'm not trying to make you feel bad."

A small, slightly melancholy smile touches my lips at the affection behind his words. "I know you're not, but I mean, I do hate that this job is getting between us and—"

My words are stopped dead in their tracks as a large, warm hand plants itself over my mouth. My eyes fly up to meet his, and when I see the sparkling laughter behind his gaze, I know my babbling is as unnecessary as the guilt behind it.

"First off," he says firmly, his hand still clamped over my mouth, "your job is not getting between us. *Nothing* will ever get between us. Understand?"

The bossiness in his tone has my eyes glazing over and my body thrumming with desire for him, his macho side as appealing to me as his sensitive side. I nod slowly in agreement as he pulls his hand away and says, "I'm saying this because I have an idea... a proposition. To fix this. To let me have you all the time."

Every single breath in my body abruptly flees.

He continues, "Your job needs you close to Baton Rouge. My job needs me close to here. But right now, fortunately, both of us live unnecessarily close to our jobs, giving us a little wiggle room."

"*West*...." I feel like I know where this is going, but don't want to risk my hopes getting up.

He shakes his head, shushing me again. "Iris, if the two of us... if we find something in that wiggle room, then everything would be okay, wouldn't it?"

"Something," I nearly stutter, reiterating his word choice. "As in... a house? To live in? Together?"

A small smile filled with nerves stretches his full, pink lips. "Yeah, a house. A condo, an apartment, a fucking tent as long as there's AC. I don't care, Iris. I just.... As pathetic as it sounds, I feel like a morning isn't really a morning unless you're there. These four months with only sleepovers on the weekends, as much as I do love those, have just not been enough. I–I need you there, with me, all the time."

By the time he's done talking, I have tears rolling down my cheeks, as what he's putting into words are things I've been feeling for months now but just haven't been able to fully grasp. The feeling of incompletion, of an inescapable void. It's not painful, it's not something overtly uncomfortable, but it's enough to make me completely aware that something, some part of me, is missing.

Maybe I've known what it was all along but was just too scared to admit it, too scared to admit that I'm not as independent as I once thought I was, too scared to admit that a part of me just *needs* Weston.

But now that he's said it out loud, now that he's spoken of the feelings I've been repressing for far too long now, I know that, whatever fears I have, the love I have for Weston beats them.

There's not even a comparison.

I can tell that the longer I go without talking, the more nervous he becomes, and the fact that I'm crying is probably not helping.

Forcing myself to speak, to say something, I start teasingly, "I don't know if I could do a tent, West." My chest burns with love for him when I see the stupid grin slowly form on his lips. "But anything else... everything else you just said, I want it. I need it—I need *you*. I just... yes. Yes to everything you said, everything you asked, everything you want."

"Yeah?" he asks a moment after, the hesitancy in his voice telling me that he's not quite accepted the fact that I've said yes to him.

I turn on his lap and swing one leg over so that I'm straddling his thighs. Completely overcome by him, by how much he loves me, by his beautiful face and by every single inch of him, I twine my arms around his neck and bury my fingers into the thick hair there. Giving him a dazed, wickedly happy smile, I say, "*Hell* yeah," and then proceed to devour him in a kiss.

# *Way* AFTER

My dad is drunk.

Just an hour ago he was telling Meg "I do" in a room full of flowers, and now he's telling the bartender about how incredible he thinks pepperoni pizza Hot Pockets are.

At first I assumed Meg would be giving him hell about being so drunk, but instead she's standing right by his side and giggling uncontrollably as my dad gets more and more excited and starts using obnoxious hand gestures.

They're undeniably and goofily in love with each other, and I couldn't be happier for them.

Just two weeks after Tim shooting my mom, my dad decided that there was no time to waste and got down on one knee in front of Meg and the rest of her diner during their busy dinner hour. She was covered in hamburger grease when she said yes and, ten months later, people in town still say it's the most romantic thing they've ever seen.

Which is why, of course, the entire town seems to be in attendance today.

It's so much fun though, that I can't really complain. Since I was one of the bridesmaids, I've been sipping on mimosas since around ten this morning, and now that it's closing in on five, I'm slowly starting to wind down on the drunken good mood.

Looking at Weston, too, the drool-inducing boyfriend of mine all wrapped up in an impeccable tux, I know he's probably feeling the same urge to go home as well. His boyish pink cheeks from earlier have faded, and now instead of his eyes being bright and slightly glossed over, they're drooping.

He's talking to Alex, the guy from the Boot and who egged us on at Meg's diner, who, as time's gone by, has become a very good friend of ours. I think they're talking about football or something; I haven't really been paying much attention, but their conversation is cut short when Jenny walks up and interrupts.

"Babe," she says to Alex, adjusting the one-month-old little blond boy on her hip. "Are there any more diapers in the car? He's been peeing like a freaking fountain since we got here."

"I think so," he says, standing to take their kid from her. "I'll hold Mr. Man here. You have the keys, right?"

"Yeah," she nods, her eyes soft as she looks at the two of them. "I'll be right back."

She gives me and Weston polite little smiles and then turns on her heel to head out, her perfectly curled blonde hair swinging over her thin, bare shoulder as she does.

"God, she's hot," Alex quips, and when I take my eyes off Jenny, I notice that Alex's eyes have been trained on her as well. "I'm so damn lucky I knocked her up."

I giggle and say, "I still don't know how the two of you ended up together."

I really do, though. Right after the shooting, word got out around town that Alex and Jenny had started dating. I was shocked at first, and I'm pretty sure everyone else was as well, but then Weston and I ran into them at dinner one weekend and as I watched the two of them interact, I realized they were both suited so well for each other.

She was so tense about so many ideas she'd created in her head, and Alex was just the kind of easygoing goofball to shake her out of that. She calmed him down, straightened him out, and he instilled in her that no-worries kind of attitude she definitely needed.

It wasn't too long after they'd started dating that she got pregnant with Holden. He was the adorable little curly-haired boy she told me so long ago that she dreamed of, and even though the two of us never got as close as we once were despite Campbell moving back to Texas, I was positively thrilled for her.

I'm lost in my thoughts until Jenny comes back and whisks Alex and Holden away from our table, leaving Weston and me alone for the first time all day today. He notices this as well, obviously, since he wastes no time in scooting his chair closer to mine and laying a heavy hand possessively over the top of my thigh.

"You okay?" he asks, leaning in close so that his breath flirts over my cheek. "You look tired."

"I'm exhausted," I say, touched that he's noticed. "But it's Sunday tomorrow so we can sleep in, and once we get home I'll make some supergreasy breakfast, and we can just chill on the couch with the dogs all day."

"Ugh, that sounds amazing," he croons, squeezing my fingers. "Having you move in has been the best decision I've ever made."

I laugh, shaking my head at him. "Why? 'Cause I spoil the hell out of you and sometimes cook you food?"

"Well, that," he says, and then winks at me, "and 'cause you're hot."

I scoff loudly, rolling my eyes. "You loser."

"A loser you're now bound to," he teases, dropping our intertwined hands so he can grab my left one and tweak the diamond ring circling my finger. "You said yes, remember?"

"Yes," I reply, trying my hardest to sound annoyed but failing since he's brought up the fact that we're engaged now. "But there's still a year until it's actually *legal*."

"Like that'll change anything," he coos, placing the back of my hand onto his thigh and then trailing his fingertips seductively over my open palm. "I know how you work, little Ms. Iris Tilley. Let's not forget I was able to keep you in bed for three days straight not too long ago."

Something shoots down my spine at the mention of our little sex fest right after he proposed, the same one in which he was able to cajole me into missing a day of work. "West, *hush*," I scold him as X-rated memories dance in my head. "If someone hears you, I will die."

As he chuckles deep in his chest, I swat his bicep and add, "You're so annoying when you've been drinking and around Alex. Like a cocky little high schooler or something."

Something in his expression flickers before he leans in and says, "It's just 'cause I love you, and seeing you get irritated is so good for me."

"Oh yeah, why's that?" I prompt, raising a brow at him.

"Because," he starts, a little introspective smile touching his mouth, "before, with me, you were always so uncomfortable and annoyingly polite, because being any other way would mean you'd opened up to me. So now, the fact you'll get pissed at me or irritated or something like that reminds me that I'm lucky to even get that from you."

I feel that familiar pinch behind my eyes, warning me that tears could soon be on their way, so I stop him before he can continue and make me ruin my makeup. Leaning up, I press a quick kiss on his mouth, my teeth nipping lightly at his lower lip, and when I pull back and meet his gaze, I say, "Well, you're about to hit the jackpot, baby, 'cause if you make me cry in front of all these people, then I'm kicking your ass."

He laughs loudly, boisterously, his eyes glazing over with that glittery green lovestruck look I still can't believe belongs to me. "Yes, ma'am."

---

It's not that much later when Jenny is dropping us off at my dad's house, having been the only appointed sober driver. Weston and my new home, a cute little two-bedroom with a front porch perfect for drinking coffee every morning, is a good half hour drive from here and both of us knew that we wouldn't be in the right state to drive back there.

So, because my dad and Meg planned to stay at a hotel tonight and because West sold his parents' house months ago, my dad offered to let Weston and me stay here.

I love it, though, because as we walk up the porch steps to the front door after telling Alex and Jenny bye, I can't help but remember the night just three weeks ago when Weston proposed to me right at this spot. We'd come to my dad's for dinner, and after dessert Weston asked if I wanted to go sit outside. It was then that he brought up our first night on these steps so long ago, when we were just two emotionally confused kids sitting on a porch with absolutely no idea where one kiss would lead.

He turned me into a sobbing, blubbering mess, just like he always does, and seconds after I said yes and he slipped the ring on my finger, Meg and my dad were barreling the door down to come and congratulate us.

It was, hands down, the best night of my life, and it's the reason I can't help but get misty-eyed as Weston unlocks and pushes the front door open.

Once we're inside, I think back to everything that happened on this dark, quiet little street and how all of that gave me Weston. I remember the pain, the hurt of my first summer back here and how all of it led me to someone who, since then, never stopped making me happy.

Someone who, upon seeing that I've stopped walking and gone incredibly quiet, walks over to me and touches the underside of my chin with his fingertips. Someone who asks me, "You all right?"

"Y-yeah," I manage to say, slightly shocked at how much being back here for the first time since the proposal has affected me. "I just.... I don't know, it's like everything just hit me."

"What do you mean?" he asks, the little crease between his brows matching the concern in his voice.

I shake my head, smiling softly at how much he cares. "I don't know. I'm thinking, like, how our one little kiss on the porch turned into something so huge, you know? How never in a million years did I think that me leaving my party to be upset would lead me to you. I'm just.... I don't know, I'm feeling very corny, I guess."

He grins at that, that soft handsome smile of his appearing and turning my heart to goo. "I love you corny, though," he says. "Out of the two of us, I feel like I'm always the sappy one."

I giggle. "Yeah, but I love that, though. You try to be such a macho man, but you're really just a hopeless romantic."

"Hey now," he scolds, that delicious blush of his staining his cheeks pink.

"I'm just kidding," I say, my grin only stretching further as I step into his arms and relax against his chest. "You're incredibly manly, West. You're *my* man."

He rests his chin against the top of my head, and I can feel his smile against my hair. "Now who's being corny?"

"Me." I laugh. "But that's only 'cause you've turned me into a lovesick loser, and for the first time in my life, I can finally say that I'm not ashamed of that."

# Acknowledgments

    First and foremost, I have to thank my mom. She encouraged my love for writing and for myself, and without her I never would have had the courage to try to publish this story. And also to my dad, whose sense of humor inspired the foundation of Steve's character. Thanks to the rest of my family and friends who never thought I was weird for wanting to be an author, but only for other reasons.

    To anyone whose ever read anything of mine online, thank you so much for your comments and critiques. I've saved so many of them and they're constantly motivating me to grow as a writer. And to the incredibly sweet and vivacious ladies in the Hot Tree Family. You decided my little story here was worth your time and because of that, I'm living my dream. Thank you!

# About the Author

CJ Miranda is a twenty-three-year-old LSU graduate with a romantic side she's never shown to the people in her life. Having grown up quiet, shy, and incredibly sarcastic in a small town she never felt a part of, CJ spent her spare time writing multiple romance novels that she posted for free online. Having done that since she was thirteen, she now feels that it's time to pursue what has always been her dream.

When she's not writing or reading, she's either working at her day job or drinking wine with her best friend/roommate and laughing at whatever their diva dogs are doing.

FACEBOOK: WWW.FACEBOOK.COM/AUTHORCJMIRANDA
WEBSITE: WWW.AUTHORCJMIRANDA.COM

# About the Publisher

Hot Tree Publishing opened its doors in 2015 with an aspiration to bring quality fiction to the world of readers. With the initial focus on romance and a wide spread of romance sub-genres, we envision opening up to alternative genres in the near future.

Firmly seated in the industry as a leading editing provider to independent authors and small publishing houses, Hot Tree Publishing is the sister company to Hot Tree Editing, founded in 2012. Having established in-house editing and promotions, plus having a well-respected market presence, Hot Tree Publishing endeavors to be a leader in bringing quality stories to the world of readers.

Interested in discovering more amazing reads brought to you by Hot Tree Publishing or perhaps you're interested in submitting a manuscript and joining the HTPubs family? Either way, head over to the website for information:

WWW.HOTTREEPUBLISHING.COM

Made in the USA
Middletown, DE
28 April 2017